V
is for
Vengeance

## ALSO BY SUE GRAFTON

Kinsey Millhone mysteries

*A is for Alibi*
*B is for Burglar*
*C is for Corpse*
*D is for Deadbeat*
*E is for Evidence*
*F is for Fugitive*
*G is for Gumshoe*
*H is for Homicide*
*I is for Innocent*
*J is for Judgment*
*K is for Killer*
*L is for Lawless*
*M is for Malice*
*N is for Noose*
*O is for Outlaw*
*P is for Peril*
*Q is for Quarry*
*R is for Ricochet*
*S is for Silence*
*T is for Trespass*
*U is for Undertow*

# Sue Grafton

First published 2011 by G. P. Putnam's Sons,
a member of Penguin Group (USA) Inc., New York

This edition published 2011 by Mantle
an imprint of Pan Macmillan, a division of Macmillan Publishers Limited
Pan Macmillan, 20 New Wharf Road, London N1 9RR
Basingstoke and Oxford
Associated companies throughout the world
www.panmacmillan.com

ISBN 978-0-230-75621-2



1 3 5 7 9 8 6 4 2

A CIP catalogue record for this book is available from
the British Library.

Printed and bound by CPI Group (UK) Ltd, Croydon, CR0 4YY

This one is for the Humphrey clan to honor all the years we've been together.

Chuck and Theresa

Pam and Jim

Peter, Joanna, and baby Olivia

Meredith

Kathy and Ron

Gavin

and, of course, my darling Steven

with love.

# 1

# BEFORE

## Las Vegas

## August 1986

Phillip Lanahan drove to Vegas in his 1985 Porsche 911 Carrera Cabriolet, a snappy little red car his parents had given him two months before, when he graduated from Princeton. His stepfather bought the car secondhand because he abhorred the notion of depreciation. Better that the original owner take that hit. The car was in pristine condition, with 15,000 miles on the odometer, a black leather interior, fully accessorized, with four brand-new tires. The car could jump from 0 to 60 in 5.4 seconds.

With the top down, he hugged the coastline and then continued traveling east through Los Angeles on the 10. From the 10 he picked up the 15, which took him straight into Vegas. The sun was harsh and the wind whipped his hair to a wild tangle of black. At the age of twenty-three, he knew he was good-looking and he carried the knowledge like a rabbit's foot for luck. His face was lean, clean-shaven; his dark eyebrows straight; ears tucked close to his head. He wore jeans and a short-sleeve black polo shirt. His white linen sport coat lay folded beside him on the passenger's seat. In his duffel he had ten grand in hundred-dollar bills, compliments of a loan shark he'd recently met.

This was his third trip to Vegas in as many weeks. The first time, he'd played poker at Caesars Palace, which, though vulgar and overblown, had everything you'd ever want in one sprawling complex. That trip had been magical. He could do no wrong. The cards fell into place, one hand after another. He read his opponents, picking up tells so subtle he felt psychic. He'd driven to Vegas with three thousand dollars he'd pulled from a savings account and he'd run it up to eight with no sweat.

The second trip had started out well but then he lost his nerve. He'd returned to Caesars, thinking the same gut-level instincts would come into play, but his reads were off, the cards wouldn't come, and he couldn't regain ground. He left the casino a miserable five grand down. Thus the meeting with the loan shark, Lorenzo Dante, who (according to Phillip's friend Eric) referred to himself as a "financier." Phillip assumed the term was meant tongue-in-cheek.

He'd been uneasy about the appointment. In addition to Eric's filling him in on Dante's sordid past, he'd assured Phillip the exorbitant fees for the loan were what he called "industry" standard. Phillip's stepfather had drilled into him the need to negotiate all monetary matters, and Phillip knew he'd have to tackle the issue before he and Dante came to an agreement. He couldn't tell his parents what he was up to, but he did appreciate his stepfather's counsel in absentia. He didn't like the man much, though he had to admit he admired him.

He'd met Dante in his office in downtown Santa Teresa. The space was impressive, all glass and high-gloss teak, leather-upholstered furniture, and soft gray wall-to-wall carpeting. The receptionist had greeted him warmly and buzzed him through. A sexy brunette in tight jeans and spike heels had met him at the door and escorted him past ten interior offices to a large corner suite at the end of the corridor. Everyone he caught sight of was young and casually dressed. He imagined a cadre of tax attorneys, as well as accountants, financial hotshots, paralegals, and administrative assistants. Dante was under indictment on racketeering charges, and Phillip had expected an atmosphere both tense and sinister. He'd worn an expensive sport coat, thinking to show respect, but now he realized the image was all wrong. Everyone he saw wore casual attire, stylish but understated. He felt like a kid dressing up in his daddy's clothes, hoping to be taken for an adult.

The brunette showed him into the office, and Dante leaned forward across the desk to shake hands, then motioned Phillip into a seat. Phillip was startled by the man's good looks. He was in his midfifties, a big guy, probably six foot two, and handsome: soulful brown eyes, curly gray hair, dimples, and a cleft in his chin. He appeared to be in great shape. The warm-up conversation had covered Phillip's recent graduation from Princeton, his dual major (business and economics), and his job prospects. Dante listened with apparent interest, prompting him now and then. Actually, nothing in the way of employment had materialized as yet, but the less said about that the better. Phillip spoke about his options, not mentioning he'd been forced to move back in with his parents. That was too lame to bear thinking about. Phillip began to relax, though his palms were still damp.

Dante said, "You're Tripp Lanahan's boy."

"You knew my dad?"

"Not well, but he did me a good turn once upon a time . . ."

"Excellent. I'm glad to hear that."

". . . Otherwise, you wouldn't be sitting here."

"I appreciate your time."

"Your friend Eric says you're quite the poker player."

Phillip shifted in his seat, steering a course between modest and boastful. "I played all through college, starting my freshman year at Princeton."

Dante smiled and his dimples flashed briefly. "No need to mention Princeton again. I know where you went to school. Was this high stakes or you taking change off a bunch of donkeys at some frat house?"

"Actually, I played in Atlantic City and picked up enough change most weekends to cover my expenses."

"You didn't work your way through school?"

"I didn't need to."

"Lucky you," Dante said, "though, just off the top of my head, poker parlors couldn't be the lifestyle your dad had in mind for you."

"Well, no, sir. I expect to work. That's why I got my degree. At this point, I'm just not sure what I want to do."

"But you'll decide soon."

"I hope. I mean, that's certainly my intention." Under his sport coat, Phillip felt his shirt dampen, sticking to his back. There was something fearsome about the man, almost as though there were two of him, the one benevolent, the other pitiless. On the surface he seemed affable, but underneath, a shadow personality was in play, prickly and sharp. Phillip was anxious, uncertain from moment to moment which of the two he was dealing with. Now Dante's smile faded and the alternate took over. Maybe it was in business matters that Dante became dangerous.

"And you've come to me for what?"

"Eric says you sometimes advance him cash if he's experiencing a shortfall situation. I was hoping you'd do the same for me."

Dante's tone was pleasant, but the benevolence didn't reach his eyes. "A sideline of mine. I lend money to people the banks won't touch. For this I charge fees and administrative costs. How much are you looking for?"

"Ten?"

Dante stared at him. "Lot of money for a kid."

Phillip cleared his throat. "Well, ten . . . you know, ten gives me breathing room. That's how I look at it, at any rate."

"I take it Eric explained my terms."

Phillip shook his head. "Not entirely. I thought I should hear it from you."

"The charge is twenty-five dollars per hundred per week, payable along with the principal when the note comes due."

Phillip's mouth was dry. "That seems steep."

Dante opened his bottom drawer and pulled out a sheath of papers. "If you like, you can take your chances at the Bank of America two blocks down State. I've got the application forms right here." He tossed a BofA loan application on the desk.

"Hey, no. I understand and I appreciate the position you're in. You have expenses like everybody else."

Dante made no response.

Phillip leaned forward, trying for solid eye contact, two men of the world getting down to business. "I'm wondering if twenty-five per hundred is the best you can do?"

"'The best I can *do*'? You want to *haggle* with me?"

"Oh, no, sir. Not at all. That's not what I meant. I just thought there might be some wiggle room." He could feel the heat as a belated flush crept into his cheeks.

"Based on what? Our long and productive association? Your prowess at the table? Word has it, you got stuck for five grand at Caesars last week. You want my ten so you can recoup your losses and run up the rest. You think you'll pay me off, including the juice, and keep the balance for yourself. Is that about it?"

"Actually, that's how I've done it in the past."

"'Actually' you can kiss my ass. All I care about is getting my money back."

"Absolutely. No problem. You have my word."

Dante stared at him until he looked away. "How much time are we talking here?"

"A week?"

Dante reached over and flipped a page on his desk calendar. "Monday, August 11."

"That'd be great."

Dante made a note.

Phillip hesitated, unsure what came next. "Is there paperwork?"

"Paperwork?"

"An IOU or contract you want me to sign?"

Dante waved off the idea. "Don't worry about it. Gentlemen's agreement. We shake hands and it's done. Check with Nico on your way out and he'll give you the cash."

"Thank you."

"You're welcome."

"I mean that."

"You can thank your old man. I'm returning a kindness from way back," Dante said. "Speaking of which, I have a friend in management at Binion's. You play there, he'll comp you a room. You can tell him I said so."

"I'll do that, and thank you so much."

Dante stood up and Phillip followed suit. As they shook hands, Phillip felt himself breathing a sigh of relief. In his fantasy, he'd played hardball with the vig, and Dante had come down two percentage points, impressed by his bargaining skills. Now he felt sheepish having broached the subject with a man of Dante's reputation. He was lucky he hadn't been thrown out on his ass. Or worse.

As though on cue, the door opened and the brunette appeared.

"One word of advice . . ." Dante added.

"Yes, sir?"

"Don't mess up. You dick with me, you'll be sorry."

"Got it. I'm good for it. I guarantee."

"That's what I like to hear."

Binion's had seen better days, but Phillip's room was nice enough. Looked clean at any rate. He dropped his duffel, put seven of his ten-grand stake in his pocket, and went down to the floor, where he traded the cash for chips. He spent a few minutes circling the poker room, getting a feel for the place. He was in no particular hurry. He was looking for a loose table, one where a lot of money was being tossed out on each hand. He bypassed a table where the player with all the chips in front of him wore a Rolex watch. Forget that. The guy was either too wealthy or too good, and Phillip didn't want to go up against him.

He paused at a table filled with seniors who'd been bussed in from a retirement home. They wore matching T-shirts, red with the silhouette of a setting sun in white. Play was passive, the betting haphazard, and one elderly woman had trouble remembering how hands were ranked. The guy next to her kept saying, "Alice, for god's sake. How many times I gotta tell you, flush beats a straight and a full house beats a flush." Small chip stacks at a table like that would probably take him weeks to get unstuck.

Once he'd made the rounds, he had the board person put his name on the list for the no-limit game on table number 4 or 8. This was No-Limit Texas Hold'em with a five-grand buy-in, rich stakes for his blood, but it was the only way he could think of to recoup his losses and put himself back on top. He preferred to play at the even-numbered tables, four being his lucky number. The first opening was seat 8 at table number 8, which he decided to view as a good omen, both being multiples of four. Phillip placed his chips to his right and ordered a vodka tonic. There were six guys already in the game and he entered in late position, which gave him a nice preview of the action. He let a couple of hands go by, showing discipline by folding on a jack-queen and then a pair of 5's. Small pocket pairs, which rarely hit the flop, were tempting to bet and therefore dangerous.

Playing with borrowed money, he felt a certain burden to perform. Ordinarily, he liked the pressure of play because it sharpened his wits. Now he found himself tossing in hands that on other occasions he might have pushed. He picked up a small pot on two pair, and six hands later won fifteen hundred dollars on a wheel. He hadn't lost anything to speak of, four hundred dollars max, and he felt himself grow calmer as the vodka flowed into his system. While the long, dull stretch was unproductive, it gave him the chance to watch how the others at the table operated.

The fat fellow in the blue shirt too small for him affected boredom when he had a strong hand, implying it was a bust and he could hardly wait to get it over with. There was a pinch-faced older man in a gray sport coat, whose every gesture was contained. When he looked at his cards, he barely lifted the corners, glanced at them once, and then stared off in the opposite direction. Phillip kept an eye on him, watching for involuntary tells. There was a fellow in a green flannel shirt, built like a lumberjack, who called anytime he thought he was behind in the hand, hoping to hit some good board cards. Phillip wasn't worried about the remaining three, who were either too tight or too timid to constitute a threat.

He played for an hour, pulling in five more small pots. He hadn't hit his rhythm, but he knew patience would pay off. The older man left his seat and a woman sat down, a pale blonde in her forties with a scar across her chin. She was either drunk, an amateur, or the worst poker player he'd ever seen. He watched her out of the corner of his eye, puzzled by her erratic play. He lost an eight-hundred-dollar pot to her when he misread a bluff. Then he overestimated her by folding when he should have hung in. It occurred to him she might fall into another category altogether, that of a seasoned pro and superb actress, far tougher than she first appeared. The signals were mixed. He red-flagged her in his mind and focused on his cards, letting his awareness of her fade into the background. There was a particular kind of quiet he experienced when the game started working for him. It was like being in a sound booth. He picked up table talk, but only from a distance and with no impact.

After two hours, he was up two grand and just beginning to sail into the zone. He was dealt the ace of hearts and the 4 of clubs. Ordinarily, he'd have dumped his hand at that point, but he could feel a whisper of intuition, an uncanny feeling something might be coming up for him. The blonde, sitting in early position, was operating largely in the dark, with no hint of what lay ahead. With a weak hand, she could always steal a pot by betting, but in the long run she'd lose money. In this case, she glanced at her hole cards and made a big bet pre-flop, which suggested pocket rockets—two aces, affectionately known as "bullets." Chances of getting a pair of aces in the hole were approximately 1 in 220 hands.

The fat guy called. The guy in the green flannel shirt pondered his options while he aligned the stacks of chips in front of him. He called, but without conviction. Phillip had an urge to look at his hole cards again, but he knew exactly what they were. He tested his gut-level instincts and decided he'd call for one round and fold the next if nothing developed. The button seat, the small blind, and the big blind folded without putting up a fight.

The dealer burned the top card and the flop came down 3 of diamonds, 5 of spades, and the 2 of spades, and Phillip felt his heart skip. He was suddenly looking at a wheel. Ace-2-3-4-5. He watched the betting as it went around the table, gauging the strength of the other players' hands. The woman checked that round, as did the fat guy and the guy in the green flannel shirt. Phillip bet, taking control of the hand. The betting went around again and everybody called him. The dealer burned a card. The turn was the ace of spades. The blonde bet, suggesting three of a kind or a flush. A set he could beat. He revised his original assessment. With one ace in his hand, one ace on the board, and seven players sitting at the start of the deal, the odds were she wasn't holding the remaining pair of aces. He flicked a look at her, but couldn't get a reading. She tended to play with a slight smile on her face, as though reacting to a private joke. He had a stepsister like her, superior, competitive, taunting. He never could get the best of her and it galled him. Phillip set the thought aside and concentrated on the play. The fat guy and the guy in the green flannel shirt folded. Phillip called.

When the river came down, it was the 8 of spades, making a flush for her a distinct possibility, in which case his straight wouldn't mean shit. Essentially his hand hadn't improved since the flop came down, but what did that mean? He could still be high man at the table. The question was whether to push, and if so, how hard. There were only two of them left in the hand. The blonde bet. He raised and the blonde re-raised. What kind of monster hand did she have? He tried to keep his mind blank, but he knew a fine sheen of sweat had appeared on his face and there was no way to disguise the tell. He counted eight grand in the pot. If he called, it was going to cost him two grand, which meant the pot odds were four to one. Not bad. If he won, he'd pick up four times what the call had cost him. All eyes were on him. His hand was good, but not that good. She had to have a flush or a set. He'd been on a winning tear, but he knew it couldn't last. He probably shouldn't have gone this far, but he hated to back away from her. For all he knew, she was laying a trap for him and this was his last chance to dodge. Agonizingly, he pushed his hole cards toward the center, mucking his hand. The dealer pushed the pot to the blonde and she pulled it in, smiling her enigmatic smile.

He tried telling himself it was a poker hand, not a pissing contest between him and the woman across the table. It was the smirk that got to him. He stared at her. "Was that a bluff?"

"I don't have to tell you," she said.

"I know. I'm curious. Were you holding a flush or a set?"

She raised two fingers, as though making a peace sign. "Two cards, a jack and a six."

He felt the blood drain from his face. She'd outfoxed him and his rage was keen. Mentally, he shook himself off. No point in chiding himself. What was done was done. Though it had cost him, he'd learned a valuable lesson and he'd use it next time he went up against her.

He took a break, leaving his chips on the table while he went up to his room. Once there, he took a piss, washed his hands and face, and picked up the rest of his stake, which he then turned into chips when he returned to the poker room.

After six additional hours of play, there was serious money on the table—maybe fifteen grand. He hadn't seen the blonde leave the table for so much as a bathroom break or a breath of fresh air. Her betting was aggressive and unpredictable. He didn't like her at all and her recklessness was getting on his nerves.

The next hand, he was dealt pocket aces. The flop came down: 2 of diamonds, then the 10 of diamonds, and the ace of clubs. He and the blonde were suddenly engaged again, upping each other's bets. The turn was the queen of diamonds. The river was the 2 of spades, which put a pair on the board. He figured the woman had pocket kings or queens. If she held a king and a jack or two diamonds, she'd be looking at a straight or a flush.

He had a full house, aces full of 2's, and that hand would beat either. He locked eyes with the blonde. More than anything in the world, he wanted to grind her face into the felt. She was bluffing again. He knew she was. He was right back at the same place he'd been six hours before, only this time his hand was strong.

He sat there trying to anticipate what she held. Any way he looked at it, he was in the superior position. He studied the cards on the table, imagining every possible combination, given what he could see and the pocket aces he knew he had. She was bluffing. She had to be. He raised—nothing dramatic because he didn't want her backing away. She hesitated and then matched his bet and raised him another two hundred. He was going to make a mistake. He could feel it in his bones. But which way would his error lie? Would he fold as he had before and let her take a pot like that with a piss-poor hand? Or would he push her to the wall? Was he underestimating her hand? He didn't see how he could be, but he'd lost touch with his intuition. He couldn't reason. His mind was empty. When he was on a roll he could see the cards. It was like having X-ray vision. The odds would dance in his head like sugarplum fairies and he'd feel the magic at work. Now all he could take in was the green felt and the harsh lights and the cards, which lay there inert and whispered nothing to him. If he picked up this pot he was home free. He could picture it, his holding to etiquette and not reaching for the pot at first even though it was his. The dealer would push the chips in his direction. He wouldn't even look at the blonde, because who cared about her? This was his moment. Doubt had obscured his initial fleeting instincts. He couldn't remember what his gut had been telling him. Time seemed to stretch. She was waiting, and the dealer waited, and the other players measured his chances in the same way he did. If he won the pot, he'd quit. He made a promise to himself. He'd get up, collect his winnings, and walk out a free man.

She was a woman who bluffed. She'd gotten him once and if she was a killer, she'd do it again. What were the chances of the two of them going head-to-head like this and her bluffing a second time? How much nerve did she have? How calculating was she? She wouldn't do that, would she? He had to make a decision. He felt like he was standing on a ten-meter board, teetering on the brink, trying to work up the courage to go flying off the edge. *Fuck it*, he thought, and he went all in. He was not going to let the bitch get the best of him.

He turned over his pocket cards, watching every player at the table put the hand together: pocket aces, plus an ace of clubs and the pair of 2's on the table, giving him his full house. The look she turned on him was odd. He didn't understand until he caught sight of the cards she'd fanned out in front of her. There was a collective intake of breath. She was holding pocket 2's. Adding those to the 2's on the table gave her four of a kind. He stared with disbelief. Pocket deuces? Nobody pushed pre-flop with a pair like that. She had to be insane. But there they sat, four 2's . . . four sharp arrows in his heart.

The dealer said nothing. He pushed the blonde's winnings forward and she gathered them in. Phillip was in shock, so convinced the hand was his that he couldn't absorb the fact of her four of a kind. What kind of lunatic held on to pocket 2's and pushed all the way to the end? His mouth was dry and his hands had started to shake. The gaze she fixed on him was nearly sexual, soft with satisfaction. She'd played him and just as he thought he'd gotten off, she pulled the rug out from under him again. He got up abruptly and left the table. Of his original ten grand, he had four hundred dollars in chips.

He took the elevator to the fourth floor, surprised when he realized it was dark outside. His hands shook so badly, it took him two tries to get his key to work. He locked the door behind him and stripped off his clothes, leaving a trail across the floor: shoes, socks, pants, shirt. He smelled of flop sweat. In the bathroom, he dropped two Alka-Seltzers into a glass of water and drank down the still-fizzing mix. He showered and shaved, then pulled on the hotel robe, a white terry cloth garment that hit him at the knee and gaped unbecomingly when he perched on the edge of the bed. He punched in the number for room service, ordering an Angus steak sandwich, medium rare, hand-cut fries, and two beers.

Forty-five minutes passed before the food arrived and by then both the fries and the steak were cold. The beef was choice instead of prime and too tough to bite through. He'd had to discard the bun and cut the meat with his steak knife. He chewed until the meat was a flavorless wad. He had no appetite. He was sick at heart. He pushed the cart to one side. He'd nap for an hour and then go down to the casino and try his luck again. He really had no choice. With four hundred dollars in chips, he had no idea how he'd get back on top, but there was no way he'd leave town without Dante's money in hand.

There was a knock at the door. He glanced at the clock. 9:25. He'd had the presence of mind to put the Do Not Disturb sign on the outside knob and he was tempted to ignore the intrusion. Probably a complimentary fruit bowl or a bottle of bad wine. Amenities of that sort were always delivered at odd hours when you had no use for them. The knock came again. He crossed the room and put an eye to the spy hole.

Dante was standing in the corridor. Phillip could see two more men approaching from down the hall. When he'd returned to his room earlier, he'd flipped the dead bolt into the locked position and swung the elongated V of the safety lock into place. What were the chances of the three going away if he didn't answer the door? Dante had no way of knowing he was in his room. He might have gone out without removing the plastic tag that hung over the knob. He debated briefly and decided it was better to face him. His only hope was to ask for an extension. Dante would almost have to agree. What else was he going to do? Phillip didn't have the money and if he didn't have it, he didn't have it.

Phillip undid the locks and opened the door.

Dante said, "I was beginning to think you weren't here."

"Sorry about that. I was on the phone."

There was a moment of silence.

"You going to let me in?" Dante asked. His tone was mild, but Phillip detected the edge.

"Of course. Absolutely."

Phillip stepped back and Dante entered the room, with his two companions sauntering in behind him. The door was left open and Phillip didn't like the feeling that anyone passing down the hall could see in. He felt vulnerable, barefoot, wearing the hotel robe, which barely covered his knees. His clothes were still strewn across the floor. The remains of dinner on his room-service tray smelled strongly of ketchup and cold fries.

Dante wore a dove gray silk shirt, open at the collar, and fawn-colored slacks. His loafers and belt were made of the same honey leather. The two men with him were more casually dressed.

Dante nodded at one. "My brother, Cappi," he said. "That's Nico. You met him."

"I remember. Nice seeing you again," Phillip said. Neither man acknowledged him.

Cappi was in his forties, a good eight years younger than his brother; five foot nine, maybe, to Dante's height of six two. He was fair, his hair an unruly thatch of dark blond, spiked with gel. He had a fashionable two-day growth of beard, light eyes, and a jaw that jutted forward slightly. The malocclusion offset his otherwise good looks. He wasn't the same natty dresser as his brother. Where Dante's clothes were high quality and tailored to fit, Cappi's gray-and-black polyester shirt was worn loose over stone-washed jeans. Phillip wondered if he carried a gun.

Nico, the third guy, was heavyset and soft, wearing jeans and a T-shirt too tight for his bulging gut. Cappi moved to the open door while Nico popped his head into the bathroom, checking to see that it was empty. Dante crossed to the window and turned to survey the accommodations, taking in the eight-foot cottage-cheese ceiling, the furnishings, the drab wall-to-wall carpeting, the fourth-floor view. He said, "Not bad. Wouldn't hurt 'em to sink serious money into the place."

Phillip said, "It's nice. I appreciate your putting in a good word for me."

"They treating you well?"

"Great. Couldn't be better."

"Glad to hear that," Dante said. "I flew in an hour ago. It's been a while since I was here and I figured as long as I was in the neighborhood, I'd see what you were up to."

Phillip couldn't think of an appropriate response so he said nothing. He watched to see which Dante was in evidence, the kind man or the hidden one with his malicious heart and dead eyes. He thought the good one was in charge, but he knew better than to make assumptions.

Dante leaned against the chest of drawers. "So how's it going? You said you'd be coming in to see me. We had a date. What was it, August 11? Day before yesterday."

"I know. Sorry I didn't make it, but something came up."

There was a moment's pause while Dante absorbed the news. He didn't seem upset. "Happens to all of us. A phone call would have been nice, but here you are." His manner was casual, as though he couldn't have cared less. Phillip felt a cautious relief. He'd been aware of the deadline he'd missed and half expected Dante to make a fuss.

He said, "I appreciate your understanding."

"Would you quit with the fucking appreciation? It's getting on my nerves."

"Sorry."

Dante moved away from the chest of drawers. He put his hands in his trouser pockets and ambled along the periphery of the room, checking the room-service menu still sitting on top of the television set. "What exactly *came up*? You had a social engagement, something you couldn't tear yourself away from?"

"I meant to call, but I got sidetracked."

"Well, that explains everything," Dante said. "So how's it going now that you're on point? You don't look happy."

"I played well at first, but I've had a stretch of bad luck. I didn't want to short you so I was waiting until I had the full amount."

"Fair enough. Which is when?"

"I was just on my way down to the casino. I was at the table all day and came up to rest, you know, freshen up . . ."

"Empty your pockets and let's see what you've got."

"This is it for now." He picked up his chips and held them out to Dante, who stared.

"Four hundred dollars' worth? Out of the ten grand I trusted you with—you got four hundred left? Are you out of your mind? I made you a loan. I told you how much it was going to cost you. Any ambiguity? I don't think so. You're into week two and the vig's up to five grand. What am I supposed to do with *this*?"

"That's all I have. I can get the rest of it in a week."

"I didn't offer you a layaway plan. You knew the terms of the deal. I did what I could to help you. Now you help me."

"I'm not able to do that, Mr. Dante. I'm sorry, but I can't. I feel terrible."

"As well you should. How do you propose to raise the rest of it? You've got no credit left."

"I was hoping you'd give me an extension."

"I already did that and this is what I get. You told your parents about the money you owe me?"

"Oh, no, sir. Absolutely not. I promised to give up gambling after they bailed me out last time. I'll tell 'em if I have to, but I'd prefer not."

"What about your girlfriend?"

"I told her I was going camping with a friend."

"You call this camping?" Dante shook his head. "What am I going to do with you? You're a moron, you know that? Big ego, hot talk, but in the end you're a putz. You pissed all your money away and now it's my money you've blown. And for what? You think you're a poker champ? There's no way. You don't have the skill, the talent, or the brains. You owe me twenty-six grand."

Phillip said, "No, no. That's not right. Is that right?"

"You're on the hook for my expenses getting over here."

"Why?"

"Because I came on your account. How else am I going to talk to you when you don't show up when you said you would? You missed our appointment so I had to come on short notice, which meant chartering a flight. Plus, I got these two goons to pay."

"I can't do it. You told me twenty-five dollars per hundred on ten grand . . ."

"Per week."

"I understand, but that's only five grand. You just said so yourself."

"Plus interest on the interest, plus the late fees, plus expenses."

"I don't have it."

"You don't have it. You have nothing of value anywhere in the world. You own nothing. Is that what you're telling me?"

"I could give you my car."

"Do I look like a guy who owns a used-car lot?"

"Not at all."

Dante stared at him. "What's the make and model?"

"1985 Porsche 911, red. It's worth over thirty thousand dollars. It's in pristine condition. Perfect."

"I know the definition of 'pristine,' you asshole. What do you owe on it?"

"Nothing. It's paid for. My parents gave it to me for graduation. I'll sign the pink slip right now and hand it over to you."

"And it's where, this fancy paid-for car of yours?"

"In the parking garage."

"Valet?"

"I parked it myself to save the expense."

"Well, aren't you the frugal one. How far up?"

"The top."

"I ought to have my head examined." He glanced at his brother. "You two go up with the kid here and take a look at his car, tell me what you think. I want it checked out. Find a local mechanic if you have to." He turned to Phillip. "The car better be as advertised. I'm running out of patience."

"I swear it is and thank you."

"Take a good look at yourself. Time to give up this poker shit and get a job. You're wasting your life. Are you hearing me?"

"Absolutely. Yes. This will never happen again. It's been a valuable lesson. I'm out of here. I'm gone. No more poker, I swear. This has been a wake-up call. I can't thank you enough."

"Cappi, you take care of this." Dante dismissed Phillip with a gesture. "Jesus, put some clothes on. You look like a girl."

All three men looked on without comment as Phillip gathered his clothes. He'd have preferred going into the bathroom to dress in privacy, but he didn't want to risk another round of verbal abuse. Three minutes later, Cappi, Nico, and Phillip traversed the hotel, bypassing the elevator in favor of the stairs. Phillip said, "Why can't we take the elevator?"

Cappi stopped so fast, Phillip nearly stumbled into him. Cappi poked him in the chest with his index finger. "Let me tell you something. I'm in charge now, you got that? We do it by the book, no ifs, ands, or buts."

"I didn't hear him say we had to walk up."

Cappi was in his face with his beefy breath. "You know what your problem is? You're always thinking someone has to make an exception for you. Do it your way, on your terms. That's not how it works. He says take you up. I'm taking you up. He wants to see how the car drives, okay? He wants to know what kind of shape it's in. You say pristine, but we only have your word for it. All he knows, it's a piece of shit."

Phillip dropped the protest. Ten more minutes and this would all be over with. He'd cash in his four hundred dollars' worth of chips and buy a bus ticket home. The two began to climb, Phillip clearly out of shape. After two flights he was winded. He had no idea how he'd explain what had happened to his car, but he'd deal with one problem at a time.

They reached the top level of the parking garage. While only six stories high, the night view was dramatic, lights as far as he could see. He spotted the Lady Luck two blocks over, the Four Queens across the street, so close he felt he could reach out and touch the sign. The lot was jammed with vehicles, but the Porsche stood out, gleaming red in the light, not a speck of dust on it. Cappi snapped his fingers. "Lemme see the keys."

Phillip fumbled in his pants pocket and came up with the car keys. Nico didn't seem interested. He stood with his arms crossed, looking off to one side like he had better things to do. Phillip thought he'd be the one who looked under the hood, but maybe he didn't know anything about cars. He doubted Cappi was any kind of expert.

Three guys stepped out of the elevator. Phillip thought they were mechanics or parking attendants until he noticed they wore blue latex gloves. This struck him as odd at first, and then as alarming. He backed up a step, but no one said anything and no one made eye contact. Without a word, they approached and picked him up, one grabbing him under the arms while another was lifting his feet. The third man pulled his wallet from his back pocket and flipped off his shoes. The two men hauled him closer to the parapet and began to swing him back and forth.

Phillip struggled, thrashing, his voice shrill with fear. "What are you doing?"

Irritably, Cappi said, "What's it look like? Dante says take care of it. I'm taking care of it."

"Wait! We had a deal. We're square."

"Here's the deal, Fuck Face."

The men swinging him had built up momentum. He thought they might not be serious. He thought they were trying only to scare him. Then he felt himself hoisted over the rail. Suddenly he was airborne, falling so fast he couldn't make a sound before he hit the pavement below.

Cappi peered over the wall. "Now we're square, you little prick."

# 2

So this is how it went down, folks. I turned thirty-eight on May 5, 1988, and my big birthday surprise was a punch in the face that left me with two black eyes and a busted nose. Contributing to the overall effect were the wads of gauze in both nostrils and a fat upper lip. My medical insurance sported me to the services of a plastic surgeon who repaired the old schnozz while I was blissfully sedated.

On my release, I retreated to my studio apartment, where I lay on my sofa, keeping my head elevated to minimize the swelling. This allowed me time to brood about my ill treatment at the hands of a virtual stranger. Five or six times a day, I'd check my reflection in the bathroom mirror, watching handsome red-and-purple bruises migrate from my eye sockets to my cheeks, blood settling in circles as conspicuous as rouge on a clown's face. I was grateful my teeth had been spared. Even so, I spent days explaining my sudden resemblance to a raccoon.

People kept saying, "Oh, wow! You finally got your nose done. It looks great!"

This was entirely uncalled for as no one had ever complained about my nose before, at least not to my face. My poor snout had been broken on two previous occasions and it never occurred to me that I'd suffer a repetition. Of course, the indignity was my own fault, since I was sticking said nose into someone else's business when I was so rudely assaulted by a short-arm blow.

The incident that heralded my fate seemed insignificant at first. I was standing in the lingerie department at Nordstrom's department store, sorting through ladies' underpants on sale—three pair for ten bucks, a bonanza for someone of my cheap bent. What could be more banal? I don't like to shop, but I'd seen a half-page ad in the morning paper and decided to take advantage of the bargain prices. It was Friday, April 22, a date I remember because I'd wrapped up a case the day before and I'd spent the morning typing my final report.

For those of you just making my acquaintance, my name is Kinsey Millhone. I'm a licensed private detective in Santa Teresa, California, doing business as Millhone Investigations. In the main, I deal with bread-and-butter jobs—background checks, skip tracing, insurance fraud, process serving, and witness location, with the occasional rancorous divorce thrown in for laughs. Not coincidentally, I'm female, which is why I was shopping for ladies' underwear instead of men's. Given my occupation, I'm no stranger to crime and I'm seldom surprised by the dark side of human nature, my own included. Further personal data can wait in the interest of getting on with my sad tale of woe. In any event, I have additional groundwork to lay before I reach the stunning moment that did me in.

I left the office early that day and made my usual Friday bank deposit, taking back a portion in cash to carry me over the next two weeks. I drove from the bank to the parking garage under the Passages Shopping Plaza. I generally frequent the low-end chain stores, where aisles are jammed with racks of identical garments, suggesting cheap manufacture in a country unfettered by child labor laws. Nordstrom's was a palace by comparison, the interior cool and elegant. The floors were gleaming marble tile and the air was scented with designer perfumes. The store directory indicated that women's intimate apparel was located on 3, and I headed for the escalator.

What caught my eye as I entered the sales area was a display of silk pajamas in a dazzling array of jewel tones—emerald, amethyst, garnet, and sapphire—neatly folded and arranged by size. The original unit price was $199.95, marked down to $49.95. I couldn't help flirting with the notion of two-hundred-dollar pj's against my bare skin. Most nights, I sleep in a ratty oversize T-shirt. At $49.95, I could afford to indulge. Then again, I'm single and sleep alone so what would be the point?

I found a table piled with scanties and picked my way through, debating the merits of high-cut briefs versus boy-shorts versus hip-huggers, distinctions that meant absolutely nothing to me. I don't often buy undies, so I'm usually forced to start from scratch. Styles have changed, lines have been discontinued, entire manufacturing plants have apparently burned to the ground. I vowed if I found something I liked, I'd buy a dozen at the very least.

I'd been at it ten minutes and I was already tired of holding lacy scraps across my pelvis to judge the fit. I scanned the area, looking for assistance, but the nearest clerk was busy advising another customer, a hefty woman in her fifties, in spike-heel shoes and a tight black pantsuit that made her thighs and butt bulge unbecomingly. She would have done well to emulate the sales clerk, younger by a good ten years, in her conservative dark blue dress and sensible flats. The two stood in front of a rack of matching lacy bra-and-bikini sets on little plastic hangers. I couldn't imagine the chunky woman in bikini underwear, but there's no accounting for taste. It wasn't until the two parted company that I saw the younger woman's big leather purse and shopping bag and realized she was simply another customer, shopping for lingerie like everyone else. I returned to my task, decided a size small would do, and gathered an assortment of pastels, adding animal prints until I had forty dollars' worth.

A girl-child of about three scurried past and concealed herself in the inner recesses of a rack of loungewear, knocking several hangers to the floor. I could hear the raised voice of an anxious mother.

"Portia, where are you?"

There was a movement in the loungewear; Portia wiggling deeper into her hiding place.

"Portia?"

The mother appeared at the end of the aisle, a woman in her twenties, probably trying not to sound as anxious as she felt. I raised a hand and pointed at the rack, where I could still see a pair of black patent leather Mary Janes and two sturdy legs.

The mother pushed the clothes aside and dragged the child out by one arm. "Goddamn it! I told you not to move," she said, and swatted her once on her backside before she retreated to the elevators with the little girl in tow. The child seemed totally unaffected by the reprimand.

A woman standing nearby turned with a disapproving look and said to me, "Disgusting. Someone should call the floor manager. That's child abuse."

I shrugged, remembering the many swats I'd endured at my Aunt Gin's hands. She always assured me she'd really give me something to cry about if I wanted to protest.

My attention was drawn back to the woman in the black pantsuit, who was now peering wistfully at the silk pajamas, much as I had. I confess I took a certain proprietary interest, having lusted after them myself. I glanced at her and then I blinked with disbelief as she slid two pairs of pajamas (one emerald, one sapphire) into her shopping bag. I shifted my gaze, wondering if the strain of panty buying had caused me to hallucinate.

I paused, feigning interest in a rack of house robes while I kept an eye on her. She rearranged the display to disguise the gap where the stolen pajamas had been resting mere moments before. To the average observer, she appeared to be restoring order to an untidy tabletop. I've done the same thing myself after rooting through a pile of sweaters in search of my size.

She glanced at me, but by then I was scrutinizing the construction of a house robe I'd removed from the rack. She seemed to take no further notice of me. Her manner was matter-of-fact. If I hadn't just witnessed the sleight of hand, I wouldn't have given her another thought.

Except for this one tiny point:

Early in my career, after I'd graduated from the police academy and during my two-year stint with the Santa Teresa Police Department, I'd worked a six-month rotation in property crimes—the unit handling burglaries, embezzlement, auto theft, and retail theft, both petit and grand. Shoplifters are the bane of retail businesses, which lose billions annually in what's euphemistically referred to as "inventory shrinkage." My old training kicked in. I noted the time (5:26 P.M.) and studied the woman as though I were already leafing through mug shots, looking for a match. Briefly, I thought back to the younger woman in whose company I'd first seen her. There was no sign of the younger woman now, but it wouldn't have surprised me to find out they were working in tandem.

With the older woman now in close range, I upgraded her age from midfifties to midsixties. She was shorter than I and probably forty pounds heavier, with short blond hair back-combed to a puff and sprayed to a fare-thee-well. In the clear overhead light, her makeup glowed pink while her neck was stark white. She crossed to a table display of lace teddies, touching the fabrics appreciatively. She checked the whereabouts of the sales staff and then, with her index and middle fingers, she gathered one of the teddies, compressing it into accordion folds until it disappeared like a handkerchief crumpled in her hand. She eased the garment into her shoulder bag and then removed her compact as though that had been her intent. She powdered her nose and made a minor correction to her eye makeup, the teddy now safely deposited in her purse. I glanced at the rack of bras and panties where I'd first seen the two women. The rack had been thinned considerably, and I was guessing she or the other woman had added any number of items to her cache of stolen goods. Not to criticize, but she should have quit while she was ahead.

I went straight to the register. The sales clerk smiled pleasantly as I placed my selection on the counter. Her name tag read CLAUDIA RINES, SALES ASSISTANT. We were nodding acquaintances, in that I saw her from time to time at Rosie's Tavern, half a block from my apartment. I frequented the place because Rosie was a friend, but I couldn't think why anyone else would go there, aside from certain undiscerning neighbors of the alcoholic sort. Tourists shunned the restaurant, which was not only shabby and outdated, but devoid of charm; in other words, innately appealing to the likes of me.

Under my breath, I said to Claudia, "Please don't look now, but the woman over at that table in the black pantsuit just stole a lace teddy and two pairs of silk pajamas."

She flicked a look at the customer. "The middle-aged blonde?"

"Yep."

"I'll take care of it," she said. She turned and picked up the house phone, angling her body so she could keep an eye on the woman while she spoke in low tones. Once alerted, an agent in the security office would check the bank of monitors in front of him, searching for the suspect in question. Strategically placed cameras picked up overlapping views that covered all three floors, forty thousand square feet of retail space. When he had her in view, he could pan, tilt, and zoom to keep her under continuous observation while the loss-prevention officer was dispatched.

Claudia returned the receiver to the cradle, her professional smile still in place. "He's on his way. He's one floor down."

I handed her my credit card and waited while she removed price tags and rang up the sale. She placed my purchases in a shopping bag and came around the end of the counter to hand it to me. She was doubtless as conscious of the shoplifter as I was, though both of us tried not to call attention to the fact that we were tracking her. On the far side of the floor, the elevator doors opened and a man in a dark gray business suit emerged with a walkie-talkie to his lips. He might as well have worn a sandwich board announcing his status as a loss-prevention officer.

He made his way past infant and children's wear and into lingerie, where he paused to engage Claudia in conversation. She relayed what I'd told her, saying, "This is Mr. Koslo."

We nodded at each other.

"You're sure of this?" he asked.

I said, "Quite." I took out a photocopy of my PI license and placed it on the counter where he could view it. While none of us looked directly at the woman in the pantsuit, I could see the color draining from her face. Shoplifters are nothing if not canny in their assessment of jeopardy. In addition to closed-circuit television cameras, sales staff and the store's plainclothes floor walkers were all a source of peril. I'd have been willing to bet she had close to a photographic memory of every shopper in the area.

Nearby customers seemed unaware of the drama being played out, but I was transfixed. The shoplifter's gaze flicked from the loss-prevention officer to the escalators. A direct path would have forced her to walk right past him. I thought a move was ill advised and, apparently, she did too. Better to keep her distance and hope the threat evaporated of its own accord. In most stores, policy dictates that no one make contact with a customer under surveillance as long as she is still on the premises and has the opportunity to pay. For the moment, the woman was safe, though her agitation surfaced in a series of random gestures. She looked at her watch. She glanced toward the ladies' room. She picked up a half-slip, studied it briefly, and then replaced it. The items she'd stolen must have felt radioactive, but she didn't dare return them lest she call attention to herself.

The prospect of being apprehended must have obliterated the alternatives she'd planned if the caper turned sour. Her best course of action would have been to adjourn to the ladies' room and toss the stolen merchandise in the trash. Failing that, she could have abandoned her shopping bag and headed for the elevators in hopes of stepping into the next available car. Without the pilfered items in her possession, she'd be home free. Until she left the store without paying, no crime had been committed. Perhaps with something of the sort in mind, she removed herself from Mr. Koslo's line of sight and ambled into the women's plus-size department, where she looked right at home.

Koslo moved away from the counter without visual reference to the woman. I watched as he circled behind her in a wide arc, herding her from the rear. Claudia moved directly to the escalator and went down, probably to intercept the woman if she tried leaving by that means.

The shoplifter's gaze darted from one area to the next as she considered viable escape routes. Her only choices were the elevators, the escalators, or the fire stairs. With Koslo ten yards behind her, the elevators and the fire stairs must have seemed too far away to chance. From her current location, the aisle widened to form a generous apron of pale marble that led to the escalators, tantalizingly close. She strolled out of the plus-size department and crossed the open floor at a leisurely pace. Behind her, Koslo adjusted his speed to correspond with hers.

On the far side of the escalators, I saw the younger woman in the dark blue dress appear at the mouth of the short corridor leading to the ladies' room. She halted abruptly, and as the shoplifter reached the top of the escalator a look flashed between them. If I'd entertained doubts about their being in cahoots, I was convinced of it now. Maybe they were sisters or mother and daughter on a regular late-afternoon outing, ripping off retail goods. In that brief freeze-frame, I took a mental inventory of the younger woman. She was fair, forty by my guess, with untidy, shoulder-length blond hair and little or no makeup. She turned on her heel and returned to the ladies' room while the older woman moved on to the escalator; Koslo seven steps behind her. The two of them sank from view, first the woman's head disappearing and then his.

I crossed to the balustrade and peered down, watching them glide slowly from the third floor to the second. The woman must have realized she was boxed in because the knuckles of her right hand were white where she clutched the rail. The sluggish speed of the moving staircase must have sent her heart into overdrive. The fight-or-flight instinct is almost irresistible and I marveled at her self-control. Her partner would be of no help to her now. If the younger woman intervened, she risked being caught in the same net.

Claudia was waiting on the second floor at the foot of the moving stairs. The shoplifter kept her attention fixed straight ahead, perhaps thinking if she couldn't see her two trackers, they couldn't see her. Once on the second floor, she took a hard turn and stepped onto the next down escalator. Claudia stepped on after she did, so that now there were two store employees in that slow-motion foot chase. The fact that the shoplifter was aware of them took away their home court advantage. By this time, however, the game was in progress and there was no way to abandon the pursuit. I could see a thin pie-shaped portion of the first-floor shoe department, which I knew was only a short stretch away from the automatic doors that opened onto the mall. I left the three of them to their own devices. By then, the older woman was no concern of mine. I was interested in her companion.

I crossed to the short corridor that led to the ladies' lounge and pushed open the door. I was hoping she was still there, but she might well have slipped past me while I was watching her friend. To my right, an anteroom had been set aside for mothers with babies, affording them privacy to nurse, change stinky diapers, or collapse on a well-upholstered couch. That area was empty. Across from it, there was a room where sinks lined the two opposite mirrored walls, with the usual paper towel dispensers, hand blowers, and plastic-lined waste bins. An Asian woman foamed her hands with soap and rinsed them under running water, but she seemed to be the only customer present. I heard a toilet flush, and a moment later the younger woman opened the door to the second stall. She now sported a red beret and wore a white linen jacket over her navy blue dress. She still carried the shopping bag and her big leather purse. The only oddity I noted was a short horizontal scar between her lower lip and her chin, the sort of mark left when your teeth are driven through your lower lip on impact. The scar was old, with only a white line remaining to suggest a tumble from a swing or a fall against the corner of a coffee table, some childhood misfortune she'd carried with her since. She averted her face as she brushed by me. If she recognized me from the lingerie department, she gave no sign.

I kept my expression blank and headed for the stall she'd just vacated. It took me half a second to peer into the wall-mounted receptacle meant for used sanitary supplies. Six price tags had been clipped from articles of clothing and tossed into the bin. I listened to the sound of her retreating footsteps. The outer door closed. I scurried after her and opened the door a crack. I didn't see her, but I knew she couldn't have gone far. I proceeded to the mouth of the corridor and peered to my right. She stood in front of the bank of elevators, pushing the down button. Her head came up, as mine did, at the sound of a persistent high-pitched *whoop* from the ground floor. The older woman must have breached the transmitter-receiver system at the exit doors, where electronic surveillance tags had activated the alarm. Once she stepped outside, it would at least allow the loss-prevention officer to stop her and ask her to return.

The younger woman pressed the down button repeatedly as though to speed the arrival of the car. The elevator doors opened and two pregnant mothers emerged side by side, pushing strollers ahead of them. The younger woman pushed her way past them, and one turned to look at her with annoyance. Another shopper approached in haste and called out, not wanting the doors to close before she had a chance to get on. One of the pregnant women reached back and put a hand against the doors to stall their closure. The shopper smiled gratefully as she stepped in, murmuring her thanks. The elevator doors closed as the two pregnant women ambled off toward infant and children's wear.

I made a beeline for the fire exit, laid one hip against the push-bar, and entered the stairwell. I went down as rapidly as possible, dropping two steps at a time while I calculated the younger woman's escape alternatives. She could take the elevator as far as the second floor or the first, or proceed all the way down to the basement level, where the parking garage was located. If she realized I was on her tail, she might leave the elevator on 2 and take the escalator up to 3 again, in hopes of throwing me off course. On the other hand, she probably wanted to get out of the store as quickly as possible, which made the first floor the obvious choice. Once she slipped into the busy mall, she could doff the white linen jacket and the red beret and hurry away, knowing there was no chance I'd reach the exit doors before she'd been swallowed into the crowd. I reached the second-floor landing and used the railing as a pivot as I took the next flight down, muffled footsteps echoing as I ran. Another possibility occurred to me as I galloped down the stairs. If she'd arrived at the store with an eye to a leisurely day of thieving, she might have wanted her car handy, with a trunk capacious enough to accommodate multiple shopping bags stuffed with stolen goods. How many times had I seen shoppers dropping bags off at the car before returning to the mall?

I rounded the landing at the first floor and bypassed the exit as I sped toward the parking garage. I took the final short flight of stairs in two leaps. The door at the bottom opened into a small carpeted lobby with offices visible behind a set of glass doors. The exit doors slid open as I reached them and then politely closed behind me. I paused to take in the vast underground garage. I was standing in a dead-end bay, circumscribed by a short loop of parking spaces coveted because of their proximity to the store's entrance. I've watched cars circle endlessly, hoping to snag one of these treasured slots. Now all of them were taken and there was no sign of backing-out taillights to suggest a vacancy coming due.

I trotted into the empty lane and scanned the straightaway that shot to the far end of the garage, where a shadowy two-lane ramp curved up to the street level above. The space was illuminated by a series of flat fluorescent fixtures mounted against the low concrete ceiling. There was no sound of running footsteps. Cars entered and departed at regular intervals. Ingress was impeded by the need to push a button and wait for an automated ticket to emerge from the slot. Egress was governed by the need to surrender that same ticket on exiting, pausing long enough for the attendant to check the date-and-time stamp to see if parking fees were due. To my right was the nearest exit, a short upward incline that spilled out onto Chapel Street. The sign posted at the top read WATCH FOR PEDESTRIANS. NO LEFT TURN. As I waited, two cars passed me, one coming down the ramp, the other on its way up. I gave the departing driver a quick look, but she wasn't the woman I was looking for.

I heard a car engine spark to life. I squinted and tilted my head as I tried to track the sound to its origin. In the artificial light of the garage with its gloomy acres of concrete, it was almost impossible to pinpoint. I turned and looked behind me, where twenty feet away, I caught the wink of red taillights and a white flash of backup lights. A black Mercedes sedan accelerated out of the slot, swung sharply, and careened backward in my direction. The younger woman had an arm over the front seat, zeroing in on me, the car zigzagging as she corrected her aim. The rear of the Mercedes fishtailed and bore down on me with surprising speed. I leaped between two parked cars, banging my shin against the front bumper of one. I stumbled and toppled sideways, extending my right hand in hopes of breaking my fall. I went down on one shoulder and then staggered to my feet again.

The woman rammed the gear into drive and took off with a chirp of her tires. Of necessity, she slowed at the kiosk, handing over her ticket while I limped gamely after her with no hope of catching up. The attendant glanced at her ticket and waved her on, apparently unaware that she'd just tried to run me down. The traffic arm lifted and the woman sent me a satisfied smile as she sailed up the ramp and hung a left at the street.

Wincing, I stopped and leaned over, putting my hands on my knees. I realized belatedly that my right palm was badly scraped and bleeding. My right shin throbbed and I knew I'd be nursing a nasty bruise and a knot along the bone.

I looked up as a man approached and handed me my shoulder bag, eyeing me with concern. "Are you all right? That woman nearly hit you."

"I'm fine. Don't worry about it."

"You want me to notify mall security? You really ought to file a report."

I shook my head. "Did you catch the license plate?"

"Well, no, but she was driving a Lincoln Continental. Dark blue, if that helps."

I said, "Good call. Thanks."

As soon as he was gone, I pulled myself together and went in search of my car. My shin throbbed and the palm of my hand stung where grit was embedded in the wound. I'd gained precious little for the price I'd paid. So much for the eyewitness account. I'd already identified the black Mercedes. It was the plate number I'd missed. Shit.

# 3

Fifteen minutes later I was turning off Cabana Boulevard onto Albanil. I parked my Mustang half a block from my apartment and limped the rest of the way, still rerunning the episode in my head. It's amazing what you miss when someone's trying to score a traffic fatality at your expense. There was no point in berating myself for failing to pick up the number on the license plate. Well, okay, I chided myself a little bit, but I didn't go overboard. I could only hope the woman in the black pantsuit had actually been arrested and was at the county jail being booked, fingerprinted, and photographed. If she was a novice, a night in jail might cure her of the urge to steal. If she was an old hand at shoplifting, maybe she'd lay off, at least until her court date came up. Her friend might also take a lesson.

Turning up the front walk, I saw that Henry had already put his garbage bins at the curb, though the regular weekly pickup wasn't until Monday. I went through the squeaky gate and around to the rear, where I unlocked my studio door and dropped my shoulder bag on a kitchen stool. I turned on the desk lamp and pulled up my pant leg to examine my injury, a move I immediately regretted. My shin now sported a bony protrusion that had an eerie sheen to it, flanked by two wide bruises the color of eggplant. I don't like playing tag with a luxury sedan. I don't like being forced to leap between cars as though rehearsing a stunt. I was more pissed off in retrospect than I'd been at the time. I know there are people who believe you should forgive and forget. For the record, I'd like to say I'm a big fan of forgiveness as long as I'm given the opportunity to get even first.

I crossed the patio to Henry's place. The kitchen lights were on and the glass-paned door stood open, though the screen was hooked shut. I picked up the scent of split pea soup simmering on the stove. Henry was on the phone. I tapped on the frame to let him know I was there. He waved me in and when I pointed at the door, he stretched the long coiled telephone line to the maximum to unhook the screen. He went back to his conversation, which he conducted while gesturing with a ticket envelope, saying, "By way of Denver. I have an hour-and-thirty-minute layover. Connecting flight gets me in at 3:05. I left the return open so we can play that by ear."

There was a pause while the other party responded in such loud tones, I could almost distinguish the content from where I stood. Henry held the handset away from his ear and fanned himself with his itinerary, rolling his eyes.

After a moment, he cut in. "That's fine. Don't worry about it. I can always take a cab. If I see you, I see you. If I don't, I'll show up at the house as soon as I can."

The conversation went on for a bit while I held up my skinned palm, the butt of which was scored with skid marks. He peered at it closely and made a face. Still chatting, he tossed the plane ticket on the counter, opened a drawer, and took out a bottle of hydrogen peroxide and a box of cotton balls.

When his conversation ended, he returned the handset to the wall-mounted cradle and motioned me into a chair. "How'd you do this?"

I said, "Long story," and then regaled him with a condensed version of the shoplifting incident and my attempt to pick up an ID on the younger woman. "You should see my shin," I said. "It looks like somebody hit me with a tire iron. Weird thing is I don't even know how it happened. One minute she was steering straight for me. Next instant I'd levitated, getting out of her way."

"I can't believe you went after her. What were you going to do, make a citizen's arrest?"

"I hadn't thought that far ahead. I was hoping to pick up her plate number, but no such luck," I said. "What's going on? It sounds like you're taking a trip."

"I'm flying to Detroit. Nell took a spill. Lewis called first thing this morning and woke me out of a sound sleep."

"She fell? That's not like her. She's usually steady as a rock."

He saturated a cotton ball with peroxide and dabbed my wound. A light foam bubbled on the edge of the scrape. The wound no longer hurt, but there was something lovely about being tended to by a bona fide mother substitute. He frowned. "She was opening a can of tuna and the cat was winding back and forth between her legs. You know how they do. She went to set his bowl on the floor, tumbled over him, and came down on her hip. Lewis said it sounded like a well-struck baseball flying out of the park. She tried to pull herself up but the pain was excruciating, so the boys called 9-1-1. She went from the ER straight into surgery, which is when he called me. I contacted my travel agent as soon as the office opened and she got me a seat on the first flight out."

"What cat? I didn't know they had a cat."

"I thought I told you about him. Charlie took in a stray a month ago. Skin and bones from all reports, no tail, and half of one ear gone. Lewis was adamant about turning the scruffy guy over to the pound, but Charlie and Nell ganged up and voted him down. Lewis made his usual dire predictions—mange, cat scratch fever, septicemia, ringworm—and sure enough, this morning 'tragedy struck,' as he put it. Most of his report was taken up with I-told-you-so's." He returned the first-aid items to the drawer.

"But Nell's okay?"

Henry wagged his hand. "Lewis says they put a fourteen-inch titanium pin in her femur and I don't know what else. It was tough to keep him on point. I gather she'll be in the hospital for a few days and then go to rehab."

"Well, the poor thing."

Henry's sister, Nell, was ninety-nine years old and ordinarily the picture of health, not only active but vigorous. The only other hospitalization I'd heard about was nineteen years before, when she'd developed "female trouble" and had undergone a hysterectomy. Afterward she'd declared that while at eighty she was fully reconciled to the notion that her childbearing days were done, she was sorry to lose the organ. She'd never had a body part removed and she'd been hoping to leave the world with all her original equipment intact. Nell had never married and had no children of her own. Her four younger brothers had served as surrogates, aggravating the life out of her as kids are meant to do. Henry, as the youngest, was more closely allied with Nell than any of the intervening sibs. The two of them were like bookends, holding the three middle brothers upright. After Nell, Henry was the take-charge member of the family. In truth, he sometimes served in that capacity in my life as well.

William, age eighty-nine and senior to Henry by one year, had relocated to Santa Teresa four years before and had subsequently married my friend Rosie, who owns the neighborhood tavern where I hang out. As for Lewis and Charlie, still living at home, they were entirely capable of taking care of themselves. It was Nell, the temporary invalid, they'd find difficult to accept. All the boys deferred to her, giving her full command over their lives and well-being. If she was out of commission, even briefly, Lewis and Charlie would be lost.

"What time's your flight?"

"Six thirty. Means getting up at four thirty, but I can sleep on the plane."

"Is William going with you?"

"I talked him out of it. He's been complaining about his stomach, and the news of Nell's fall threw him into a tizzy. If he went, I'd end up with two patients on my hands."

William was a born-again hypochondriac and couldn't be trusted around the sick or infirm. Henry had told me that in the months before Nell's hysterectomy, William suffered from monthly cramps, which were later diagnosed as irritable bowel syndrome.

"I'll be happy to take you to the airport," I said.

"Perfect. That way I won't have to leave my car in the long-term parking lot." He put the oven on preheat and fixed a blue-eyed gaze on me. "You have dinner plans?"

"Forget it. I don't want you worrying about me. Have you packed?"

"Not yet, but I still have to eat. After supper I'll haul out a suitcase. I have a load in the dryer so I can't do much anyway until it's done. Chardonnay's in the fridge."

I poured myself some white wine and then took out an old-fashioned glass and filled it with ice. He keeps his Black Jack in a cabinet near the sink, so I added three fingers. I looked at him and he said, "And this much water." He held his thumb and index finger close together to specify the amount.

I added tap water and passed him the drink, which he sipped while he continued dinner preparations.

I set the table. Henry pulled four homemade dinner rolls from the freezer and put them on a baking sheet. As soon as the oven peeped, he slid the pan in and set the timer. Henry's a retired commercial baker who even now produces a steady stream of breads, rolls, cookies, cakes, and cinnamon buns so tasty they make me whimper.

I sat down at the table, catching sight of a list of items he needed to handle before he left town. He'd already canceled the newspaper, picked up his cleaning, and rescheduled a dental appointment. He'd drawn a happy face on that line. Henry hates dentists and postpones his visits for as long as he can. He'd crossed out a reminder to himself to roll out the garbage bins for Monday pickup. He'd also put his interior lights on timers and shut down the water valve to the washer so the machine wouldn't suffer a mishap in his absence. He intended to ask me to water his plants as needed and cruise through his place every two days to make sure things were okay. I checked that item off the list myself. By then the salad had been made and Henry was ladling soup into bowls. We snarfed down our food with the usual dispatch, competing for the land speed record. So far I was ahead.

After supper I helped him with the dishes and then went back to my place, toting a brown paper bag full of perishables he'd passed along to me.

In the morning, I woke at 5:00, brushed my teeth, washed my face, and pulled a knit cap over my mop of hair, which was mashed flat on one side and stood straight up everywhere else. Since it was Saturday, I wouldn't be doing my usual three-mile jog, but I stepped into sweats and running shoes for simplicity's sake. Henry was waiting on the back patio when I emerged. He looked adorable, of course: chinos and a white dress shirt with a blue cashmere sweater worn over it. His white hair, still damp from the shower, was neatly brushed to one side. I could picture "widder" women in the airport waiting room, angling for the chance to sit next to him.

We chitchatted on the twenty-minute drive to the airport, which allowed me to repress the feelings of melancholy I experienced the minute I dropped him at the gate. I made sure his flight was on time and then I waved once and took off, swallowing the lump in my throat. For a hard-assed private eye, I'm a wienie when it comes to saying goodbye. Home again, I pulled off my shoes, stripped my sweats, crawled into bed, and pulled the covers up to my chin. The Plexiglas skylight above my bed was streaked with the pink-and-blue streamers of a burgeoning dawn when I finally closed my eyes and sank into the warmth.

I woke again at 8:00, showered, dressed in my habitual jeans, turtleneck, and boots, and watched a segment of the news while I finished my cereal and washed my bowl. Neither the newspaper nor the local television station made reference to the shoplifting episode, not even as a tiny two-line report on an inside page. I would have appreciated learning the woman's name and age, along with some hint of what had happened to her. Was she arrested and charged, or kicked out of the store and told never to return? Policy varied from one retail establishment to the next and ranged from warn-and-release to criminal prosecution—the alternative I'd vote for if it were up to me.

I don't know why I thought the disturbance would warrant a news story. Crimes take place daily that don't generate a smidge of interest in the public at large. Minor matters of burglary and theft are relegated to the back page, break-ins reported by neighborhood with a cursory list of items stolen. Vandalism might be elevated to a one-inch squib. Depending on the political climate, taggers might or might not be accorded column space. White-collar crime—especially fraud and embezzlement of public funds—are more likely than murder to inspire irate letters to the editor and the denunciation of corporate greed. My shoplifter and her coconspirator were probably long gone, my bruised shin the only testimony that remained, painful witness to their skullduggery. For the foreseeable future, I'd be scanning pedestrians, alert to the presence of any black Mercedes sedan, all in hopes of spotting one or the other of the two women. Mentally, I sharpened the metal toes of my boots.

In the meantime, I loaded my car with cleaning equipment in anticipation of my Saturday chores. I was at the office by 9:00, happy to find a parking place out front. There was a period of time when I'd hired a service, the Mini-Maids, to clean my office once a week. There were usually four of them, though never the same four twice. They wore matching T-shirts and arrived toting mops, dust cloths, vacuums, and assorted janitorial products. The first time they cleaned for me they took an hour, their efforts thorough and conscientious. I'd been thrilled to pay the fifty bucks because the windows shone, all the surfaces gleamed, and the carpet was as clean as I'd ever seen it. Every visit thereafter, they accelerated the process until they became so efficient, they were in and out again in fifteen minutes, dashing off to the next job as though their very lives depended on it. Even then, much of their time on the premises was spent chatting among themselves. Once they departed, I'd find a dead fly on the windowsill, spider silk trailing from the ceiling, and coffee grounds (or were those ants?) littering the counter in my kitchenette. I figured fifty bucks for fifteen minutes (fraught with giggles and gossip) was the equivalent of two hundred bucks an hour, which was four times more than I earned myself. I fired them with a giddy sense of piety and thrift. Now I made a point of going in at intervals to do the job myself.

It wasn't until I hauled my vacuum cleaner from the trunk of my car that I noticed the fellow sitting on my steps, smoking a cigarette. His blue jeans had faded to white at the knee and his brown boots were scuffed. He had wide shoulders, and his shirt was a royal blue satin, unbuttoned to the waist, the sleeves rolled up above his biceps. The name Dodie was scrawled in cursive along his right forearm. For a moment I drew a blank, and then his name popped to mind.

He grinned, gold incisors flashing in his weathered face. "You don't recognize me," he remarked as I came up the walk.

"I do too. You're Pinky Ford. Last I heard, you were in jail."

"I've been a free man since last May. I admit I was picked up Friday on a DUI, but I got sprung. That's what friends are for is how I look at it. Anyways, I had business over at the jail this morning and seeing's how I was in the neighborhood, I decided to stop by and see how you were doing. How you been?" His voice was raspy from a lifetime of smoking.

"Fine, thanks. And you?"

"Good enough," he said. He didn't seem to register the Hoover upright and I didn't explain. It wasn't any of his business if I was working as a part-time char. He flipped his cigarette onto the walkway and stood up, brushing off his jeans. He was my height, five six, wiry, bowlegged, and brown from too much sun. His arms and chest were muscular, veins running across like piping. He'd been a jockey in his youth until he got tossed one time too many and decided he'd better find another line of work. He'd started smoking when he was ten and continued the habit as an adult because it was the only way to keep his weight including tack under the 126 pounds required for the Kentucky Derby, which he'd ridden in twice. This was long before his personal fortunes had gone into reverse. He'd kept on smoking for much the same reason any habitual criminal does, to break up the time while he was in the joint.

I put down my vacuum cleaner and unlocked the door, talking to him over my shoulder. "You're lucky you caught me. I don't usually come in on Saturdays."

I ushered him into the office ahead of me, noting that his limp was pronounced. I knew how he felt. Pinky was in his sixties, coal black hair, black brows, and deep lines around his mouth. He sported the ghost of a mustache and the shadow of a goatee. There was a band of white on his left wrist where he'd shed a watch.

"I'm about to put on a pot of coffee if you'd like a cup."

"Couldn't hurt."

After his passion for racing was squelched, his second calling was a long, inglorious career as a nonresidential burglar. I did hear he'd eventually taken to burgling houses, but I hadn't had that confirmed. He was the man who'd given me a set of key picks in a leather case years before, essential tools on those occasions when a locked door stands between me and something I want.

He'd hired me during one of his stints in prison when he'd been worried about his wife, the aforementioned Dodie, convinced she was dallying with the guy next door. She was actually being faithful (as far as I could tell), which I'd reported after sitting surveillance off and on for a month. He gave me the picks in lieu of payment, since his cash reserves were all illegally acquired and had to be returned.

"Why burglary?" I'd asked once.

He'd flashed me a modest smile. "I'm a natural. You know, because I'm a skinny guy and agile as a cat. I can squeeze in through places lot of other fellows can't. Job's more physical than you'd think. I can do a hundred one-arm push-ups, fifty either side."

"Good for you," I'd said.

"There's actually a trick to it, something a fellow taught me up in Soledad."

"You'll have to show me sometime."

I put on a pot of coffee and went to my desk, where I sat down in my swivel chair and propped my feet on the edge. Meanwhile, Pinky remained standing, scanning my office with an eye to where the valuables might be kept.

He shook his head. "This is a comedown. Last I saw, you had an office over on State Street. Nice location. Very nice. This—I don't know so much. I guess I'm used to seeing you in classier digs."

"I appreciate the vote of confidence," I remarked. With Pinky, there wasn't any point in taking offense. He might be a repeat offender but he was never guilty of subterfuge.

When the coffee was done I filled two mugs and handed him one before I returned to my swivel chair. Pinky finally settled into one of my two visitor's chairs, sucking in hot coffee with a series of slurping sounds. "This is good. I like it strong."

"Thanks. How's Dodie?"

"Good. She's great. She's gone into direct sales, like an entrepreneur."

"Selling what?"

"Nothing door-to-door. She's a personal beauty consultant for a big national company, Glorious Womanhood. You probably heard of it."

"Don't think so," I said.

"Well, it's bigger than Mary Kay. It's Christian-based. She sets up these home parties for bunches of women. Not our place but someone else's, where they serve food. Then she'll do makeovers, demonstrating products you can order on the spot. Last month, she edged out the regional manager for top sales."

"Sounds like she's doing well. I'm impressed."

"Me too. I guess the regional manager was fit to be tied. Nobody ever beat her out before, but Dodie's purpose-driven when she puts her mind to it. Used to be when I was gone, she'd get all mopey and depressed. I'd be doing hard time and she'd be laying around watching TV and eating fatty snacks. We'd talk on the phone and I'd try to get her motivated—you know, building up her self-esteem—but it never did much good. Then she hears about this business opportunity, similar to a franchise or something like that. I didn't think much of it at the time because she never stuck to anything until this came along. This past year, she's earned enough to buy a Cadillac and qualify for a free vacation cruise."

"Where to?"

"The Caribbean . . . St. Thomas . . . and around in there. A flight to Fort Lauderdale and then onto the ship."

"You going with her?"

"Sure. If I can get myself set. Two of us have never been on a vacation together. It's tough to make plans when we never know if I'll be in jail or out. Something like this, I don't want to be dependent on her moneywise. The trip is all-expenses-paid, but there's incidentals—on-shore excursions and the casino when you're out at sea. Two of the six nights formal wear's required so I'll have to rent me a tux. Can you picture it? I always swore I'd have to be dead before you caught me in one, but she's all excited about the dress she had made. Not that she'd show me. She says it'd be bad luck, like seeing a bride decked out in her wedding finery before you get to the church. It's a knockoff of a gown Debbie Reynolds wore one year to the Academy Awards. There's even a good possibility she'll be crowned Glorious Woman of the Year."

"Wouldn't that be something," I said. I let him go on telling the story his way. I knew he had a problem—why else would he be here?—but the faster I pushed him, the sooner I'd be in the bathroom, scrubbing the toilet bowl. I figured that could wait.

"Anyways, I'm giving you the background."

"I assumed as much."

"Thing is, my wife's got this engagement ring. One-point-five-carat diamond set in platinum, worth three grand easy. I know, because I had it appraised two days after it came into my possession. This was in Texas some time ago. She hasn't been wearing it because she says it's too loose and bothers her every time she goes to wash her hands."

"I can't wait to see where you're going with this."

"Yeah, well, that's the other thing. She's lost a lot of weight. She looks like a runway model only bigger in the tush. You probably don't remember, but she used to be . . . I won't say fat, but on the far side of plump. The past fifteen months, she's taken off sixty pounds. I came home, I didn't recognize her. That's how good she looks."

"Wow. I love success stories. How'd she manage it?"

"Diet supplement, an over-the-counter upper that's not FDA regulated because, technically speaking, it's not a drug. She's so buzzed all the time, she forgets to eat. She has to be on the go every minute or she gets whacked out from too much nervous energy. As a side benefit, the house's never looked so good. Drop of a hat, she'll do all the windows, inside and out. Anyways, she tossed the ring in her jewelry box six months back and she hasn't touched it since. Now she wants to have it sized so she can wear it on the cruise. She's all stressed out because she can't find it anywhere, so I said I'd look."

"You hocked it."

"Pretty much. I want to do right by her, but I'm low on funds and it's tough to find work. I don't like taking handouts from the woman I love. Problem is, the skills I have aren't exactly in demand. What happened was, I put together a stake using the ring as collateral on a four-month loan. This was way last spring after I got out of Soledad. I went down to Santa Anita to play the ponies. I don't get to the track every couple of months, I tend to brood. I'm a moody guy to begin with and the nags take my mind off."

"Let me guess. You lost your shirt and now you need to get the ring back before she figures out what you did."

"There you have it. I couldn't come up with the principal so I paid the interest and rolled it over for another four months. Now that's up and the ten-day grace runs out Tuesday of next week. I don't pay, that's the last I see of it, which would break my poor heart. Hers, too, if she found out."

"How much?"

"Two hundred."

"That's all you got for a ring worth three grand?"

"Sad, but true. The guy lowballed me on the deal, but it's not like I had any choice. I can't borrow from a bank. I mean, picture the loan docs, me wanting two hundred dollars for a hundred and twenty days. Can't be done. So now I owe the two in cash plus another twenty-five in interest. Be honest about it, I might not get the money back to you right away. I mean, eventually, sure."

I stared at him while I considered his request. I had cash in my wallet so I wasn't worried about that. The key picks he'd given me had served me well, as had the tutorial he'd provided before he got sent up. Also counting in his favor was the fact that I liked the man. Profession aside, he was a good-hearted soul. Even a burglar suffers the occasional financial woes. Finally, I said, "How about this? I won't give you the cash, but I'll go with you to the pawnshop and pay the guy myself."

His look was pained. "You don't trust me?"

"Sure I do, but let's not tempt fate."

"You're tough."

"I'm a realist. Your car or mine?"

"Mine's in the shop. You can drop me off there afterward and I'll pick it up."

# 4

Santa Teresa Jewelry and Loan is located two doors down from a gun shop on lower State Street. There's a gas station across the street and a tattoo parlor around the corner. The area is short on tourists and long on bums, perfect for urban renewal if the city ever gets around to it. The pawnshop itself is narrow, wedged between a thrift shop and a package liquor store. Pinky held the door for me and I went in.

Inside, the air carried the faint scent of alcohol, which stirred when the door closed behind us. A percentage of the cash out on loan probably traveled next door to the liquor store, where the exchange rate was keyed to red wine of the lowest denomination. A green neon sign with the three-ball symbol for a pawnshop sputtered at a speed that would cause seizures in the unsuspecting.

To my right, high up on the wall, fifteen hocked paintings had been mounted, artfully arranged around a security camera, angled on the two of us. This allowed me to view myself in full color as seen from above, me checking out the camera while the camera checked me. In my jeans and turtleneck I looked like a homeless person down on her luck. Below the paintings, shelves held an assortment of power tools, air tools, hand tools, nail guns, and socket wrench sets. The lower shelves were crowded with secondhand electronics: clocks, headphones, stereo speakers, turntables, radios, and big clunky television sets with screens the size of the windows in airplanes.

On the left, a row of guitars hung behind the counter, along with enough violins, flutes, and horns to constitute a small-town orchestra. A series of glass display cases ran the length of the shop, holding tray after tray of rings, watches, bracelets, and coins. Dispirited household items—a child's bone-china tea set, a ceramic vase, a cut-crystal figurine, and four graduated teak nesting bowls—sat together on a shelf. There were no books, no weapons, and no articles of clothing.

This was where once-cherished items came to roost, sentiment surrendered for cash. I pictured a constant round-robin of relinquishment and redemption, items converted into currency and then claimed again as personal fortunes improved. People moved, people died, people retired into nursing homes where there was so little space that much of what they owned had to be sold, given away, or abandoned at the curb.

The place was doing better business than I'd expected. One man took down a wall-mounted leaf blower that he examined for some time before he carried it to the counter to purchase. A second man browsed the electronics while a third at the rear labored to affix his signature to a document with a shaky hand. Of the four employees I counted, two greeted Pinky by name.

The woman who stepped forward to assist him was middle-aged, with wavy red-gold hair that she parted on the side. A two-inch-wide swath of gray hair showed at the roots. Her eyeglasses were framed in thick black plastic that seemed too emphatic for her fair coloring. She wore slacks and a white cotton blouse with a bow at the collar, apparently meant to disguise the width of her neck, which put her in a league with weight lifters given to heavy steroid use. She winked at him, held up a finger, and then retired to the back room. She returned moments later with a padded tray covered in black velvet.

"This is June," he said of her and then nodded at me. "Kinsey Millhone. She's a private detective."

We shook hands. "Nice meeting you," I said.

"Same here."

Pinky watched as she untied a ribbon and opened two cloth flaps. In the center was the ring, which to me looked small and unremarkable. Then again, Pinky never claimed it was a family heirloom, at least not in his family. The diamond was the size of a wee rhinestone stud, not that I owned anything so grand.

He smiled at me shyly. "You want to try it on?"

"Sure." I slipped it on my finger and held it to the light, turning it this way and that. "Gorgeous."

"Isn't it?"

"Absolutely," I said, practicing my lying skills.

Shortly after that we got down to business. I handed over the $225 in cash while the two of them dealt with the paperwork.

Afterward I drove Pinky to the car-repair shop, which was six blocks away. As I pulled over to the curb, I peered past him through the passenger-side window. There was no sign of activity. The doors to the service bays were down and the office was dark. "Are you sure someone's there?"

"Doesn't look like it, does it? I must have misunderstood."

"You want me to drop you off at your place?"

"No need. I'm up on Paseo. It's an easy walk."

"Don't be silly. It's right on my way."

I drove eight blocks north on Chapel until I reached Paseo, where I hung a left. He pointed to a dark gray frame duplex and I slowed to a stop. There was no room to park so he got out while the engine idled. He closed the car door and waved me on. I wiggled my fingers at him in the rearview mirror by way of a farewell, though he was gone by then.

I returned to the office, where I donned a pair of rubber gloves and gave the premises a thorough going-over. Then I went back to my place and started a load of laundry. As a youngster, I was taught that Saturday was for chores and you couldn't go out to play until your room was clean. The critical lessons in life hold sway whether you like it or not.

At 5:30, I put on my windbreaker, slid my paperback novel down in my shoulder bag, locked the studio, and walked the half block to Rosie's. Another woman approached the entrance at the same time I did and we reached for the door simultaneously. When our eyes met, I pointed at her. "You're Claudia."

She smiled. "And you're Kinsey Millhone. Twelve pairs of size small high-cut briefs."

"I can't believe you remembered."

"You were just in yesterday."

I held the door, allowing her to pass in front of me. Her hair was coal black, shiny, and carelessly arranged. Her eyes were bright brown and her gaze was direct. She was probably in her late forties and stylishly put together. She wore a two-button designer jacket, well-cut slacks, and a crisp white shirt. Working for Nordstrom's gave her access to the latest fashions, as well as an employee discount.

I said, "You must live close by. I can't think why else you'd frequent the place."

She smiled. "Actually, we live on the upper east side. Drew's the manager at the Ocean View Hotel. We meet here on nights when he's working late and only has a short dinner break. I got off work early and decided to come in and wait for him. What about you?"

"I'm half a block down. I'm here two or three nights a week when I'm too lazy to cook."

"Same for me. Nights he's not home, I tend to graze," she said. "You want to join me for a drink?"

"Sure, I'd like that. I've been dying to find out what happened to the shoplifter."

"I'm glad you were there when Mr. Koslo showed up."

"Absolutely. I loved every minute of it. What are you drinking?"

"Gin and tonic."

"I'll be right back."

William had seen me come in, and by the time I reached the bar he'd already poured me a glass of bad Chardonnay. I waited until he'd made Claudia's gin and tonic and then carried both drinks to the table and sat down. I wasn't sure how much Claudia was at liberty to disclose about store business, but I took up the conversation where we'd left it, behaving as though the matter was open for discussion.

I said, "I thought I was seeing things when she slid those pajamas in her bag."

"What nerve! I thought she was acting odd the minute she showed up, so I kept an eye on her. Shoplifters always think they're cool, but they tend to telegraph their intent. I'd just finished ringing up a customer when you came up and told me what was going on. When I called Security, Ricardo picked her up on the monitor and notified Mr. Koslo. He sent me to wait by the second-floor escalator in case she came down. Ordinarily he'd have handled the situation on his own, but there was an occasion not too long ago where a female customer accused him of using excessive force. It wasn't true, of course, but since then, he's made a point of having a witness on hand."

"I heard the alarm go off but I never saw the follow-up. Was she arrested?"

"Oh, yes, ma'am," she said. "He caught up with her in the mall and asked her to accompany him into the store. She played dumb, like she had no idea what he wanted with her. They usually start out pretending to cooperate, so she did as he asked though she protested the whole time."

"About what? She had the stolen items right there."

"He didn't ask her to open the shopping bag until they reached the security offices. No one wants to subject a customer to public embarrassment in case it turns out to be a bad stop. Once in private, he had her empty the contents of her bag and out came the two pairs of pajamas and . . . oops, no receipt. Then he asked her to open her purse and there was the lace teddy, again with no evidence she'd paid. Completely baffling to her."

"I can't believe she had the gall to deny it."

"That's the standard MO. Did you ever see the surveillance tape that shows the nurse's aide stealing money from an elderly patient? Once in a while they run it on one of those true-crime shows. You can see the aide clear as day. She gets into the woman's purse and takes the cash, which she stops to *count* before sticking it in her pocket. When the police showed her the tape, she sat right there with the detective, swearing up and down she didn't do it."

"Falsely accused."

"You got it. Same thing here. At first she was all innocence. Then—well, talk about irate! She was a loyal Nordstrom's customer. She'd been shopping there for years. She couldn't believe he'd accuse her of stealing when she did no such thing. He said he hadn't accused her of anything. He was just asking her to account for the items in her possession. She said she certainly hadn't *stolen* them. Why would she do that when she had money in her wallet? She insisted she intended to buy the items, but then changed her mind. She had an appointment and she was in a hurry so she ended up leaving the store without realizing she hadn't returned the items to the display.

"Mr. Koslo didn't say a word. He just let her run on because he knew he had her on tape. She went from huffy to belligerent, full speed ahead, yelling about her rights. She was going to contact her attorney. She'd sue the store for slander and false arrest. He was polite, but he didn't budge an inch. She broke down at that point and started sobbing. You've never seen anyone so pitiful in your life. She just about got down on her knees, begging him to let her go. The tears were the only part of the whole performance I thought was sincere. When that didn't work, she tried to bargain her way out. She offered to pay for the items and said she'd sign a conditional release. She also swore she'd never come in again. On and on it went."

"She used the phrase 'conditional release'?"

"She did."

"Sounds like she's an old hand at this—or how'd she know the term?"

"Oh, she knew what notes to hit. Not that it did any good. Mr. Koslo had already told Ricardo to call the police, so he said she might as well calm down and save her arguments for the judge. That set off a whole new round of weeping and wailing. I didn't see the end of it because I went back to the floor when the officer arrived. Ricardo told me by the time they put her in the cop car, she was white as a sheet."

"Were you aware she was working with someone else?"

Claudia seemed taken aback. "You're not serious. There were two of them?"

"Absolutely. You might have noticed her partner without realizing who she was. A younger woman in a dark blue dress."

Claudia shook her head. "Don't think so."

"When I first saw them they were standing together, chatting. I mistook her for a sales clerk. I assumed the younger one was a Nordstrom's employee and the older a customer. Then I realized the second woman had a shopping bag of her own, so I figured they were both customers making idle conversation."

"Probably deciding what to take."

"I wouldn't be surprised. After that they split up, and by the time your security guy arrived, the other woman had gone off to the ladies' room. She was on her way back when she caught sight of her friend stepping onto the escalator with Mr. Koslo hard on her heels. She knew exactly what was going on. She went straight back to the ladies' room and locked herself in a stall. Then she clipped the price tags off the articles she'd cribbed and tossed 'em in the trash. I went in there right afterward, and when I saw what she'd done, I made a beeline for the fire stairs and followed her, but not fast enough. She managed to peel out of the parking garage before I got a look at her license plate."

"Funny you should mention the tags. Ricardo told me the cleaning crew found tags when they were picking up trash. The supervisor turned them over to Mr. Koslo and he included them in his report. I think both he and Ricardo assumed it was the same woman."

"Well, if he needs a corroborating witness, I'd be happy to oblige."

"I doubt he'll take you up on it, but if the DA files charges, you can talk to him."

"I just hope the one woman gets nailed, even if her pal got away."

"You and me both."

At that point Claudia's husband arrived, and after a brief introduction, I excused myself. I returned to the bar and when I asked for a second glass of wine, William caught sight of the skid marks across my right palm. "What happened to you?"

I looked down and made a wry face, holding up my hand to show him the full effect. "I fell while I was chasing a thief."

I gave him the short version of the incident and then, since there was so little in it to recommend my private detecting skills, changed the subject. "I was sorry to hear about Nell's tumble. Have you talked to her?"

"Not yet. I had a call from Henry when he arrived at the house. He said his flight was uneventful and he was going to the hospital as soon as he dropped his bag."

"I'm glad he made it with no problems. How's she doing?"

"Fair, at least from what I've been told. The head of the femur was broken off and the shaft was in pieces, probably the result of osteoporosis."

"That wouldn't surprise me—at ninety-nine years old. Henry told me about the pin they put in."

His tone turned from somber to gloomy. "Let's just hope it ends there. If she's immobilized for any length of time, her muscles will atrophy and she'll develop bedsores. Next comes pneumonia and after that . . ." He fixed me with a bleak look and let the sentence trail off.

"I'm sure they'll get her up within a day. Isn't that the current thinking?"

"One can only hope. You know the theory about bad things coming in threes."

"There was something else bad?"

"I'm afraid so. I received a call from my doctor with the results of my latest blood tests. My blood sugar's elevated. The doctor said fifty percent of people in the same range end up with diabetes in five years."

From somewhere under the bar he pulled out a piece of paper and placed it in front of me, pointing at the relevant column. Normal for glucose was 65–99. His was 106. I had no idea if that put him in the danger zone, but he seemed to think so.

I said, "Wow. What's the doctor suggesting?"

"Nothing. He did mention that stress hormones are sometimes responsible for an inappropriate elevation of blood glucose. I went straight to my *Merck Manual* and looked it up." He gazed upward, apparently quoting directly. "'Diabetic amyotrophy is found characteristically in elderly men, producing a predominant muscle weakness around the hip and upper leg.'"

"And you *have* that?"

"I've been experiencing a weakness off and on this past month, which is why I went to see him in the first place. After a thorough examination, he was at a loss. He had absolutely no idea what was wrong with me." He leaned forward. "I saw him write 'etiology unknown' on my chart. It was chilling. My *Merck* says the absence of a precise diagnostic marker for diabetes mellitus 'continues to be a problem.' 'Onset tends to be abrupt in children,' it says, '*Insidious* in older patients.' I shudder to think of the word 'insidious' applied to me."

"But surely there's something you can do for yourself. What about dietary changes?"

"He gave me a pamphlet, which I haven't had the heart to read. In addition to muscle weakness, I've been having stomach problems."

"Henry mentioned that last night."

He lifted his brows. "Of course, abdominal tenderness is another indicator for diabetes, as is fruity breath." He cupped his hands around his mouth and blew. I thought he'd offer me a sniff, which I was prepared to decline. "Fortunately, it hasn't come to that, but I *am* urinating more frequently. I'm up half the night."

"Don't tell me about the stream," I said, hastily. "I thought that was related to your prostate."

"That was my first thought as well. Now I'm not so sure."

Mentally, I squinted, trying to judge the truth value of his claim. I knew *he* believed it, but was there foundation in fact? One of these days, despite his tendency to dramatize, William was going to be afflicted with something real. "Do you have a family history of diabetes?" I asked.

"How would I know? There are only five of us left. The sibs and I take after our mother's side of the family. Her maiden name was Tilmann, hardy German stock. Our grandmother on our father's side was a Mauritz by birth. There were five other brothers and sisters who carried her genetic line. They all died within days of each other in the influenza epidemic of 1917. Who knows what health problems they'd have developed had they lived?"

"What's Rosie think about all this?"

"She has her head in the sand as usual, convinced nothing's wrong. It's right there in the *Merck* . . . every word of it . . . under 'Endocrine Disorders,' page 1289. On the facing page, there's talk of 'Precocious Puberty,' which I was mercifully spared."

"I'm not sure you should consult medical texts on your own. Most of the terminology makes no sense to the average person."

"I was a Latin scholar as a youth. *As praesens ova cras pullis sunt meliora.*"

He fixed me with a look to see if I was following. My face must have been blank because he went on to translate. "'Eggs today are better than chickens tomorrow.'"

I let that one pass. "But what if you're misinterpreting? I mean, the doctor didn't actually *say* you were diabetic, did he?"

"He's probably giving me time to adjust. Most doctors don't want to burden a patient in the early stages. I thought he'd order additional lab work, but apparently he couldn't see the point. He told his nurse to make me an appointment for the *week after next*. It's probably going to be like that from now on."

"Well, if Henry's home by then, he should go with you for moral support. When you're upset, you don't always hear what's being said."

Rosie opened the swinging kitchen door and stuck her head out. "I'm make stuffed kohlrabi. Whatever you got, it's gonna fix," she said to him. And then to me, "You gonna hev some, too, with mutton. Sauce is best I ever make."

I took the interruption as an opportunity to retire to my favorite booth, bad wine in hand. I shrugged off my jacket and slid into the seat, hoping I wouldn't get a splinter in my butt. I pulled out my paperback and found my place, trying to look engrossed so William wouldn't follow me across the room to amplify his complaints. I was apprehensive about dinner. Rosie's Hungarian by birth and favors strange native dishes, many composed of animal organs smothered in sour cream. Earlier that week, she'd served me sautéed sweetbreads (a calf's thymus gland, if you want the offal truth). I'd eaten with my usual oinky appetite. I was mopping up the plate with half a dinner roll when she told me what it was. Thymus gland? What could I do about it when I'd already eaten it? Short of running to the ladies' room to jam a fork down my throat, I was stuck. It didn't help that I'd enjoyed it.

She appeared with my dinner plate, setting it down in front of me.

She waited with her hands clasped while I tasted a small bite of meat and faked enthusiasm. She didn't seem convinced.

"Yummy," I said. "Really. It's fabulous."

She remained skeptical, but she had other orders coming up and she returned to the kitchen. Once she was gone, I picked up my fork and knife and started sawing away. The mutton required more work than I'd anticipated, but the effort took my mind off the sauce, which was not as sublime as she'd indicated. The kohlrabi looked like a little alien spacecraft and tasted like a cross between a turnip and cabbage, a perfect complement to the badly fermented sugar water I was using to wash it down. I wrapped a chunk of mutton in a paper napkin that I then tucked in my shoulder bag. I caught William's eye and made the universal gesture for the check. I exchanged a few parting remarks with Claudia and Drew, and then headed for home.

I was in bed by 9:00, thinking that was the end of the shoplifting episode. Silly me.

# 5

# NORA

For Nora, the weekend had started on a sour note. She'd spent the early part of the week in Beverly Hills, taking care of routine appointments. She had her hair done, manicure, pedicure, massage, and her annual physical, which she was happy to have out of the way. She returned to the house in Montebello on Thursday afternoon. She and Channing had bought their second home the year before and she loved every minute of their time away. Though the new place was only a hundred miles north of their permanent residence, she felt she was traveling to another country. She could hardly wait to get there. This was a second marriage for each of them. When she and Channing met, he had shared custody of his twin girls, age thirteen. Her son was eleven. They'd decided against having children of their own, opting instead to keep life simple. Summers, all three kids would be under the same roof with them, and that was sufficient chaos, especially as puberty struck, bringing with it the squabbles, the shrieking, tears, accusations of unfairness, and doors slamming upstairs and down. While appreciating the current household peace, Nora looked back on that era with fondness. At least the family was intact, however bumptious and loud.

Channing had intended to join her Friday in time for dinner and stay until Monday morning. At the last minute, however, he'd called to say that he'd be bringing the Lows. Abner was a senior partner in Channing's law firm and one of his best friends. Meredith was Abner's second wife, the woman responsible for the breakup of his first marriage ten years before. He was a serial womanizer, currently cheating on Meredith with the woman who'd doubtless turn out to be wife number three—if she was smart and played her cards right.

Nora and Meredith had met in a Jazzercise class early in their fifteen-year friendship, and they'd loved nothing better than dishing about the various scandals in their social set. They'd bonded initially over the revelation that the wife of a pretentious bank president had had when she returned home unannounced and caught her husband cross-dressing, decked out in an Armani suit and designer heels. On another occasion, a mutual acquaintance was accused of appropriating large sums of money from the charity for which she volunteered as treasurer. Charges were filed but the case never went to trial. An agreement was reached and the business was swept under the carpet.

At least twice a year some outrageous impropriety would come to light, and the two would busy themselves trading rumors and howling with delight. Nora and Meredith had built an entire relationship on salacious gossip. This allowed the two women to compare notes, test their mutual values, and reinforce shared attitudes, to swap any number of snobbish put-downs. Not that they considered themselves snobs.

Then Meredith met Abner and within a year the two had abandoned their respective spouses. Nora and Channing had stood for them at a simple ceremony at city hall, followed by an elegant lunch at the Bel-Air Hotel. As Channing and Abner were such good friends, the two women became even closer. Nora had been a staunch support to Meredith after she'd caught Abner in the first affair. The irony wasn't lost on either one of them. They'd forged a bond based on the misfortunes of others, and Meredith's suffering now occupied front and center. Nora became her sounding board, counseling her during hour-long telephone conversations and drunken lunches, wherein Nora played life coach and marriage counselor, feeling wise and superior and above it all. Together they analyzed every nuance of Abner's infatuation with the other woman, who (to their way of thinking) was not only coarse, but had put herself in the hands of the wrong cosmetic surgeon. Problematic was the fact that Meredith loved the lifestyle Abner provided, so once she'd exhausted her emotional responses, she managed to make her peace with his infidelity. Though he never admitted to the affair, he bought her an armload of expensive jewelry and took her on a Silver Seas cruise through the Mediterranean.

With Meredith's discovery of affair number two, the same scenes played out. A renewed cycle of tears, rage, and vows of revenge continued during the next few months. Nora found herself bored, though it took her a while to admit it to herself. She wanted to be loyal and sympathetic, but the drama soon became tedious, and she was impatient with the ineffectual anguish and spite. Meredith would never file for divorce so why make such a big deal of it? The breaking point was when Meredith made a scene at a dinner party where the other woman was in attendance. The hostess quickly put a stop to Meredith's drunken catcalling, but not before she'd made a thorough fool of herself. This offended Nora, who thought Meredith's conduct was unseemly and unbecoming. Regardless of the righteousness of Meredith's position, there was the matter of etiquette. In their social circle, everybody was supposed to be too well-bred to expose any unhappiness to public view. Whatever their marital status, whether delirious or disaffected, couples were expected to maintain at least a *facade* of amicability. No sniping, no zingers, no hostility expressed as teasing or bantering. Nora realized that Meredith had become hooked on playing victim because she loved to occupy center stage. Nora confided this sentiment in a candid conversation with a mutual friend, a moment of openness that turned out to be a miscalculation on her part. She knew it was indiscreet to pass along information she should have kept to herself, but the other woman had brought it up and Nora couldn't resist. Somehow Meredith had gotten wind of it, and she and Nora had had a huge falling-out. Over time they'd mended their fences, but Nora was uncomfortably aware of having failed her friend and was therefore happier keeping her at a distance.

Channing had invited them up once before without consulting Nora, and she had bitten her tongue. She'd spent two days walking on eggshells, and once Abner and Meredith were out the door, she'd made her feelings known. "Jesus, Channing, the last thing in the world I want is her unloading on me. I feel sorry for her, but I don't want to be in the position of having to commiserate. If you can avoid inviting them again I'd be grateful."

This had apparently annoyed him, though his tone of voice was light. "Just because you and Meredith had a parting of the ways doesn't mean Abner and I should be penalized."

"It's not a question of *penalizing* anyone. You have to admit it's uncomfortable, knowing what Abner's up to. I mean, what if she asks me outright? What am I supposed to say?"

"What he does and how she feels about it is none of our business."

"Maybe not, but the man's a shitheel."

"Agreed, now let's drop the subject, please."

From that point on, Nora had kept her observations to herself.

She had no way to guess if Meredith knew about affair number three, and this put her in the awkward position of editing her words. She didn't like keeping secrets. Even though the friendship had cooled she was conflicted. Should she raise the issue or not? If Meredith already knew about the liaison and Nora mentioned it, the weeping and hand wringing would erupt and the weekend would be shot. By the same token, if Meredith was in the dark and Nora failed to alert her, she'd be setting herself up for recriminations: *Why didn't you tell me? How could you have let me go on when you knew what was happening?*

Nora made sure the housekeeper, Mrs. Stumbo, readied the guest room, setting out fresh flowers, distilled water in a crystal carafe with matching glasses, and two sets of Egyptian cotton towels folded together and tied with color-coordinated satin ribbon. Though it was April, evenings were still chilly, and she made sure all the fireplaces were laid with wood. Meals might be a problem. She and Channing had recently lost their personal chef, and Mrs. Stumbo couldn't be counted on to cook for the four of them. Nora checked the freezer, where she still had several dishes the chef had prepared before she left their employ "to pursue other goals." She'd actually jumped ship in order to work for another couple in Montebello, who'd offered a thousand dollars more a month. Nora had bid the chef a fond farewell and cut the couple from their social list.

She decided she'd thaw the casserole of *boeuf bourguignon* and serve it that night with salad, french bread, and berries for dessert. Saturday night, she'd make reservations for the four of them for dinner at the country club. She wrote out a grocery list and sent Mrs. Stumbo off for items to cover breakfasts on Saturday and Sunday mornings and one lunch. Abner would insist on reciprocating their hospitality, taking them out for a meal on Sunday, and that would be that. The Lows would be on their way back to Bel Air by 2:00, and with luck she and Channing would have Sunday evening to themselves.

She'd hoped he'd arrive first so she could find out from him what, if anything, Meredith knew about Abner's latest fling. She wanted to be in the proper frame of mind so she could play her part. She also wanted to chide him for springing guests on her at the last minute when he knew she'd been looking forward to time alone. She'd have to underplay any suggestion of criticism. If Channing started feeling defensive, he'd trot out that little-boy-pouting act of his. He had a knack for sounding pleasant when he was actually being chilly and withdrawn.

As it turned out, the opportunity for conversation didn't present itself because Channing and the Lows arrived at the same time. First his car then theirs pulled into the courtyard, and from that point on she had no chance to quiz him. Her irritation was quickly dispelled by cocktails and conversation. Who could hold on to a bad mood in the presence of expensive wine?

Abner was at his most charming, a sure sign he was otherwise engaged. Meredith surely sensed what his behavior signified. Nora could tell Meredith yearned for more of the sympathy she had once lavished on her. Nora kept her manner light and saw to it that exchanges between the two of them were firmly anchored in the superficial. Twice Meredith gave her hangdog, beseeching looks, and once seemed on the verge of speaking up, but Nora sailed on.

Finally, when Channing and Abner were off making fresh drinks, Meredith touched Nora's arm and said in a woebegone tone, "We need to talk."

"Sure. What's up?"

"I don't even know where to start. Maybe we can do a beach walk in the morning. Just the two of us. I really miss you."

"Fine. Let's see what the guys have in mind and maybe we can carve out some time," Nora said brightly. Inwardly, she felt a little stubborn streak kick in. She didn't relish the idea of an intimate chat with Meredith, and she would make sure it never happened. Really, it was time for Meredith to take responsibility for the bargain she'd made when she married the man. She was the reason Abner was unfaithful to his first wife so what did she expect? She should suck it up or move on. Wallowing in misery was self-indulgent, especially when her woes were those she'd brought on herself.

To Nora's great relief, the weekend had finally wound to a close without the much-dreaded beach walk. When Abner and Meredith pulled out of the driveway at 1:00, Nora finally felt herself relax. Unfortunately, the rest of Sunday was cut short by a call from the office that came in just after the Lows left. Something had come up with one of

Channing's celebrity clients, and he would have to dance attendance. No explanation or apology was needed because Nora understood. That was the nature of the beast. Channing was an entertainment lawyer, and his roster of clients included the up-and-coming talent, along with the longtime players, in the industry. He'd made a fortune on the basis of personal service. Like a doctor, he was ready to roll, at any hour, if the phone rang.

Which meant that the personal matter she wanted to discuss was squeezed into the last few minutes of his visit, when he was literally packing files in his briefcase on his way to the car. What she'd wanted to clarify was the recent tiff she'd had with his personal assistant. Thelma (whose last name she had trouble remembering) had been with him two years, and while Nora had had trifling problems with her in the past, there was never any overt insubordination.

She'd met Thelma when she first came to work for him. Nora made a point of putting in an appearance at the office whenever there was a new hire on board. That personal connection, even if it was only once, ensured a better phone relationship. Nora seldom called the office but occasionally something came up about the house, or his twin daughters. Channing's taste was consistent when it came to underlings. Secretaries, bookkeepers, administrative assistants, even housekeepers, were cut from the same cloth—women of a certain age who grew up during the Great Depression in an era of deprivation and want. These women were grateful to have well-paying jobs; they were schooled in old-fashioned values of hard work, loyalty, and thrift. His previous "girl," Iris, had been with him for seven years when she suffered a stroke that forced her into retirement. Thelma was the exception, some twenty years younger, plain, slightly overweight, and ever so faintly officious.

Nora had talked to her on countless occasions since their first meeting, and there was never a suggestion of friendliness on the woman's part. To be fair, Channing did discourage chumminess. He'd often complained about his ex-wife, Gloria, who was forever befriending the hired help, becoming enmeshed in their personal upheavals. The cleaning lady, a drunk, had taken to calling Gloria in the middle of the night, asking for advances on her salary. The gardener talked her into buying him new equipment when his was stolen from another job site. When the cook's daughter got pregnant, Gloria was the one driving the girl to her doctor's appointments because she was too sick to ride the bus. Channing thought it absurd that Gloria was at the beck and call of people on the payroll. With Nora, he'd put his foot down and she'd been happy to comply. She assumed he'd given Thelma the same stern talking to, which was why her tone of voice bordered on the chilly.

Thelma, either unsure of herself or obsequious by nature, insisted on consulting Channing when Nora made even a minor request. Now when Nora called the office to talk to him, she was greeted by a wall of cobwebs. Thelma was subtle about it, putting up a nearly imperceptible resistance that Nora couldn't call her on. If Nora asked her to cut a check, Thelma would sidestep until she could clear it with him. The second time it happened, Nora complained to Channing, and he'd said he'd speak to her. For a while Thelma's attitude had improved, but then she'd reverted to the same sullen behavior, leaving Nora in the uncomfortable position of saying nothing or having to object yet again, which made her seem churlish. Thelma refused to recognize Nora's authority. Channing was her boss. Nora might be the boss's wife at home, but not where Thelma was concerned.

Nora was ready to lower the boom. "Channing, we really need to talk about Thelma."

"We can do that later. Right now, I'm trying to get to this meeting before the situation blows up in my face," he said as he headed out the door. "I'll see you Wednesday. Traffic probably won't be heavy. If you're in Malibu by five o'clock, it should give you plenty of time to get ready."

Nora stopped in her tracks. "For what? I'm not coming down at all this week."

"What are you talking about? We have the fund-raiser for the Alzheimer's Association."

"A fund-raiser? In the middle of the week? That's ridiculous!"

"The annual dinner dance. Don't play dumb. I told you last week."

Nora followed him down the front steps. "You never said a word."

He glanced back at her, irritation surfacing. "You're kidding me, right?"

"No, I'm not kidding. I have plans."

"Well, cancel them. My presence is required and I want you there. You've begged off the last six events."

"Pardon the hell out of me. I didn't realize we were keeping score."

"Who said anything about keeping score? Name the last time you went anyplace with me."

"Don't do that to me. You know I can never think of an example in the moment. The point is, Belinda's sister's coming into town from Houston. She's here one day and we have tickets for the symphony that night. We had to pay a fortune for the seats."

"Tell her we had plans and it totally slipped your mind."

"An Alzheimer's event and it 'slipped my mind'? How tacky is that?"

"Tell her anything you like. She can give your ticket to someone else."

"I can't cancel at the last minute. It's inconsiderate. Besides, you know how much I hate those things."

"This is not meant as entertainment. I bought a table for ten. We've gone every year without fail for the last ten."

"And I'm always bored out of my mind."

"You know what? I'm tired of your excuses. You pull this shit at the last minute and it leaves me scrambling around, trying to find someone to fill in. You know how embarrassing that is?"

"Oh, stop. You can go by yourself. It's not going to kill you for once."

"Screw you," he said.

He tossed his briefcase and a duffel in the trunk and then moved to the driver's side with Nora close behind. She was exasperated having to trot after him, which reduced their conversation to fits and starts.

Channing slid in under the wheel and slammed the car door. He turned his key in the ignition so he could power down the window. "You want to talk about Thelma? Fine. Let's talk about Thelma. She said you called on Friday, asking her to cut you a check for eight grand. She said you were very frosty when she said it would have to go through me. She was worried she'd offended you."

"Good. Perfect. She did offend me. That's what I wanted to talk to you about. You should have told me she controlled the purse strings. I had no idea."

"Stop. You know better. Every expenditure gets funneled through her and then through me before it goes on to the accountant's office. With seventeen attorneys in the firm, it's the only way I can keep track. She doesn't say yea or nay to anyone without checking with me first. That's just a fact."

"Fine."

"There's no reason for you to get all prickly about it. She's doing her job."

"I don't want to discuss it."

"That's unlike you. You're usually hell-bent on talking everything to death."

"Why are you acting so put-upon? It's a goddamn dinner dance in L.A. It's not the White House."

"I told you twice."

"No. You did not. You're bringing it up now because you're hoping to deflect the issue."

"What issue?" he said.

"I don't see why I should have to justify myself to her."

"You didn't offer an explanation. You told her to cut you a check. Is it too much to ask what you have in mind? Believe it or not, an eight-thousand-dollar check isn't trivial."

"I don't want to talk about it now."

"And why is that?"

"Six months ago, I wanted to buy shares of IBM. You pooh-poohed the idea and the stock jumped sixteen points in two days. If I'd had access to even a modest sum of money, I could have cleaned up."

"And two days later, it tanked. You'd have lost it all."

"I'd have sold before the price dropped and then bought it again at the new low. I'm not stupid about these things, whatever you might think."

"What's this really about? Clearly, you've got your nose out of joint."

"I wanted the eight thousand dollars to buy shares of GE. Now it's too late. By the time the market closed on Friday, the stock had jumped from 82 to 106."

"Eight grand? What good would that have done?"

"That's irrelevant. I shouldn't have to beg."

"There's no point in throwing a tantrum about good business practice. You want money, I'll set up an account for you."

"You'll open an *account* for me, like you're my father?"

Channing's sigh was accompanied by a rolling of his eyes. High theater for him. He lowered his head, shaking it with resignation. The window slid up. He put the car in reverse and backed across the courtyard until he had the necessary clearance to pull out, which he did with a testy chirp of his tires.

The next thing she knew he was gone.

She returned to the house and closed the door behind her. It wasn't the first time they'd clashed and it certainly wouldn't be the last. The emotional uproar would fade and cooler heads would prevail, but she wasn't going to drop the matter. For the most part, they were capable of settling their differences, but she'd learned to avoid negotiations when one or the other of them was in high dudgeon.

She went into the kitchen and cleared the counter of stray martini glasses, which she placed in the machine. She loved having the house to herself again. Monday morning, Mrs. Stumbo would do a thorough cleaning, changing sheets, doing four loads of laundry, and generally restoring order. For now, Nora was free to enjoy the quiet. Briefly, she checked the guest room with its spacious adjoining bath, making sure the Lows hadn't overlooked personal items. Nora didn't like other people's stray shampoo bottles accumulating in the shower, and there was always the chance someone had forgotten the odd piece of jewelry or a garment hanging in the closet. Meredith had left a copy of *Los Angeles Magazine* on the bed table.

Nora scooped it up, intending to toss it into the trash. Instead she took it with her to the kitchen, where she made herself a cup of tea. She carried both teacup and magazine to the sunroom and sank into an upholstered chair. She put her feet up on the ottoman, grateful for the rare moment of relaxation. She leafed through glossy pages, checking the advertisements for shops on Rodeo Drive, expensive salons, art galleries, and boutique clothing stores. There was a six-page spread on the mansion of the month, some overblown though tastefully done palace built by one of the hot new movie producers. She also read the feature-length profile on an actress she'd met and disliked, taking a wicked satisfaction in the journalist's acid observations. What was meant to be a puff piece was devastatingly snide and unkind.

When she reached the society section, she checked to see who'd been in attendance at various charity events. Channing was right about her begging off the last six occasions. She knew many of the couples who'd been photographed, usually paired with friends, or linked with board members or celebrities, drinks in hand. The women were all decked out in full-length gowns and fabulous jewelry, posed side by side with their self-important husbands. The men did look elegant in their tuxedos, though the pictures, two inches by two, were monotonously similar. The photographs represented the Who's Who of Hollywood society with some couples in attendance at every event.

She was secretly congratulating herself for ducking out on so many tedious evenings when she spotted a photograph of Channing with Abner and Meredith at the Denim and Diamonds Ball, which she'd also missed. The Lows beamed as though blissfully happy. Now that was a laugh. She looked at the voluptuous redhead on Channing's arm. She didn't recognize the woman, but the dress she wore looked like a knockoff of the strapless white Gucci Nora kept at the house in Malibu. It couldn't be an original because she'd been assured hers was one of a kind. Briefly she considered how awful it would have been if she'd showed up at the same party in a similar gown.

She looked back at the redhead, alerted by the doting smile the woman was lavishing on Channing. It was the only photograph on the entire page where a woman was gazing at her companion instead of smiling directly at the camera. She read the caption and felt a silvery chill, like a veil of mercury, envelop her from head to toe. Thelma Landice. She had her hand tucked in the crook of Channing's arm. His right hand covered hers. Thelma was still overweight, but she'd managed to compress and confine every excess pound into a bloated approximation of the hourglass figure Marilyn Monroe had made famous thirty years before. Gone were Thelma's yellowing teeth and the drab, ill-cut hair. Now her gaudy dyed red tresses were smoothed into a french roll. She wore diamond earrings, and the smile she flashed showed several thousand dollars' worth of snow white caps.

Nora felt the heat rise in her face as comprehension flooded her frame. She'd misunderstood. She'd misread the signs. Meredith hadn't sent her those beseeching looks in hopes of confiding her own marital misery. She'd pitied Nora for what she and half of Hollywood knew was going on between Channing and Thelma Landice, the *fucking typist* who worked for him.

# 6

# DANTE

Dante had taken up swimming for the second time in his life when he bought the estate in Montebello eighteen years before. He was actually Lorenzo Dante Junior, commonly referred to as Dante to distinguish him from his father, Lorenzo Dante Senior. For security reasons, he avoided exercising in the open, which meant jogging, golf, and tennis were out. He'd set up a home gym, where he lifted weights three times a week. For cardio, he swam laps.

The thirty-two-acre property was surrounded by a stone wall, with entrance effected through electric gates, one set at the front and a second set at the rear, each with its own small stone guardhouse complete with a uniformed armed guard. There were six men altogether, working eight-hour shifts. A seventh oversaw the security cameras, which were monitored in situ by day and remotely by night. There were five buildings on the compound. The two-story main house had a detached five-car garage, with two apartments above. Tomasso, Dante's chauffeur, lived in one, and the other was occupied by his personal chef, Sophie.

There were also a two-bedroom guesthouse and a pool house, which included Dante's home gym and a twelve-seat theater. Dante's home office was in a sprawling bungalow, referred to as "the Cottage," which had its own living room, bedroom, one and a half baths, and a modest kitchen. He also had a suite of offices in downtown Santa Teresa, where he spent the better part of his workday. The Cottage and the pool house appeared to be separate from the main house but were actually connected by tunnels that branched off in two directions under the tennis court.

Dante had added the indoor lap pool across the back of the main house: two lanes wide and twenty-five yards long with a retractable roof; the bottom and sides were lined with iridescent glass tiles, and when the sun shone overhead, it was like moving through a shimmering rainbow of light. His mother had taught him to swim when he was four years old. She'd been fearful of the water as a child, and she made certain her own children were skilled swimmers from an early age. Dante did twenty-five laps a day, starting at 5:30 in the morning, counting backward from twenty-five to zero. He kept the water temperature seventy degrees, the surrounding air at eighty-four. He loved the way sound was muffled by the water, loved the simplicity of the crawl stroke, loved how clean and empty he felt when he was done.

He and Lola, his girlfriend of eight years, had returned the night before from a ski trip to Lake Louise, where a fluke in temperatures made the runs almost too sloppy to ski. He hated cold weather anyway, and if it had been up to him, he'd have cut the trip short, but Lola was adamant and wouldn't even entertain the idea. He found vacations stressful. He didn't like to be idle and he didn't like being separated from his business dealings. He was looking forward to getting back in the swing of things.

At 7:00 that Monday morning, he showered and dressed. He could smell coffee, bacon, and something sugar-scented. He looked forward to eating in solitude, catching up on the news while he lingered over his meal. Before he went down to breakfast, he stopped by his father's quarters on the second floor. The door was open and the nurse was in the process of changing his sheets. She told him his father had had a rough night and had finally abandoned any hope of sleep. He'd put on his suit and had Tomasso take him into the office in Santa Teresa. Most days, the old man sat at his desk for hours, drinking coffee, reading biographies of long-dead political greats, and working the *New York Times* crossword puzzle until it was time to go home.

Dante went down to the basement level and took the tunnel from the main house to the Cottage. Coming up from below, he crossed a short stretch of lawn to the guesthouse to pay his morning visit to his Uncle Alfredo, who'd been living there since he was discharged from the hospital after cancer surgery the year before. Originally, the guesthouse had been set up to accommodate a series of nannies who worked for the previous owner. Now one of the two bedrooms was outfitted with a hospital bed and the second bedroom was available for the night nurses. A nurse's aide came in days to help with his care.

Alfredo was his father's sole surviving brother and virtually penniless. Two younger brothers, Donatello and Amo, at ages nineteen and twenty-two, had died the same day, February 7, 1943, two days before the Battle of Guadalcanal came to an end.

Dante couldn't figure out what had happened to Pop and his Uncle Alfredo. How could you reach the end of your life and have nothing to show for it? Pop claimed it was bad financial advice from an accountant who was "no longer with the firm," meaning six feet under. Dante suspected what his father referred to as bad financial advice was really the function of his living perpetually beyond his means.

Lorenzo Senior was a local boy who'd risen to prominence during Prohibition, smart enough to cash in on the boom. The market was wide open with a premium placed on rotgut liquor. Gambling and prostitution seemed to flourish in the same spirit of excess. He'd never regarded the major syndicate mobsters as his allies. New York, Detroit,

Chicago, Kansas City, and Las Vegas seemed remote. He was distantly related to many of the players, but his ambitions were strictly provincial, and Santa Teresa was the perfect small community for promoting the sin trades. His organization became a feeder to San Francisco and Los Angeles. Beyond those two cities, he had little interest. He didn't interfere with the big boys and they didn't interfere with him. He had an open-door policy, offering safe haven for any made man who needed to lay low for a while. He also entertained his Midwest and East Coast cronies with a generous hand. The West Coast was already a magnet to rich and restless citizens who came from every part of the country, looking for sunshine, relaxation, and sheltered surroundings in which to indulge their low appetites.

For six decades, Lorenzo Senior had enjoyed his status. Now he was treated with all the deference due a man who'd once wielded power but wielded it no more. Times had changed. The same money could be made from the same sordid activities but with a firewall of paid protection. The legal profession and big business now provided all the cover that was needed, and life went on as before. Control had passed to his oldest son, Dante, who'd worked for years papering over the cracks with a veneer of respectability.

Lorenzo had taken for granted he'd die young and therefore had no need to provide for himself in his old age. Alfredo was the same way, so maybe it was something they'd learned in their youth. Whatever the source of their poor decisions, they now lived on Dante's dime. He also supported his brother, Cappi, who was supposedly "getting on his feet" after an early release on a five-year bid at Soledad. Three of Dante's four sisters were spread out across the country, married to men who did well (thank god) with twelve children among them, democratically distributed at three apiece. Elena lived in Sparta, New Jersey; Gina in Chicago; and Mia in Denver. His favorite sister, Talia, widowed two years before, had moved back to Santa Teresa. Her two sons, now twenty-two and twenty-five, were college graduates with good jobs. Her youngest, a daughter, was attending Santa Teresa City College and living at home. Talia was the only one of his sisters he talked to with any regularity. Her husband had left her megabucks and she didn't look to Dante for financial support, which was a blessing. As it was, he had twelve full-time and five part-time employees at the house.

Dante tapped on Uncle Alfredo's door and the nurse admitted him. Cara had worked the morning shift, making sure the old man was clean, freshly dressed, and had taken his daily regimen of medications. Alfredo was in pain much of the time, but there were moments when he was able to sit out on the patio surrounded by the roses Dante had planted for him when he first arrived. That's where Dante found him now, his white hair still damp from his sponge bath. He had a shawl pulled over his shoulders and he had his eyes closed, enjoying the early morning sunshine.

Dante pulled up a chair and Alfredo acknowledged him without bothering to look.

"How was Canada?"

Dante said, "Boring. Too warm to ski and too cold to do anything else. Two days in, my knees were killing me. Lola claimed it was psychosomatic so I got no sympathy. She said I was just looking for an excuse to go home. How are you?"

His uncle managed a half smile. "Not wonderful."

"Mornings are tough. It'll get better as the day goes on."

"With enough pills," he said. "Yesterday, Father Ignatius came to the house and heard my confession. First time in forty-five years, so it took a while."

"Must have been a relief."

"Not as much as I'd hoped."

"Any regrets?"

"Everybody has regrets. Things you did, you shouldn't have. Things you didn't do, you should have. Hard to know which is worse."

Dante said, "Maybe in the end, it doesn't matter."

"Believe me, it matters. Tell yourself it doesn't, but it does. I repented my sins, but that don't repair the damage."

"At least you had a chance to come clean."

Alfredo shrugged. "I wasn't entirely candid. Close as I am to leaving this earth, there are some secrets I'm reluctant to give up. It's a burden on my soul."

"You still have time."

"Don't I wish," he said mildly. "How's Cappi doing?"

"That fuck's got more ambition than brains."

Alfredo smiled and closed his eyes. "So use that to your advantage. You know Sun-Tzu, *The Art of War*?"

"I do not. He says what?"

"'To secure ourselves against defeat lies in our own hands, but the opportunity of defeating the enemy is provided by the enemy himself.' You understand what I'm saying?"

Dante studied his uncle's face. "I'll give it some thought."

"You better do more than that." Uncle Alfredo fell silent.

Dante watched the rise and fall of his chest, shoulders now spindly, arms as white as bone. His knuckles were red and swollen, and Dante imagined they'd be hot to the touch. A gentle snoring began, which at least signaled that the old man was alive if not attentive. He admired Alfredo's stoicism. The fight was wearing him down, the pain grinding away at him, but he didn't complain. Dante had no use for people who whined and bellyached, an attitude he'd learned from Pop, who wouldn't tolerate complaints from him or from anyone else. Dante had lived his life listening to his father's admonitions about people whom he considered weak and stupid and conniving.

Dante was the eldest of six. Cappi was the youngest with the four girls between them. After his mother had walked out, Lorenzo had taken to beating Dante with a savagery that was unrelenting. Dante took the punches, thinking to protect his little brother. He knew Lorenzo would never lay a hand on the girls. Between the ages of twelve and fourteen, Cappi was subject to the same abuse, but then something changed. Cappi began to fight back, refusing to take the old man's crap. For a brief period, the violence escalated and then, suddenly,

Lorenzo backed off. Whatever the strange dynamic between them, Cappi had ended up just like Pop, careless, mean, and impulsive.

The dining room was empty when Dante sat down. Sophie had laid out the *New York Times*, the *Wall Street Journal*, the *Los Angeles Times*, and the local paper that Dante occasionally scanned for gossip. Lola wouldn't be joining him. She'd use jet lag as today's excuse for sleeping in. Lola was a night owl, staying up until all hours watching TV, old black-and-white movies shown nightly on an off channel. Most days she wouldn't emerge from the master suite until early afternoon. One day a week she went into the office and made a show of being useful. He'd put her on the payroll and he insisted she do something to earn her keep.

She was the first woman who'd been in his life longer than a year. He'd always been wary of women. He made a point of keeping his distance, which most women found intriguing at first, then infuriating, and finally intolerable. Women wanted a relationship that was concrete and clearly defined. The commitment talk would begin after the first few months and accelerate until he shut it down and the women moved on. He never had to break up with them. They broke up with him, which suited him just fine. It had been pointed out to him more than once that he was attracted to the same type over and over: young, dark-haired, dark-eyed, and thin; in effect, his mother at thirty-three when she'd left without a word.

Lola was different, or so it seemed. They'd met in a bar on her twenty-eighth birthday. He'd stopped in for a drink, bringing his usual contingent: chauffeur, bodyguard, and a couple of pals. He'd noticed her the minute he walked in. She was there celebrating with friends, in the midst of a Champagne toast when he sat down at the next table. Dark mane of hair, dark eyes, a voluptuous mouth. She was long-limbed and rail thin in tight jeans and a T-shirt through which he could see the shape of her small breasts. She'd spotted him about the same time, and the two had played eye-tag for an hour before she walked over and introduced herself. He'd taken her back to his place, thinking to impress her. Instead, she'd been amused. He learned later that her tablemates had warned her about him . . . for all the good it did. Lola was attracted to bad boys. Until she met Dante, she'd spent years bailing guys out of jail, believing their promises, waiting for them to change. Lola stuck with them through their prison sentences and stints in rehab. Her faith in them rendered her only more gullible in the face of the next unlucky loser.

Dante was "clean" by comparison. He made big money and he was generous. He offered her the same whiff of danger, but he was smarter and better insulated. Lola teased him about his armor-plated limousine and his bodyguards. He liked her sassiness, the fact that she'd sooner flip him off than do his bidding.

After the first six years, talk of marriage began to filter into her conversation. She was impatient with the status quo. Dante had sidestepped the issue, holding her off for another two years, but he could feel himself weakening. What difference would it make? They'd been living as husband and wife since the beginning of their relationship. To date, his argument had been that a marriage license was superfluous. Why insist on a piece of paper when she already enjoyed all the perks and benefits? Lately, she'd been turning it around on him, pointing out that if marriage meant so little, why was he making such a big deal of it?

At 9:00 he pushed the newspapers aside and finished his coffee. Before walking out of the kitchen, he buzzed Tomasso on the intercom. "Would you bring the car around?"

"I'm waiting at the side door. Hubert's riding shotgun."

"Just what I like to hear."

As Dante passed through the sheltered portico off the library, Tomasso opened the back door of the stretch limousine and watched him slide into the backseat. Drive time to the office would be fifteen minutes even as Tomasso varied the routes. Hubert, Dante's hulking bodyguard, shifted in the front seat and nodded a greeting. Hubert was Czechoslovakian and spoke very little English. He was good at what he did and his minimal comprehension meant he couldn't eavesdrop when Dante and Tomasso discussed business. At six foot five, weighing the better part of three hundred pounds, Hubert had a presence that was reassuring to his employers, like owning a Rottweiler with a placid disposition and vicious territorial instincts.

Dante noticed Tomasso eyeing him in the rearview mirror. "What's up?" he asked.

Tomasso said, "I thought you'd be windburned."

"Hardly left the hotel. Next time I talk vacations, remind me how much I hate being away."

"Resort was okay?"

"For two grand a night, it was so-so."

"How about the guys we hired to look after you?"

"Not as competent as you two, but I'm alive and well."

Tomasso was quiet for the duration of the drive. He pulled into the underground parking garage that ran beneath the Passages Shopping Plaza on the Macy's end of the mall. Hubert emerged from the car and did a quick scan, searching the nearly empty space for potential danger before he opened the back door and Dante got out.

Tomasso lowered the window. "Hey, Boss? You might want to check with Mr. Abramson before you do anything else."

Dante paused, leaning down to peer into the driver's-side window. "And why is that?"

"All I know is he said you should talk to him soon as you got in. He's not one to run off at the mouth, but his body language was on the urgent side of tense."

"You know what it's about?"

"Better you should hear it from him . . . killing the messenger being what it is. What time you want to be picked up?"

"I'll call. You can take Pop back to the house whenever he's ready to go. Might be a long day for me depending on what went down while I was gone."

Tomasso seemed on the verge of saying more, but Dante didn't like to linger in the open, so with Hubert close on his heels he crossed to the elevators and pushed the up button. The two of them took the elevator to the top floor. Once Dante left the elevator, Hubert returned to the car. Passing through the reception area, Dante noticed a slim brunette ensconced in one of the big leather chairs, leafing through a magazine.

He paused at the receptionist's desk. "Morning, Abbie. Is Saul in?"

"No, sir. Mr. Abramson had a dental appointment. He should be back by ten."

"Tell him I want him in my office," he said, and then flicked a look at the visitor. "Who's she?"

"Mrs. Vogelsang. Mr. Berman referred her."

"Give me five minutes and then you can show her in."

On his way down the corridor, he tapped on his father's office door and stuck his head in. Lorenzo, fully dressed in a three-piece suit and black wingtips, was stretched out on the couch asleep, a biography of Winston Churchill open facedown across his chest. Dante eased the door shut and left him to his rest.

He sat down at his desk and put in a call to Maurice Berman, who owned a small chain of high-end jewelry stores. When Berman picked up, Dante said, "Hey, Maurice. Dante. I got a gorgeous woman waiting in reception. What's the story?"

"Channing Vogelsang's wife. You know the name?"

"I don't."

"Hotshot Hollywood attorney. They have a house in Malibu and a second home in Montebello. They split time between the two. I bought a couple of pieces from her—nice, high quality, and the price was fair. Then she shows me a ring I have problems with. I'm thinking who am I to bring bad tidings to a beautiful woman? Money she's asking, it was out of my league anyway. I told her you were the only guy in town with the resources to take it off her hands."

"What's she need the money for?"

"Beats me. She's a cool customer. Not a lot of small talk and no explanation."

"Drugs?"

"I doubt it. Could be gambling, but she doesn't look like the type. I handed her a check for seven on jewelry appraised at forty-two."

"Nobody ever said you weren't generous," Dante said. "Tell me about the pieces you bought."

"A pair of cabochon sapphire-and-diamond earrings, probably worth seventeen grand, and an Art Deco sapphire-and-diamond line bracelet worth twenty-five easy. The ring, I don't like."

"I'm willing to take a look."

"I thought you'd see it that way. Let me know what comes of it."

Dante hung up and buzzed Abbie, asking her to bring in Mrs. Vogelsang. He crossed to the door and watched the two approach. When Abbie showed her into the office, he held out his hand. "Mrs. Vogelsang. A pleasure. I'm Lorenzo Dante. My father's Lorenzo Senior, so I'm Dante to most. Come in and have a seat."

"It's Nora," she replied, and the two shook hands. Her fingers were cool and slim, her grip strong. Her smile was tentative, and he realized she was ill at ease.

"Coffee?" he asked.

"Yes, please. I'd like milk if you have it. No sugar."

"Make that two," he said to Abbie.

While she went off to the break room, Dante gestured toward a leather-upholstered chair that was part of a seating arrangement in front of the three big circular windows that looked out onto State. She sat down, placing a large, expensive-looking black leather handbag on the floor next to her. She was trim, petite, in a well-cut black suit that suggested more than it revealed. A delicate scent trailed into the room after her. He settled on the couch, trying not to stare. She was so beautiful he could hardly take his eyes off her. There was an elegance about her, a reserve, he found unsettling. He manufactured small talk while they waited for the coffee, happy to have an excuse to study her at close range. Solemn, dark eyes; sweet mouth. Her gaze traveled across the room, which was awash in tones of gray. The upholstered pieces were covered in Ultrasuede in a deep charcoal shade; the rug a softer gray; the walls paneled in whitewashed walnut.

She turned a curious gaze on him. "May I ask what you do? I assumed you dealt in estate jewelry. This looks like an attorney's office."

"I'm a private banker of sorts. I lend money to clients who don't qualify for loans from traditional institutions. Most prefer to keep their finances out of the public eye. I also own a number of commercial businesses. What about you?"

"My husband's a lawyer in the industry."

"The 'industry' meaning the film business. So I've heard. Channing Vogelsang. You live in Los Angeles?"

"Malibu. We have a second home in Montebello."

"Nice. You belong to the Montebello Country Club?"

"Nine Palms," she said, correcting him.

"Maybe you know the Hellers, Robert and his wife?"

"Gretchen. Yes. They're good friends. As a matter of fact, we're meeting for dinner at the club next Saturday. How do you know them?"

"Robert and I had business dealings in times past," Dante said. "It's possible I'll see you there."

"At the club?"

"You don't have to sound so surprised. You're not the only one with friends," he said. "At any rate, I talked to Maurice Berman this morning. He says you have a ring you'd like to sell. May I see it?"

"Certainly." She reached into her bag and took out a ring box, which she handed him.

He opened the box and found himself looking at a radiant-cut pink diamond, flanked by two white diamonds. "Five carats?"

"Five point four six. The setting is platinum and eighteen-carat gold. The smaller stones total one point seven carats. My husband bought it from a New York dealer several months ago."

"You know what he paid?"

"A hundred and twenty-five thousand."

"You have the bill of sale?"

"I don't have access to it. My husband keeps financial records at the office."

Dante let that pass, wondering if Channing Vogelsang knew what she was up to. "You mind if I get an outside opinion? I've got a gal in the office who's a trained gemologist."

"If you like."

Abbie returned with a tray that held a coffee carafe, two cups and saucers, spoons, and a creamer and a sugar bowl. She placed the tray on the glass-topped coffee table and passed Nora a saucer and cup. Abbie filled hers, being careful not to get the steaming liquid too close to the rim. Nora helped herself to milk from the pitcher while Abbie poured coffee for Dante. Before she left, Dante held out the ring box. "Give this to Lou Elle and have her take a look."

"Yes, sir." Abbie left the office with the ring box and closed the door behind her.

"This shouldn't take long," he said. There was silence while she sipped her coffee. He set his cup aside untouched. "You mind if I ask a few questions?"

She tilted her head in a move that he took as assent.

"The ring was a gift from your husband?"

"Yes."

"I'm guessing an anniversary. Tenth?"

"Fourteenth. Why do you ask?"

"I'm trying to understand what's happening here."

"Nothing complicated," she said. "I'd prefer the cash."

"And for this, you'd go behind his back?"

"I'm not *going behind his back.*"

He lifted one brow. "So he knows you're doing this?"

"I don't see that it's any of your business."

"I'm not trying to be fresh. I'm confused. I thought marriage was about having someone you rely on. Someone you can say anything you want to. No secrets and no holding back. Otherwise what's the point?"

"This has nothing to do with him. The ring is mine."

"He won't notice you're not wearing it?"

"He knows I don't care for it. It's not my style."

"How much are you asking?"

"Seventy-five."

Dante watched her face, which was more expressive than she knew. In her life, for some reason, the stakes had gone up. He waited but she didn't expand. "I'm surprised you're willing to part with it. No sentiment attached?"

"I'm not comfortable discussing it."

He smiled. "You want seventy-five grand and it's not worth a conversation?"

"I didn't mean it that way. It's personal."

He watched her with interest, amused at her refusing to meet his eyes. "Must be very personal to have you salting money away."

Startled, her gaze came up to his. "What makes you think I'm doing that?"

"Because you sold two other pieces of jewelry. Nothing as pricey as this from what Maurice says."

"I had no idea he'd discuss it with you. I consider that indiscreet."

"What, you think there's a confidentiality clause in a deal like this? Business is business. I figure you're stockpiling cash and I'm curious."

She hesitated, not meeting his eyes. "Call it insurance."

"Mad money."

"If you like."

"Fair enough," he said.

Dante's phone rang. He reached over to the end table and picked up the handset, saying, "Yes, ma'am."

Lou Elle said, "Can I see you in my office?"

"Sure thing," he said and hung up. To Nora, he said, "Would you excuse me? This should only take a minute."

"Of course."

He closed the door behind him and proceeded to Lou Elle's office in the same corridor. She'd been the company comptroller for the past fifteen years. He found her sitting at her desk, the ring box open in one hand. She held it up. "What's the story?"

"Lady in my office is selling it."

"How much?"

"Seventy-five. She tells me her husband bought it from a New York dealer for one twenty-five. No bill of sale, but she seems sincere."

"Guess again. It's bullshit. The diamond's flawed. It's been subjected to a process called clarity enhancement, in which a resinlike material is used to correct imperfections. If he paid one twenty-five, he was robbed."

"Maybe he didn't know."

"Or maybe he paid less and lied to her. The color's bullshit too. The diamond probably didn't score well so it's been irradiated, which gives it the pink tint."

"We're still talking five point four six carats."

"I didn't say it was junk. I said it wasn't worth seventy-five."

He smiled. "How much did I pay for your training?"

She handed him the ring box. "Nineteen thousand for the certification as a gemologist, with an additional thirteen grand for certification in colored stones."

"Money well spent."

"At the time, you complained."

"Shame on me."

"That's what *I* said."

He put the box in his suit coat pocket and patted the bulge. "Remind me and I'll give you a bonus at the end of the year."

"I'd rather have it now."

"Done," Dante said. "Give Maurice Berman a call and tell him what you told me."

When he got back to his office, Nora was standing at one of the circular windows, watching the pedestrians passing on the far side of the street.

"Good for spying purposes," he said. "Glass looks opaque from the outside, smoke black."

"I've seen the windows from the street. Odd to be seeing them from this side." She smiled briefly and returned to her seat. "Is everything okay?"

"It's fine. This was another matter altogether. Nothing to do with you."

He stopped at his desk and removed a big padded mailer from the bottom drawer and then crossed to the side wall and triggered the panel that concealed his office safe. He shielded the contents of the safe from view while he removed seven thick bundles of hundred-dollar bills bound in packets. He added one smaller bundle and placed all eight in the mailer. He returned to his seat before he gave it to her.

She opened the mailer and glanced at the contents. She seemed startled and the color rose in her cheeks.

"Seventy-five," he said. "It's all there."

"I expected a wire transfer or maybe you'd pay by check."

"You don't want seventy-five grand showing up in your bank account. A deposit that size generates a report to the IRS."

"Is that a problem?"

"I don't want to create a paper trail that starts with me and ends up with you. I'm under investigation. The IRS finds out you've done business with me, they'll beat a path to your door. You don't want our association coming to light."

"There's nothing illegal about selling a ring."

"Unless you sell it to a guy the Feds are hot to prosecute."

"For what? You said you were a private banker."

"A private banker *of sorts*."

She stared at him. "You're a loan shark."

"Among other things."

She held up the bulky mailer. "Where did this come from?"

"I told you. I operate a number of businesses that generate cash. I'm passing some of it on to you."

"That's why you didn't haggle. I said seventy-five and you never batted an eye. You're laundering money."

"It's only 'laundering' if dirty money's been integrated and it comes out clean. All you have to do is hang on to it."

"That's ridiculous. What good's the cash if I can't use it?"

"Who said you couldn't use it? Stash it in a safe-deposit box and move it into a checking or savings account in increments of less than ten grand. It's no big deal."

"I can't do that."

"Why not? I have the ring. You have the cash. As long as you don't call attention to it, we both benefit. The point is, it's yours."

"I'm not that desperate."

"I think you are. I don't know what's happened in your life, but your husband's a fool if he's giving you grief."

"That's no concern of yours."

Nora rose from her chair and retrieved her handbag. Dante stood up at the same time. She pushed the padded mailer toward him. He held up his hands, refusing to accept the package. "Why don't you think about it overnight?"

"I don't need to think about it," she said, and tossed the mailer onto the chair.

There was a brief knock at the door and Abbie appeared. "Mr. Abramson is here."

Nora said, "I'll let you get back to work."

Dante took the ring box from his pocket and placed it in her palm. "Change your mind, let me know."

Nora broke off eye contact, saying nothing as she left the room. Dante watched her depart, hoping she'd look back at him, which she refused to do.

Abbie remained in the room.

Dante looked at her. "Something else?"

"I just wanted to remind you I'll be out of town Thursday and Friday of this week. I'll be back at work next Monday."

"Fine. Enjoy yourself."

Once she was gone, he returned to his desk and settled into his chair. Abramson came in and closed the door. He'd been in partnership with Dante for twenty years and he was one of the few men Dante trusted. He was in his fifties, balding, with a long, solemn face, and glasses with dark frames. He was tall and trim in a custom-made suit. He'd apparently had Novocaine on the left side of his mouth and it hadn't worn off. There was a puffiness and a droop to his lip on that side as though he'd suffered a stroke. He said, "Audrey's dead." No preamble.

It took Dante half a beat to shift his focus from Nora to Abramson. "Shit. When was this?"

"Sunday."

"Yesterday? How?"

"She got picked up for shoplifting. This was Nordstrom's, Friday afternoon. I guess she couldn't talk her way out of it so she was thrown in the clink. Her boyfriend put up bail, but by then she was hysterical. Word reached Cappi she was close to cutting a deal, so he and the boys took her up to Cold Spring Bridge and tossed her over the rail."

"Fuck."

"I've been telling you for months the kid is out of control. He's reckless and dumb and it's a dangerous combination. I think he's leaking information to the cops."

"I'm too old for this shit," Dante said. "I can't have him whacked. I know it needs doing, but I can't. Maybe once upon a time, but not now. I'm sorry."

"Your call, but you buy into the consequences. That's all I'm saying."

# 7

Monday morning, I dragged my sorry butt out of bed at 6:00, assembled myself, and went out for my jog. I wasn't limping, but I was conscious of my bruised shin, which, the last time I peeked, was as dark and ominous as a thundercloud. My palm had scabbed over, but I'd be picking grit out of the wound for days. On the plus side, the sun was up and the April sky above was bright blue. There was talk of a storm coming in, a phenomenon known as the Pineapple Express—a system that rotates in from the South Pacific, picking up tropical moisture as it moves toward the coast. Any rain would be warm and the air would be balmy, my concept of spring in the south. We weren't yet feeling the effects, except for the ragged rim of clouds piled up on the horizon like trash against a fence.

Jogging was a chore, but I chugged on, feeling leaden to the bone, probably due to the change in barometric pressure. These are the days that require discipline, when exercise is pure duty and the good feeling only comes later, consisting solely of self-congratulations for having done the job at all. I walked the final block home. I'd barely broken a sweat, but my body temperature was dropping rapidly and I was cold. I reached the front gate and when I bent to pick up the morning paper, I experienced a whisper of depression. Henry's copy of the *Dispatch* was usually lying on the sidewalk next to mine. He'd canceled for the duration of his out-of-town stay, leaving my paper all alone and looking forlorn. Amazing the things I miss about the man when he's gone.

I let myself into my studio and put on a pot of coffee, then went up the spiral stairs to the loft. Once I'd showered and dressed, I trotted down again, spirits on the rise. I leafed through the paper until I found the obituaries and then flapped the section open and folded the pages back. I poured myself a bowl of cereal and added milk, spooning up breakfast while I read. I can't remember when the daily death list became a matter of such interest. Usually, the names mean little or nothing. In a town of eighty-five thousand, the chances of being acquainted with the newly departed aren't that great. I scan for ages and birth years, checking to see where mine falls in relation to the deceased. If the dead are my age or younger, I read the notices with close attention to circumstances. Those are the deaths I ponder, reminded every morning that life is fragile and not as much in our control as we'd like to think. Personally, I don't endorse the notion of mortality. It's fine for other folk, but I disapprove of the concept for me and my loved ones. Seems unfair that we're not allowed to vote on the matter and not one of us is excused. Who made up that rule?

I'd scarcely opened that section when I spotted a photograph in the middle of the page and found myself staring at the shoplifter I'd observed Friday afternoon. I drew back, looked again, and then read once quickly to get the gist. Audrey Vance, sixty-three, had passed away unexpectedly the day before, Sunday, April 24. The midsixties age range was about where I'd placed the woman, and the likeness was unmistakable. How odd was that? I skipped to the last line, which suggested that in lieu of flowers, donations should be made to the American Heart Association in Audrey's name.

The notice was short and on the stingy side. I went back to the beginning and read again with care. Audrey was described as "vivacious and fun-loving, admired by all who knew her." Not a word about her parents, her education, her hobbies, or good deeds. Her survivors included a son, Don, of San Francisco, and a daughter, Elizabeth, also living in San Francisco. There were numerous unnamed nieces and nephews "left to mourn her passing." In addition, she would be greatly missed by her fiancé and loving companion, Marvin Striker. The visitation was at Wynington-Blake Mortuary, Tuesday, 10:00 to noon, with a service to follow at 2:00 at Wynington-Blake. There was no mention of the burial.

I could hardly take it in. I wondered if the trauma of her arrest had triggered her collapse. It was not beyond the realm of possibility. Audrey had looked matronly and middle class, not out of place in an upscale department store. Until I saw her shoplift, I'd have pegged her as the type who returned her library books on time and wouldn't have dreamed of fudging on her income tax forms. What a shock she must have experienced when the loss-prevention officer caught up with her. She'd made it as far as the mall and must have thought she was in the clear, even with the store alarm bleating behind her. From what Claudia had said about her weeping and wailing, she was either a first-rate actress or truly desperate. Sincerity aside, she must have felt humiliated being hauled off in handcuffs. I was thrown in jail once myself and I can tell you it's not an experience you want to repeat. Habitual criminals are probably undismayed by the booking process, associating as they do with other miscreants for whom pat-downs and strip searches are the norm. All they care about is finding a bail bondsman as fast as possible so they can fork over the 10 percent and get themselves cut loose. Poor Audrey Vance. What a strange turn of events. I wondered how much, if anything, her fiancé knew about her ordeal.

Following on the heels of my initial surprise, I experienced a twinge of guilt. I'd been thrilled to hear about her arrest, happy to know she was being called to account. The idea that she'd been slapped with consequences suited me just fine. We're each responsible for our own choices, and if she'd elected to break the law, why should she have been spared? At the same time, as much as I'd rejoiced at her comeuppance, I hadn't expected her to *die*. In this country (at least as far as I know), shoplifting isn't deemed a capital offense. I didn't imagine wielding such influence in the universe that my very enmity had pushed her into the grave. Where I faulted myself was in my sense of moral superiority.

Idly, I wondered if she'd been charged with a felony or a misdemeanor. The two pairs of pajamas at full price (including tax) would have pushed her over the four-hundrd-dollar limit, shifting her offense from petit to grand theft. But what about the sale? Was she more or less culpable in the eyes of the law? At 75 percent off, was a felony discounted down to a lesser charge?

In either case, the poor woman was dead and that seemed bizarre. Maybe she'd suffered from a chronic medical condition that left her vulnerable to stress. Or maybe she'd experienced chest pains and (like so many women) had decided to say nothing because she didn't want to make a fuss. Even if she was under a doctor's care, death might have come as a surprise. She might have appeared to be in perfect health, asymptomatic, and still toppled over dead with little apparent provocation. I'd been a witness, standing by in the final days of her life, with no idea how little time she had left. It was freakish to contemplate and I could hardly get it out of my mind.

I grabbed my jacket and car keys, taking the paper with me. I drove to the office in hopes of distracting myself with the business of doing business. Once at my desk, I caught up with my paperwork. I was doing okay until the telephone rang. "Millhone Investigations."

"Kinsey?" A woman's voice.

"Yes, ma'am."

"This is Claudia Rines. Did you see the article in this morning's paper?"

I put an automatic hand against my heart. "I did and I feel like such a *turd*. What are the odds of a heart attack? Jesus. I wonder if she knew what was happening to her."

There was a moment of quiet. "You didn't see the article."

"I did too. Audrey Vance, sixty-three years old. Two grown kids and she was engaged to some guy. I have the newspaper right here."

"Fine, but she didn't die of a heart attack. She jumped off the Cold Spring Bridge."

"What?"

"The *Dispatch*. Front page of the second section, just below the fold. If you have it handy, I can wait."

"Hang on." I tucked the receiver against my ear and secured it with one shoulder while I dragged my bag from under the desk and pulled out the paper I'd brought from home. The obituaries were uppermost. The photograph of Audrey still occupied center stage. I put the phone down on the desk and used both hands to flap the pages back to their original configuration. I leaned close to the mouthpiece, saying, "Sorry about that. Hang on a minute."

First page, bottom left. There was no photograph of the victim and Audrey's name wasn't mentioned. According to the article, a Santa Teresa man was coming over the pass Sunday afternoon when he noticed a car parked on the berm. He stopped to investigate, thinking the vehicle was disabled and the motorist might need help. There was no sign of a flat tire and no note on the windshield indicating the driver had gone in search of the nearest service station. The car was unlocked and he could see the keys in the ignition. What caught his attention was the handbag on the front seat. A pair of high heels had been placed neatly on the seat beside the bag. This was not good.

He'd walked to the nearest call box and notified the county sheriff's department. An officer arrived seven minutes later and assessed the situation in much the same way the motorist had. He called for backup and a ground search was instigated. The chaparral below the bridge was so dense that both the Santa Teresa County Sheriff's K-9 unit and a search-and-rescue team were brought in. Once the dog had located the body, it was a forty-five-minute struggle across treacherous terrain to bring it out. Since the bridge was completed in 1964, seventeen people had made the leap and none had survived the four-hundred-foot drop. The victim's driver's license was in her handbag. Identification was withheld, pending notification of the next of kin.

"Are you sure it was her?"

"I am now. When I first read the article, I didn't put it together with the obit. The police made the connection when they ran her name through their computer system. They called and talked to Mr. Koslo, who'd filed the charges against her. Mr. Koslo mentioned it to the guy who monitors the closed-circuit security cameras. Ricardo rang me up as soon as Mr. Koslo was out the door."

"This is *terrible*," I said. I could see where someone in the throes of mental or physical anguish might view suicide as a form of relief. The problem was, there was no backing up. The remedy was harsh and precluded alternatives. Life might have looked better in a day or two. "Why would she *do* such a thing? It's just so weird."

"I guess she wasn't faking the hysteria."

"No kidding. And here I was feeling so *gleeful*."

"Hey, me too," Claudia said. "I mean, what if I hadn't notified Security? Would she be alive today?"

"Oh, man. I wouldn't head down that road if I were you. I wonder what her accomplice is going through."

"Nothing good," she said. "Anyway, I gotta scoot. I'm on my break. I'll give you my number and you can call me later if you want to talk."

I made a note of the number, though I couldn't imagine having anything more to say. For the moment, I was hung up on the idea that the woman had killed herself. Built into bad news is that sense of profound disbelief. The mind struggles to absorb the bare facts, defending itself against the larger implications. I didn't feel responsible for what had happened, but I did feel ashamed that I'd wished the woman ill. I harbor a huffy dislike of scofflaws, unless the breach is mine, of course, in which case I find ways to justify my bad behavior. Who was I to judge? I'd pointed a pious finger and now the woman I'd so heartily condemned had hurled herself off a bridge.

I spent the remainder of the morning and half the afternoon organizing my files, a self-inflicted penance that pulled my attention down to the mundane. *Where did this receipt go? Which of these folders could I relegate to the box I was retiring to storage? Whose phone number was this scratched on a stray piece of paper? Keep it or toss?* I'm not sure which I hate more, the pig piles on my desk or the task of dismantling the mess and setting it to rights. By 4:00, the surfaces in my office were clear and my hands were filthy, which seemed appropriate. I washed up, and when the mail was delivered I busied myself sorting the bills from the junk. There was a notice from the water department, letting me know the water to the office would be shut off for eight hours the following Monday to replace a leaky water main. I made a mental note to work from home that day so I wouldn't be stranded in an office with no working toilet.

I found Henry's number in the Detroit area and placed a call. It was close to 7:00 his time. He and his brothers had been home for ten minutes after a day with Nell, who'd been transferred to an in-patient recovery center.

"So how's she doing?"

"Not bad. In fact, I'd say she's good. She's in a lot of pain, but she managed to sit up for an hour, and they're teaching her to use a walker. She can't put any weight on her leg, but she's managing to hobble ten feet or so before she has to sit down again. What's happening there?"

I filled him in on my shoplifter's demise, giving him the long version just so he could appreciate how stunned I was and how stricken I felt about my lack of charity. Henry made all the appropriate clucking sounds, which alleviated my guilt to some extent. We agreed to talk in a couple of days and I hung up the phone feeling better, though not absolved. Despite my efforts to deflect the subject, the specter of Audrey Vance continued to hover at the back of my mind. I couldn't resist the urge to brood. Granted, my connection to her was peripheral. I doubted she'd even noticed me despite our being in range of each other in the lingerie department. The younger woman was certainly aware of me, but there was no point in worrying about *her*. Without a license plate number, I had no way to track her down.

At 5:30, I locked the office and stopped at McDonald's on my way home. When it comes to comfort food, nothing tops a Quarter Pounder with Cheese and a large order of fries. I made a point of asking for a diet soda to mitigate my nutritional sins. I ate in my car, which for a week afterward smelled of raw onions and fried meat.

Once home I left my Mustang in Henry's driveway and headed for Rosie's. I wasn't (necessarily) interested in a glass of bad wine. I wanted familiar faces and noise, maybe even a bit of bullying if Rosie had some to spare. I wouldn't have minded chatting with Claudia, but she didn't make an appearance, which was probably just as well. I flirted with the notion of using William as a sounding board, but quashed the idea. While I felt a need to discuss Audrey Vance's untimely end, I didn't want to get him in a lather about death and dying. In the wake of Nell's fall and his own elevated glucose, he was already feeling vulnerable. In his mind, it was a hop, skip, and a jump from the idea of death to its imminent arrival.

William was a funeral junkie, presenting himself at visitations, services, and graveside ceremonies once or twice a week. His interest was a natural extension of his obsession with his health. It didn't matter to him whether he knew the deceased. He'd put on his three-piece suit, tuck a fresh hankie in his pocket, and set forth. Usually he walked. Several Santa Teresa mortuaries are located downtown, within a ten-block radius, which allowed him his constitutional at the same time he was seeing someone off.

I'd told him about the shoplifter when I was in on Saturday night. Under the circumstances, I didn't think it would be wise to introduce the fact of her toppling over the rail. As it turned out, I needn't have worried. The place was quiet, with only a scattering of patrons. Above the bar, the color television set was on, though the sound had been muted. The channel was fixed on some off-brand game show, to which no one was paying the slightest attention. There was none of the usual background music coming through the speakers and the energy level seemed flat.

Henry's table was empty. One of the day drinkers sat alone in a booth, sipping a whiskey neat. Rosie was perched on a stool at the far end of the bar folding white cloth napkins. A young couple appeared in the doorway, checked the menu posted on the wall, and quickly withdrew. William was behind the bar, leaning forward on his elbows, a ballpoint pen in hand. I thought he might be working on a crossword puzzle until I saw Audrey's photo in the middle of the page. He'd circled three names, hers among them, and underscored the last few lines of the relevant obituaries.

I perched on a stool and peered over the bar. "What are you doing?"

"Working on my short list."

I meant to keep my mouth shut but I couldn't help myself. "Remember the shoplifter I told you about?" I pointed to Audrey's photograph. "That's her."

"Her?"

"Uh-hun. She threw herself off the Cold Spring Bridge."

"Oh, my. I read about that, but had no idea she was the one. Did the paper mention her by name?"

"ID was withheld pending notification of the next of kin," I said. "I didn't see the article at all until someone told me where to look."

He tapped his pen on the paper. "That settles it. There's a scheduling conflict so I can't attend all three of these anyway. Audrey Vance it is. You'll be going, of course."

"Absolutely not. I didn't know the woman."

"Nor did I, but that's hardly the point."

"What *is* the point?"

"Seeing she gets a proper send-off. It's the least we can do."

"You're a total stranger. Don't you think it's bad form?"

"But they don't know that. I'll make it clear we weren't terribly close and therefore I can be more objective about her unfortunate choice. With a suicide, family members are often at a loss. It will help if they can talk about the situation with someone and who better than me? Surely there are details they wouldn't share with friends. You know how it is. A veil of privacy descends. I'm both dispassionate and sympathetic. They'll appreciate the opportunity to sort through their feelings, especially when they learn I'm an old hand at this."

The way William described it, I was inclined to agree.

"What if they ask how you knew her?"

His tone was incredulous. "At a funeral? How *rude*. The right to pay one's respects isn't reserved solely for the next of kin. If someone's gauche enough to inquire, I'll tell them we were distant acquaintances."

"So distant you never met."

"This is a small town. How can anyone be sure our paths didn't cross half a dozen times?"

I said, "Well, don't go on my account. I didn't even know her name until this morning."

"What's the difference?" he asked. "You should join me. We could make an afternoon of it."

"Thanks, but no thanks. Too ghoulish for my taste."

"What if her criminal confederate is there? I thought you were interested in tracking her down."

"Not now," I said. "I'm convinced she was involved, but I don't have a shred of proof, so what's it to me?"

"Don't be callous. Audrey's accomplice bears some responsibility for her demise. I should think you, of all people, would want to see justice done."

"What justice? I saw Audrey shoplift, but I didn't see the other gal steal anything. Even if I did, it would still be her word against mine. The salesclerk at Nordie's didn't have a clue there were two of them."

"Maybe the accomplice was picked up on one or more of the store's security cameras. You could have them print a still shot and take it to the police."

"Trust me, the loss-prevention officer won't invite me in to review the tapes. I'm not even law enforcement. Besides, from his perspective, it's the store's business, not mine."

"Don't be stubborn. If the second woman showed up at the funeral home, you could follow her. If she shoplifted once, she's bound to do it again. You could catch her in the act."

He pulled out the jug of bad wine and poured me a glass.

I considered his proposal, remembering the younger woman's failed attempt to run me down. It *would* be satisfying to see the look on her face if the two of us turned up at the same place. "What makes you think she'll be there?"

"It just stands to reason. Imagine the guilt she must feel. Her friend Audrey is dead. I should think she'd put in an appearance to appease her conscience, if nothing else. You could do the same."

"My conscience doesn't bother me. Who said it did?"

William arched a brow as he screwed the cap on the jug. "Far be it from me."

# 8

Tuesday morning I skipped my run. The pain in my bruised shin felt worse, but that wasn't my excuse. The visitation for Audrey Vance was scheduled for 10:00 A.M. If I went into the office early, I'd have time to make a few calls and open mail before I had to break away. I brushed my teeth, showered, and washed my hair, after which I took my all-purpose black dress out of the closet and gave it a shake. Nothing dropped on the floor and skittered away so I thought I was safe in assuming insects hadn't taken up residence. I inspected the dress, turning it this way and that on the hanger. There was dust on both shoulders and I brushed that away. No buttons missing, no split seams, and no dangling threads. The fabric in this garment is wholly synthetic, probably a petroleum derivative that will one day be pulled off the market owing to its newly discovered carcinogenic properties. In the meantime, it never wrinkles, never shows dirt, and never looks out of date, at least to my untutored eye.

At the office, I accomplished what I could in the brief time allotted. At 9:30, I locked up and drove back to my neighborhood. William, sharply dressed in one of the more somber of his three-piece suits, was waiting outside Rosie's when I swung by to pick him up. Now that he was "pre-diabetic," he'd affected a cane, a handsome ebony affair with a thick rubber tip. We did the crosstown drive in a little less than ten minutes.

There were only two other cars on hand when we pulled into the side lot at Wynington-Blake Mortuary: Burials, Cremation, and Shipping, Serving All Faiths. I chose a spot at random. William could hardly contain himself. As soon as I shut down the engine, he hopped out and approached the entrance with a jaunty step, which he corrected moments later when he remembered his condition. I took my time locking the car, wishing I hadn't come. The facade of the building was blank. All the window openings on the ground floor had been bricked up, and I could feel a creeping claustrophobia before I'd even set foot inside.

Wynington-Blake occupies what was formerly a substantial single-family home. The spacious entry hall now served as a communal corridor, from which seven viewing rooms opened up, each capable of seating as many as a hundred people in folding chairs. Each room had been given a suitably funereal name: Serenity, Tranquility, Meditation, Eternal Rest, Sojourner, the Sunrise Chapel, and the Sanctuary. These rooms had probably once been a front parlor, a living room, a dining room, a library, a billiard room, and a large paneled study. An easel had been placed outside of Tranquility and Meditation, and I was guessing the others were unoccupied.

As we entered, the funeral director, Mr. Sharonson, greeted William warmly. William mentioned Audrey's name and was directed to Meditation, where her viewing was taking place. In a low tone, Mr. Sharonson said to William, "Mr. Striker just arrived."

William said, "The poor fellow. I'll have a word with him and see how he's doing."

"Not well, I'd say."

As though part of a receiving line, I stepped forward and Mr. Sharonson and I shook hands. I'd encountered him three or four times during the past six years, though I couldn't remember ever seeing him outside the current context. He held my hand briefly, perhaps thinking I was there to mourn a loved one.

In the corridor outside Meditation, there was a wooden podium holding an oversize ledger, where one was expected to sign in. The pages were largely blank. Since we'd been so prompt, only one other person had arrived ahead of us. I watched as William stepped forward and dashed off his signature, after which he dutifully printed his name and added his address. I supposed this bit of information was meant for the family so they could send out acknowledgments at a later date. Surely, such lists aren't sold to telemarketers who call you up at the dinner hour, thus ruining your appetite.

The person who'd signed in ahead of William was a Sabrina Striker, probably the daughter or the sister of Audrey's fiancé. The address she'd listed was local. Her handwriting was so small, I marveled it was legible at all. I stood, pen in hand, reluctant to announce my presence since I had no real business being there in the first place. On the other hand, refusing to sign in seemed surly. I wrote my name under William's and when I reached the space meant for my address, I left a blank. On a table nearby there was a stack of printed programs that bore Audrey's name. William took one and went into the viewing room with an air of familiarity. No telling how many times he'd been here to offer his condolences at the passing of someone he'd never met. I picked up a program and followed.

I'd attended a visitation in this very room six years before when a man named John Daggett had drowned in the surf. Not much had changed . . . for him, at any rate. To the right, a sofa and several wing chairs had been set in a semicircle, suggesting an informal living room. The color palette was a wash of mauves, grays, and drab greens. The upholstery was neutral, perhaps selected with an eye to its blending with the other furnishings. There were two sets of tasteful drapes at windows I knew had no outside view. Table lamps provided a suggestion of warmth that might otherwise have come from sunlight.

The tone of the interior was appropriate for any faith, which is to say, stripped of religious symbolism or sacred ornamentation. Even an atheist would have felt right at home. A wooden accordion door had been drawn across the room, bisecting it. With so few in attendance, the fully expanded space would have been disheartening.

To the left, three rows of folding chairs had been arranged in a staggered fashion to allow a view from every seat, probably for purposes of the service to follow in the afternoon. There were two enormous urns filled with gladioli that I later realized were fake. I picked up the scent of carnations, though that might have been the result of a judicious spraying with a room deodorant. A floral wreath had been placed on either side of the mahogany casket, which was closed. The four-hundred-foot drop must have left Audrey Vance in a tattered state of repose.

William had assessed the situation and quickly fixed his attention on a fellow seated in the front, his head bowed, weeping quietly into a handkerchief. This had to be Marvin Striker. A young woman in a white T-shirt and dark blue blazer sat to his right. When William sat down in the folding chair on his left, Striker pulled himself together and wiped his eyes. William placed a consoling hand on his arm and offered a few remarks that were apparently well received. Striker introduced William to the woman sitting next to him and the two shook hands. I had no idea what he'd said, but both Striker and the young woman turned to look at me. Striker nodded briefly. He was neatly dressed in a dark two-piece suit, a man in his midsixties, clean-shaven and balding with a selvage of closely clipped gray hair. His eyebrows were dark, suggesting that his hair had once been dark as well. He wore rimless glasses, with thin metal stems. I hoped William wouldn't insist on introducing me. I was still half expecting to be grilled about my connection with the deceased.

I took a seat in the last of the three rows, the only occupant in the line of seats on either side of the aisle. The temperature was on the chilly side and I picked up the hum of organ music so faint I couldn't identify the melody. I was ill at ease, feeling all the more conspicuous because I was alone and had nothing to occupy my time. I opened my program and read the text, disappointed to discover it was a word-for-word duplication of the obituary I'd read the day before.

Audrey's photograph was also the same, except this one was in color while the one in the newspaper was in black-and-white. She looked good for a woman of sixty-three. Her face had been smoothed by sufficient tasteful cosmetic work to take ten years off her age. Gone was the furrow between her brows, taking with it the "mad" or "sad" expressions that women are persuaded to erase. Better the blank, unmarked visage that bespeaks calm and eternal youth. Her hair was a darker shade than the blond I'd seen at Nordstrom's, though the style was the same, short and brushed away from her face. She was nicely made up. Her smile revealed good teeth, but not so uniform as to suggest caps. She wasn't that heavy, but she was short, probably five two or so, which meant that every extra pound counted against her.

The newspaper had cropped the photograph to a head-and-shoulders shot. What I saw here was the loose-fitting, claret-colored velvet jacket she wore. Her necklace was clearly costume jewelry, a strand of big stones that made no pretense of being precious. The glittering red clutch she held was shaped like a sleeping cat and looked like the very pricy handbag I'd seen at Nordstrom's locked in a glass display case. Snitching it would have been quite the accomplishment.

The formal ceremony, spelled out on the facing page, had been reduced to a bare minimum: an invocation, two hymns, and remarks by a Reverend Anderson, with no church affiliation specified. I was unclear on the protocol. Was there a Rent-a-Reverend agency for folks who weren't members of a proper congregation? I was worried William would want to attend the service and I was already casting about for an excuse.

The young woman sitting beside Striker said something to him and then rose from her seat. She left the room as though on tiptoe, wafting lily-of-the-valley cologne as she passed me and proceeded down the aisle. William was still engaged in an earnest conversation with Striker. What could he possibly have to say to him?

I risked a glance at the door, fearful that Audrey's many nieces and nephews would appear, determined to make nice by chatting with the visitors, namely me. Aside from William and Audrey's fiancé, there was not another soul in the room. It dawned on me that if her shoplifting accomplice appeared, I'd be the first person she'd see. I eased the program into my shoulder bag, slipped out of my folding chair, and went in search of a ladies' room.

As I passed Tranquility, I paused to read the name on the easel. Visitation for Benedict "Dick" Pagent was from 7:00 to 9:00 that night with a second visitation from 10:00 to noon on Wednesday, and services Thursday morning at the Second Presbyterian Church. The room was spacious and gloomy. Table lamps were turned off and the only light was the block slanting in from the hall, broken by my shadow as I peered in the open door. A similar arrangement of wing chairs and a matching sofa occupied the area to my right. Glancing to the left, I caught sight of an open casket on the far end, a man's body visible from the waist up, so still he might have been carved in stone. I pictured a bit of scene setting before the relatives arrived; lamps turned on, music made audible, anything to suggest he hadn't been lying there alone. I backed up and continued down the hall.

Around the next corner, I saw a small informal sitting room with an adjacent kitchenette, perhaps intended for the immediate family if they were in need of privacy. Restrooms marked M and W were just to the left. The ladies' lounge was immaculate, a two-stall affair with a faux marble counter, two undermounted sinks, and a prominently displayed No Smoking sign. I smelled cigarette smoke and it didn't take a professional to spot the haze wafting up from one of the stalls.

I heard a toilet flush and the young woman I'd tagged as Striker's daughter exited the stall. No cigarette in hand so she must have tossed it in the john. She glanced at me briefly and offered a polite smile as she crossed to the sink, turned the water on, and washed her hands. Along with the blazer and white T-shirt, she was wearing jeans, tennis socks, and running shoes. Not exactly funeral garb, but an outfit I'd have felt comfortable in myself.

I went into the other stall and availed myself of the facilities, hoping to delay my return to the viewing room until more mourners arrived. I expected to hear the hall door open and close, but when I emerged the woman was leaning against the counter, lighting another cigarette. I resisted the urge to point out the error of her ways. I suffered the same conflict at the bird refuge, watching tourists feed bread scraps to the ducks when a Please Don't Feed the Birds sign is posted at the site. While I'm willing to allow visitors the benefit of the doubt, I'm always tempted to say, "Do you speak English?" or "Can you read?" in slow, clear tones. I haven't done it yet, but it does irritate me when citizens ignore plainly posted municipal codes.

Sabrina Striker's face was long. Her nose was narrow through the bridge and wider at the tip, which made the whole of it seem larger than it was. She kept her dark hair tucked behind her ears, which caused them to protrude. She wore no makeup and needed a better haircut. Perhaps because of the flaws in evidence, she seemed appealing, someone nice and unpretentious.

I took my time washing my hands. It's been my experience that women in ladies' rooms will tell you anything, given half a chance. This seemed as good a time as any to test the theory. I caught her eye in the mirror. "Are you Sabrina?"

She smiled, exposing a rim of gum above her upper teeth. "That's right."

I turned off the water and pulled a fold of paper toweling from the stack. I dried my hands, tossed the towel in the trash, and then offered my hand. "I'm Kinsey."

We shook hands as she said, "I figured as much. I saw your name in the book on my way in here. You're with that older gentleman who's talking to my dad."

"William's my neighbor," I said and left it at that. I leaned toward the mirror and brushed at one eyebrow as though smoothing the arch. I could see my mop was in need of a whack and I was sorry I hadn't tucked my trusty nail scissors in my shoulder bag. I usually carry them with me in the event of a styling emergency.

She said, "So, were you Audrey's friend or was he?"

"More him than me. I actually only saw her once. He was the one who suggested we attend the visitation," I said, deftly avoiding the truth. "I believe the paper said she was engaged to your dad."

Sabrina made a face. "Unfortunately. We had no idea he was that serious about her."

"Was there a problem?"

She hesitated. "Are you telling the truth when you say you weren't Audrey's friend?"

"Not a friend at all. Cross my heart." I made a quick X on my chest by way of confirmation.

"Because I don't want to say anything out of line."

"Trust me. I'm on your team."

"Basically, what happened was my mother died last May. My parents were college sweethearts, married forty-two years. Daddy met Audrey in a bar four months after mother passed away. Next thing you know she was moving in with him."

"Tacky of her."

"Exactly."

"I take it you objected."

"I tried keeping my opinion to myself, but I'm sure he knew how I felt. I found it offensive. My sister, Delaney, thought she was a gold digger, but I disagreed. Audrey was never short of money so I had a hard time believing she was after his. She was good to him. I'll give her that." She reached over and turned on the water, extinguishing her cigarette before she tossed it in the trash. "Of course, she was a slut."

"In her age bracket, I thought they were called something else, but I can't imagine what," I said.

"A conniving old slut."

"You think she had an ulterior motive?"

"There was *something* going on with her. I mean, Daddy's adorable, but she's hardly his type."

"How so?"

"He's always been a bit of a stick-in-the-mud. Even my mother complained at times. He's a homebody. He doesn't like to go out at night. Audrey was a live wire, always on the go. Where was the common ground?"

My shrug was noncommittal. "Maybe they fell in love. He must have been lonely with your mother gone. Most men don't do well on their own, especially if they've been happily married."

"Agreed. And of course now he's done a complete turnaround . . . Mr. Gadabout. I figured far be it from me to interfere with his so-called love life. Delaney and I minimized our contact with Audrey. It was the best we could do. The times we saw her, we made a point of being polite. I'm not sure we succeeded, but it wasn't for lack of effort on our part. Whatever doubts I had, I kept to myself, not that anyone gave me credit. They assumed I was jealous, like I wouldn't have warmed to any woman who took up with him, but that's just not true."

"Who's 'they'?"

"Their bar buddies. After the service, I'm sure the lot of them will come rallying around and insist on taking him out for drinks. As nearly as I could tell, drinking was all he and Audrey ever did. I'm not saying he's over the line or anything like that. She's the one. Party, party, party. Luckily, she traveled a lot on business so she was gone half the time. Would you call that a healthy relationship? Because I don't."

"What about her kids? Did they approve?"

"I have no idea. We never laid eyes on them."

"Will they be here? I didn't see their names in the book."

"They don't even know she died. They're supposedly in San Francisco, but Daddy couldn't find a contact number for either one of them. Audrey had an address book. He saw it on more than one occasion, but he doesn't know what she did with it."

"She probably kept the numbers in her head."

"I guess. Audrey claimed her daughter, Betty, worked for Merrill Lynch, but that was bullshit. Delaney lives in the city herself so she called the office and drew a complete blank. Nobody'd ever heard of her."

"She could be married and using her husband's last name."

"That's one explanation," she said. She pulled her mouth down and ran her tongue across her upper teeth, a move that conveys disbelief, though I'm not sure why.

"What about her nieces and nephews? Wouldn't one of them know how to contact her kids?"

"There aren't any nieces or nephews. Daddy made that up for the obit because he thought it sounded better. She really didn't seem to have friends or family. With the exception of that bunch of drunks they hung out with, we're it."

"That seems odd."

"It is odd. I mean, if she had kids you'd think they'd have come down to visit at some point or at least called now and then."

"You think she lied about them?"

"It wouldn't surprise me. I had the sneaking suspicion she was pulling the wool over Daddy's eyes, acting all nicey-nice. The way she talked, she was head of a happy little family with kids who were gainfully employed. Ha!"

"Maybe she was estranged from them."

"I guess that's possible, though we may never know the truth." She lowered her voice. "You heard how she died?"

"I did and I wasn't sure what to make of it. Did she strike you as the type who'd take a dive off a bridge?"

"Ordinarily, no, but Daddy says she was arrested late Friday afternoon and spent half the night in jail."

My attempt to look astonished probably fell short, but she didn't know me well enough to catch on. I said, "Arrested? Are you serious? For what?"

"Who knows? I couldn't get it out of him. I know he posted bail and from what he said, she was on the verge of a nervous breakdown. He was furious. He said it was clearly bullshit and he intended to sue for false arrest. He's convinced her being picked up was what pushed her over the edge, literally."

"Sounds like it," I said.

She glanced at her watch. "I better get back. Are you staying for the service?"

"I'm not sure. I'll have a chat with William and see what he says."

"We can talk later if you're still around. Thanks for letting me vent."

"No problem."

When I returned to Meditation, a small group of people had arrived. By the look of them, these were Marvin and Audrey's bar pals. There were six of them, two women and four guys, all roughly the same age. I'm sure the habitual drinkers at Rosie's would have evidenced a similar air, as though bewildered to be outside and sober at that hour of the day. One of the two women was holding Marvin's hand, tears coursing down her face. While she wept, he used his free hand to pull out a handkerchief, which he handed her. She shook her head and I saw him dash tears from his own eyes. Grief is as contagious as a yawn.

William had moved to the back of the room where he was deep in conversation with Mr. Sharonson. I caught his eye and lifted a tentative hand. He excused himself and crossed the room. "How are you doing?"

"Fine. I was just wondering about the time frame. Are you staying for the service?"

"Of course. I hope you're not thinking of leaving. Marvin would be crushed."

"Crushed?"

"He's always wanted to meet Audrey's friends and he was thrilled we were here. Well, 'thrilled' isn't the word he used, but you get what I mean."

"What about the woman he's talking to now? Wasn't she a friend?"

"More like a mutual acquaintance. Several of them socialized at a neighborhood bar. He's distressed no one else has stopped by. He hoped for a respectable turnout."

"What about his older daughter?"

"She's flying in from San Francisco and should be here close to one." He lowered his voice. "Has *she* made an appearance?"

"Audrey's accomplice? So far, no, and that's what worries me. If she walks in now, she'll spot me right off the bat. I don't see how she could fail to recognize me."

"That's not a problem. She'll sign in and by the time she sees you, her name and address will be recorded in the book. You'll have all the relevant data you need to pursue her without further effort on your part."

"She wouldn't necessarily give her home address. I left that line blank myself."

"Matters not. You'll have her name. You can take that and run with it."

"But she'll have my name too. If she checks directory assistance, the only reference she'll find is Millhone Investigations, which will give her my business address and phone number. She's bound to figure out I'm onto her. Why else would a private detective come to Audrey's visitation?"

"There are four women here. Five, once Marvin's older daughter arrives. She won't know which of you is which. And why do you care?"

"She tried to kill me."

"I doubt she was serious. She probably saw the opportunity and acted on impulse."

"But suppose she tells Marvin I'm a PI?"

"He already knows."

"He does? How did that come up?"

"It didn't. I told him outright."

I stood and blinked at him. "William, you shouldn't have done that. What in the world did you say?"

"I didn't go into any *detail*, Kinsey. That would have been indiscreet. All I said was you watched Audrey steal hundreds of dollars' worth of merchandise, after which her accomplice tried to run you down in the parking garage before she made good her escape."

# 9

I arrived at my office at 9:00 the next morning, unlocked the door, and gathered up the pile of mail the postman had shoved through the slot the day before. I tossed the stack on my desk and went down the hall to the kitchenette, where I put on a pot of coffee. When the machine had gurgled to a finish, I filled my mug. I was pleased to discover the milk was still fresh when I subjected it to the sniff test. I added a dollop to my coffee. Life is good, I thought. Then I returned to my office to find Marvin Striker standing by the window, looking out at the street.

I only slopped the tiniest bit of coffee on my hand as I cycled through alarm, uneasiness, and guilt, wondering if he meant to take me to task for crashing Audrey's visitation. I said, "Ah! Mr. Striker. I didn't hear you come in."

He turned to look at me with brown eyes that in happier times might have held an impish light. His smile was subdued but at least suggested he wasn't feeling churlish. "The door was unlocked. I knocked a couple of times and then let myself in. I hope you don't mind."

"Not at all. You want coffee? It's fresh."

"I'm not much for coffee, but thank you. I'd hoped to talk to you after the service, but you were gone by then."

"I shouldn't have been there in the first place. I never met Audrey . . ."

"No need to apologize. William said he talked you into it. He didn't know her either, but I appreciated his being there. He's a good man."

"He is," I said. "How are you holding up? It's been a rough few days."

He shook his head. "The worst! I can't believe this is happening. If you'd told me a week ago my fiancée would take a dive off a bridge, I'd have laughed in your face."

"I wouldn't jump to conclusions," I said, wincing at my choice of words. "The police haven't made a determination yet, at least as far as I've heard."

"None of this makes sense to me. Does it make sense to you?"

"Not at this point, no, but I don't know the whole story."

"Neither do I, which puts us in the same boat."

I sat down at my desk, expecting him to take the chair across from me. Instead, he remained on his feet, hands in his trouser pockets. He was short and compact, wearing a navy pinstripe suit and a pale blue dress shirt. The knot in his tie had been pulled loose and the top button of his shirt was undone, as though he'd dressed properly that morning and then found himself impatient with the necessity. "You have another appointment or something? I don't want to hold you up. I know you're a busy lady."

"This is fine. Take as much time as you need."

"William said you were at Nordstrom's when Audrey was . . . you know, picked up or whatever it's called."

"I was there," I said, cautiously. I didn't want to launch into an account of the incident without first finding out what he knew and how he felt about it.

"Here's what I don't get. Audrey was a good person. She was a sweetheart. We had a lot of laughs and I don't have a clue what went wrong." He blinked and ran a hand down his face, brushing tears aside with the back of his hand. He pulled a neatly folded handkerchief from his back pocket and blew his nose. "Sorry about that. Shit catches me by surprise."

"Mr. Striker, would you like to have a seat?"

"Let's make it Marvin and Kinsey, if you don't mind."

"I'd prefer it," I said.

He was clean-shaven and I picked up a whiff of his aftershave. He blew out a big breath to calm himself. "I don't know what to do with this. I don't believe Audrey was a thief. I don't believe she killed herself. It's just not possible."

"You were the one who put up bail?"

"I did. She called and I went to the police station where they had her in a holding cell. First time I've ever been down there. I wasn't even sure where it was. I'd seen the place in passing, but who pays attention? I've never been arrested in my life and I'm not sure I know anyone who has. Until now."

"What did she say when you picked her up?"

"I don't remember. Seems like weeks ago and I'm drawing a blank. I know I'm not getting the big picture, which is why I'm here."

"You want me to tell you what I saw?"

He laughed with embarrassment. "No. Not really. But I guess I better hear it."

"Stop me if you have questions. Otherwise, I'll just lay it out the way I remember it." I went through the preliminaries: setting the scene, time of day, why I was there. "I first noticed Audrey when I was looking for sales help. She was talking to a younger woman I assumed was a clerk until I realized she had a purse and a shopping bag like everyone else. I found what I was looking for and I was on my way to the register when I saw Audrey again. This time, she was looking at a stack of silk pajamas I'd considered buying myself. As I watched, she picked up two pairs and put them in her shopping bag . . ."

"Did she seem nervous?" he asked.

"Not at all. She was casual. Completely matter-of-fact. So much so, I thought I must be seeing things. I stepped to one side and looked through a rack of house robes so I could keep an eye on her. She moved to another table and while she was sorting through the items on display, I saw her palm a teddy—"

"What's that?"

"A one-piece lacy undergarment with built-in bra and panties. She gathered it with her fingers and slipped it in her purse. I went to the nearest register and reported her to the clerk, who notified security. A couple of minutes later, the loss-prevention officer came into the department and stopped to chat with the saleswoman, whose name is Claudia Rines. She happens to be an acquaintance."

"In what respect?"

"Strictly casual. I see her occasionally at Rosie's, the tavern down the street from my place. Claudia was the one who filled me in on what happened later, which I'll get to in a bit."

Marvin had dropped his head and he was shaking it.

"Are you okay?"

"Don't mind me. Go on with your story. I'm having a hard time, but what else is new? So this loss-prevention guy comes into the department and then what?"

"Audrey seemed to sense she was the subject of conversation, and she left the lingerie department and went across the aisle to the ladies plus-size department. The loss-prevention officer sent Claudia down to the second floor in case she tried to leave on the escalator."

That apparently sparked his recollection because he snapped his fingers and pointed at me. "Yeah, yeah. I remember now what she told me and here's the deal. She had no idea why he stopped her. She wanted to be cooperative so she did what he said. She was mortified when she realized she had the stuff in her shopping bag. Because okay, she'd picked up a few things, but she decided to put 'em back. You know how it is. What do you call it, buyer's remorse. Anyway, she was thinking of something else and it slipped her mind. She said it was a simple oversight that got blown out of proportion. It was stupid of her. She admitted that."

I was already shaking my head. "Don't think so. Uhn-un. I'm not buying it."

"I'm just telling you what she said."

"I understand that, Marvin, but my guess is there's more going on. I was a police officer for two years and I dealt with situations like this. People will tell you anything to get themselves off the hook. This wasn't 'a simple oversight.' She was working with someone else, a younger woman who was stealing items from the same department."

His expression was pained and I could see his resistance surface. "What, like she and this other woman were confederates?"

"That was my take on it. Audrey headed for the escalator and just as she reached the top, the woman she'd been talking with earlier came out of the ladies' room. The two locked eyes and something flashed between them, one of those unspoken communications that happen when people know each other well. The younger woman turned around and went back to the ladies' room."

"Well, there's concrete proof," he said, snidely.

"You want to listen to me or not?"

"Describe the woman."

"Forties, messy shoulder-length blond hair, no makeup. She had a little scar across here, between her chin and her lower lip."

"Doesn't sound like anyone I know. Isn't it possible you misunderstood what was going on?"

"No."

"No doubt in your mind?"

"None."

"What makes you so sure? From what you've said, you never saw these two women before in your life. Now suddenly you have them engaged in a criminal conspiracy. I'm not arguing the point. I want to know the basis for your belief."

"How about training and experience? The last ten years, I've made a living dealing with crime and criminals. It's how I earn my keep."

"On the other hand, you're so used to looking for bad guys, maybe that's what you see regardless."

"You know something? I'm not sure it's smart to talk about this right now. You have a lot to absorb and you're still in shock. Maybe it's better if we wait until you've had time to adjust."

"Skip that. I'm fine. I'm never going to adjust so please go on. Let's get this out in the open so I know what I'm dealing with."

"Okay," I said, infusing the word with skepticism.

"Okay. So now Audrey's on the escalator and then what?"

"She set off the alarm as she left the store. The loss-prevention officer detained her just outside the door. Claudia Rines was with him when he took Audrey to the ground-floor Security offices. Once Audrey opened her bag and the stolen goods came to light, she tried to talk her way out of it. When that failed, she got hysterical."

"Well, think how she must have felt, ashamed and humiliated. When I picked her up, she was so upset she was shaking from head to toe and her hands were like ice. Once we got home, we had a couple of drinks and she calmed down some, but she was still a mess."

"Doesn't that lend support to the idea she jumped? If she was that stressed out . . ."

"No. Not so. Didn't happen that way."

"Which puts us back where we started. So now it's my turn to ask you, how can you be so sure?"

"You didn't know Audrey. I did. And don't be snotty with me, young lady."

"Sorry. That wasn't my intent," I said. I thought about what he'd said, wondering if there was another approach. "Tell me about the arrest. What was she charged with?"

"She wouldn't talk about it and I didn't press. She was already beside herself, so instead of dwelling on the bad stuff, I tried reassuring her. I said she'd be fine. We'd hire an attorney and he'd take care of it. I even told her the guy's name and said I'd call that night, but she said no."

"And when the police notified you they'd found her, what else did they say?"

He shook his head. "Not much. I could see they were trying to be kind, but they were real tight-lipped, like I wasn't entitled. Granted, we weren't married, but I was engaged to the woman, and they treated me like a stranger walking in off the street. They wouldn't have given me the time of day if I hadn't filed a police report on Saturday."

"You filed a missing-person's report the day before?"

"It wasn't anything official because they didn't take me all that seriously. I expressed my concern and they took down the information, but it's not like they put out any kind of bulletin. They said under the circumstances, they had no reason to."

"Is that how they knew to get in touch with you after she was found?"

"Sure. Otherwise, I'd still be in the dark and going out of my mind. Thankfully, some bright soul put the name on the report together with the information in her purse. Her driver's license showed a previous address, little place she rented in San Luis Obispo. The police detective contacted the north county sheriff's department and asked 'em to send a deputy to the house. Of course, the place was all buttoned up because she'd moved in with me. She'd left most of her stuff behind except for the bare necessities. She was holding off on the change of address until we were married and then she'd take care of everything at once—you know, name change, new address, and such."

San Luis Obispo, an hour and a half north, is variously referred to as San Luis, S.L.O., or SLO-town. "Your daughter didn't seem to realize you were getting married."

"We were keeping it under wraps. She was worried the girls would be upset so we hadn't said anything about it."

"What made you file the report in the first place?"

"I had to do something and that was the only thing I could think of. Audrey was punctual. That was her nature. Saturday morning, she went off to get her hair done as usual. I wanted her to cancel, but she started getting upset again so I backed down.

"We had a date at one and she said she'd be home by then. She didn't show up, which for her was unthinkable. Even five minutes late, she'd call and say where she was. She wouldn't leave me hanging. Never in a million years."

"You had a date to do what?"

"We were going out with this real estate agent friend of hers to look at houses. That's another reason I can't believe she'd, you know, do herself in. She was excited. She'd found some listings in the paper and Felicia, her agent friend, set up appointments to show us five or six properties. One fifteen, one thirty—no sign of Audrey and no call, so I let Felicia get on with her day, figuring she had better things to do. By three, I was down at the police station, talking to the guy at the desk."

"Did you think she was sick, she'd been in an accident, or what?"

"I just knew it was bad."

I shifted the subject. "How long had you known her?"

He waved as though fanning gnats away from his face. "You talked to Sabrina. She said she ran into you at the funeral home so I know where you're going with this. The answer is seven months, give or take, which might seem hasty to some. I'm still in the house my wife and I bought back in 1953. Audrey was okay with it, but once we started getting serious, I felt like we should have a place of our own. My girls thought I was out of my mind."

"What sort of work did she do?"

He shrugged. "She was in sales just like me so she traveled a lot. Maybe two and a half, three weeks out of every month. She'd put over three hundred thousand miles on her 1987 Honda. She was always on the road, which was a bit of a sore point with me. I was hoping she'd settle down. I figured a house of her own might be encouragement."

"What kind of sales?"

"I'm not sure. She didn't talk about her job. I got the impression it was soft goods. You know, clothing or something of the sort."

I was thinking for "soft goods" we could substitute the notion of teddies and silk pajamas, but I kept my mouth shut. "What company?"

"No idea. She worked on commission so she was more like an independent contractor than a nine-to-five type."

"What about you?"

"My job? I was a John Deere factory rep. I took early retirement. I worked like a dog all my life and there were things I wanted to do while I still had my health."

"How'd the two of you meet?"

"There's a bar in my neighborhood; a *Cheers* type of place, like the television show. She was there one night and so was I."

"You were introduced by friends?"

"Not really. We struck up a conversation. I'm a widower. My wife died a year ago and I was at loose ends. My girls were scandalized when I took up with Audrey, which is a laugh and a half. I had to remind them what I put up with when they were young. They'd be out until all hours, coming in drunk. The guys they dated were losers—scruffy and unemployed. Not that they stuck around for long. There was a constant turnover of bozos. I told 'em they had no business getting on my case.

"Audrey's the first woman I dated since their mother died. The only woman, I might add. Margaret was the love of my life, but she's dead now and I'm not. I'm not going to be a recluse just to satisfy the girls' sudden sense of decorum. To hell with that. I'm sure Sabrina gave you an earful."

"She told me you couldn't find contact numbers for Audrey's two kids. Have they been in touch?"

"No, and I'm sick about it. I went through everything—desk, chest of drawers, overnight bag. No address book, no letters, or any other reference to them."

"What about the house in San Luis Obispo? Maybe she kept her address book there."

"Possibly. I should probably drive up, but I'm chicken. I've never even seen the place and I can't walk in when I don't know what to expect."

"Right. For all you know, she has a husband and kids."

"Jeez. Don't say that."

"I was being a smart-ass. Don't listen to me," I said. "What about her background? Did she talk at all about where she was from?"

"Chicago originally, but she'd lived all over the place."

"Have you tried directory assistance in the Chicago area?"

"Big waste of time. I gave it a try, but there are hundreds of people with the last name Vance. I don't know if she was talking about the city itself or a suburb. Her parents were dead. This was years ago, I guess. She told me her kids worked in San Francisco, which I had no reason to doubt. She said her daughter was married. I don't know if she kept her maiden name or took his. There isn't a Don Vance in the book, but maybe his number's unlisted. Doesn't mean he isn't there."

"What about her past? Most people tell stories. She might have dropped bits and pieces that would help you work your way back."

"She didn't talk about herself. She didn't like to be the center of attention. At the time, it didn't seem important. I just figured she was shy."

"Shy? The obituary said she was 'fun-loving and vivacious.'"

"She was. Everybody loved her. She was interested in other people. You turn the subject back on her and she'd blow you off, like her life wasn't worth talking about."

"So in essence, you know nothing."

"Well, yeah, and how embarrassing is that? You think you're close and then something like this comes up. Turns out you don't know shit."

"If you know so little about her, what makes you so sure she didn't kill herself? Maybe she was mentally ill. She might have spent the last two years in a looney bin. Maybe that's why she wouldn't talk about herself."

"No. Absolutely not. She wasn't nuts and she wasn't depressed. Far from it. She had a sunny disposition. No mood swings, no PMS, no temper. Nothing like that. And she wasn't on medication. A baby aspirin a day, but that's about it," he said. "You'd think the cops would be all over the case."

"Trust me, they are. They're just not sharing anything with you."

"Tell me about it. I mean, shit. What would you do if you were in my shoes?"

"Go back to the police."

"Another big waste of time. I tried and got zip. I was hoping you'd talk to them. They'd treat you like a professional. I'm just a close personal friend with an ax to grind."

"Maybe so," I said.

"So let's say I hire you, then what?"

"Doesn't that seem like a conflict of interest when I was responsible for her arrest? You'd think I'd be the last person in the world you'd hire to do anything."

"But at least you were there and know part of the story. I'd hate to have to sit down and explain it all to someone else. Besides, you can't do any worse than me finding out what's going on."

"You have a point." I turned the subject over in my mind, looking for a starting place. "It would help if we knew what she was charged with and if she had a history of prior arrests."

Incredulously, he said, "You can't be serious! You think she might have been picked up before?"

"It's entirely possible."

He hung his head in despair. "This is just going to get worse and worse, isn't it?"

"That would be my guess."

# 10

## NORA

Wednesday morning, Nora stopped at the downtown branch of Wells Fargo Bank, where she kept a safe-deposit box. She signed in and showed her identification, then waited while the teller compared her signature to the one kept on file. She followed the woman into the vault. She and the teller each used their keys to unlock the compartment. The teller removed the box and placed it on the table. As soon as the teller stepped out, Nora opened the box. In addition to her passport, vital documents, gold coins, and the jewelry she'd inherited from her mother, she kept five thousand dollars in cash.

She spread it all out on the table. In her handbag, she had the check for seven thousand dollars Maurice Berman had given her for the earrings and bracelet he'd bought. In the past, she'd sold minor pieces of jewelry in order to have money to play the market. She'd opened a Schwab account and in the previous three years she'd made close to sixty thousand dollars in profit, ten of which she kept for emergency purposes, five at home and the other five at the bank. The rest of the money she reinvested. It was not a sum most traders would brag about, but she took a secret satisfaction knowing the proceeds were the result of her acumen. She tucked her passport in her handbag and returned the rest of the items to the box.

Her portfolio was solid and diverse, weighted toward mutual funds. She had a few income-producing stocks and a handful of options she toyed with according to her mood. She'd avoided anything too risky, but maybe it was time to venture outside of her comfort zone. She wasn't a financial whiz, by any means, but she was a devoted reader of the *Wall Street Journal* and an avid student of the ups and downs of the New York Stock Exchange. Since both she and Channing had been married before, they'd elected to keep their finances separate. Their pre-nup was straightforward: what was his was his, what was hers was hers. She used the same accounting firm, the same tax attorney, and the same financial planner she'd brought on board when her first marriage ended.

Channing was aware she had investments, but the particulars were none of his business as far as she was concerned. She'd been foolish to approach him for the eight thousand, but she'd spotted an opportunity at a time when she didn't have access to sufficient cash. While she'd been furious at Thelma's interference, in hindsight she knew the woman had saved her from a hideous mistake. Nora regarded her capital as her sole and separate property. The courts might disagree. That was an issue for another day and one she might never have to face. Legal niceties aside, comingling funds could be disastrous.

She left the bank and walked over to the Schwab offices, where she deposited the seven thousand dollars into her account.

Money matters carried a sexual charge that lifted her spirits and gave her a jolt of self-confidence. She thought about the heft and feel of the seventy-five thousand that had fallen into her hands and out again in a matter of minutes on Monday. She'd given Dante the impression she was morally scrupulous when she was really afraid. Withholding information from Channing was fine in small doses. Playing the market made her feel secure, especially when it came to the cash she was stashing away. If she had to, she'd sell everything and add that money to the money she had on hand. Seventy-five thousand was too tempting a sum, as damning in its own way as her husband's affair. When it came to keeping secrets, what was the difference between his taking a mistress and her hiding substantial assets? In truth, she was putting together funds in case she decided to leave. Seventy-five thousand in cash represented a door that had opened a crack. What she saw frightened her and she'd backed away.

Home again, she changed into her sweats and went for a four-mile walk. She'd been walking four miles a day, five days a week for the past seventeen years. Over time, the consistent low-key exercise had changed the shape of her body and reduced her weight by a pound a year where other women her age were picking up three annually. Ordinarily, she set out at 6:00 A.M. but she'd wakened to just enough early morning drizzle to make the outdoors look grim. She'd postponed the walk and now the sun was out.

Twice that week, she'd had occasion to run errands downtown. Crossing State, she couldn't help glancing up at the three circular second-floor windows that marked Dante's office, wondering if he was looking down at her. She still blushed when she thought about the man Maurice had referred her to. Dante looked respectable at first, but he was clearly accustomed to bending the rules—if he recognized the rules at all. And what was it he'd said to her? "Your husband's a fool if he's giving you grief." There was something sweet about that. He'd been protective of her, a gallantry that brought tears to her eyes when she thought of it. Once upon a time, Channing had protected her from pain. Now he was the source.

The walk dispelled some of the free-floating anxiety she'd flirted with over the past few days. Turning to Maurice Berman had helped. At least, she felt she was doing something for herself. Her conversation with Dante was disturbing in ways she couldn't identify. Staying busy was her only hope of diminishing her uneasiness. She showered and washed her hair, then wrapped herself in a robe while she considered what to wear. She was having a late lunch at the club with a woman she'd met through the friend of a friend. They'd talked about tennis afterward, but that was still up in the air. Late afternoon she had an appointment at a local spa where she was scheduled for a complimentary beauty package, whatever that consisted of. Probably not much. The masseuse in Beverly Hills had raised her rates, and Nora had lost interest in the round-trip drive through heavy traffic for something that was meant to soothe and relax. That evening, of course, she and Belinda and Belinda's younger sister had tickets for the symphony. Sorting through the hangers in her closet, she decided on a pair of close-fitting wool slacks and a cropped wool jacket—not a suit, but separates that worked well together.

Mrs. Stumbo had put the issue of *Los Angeles Magazine* on her bed table. Nora thought she'd thrown it in the trash but perhaps she had not. She picked it up and carried it to the bench in front of her dressing table. Perversely, she turned to the back of the magazine and worked her way forward, page by page, until she found the two-inch-square photograph that had changed so many things. There was Thelma with her red hair and doting smile, smug in her role as Channing's consort for the evening. The term *zaftig* came to mind, meaning the sort of blowzy female sexuality men lusted after: big breasts, narrow waist, flaring hips. The tops of Thelma's breasts bulged upward, threatening to flop out of the strapless white evening gown. The bodice was so tight that when she'd zipped it up the back, two mounds of underarm fat were forced over the edge of the dress in puffy white rolls.

Nora squinted and looked more closely at the photo. The dress had to be a Gucci. She knew the care he took with every stitch, the tucks and darts, the beading.

Shit.

She got up, took the magazine to the window, and peered again. Details came into sharper focus as the sunlight streamed in. Was that *her* gown or was she seeing things? Thelma's diamond earrings looked like duplicates of hers as well. She'd noticed the similarities when she first saw the photo, but she'd been so taken aback by Thelma's transformation she hadn't registered the fine points. For a moment, she stood stock still, immobilized by indecision.

She tossed the magazine aside and crossed the hall to the study. Her day planner was open at today's date. In the square for each appointment, she'd written the telephone number of the individual she was scheduled to see. The lunch date and the spa visit were simply dealt with. She picked up the phone and in two calls cleared her afternoon. It was as though the real Nora had stepped aside and someone else had taken her place. She was clear-headed and single-minded. The symphony tickets would be trickier to finesse. She was on the verge of dialing Belinda's number when she stopped. The symphony was at 8:00. If she left now, she'd be back in plenty of time. She checked the clock. 12:15. The chances were good she'd catch Channing at his desk.

By habit, he was in his office by 7:00 A.M. and worked through until 1:00, when he went out for lunch. His driver would ferry him into Beverly Hills or over Benedict Canyon and into the Valley where he'd meet a client at any one of a number of restaurants. La Serre was his current favorite, with its soft pink walls, pink linens, and white trellising. Most of Channing's practice was what he described as "transaction based": intellectual-property disputes, copyright and trademark infringements, contract negotiations, and talent agreements. Lunches out provided the opportunity to socialize, to see and be seen, cementing the relationships that were at the core of his success. He'd be back at his desk by 3:00 and put in another four hours before he called it a day.

She tried his number and when Thelma picked up the call, Nora used her cheeriest tone of voice. "Hello, Thelma. This is Nora. Could you put me through to my husband?"

She could almost feel the chill when Thelma realized who she was.

"One moment please. I'll see if he's available," Thelma said and put her on hold.

"You fucking do that," Nora said to the empty phone line.

When Channing picked up, he'd turned on the charm. Obviously, Thelma had alerted him she was on the line. "This is a rare pleasure," he said. "I can't think when you last called in the middle of the day."

"Don't be sweet to me, Channing, or I'll never get this out. I owe you an apology. I honestly don't remember your mentioning the dinner dance. I'm not saying you didn't tell me. I'm sure you did, but the subject must have gone in one ear and out the other. I shouldn't have been so adamant."

The brief tic of silence was one she might not have noticed if she hadn't anticipated his surprise. "I appreciate that. You were probably caught up in something else and didn't register the date. I take part of the blame myself. I should have verified that the lines of communication were open. Enough said?"

"Not quite. I've been thinking about it all week and I realize how far out of line I was. I shouldn't have ambushed you like that when you were heading out the door. You had enough on your mind."

"I was anxious to hit the road," he said, "and I didn't take the time to hear you out. I know these charity events can be tedious."

"True, but I was exaggerating a tiny bit to make my case. That said, you can't use my confession as ammunition."

He laughed. "Fair enough. I promise I won't beat you over the head with it the next time we get into an argument."

"You're a love," she said. "So how goes the quest to fill the empty seat?"

"I've put out feelers, but so far no luck."

"Good. I'm glad. Because the real reason I was calling was to offer a change of plans. I can be down there by three with no problem at all. Truly, I don't mind. It's the least I can do after being such a bitch."

Without missing a beat, he said, "No need for that. You go about your day. Sounds like you're busy enough as it is. If I can't find a tablemate, I'll do as you suggested and go on my own. It's no big deal."

Nora smiled to herself. What a liar he was. Thelma had probably been tapped as his date since the invitation crossed her desk. No telling how many social engagements she'd redirected to her own personal use. Nora knew perfectly well Channing hadn't warned her in advance because he wanted to catch her flat-footed. He made a point of putting her in a bind so her refusal to go would be her fault instead of his.

"I don't want you to have to go by yourself," she said. "You poor dear. I thought I'd put a call through to Meredith and see if she and Abner want to meet for drinks ahead of time. That way, we could all go in one car."

Channing's response was smooth, but she knew him well enough to sense his desperation. By capitulating, she'd gained the upper hand and put the burden back on him. He was committed by now. Thelma fully expected to go as his date and he could hardly turn around and tell her he'd be attending with his wife. "I appreciate the offer. Really, it's more than generous, but why don't we take a rain check. Next time our schedules conflict, I'll call in my marker."

"You promise?"

"Promise."

"Good. Then we have a deal. Next time I swear I'll go without making a fuss."

"Perfect. I'd like that."

"Meanwhile, enjoy yourself."

"I'll do my best. Full report afterward."

"Love you."

"You too," he said. "I've got another call coming in."

As soon as she was off the phone, Nora picked up her handbag and car keys. She stuck her head in the kitchen, where Mrs. Stumbo was down on her hands and knees scrubbing the floor.

"I have some appointments this afternoon, but I should be back by five. As soon as you finish, why don't you take the rest of the day off. You've been working way too hard."

"Thank you. I could use the time."

"Just be sure to lock up. We'll see you tomorrow."

Within minutes, she was heading south on the 101. She took pleasure in the drive because it gave her an opportunity to conduct an emotional self-examination. She needed to assess the situation with all the calm she could muster. She knew she was right about Thelma, but so far she had no proof. It didn't have to be evidence that would stand up in court. The situation would probably never come to that, but she wanted the satisfaction of knowing she was right. Poor substitute for having her marriage intact. Channing made a point of keeping his credit card statements at the office so there was no way to determine when he and Thelma had first hopped in the sack. Looking back, she could probably pinpoint the business trip where it all began.

Repeat encounters wouldn't have been conducted at the office because privacy there was in short supply. Half the partners worked late, showing up at all hours to finish business that couldn't be squeezed into the typical ten-hour day. Channing and his beloved Thelma, the whore, would have cavorted at the house in Malibu, thus saving the expense of a hotel room. Nora would have to boil the sheets before she slept in her own bed again.

She spotted a CHP black-and-white lurking at an overpass, invisible to northbound traffic. She glanced down at the speedometer needle, which wavered between eighty-seven and ninety miles an hour. She took her foot off the accelerator and put her racing thoughts in neutral. Maybe she was more stressed out about Thelma than she knew. In her mind, once she'd recovered from her initial humiliation, she'd felt curiously detached. The fact that her husband was involved with someone so *common* left her more insulted than devastated. From a practical standpoint, she could see how convenience and proximity made Thelma the logical choice. Channing's moral sensibilities were finely tuned. He would never screw around with another attorney in the firm and certainly not with one of his partners' wives. He was much too pragmatic to risk a breach of that magnitude. A violation of professional ethics could well blow up in his face. There were certainly countless Hollywood actresses, clients of his, who'd have jumped at the chance to seduce and be seduced, but that was another line he wouldn't cross. Thelma was a hireling, one down by definition. If the affair turned sour and he ended up firing her, she might sue for sexual harassment, but that was probably the worst she could do. Knowing Channing, he'd already set up safeguards against the day.

What puzzled her was that aside from her injured pride and innate snobbery where Thelma was concerned, she felt no sense of betrayal. There was no question Channing had deceived her. After the surprise wore off, she'd expected to feel outrage or anguish or loss, *some* fierce emotional response. In that first flash, she'd pictured a furious confrontation, accusations, recriminations, bitter tears, and remonstrances. Instead, the revelation simply allowed her to step away from her life and take another look. She had no doubt the affair would have an impact, but for the moment she couldn't anticipate the form it would take. She was operating on autopilot, going about her business as though nothing had changed.

An hour and a half later, she turned left off Pacific Coast Highway onto the steep, twisting road that led to their primary residence. Channing had purchased the last buildable half acre along the ridge. The lot was dominated by the sprawling glass-and-steel structure he'd commissioned. She experienced a strange form of agoraphobia each time she returned. There were no trees and therefore no shade. The views were stunning, but the air was dry and the sunlight was unrelenting. During the rainy season, the road would wash out and the occasional mud slide would make passage impossible. A brush fire of the most inconsequential sort could easily sweep up the hill, gaining momentum, sucking in fuel until it engulfed everything in its path.

Behind the house, mountains rose implacably, shaggy with chaparral and low-growing scrub. Paddle cactus had taken over the steep clay slopes, which were laced with old animal paths and fire roads. Most of the year, the surrounding hills were a dry brown, and the fire danger was constant. Channing's solution to the endless months without rain was to have a Japanese landscape architect create monochromatic gardens composed of gravel and stone. Boulders, chosen for their shape and size, were set in sand beds in asymmetrical arrangements that seemed studied and artificial. Lines were carefully raked from stone to stone, sometimes in straight rows, sometimes in circles meant to simulate water. Flat limestone slabs had been laid in the sand to serve as stepping stones, but they were too widely spaced for Nora's stride, which forced her to adopt a mincing gait, as though her feet had been bound.

The landscape architect had spoken to them at length about simplicity and functionality, concepts that appealed to Channing, who was no doubt congratulating himself for the reduction in his water bill. For Nora, the carefully composed patterns generated an almost overpowering desire to scuffle her feet, making a proper mess out of everything. Nora was a Pisces, a water baby, and she complained to Channing about how out of her element she felt in the arid environment. He was gone all day, happily ensconced in his air-conditioned offices in Century City. The house was also air-conditioned, but the sun pounding on the wide expanses of glass left the interior smelling stuffy. She was the one stuck on a mountaintop where the house was totally exposed. His concession was the addition of a shallow reflecting pool at the front of the house. Nora took an absurd pleasure in the stillness of the surface, like a mirror on which the cloudless blue sky shimmered with the faintest breeze.

She turned into the drive and left her car on the parking pad beside the gardener's battered pickup truck. She glanced over at the wide gravel circle where the full-time Japanese gardener, Mr. Ishiguro, squatted on his heels, removing pine needles. He'd worked for the Vogelsangs since the gardens went in. He'd come highly recommended by the landscape architect, but Nora would have been hard-pressed to describe what he did all day, fussing about with his wheelbarrow and his bamboo rake. He had to be in his late seventies, wiry and energetic. He wore a gray tunic over baggy dark blue farmer pants. A wide canvas hat shielded his face from the sun.

The next-door neighbor had trucked in a row of knobcone pine trees that he'd planted on his side of the wall that divided the two properties. The pines were meant to serve as an additional windbreak. Channing had taken a dim view of the plan because the pines shed quantities of dead brown needles that blew onto their side. Mr. Ishiguro was perpetually exasperated at having to remove the debris, which he plucked up by hand. If he managed to catch her eye, he'd shake his head and mutter darkly as though she were to blame.

She unlocked the back door and entered the house by way of the kitchen. The alarm system was off. They'd both become careless about arming the house. To Nora, it was a blessing to enter the air-conditioned space, though she knew within minutes she'd feel like she was suffocating. She put her handbag on the counter and made a quick circuit of the downstairs rooms to assure herself she was alone. The house, built twenty years before, was Channing's when she married him. She'd never cared for the place. The scale of the rooms was out of proportion to the occupants. There were no window coverings, which created the illusion of living on a stage. He'd resisted her few suggestions about making the place more comfortable. Curiously, the style of the house looked dated though there was nothing she could pinpoint that contributed to the effect. This was one reason the house in Montebello was such a welcome relief. The ceilings there were twelve feet tall instead of twenty, and the views from the mullioned windows revealed trees and shrubs of a dense, lush green.

She heard a loud banging at the back door, so ferocious and unexpected that she jumped. She returned to the kitchen, where she saw Mr. Ishiguro's face pressed against the glass. She opened the door, awaiting an explanation. He was angry and his agitated English was gibberish to her. The more she shrugged and shook her head, the more infuriated he became. Finally he turned abruptly and motioned for her to follow. He set off down the path, walking so rapidly she had to trot to keep up with him. Turning a corner, she slipped and caught herself, but not before her foot skidded off the stepping stone and onto the countless parallel rake marks meant to quiet the mind. Nora laughed. She couldn't help herself. It always struck her as funny when other people fell. There was something comical about the complete loss of dignity, the flailing attempt to recover one's balance. Even animals suffered embarrassment when they slipped and fell. She'd seen cats and dogs stumble and then shoot a quick look around to see if anyone had noticed.

At the sound of her laughter, Mr. Ishiguro turned and lashed out at her, yelling and shaking a fist. She babbled an apology, trying to compose herself, but a part of her had disconnected again. Why should she put up with the incoherent ravings of a yard man, for god's sake, whose only purpose was to maintain a stone gray landscape created to prevent the house from burning down. Laughter bubbled up once more and she faked a coughing fit to cover the sound. If he caught her laughing again, there was no telling what he would do.

Another ten feet along the path, Mr. Ishiguro stopped and pointed repeatedly, expressing his disapproval in a rapid series of what she took to be insults. On the ground there was a pile of animal feces. The compact deposit of excrement sat in the center of a composition of white pebbles he'd labored over the week before. It was coyote scat. She'd seen the pair for the past month, a big gray-and-yellow male with a smaller rust-colored female, picking their way along one of the trails, their bushy tails held down. They'd apparently established a den close by and regarded the neighborhood as one big cafeteria. The two coyotes were thin and wraithlike, and their posture suggested stealth and shame, though Nora thought they must be deeply satisfied with life. Coyotes weren't fussy about what they ate. Squirrels, rabbits, carrion, insects, even fruit in a pinch. A number of neighborhood cats had vanished, most noticeably on nights when the howling and yipping of the pair suggested a hunting free-for-all. The male wasn't above scaling the wall to drink from her reflecting pool, and Nora wished him well. Channing, on the other hand, had twice gone out with his handgun, shouting and waving his arms, threatening to shoot. The coyote, unimpressed, had loped across the patio, leaped the wall, and disappeared into the scrub. The female had been conspicuously absent for the past few weeks, and Nora suspected she had a litter of pups tucked away. Having watched Mr. Ishiguro obsess over the placement of every stone in the garden, she could see how a coyote taking an unceremonious dump on his path was the equivalent of an interspecies declaration of war.

"Get a hose and squirt it down," she said when he paused for breath.

He couldn't have understood a word of this, but something in her irrepressibly jocular tone set him off again, and she was treated to yet another tirade. She held up a hand. "Would you *stop?*"

Mr. Ishiguro wasn't finished with his complaint, but before he launched in again, she cut him off. "HEY, you fuck! I wasn't the one who crapped on your fucking rocks so get out of my face."

To her astonishment, he laughed, repeating the expletive several times as though committing it to memory. *"You fok, you fok . . ."*

"Oh, forget it," she said. She turned on her heel, went back into the house, and banged the door shut behind her. Within minutes her head was pounding. She hadn't driven ninety miles to take abuse. She climbed the stairs and went into her bathroom. She opened the medicine cabinet in search of Advil, which was sitting on the bottom shelf. She shook two into her palm and swallowed them with water. She studied herself in the mirror, marveling that recent revelations hadn't altered her outward appearance. She looked the same as she always did. Her gaze shifted to the wall behind her and she turned with a fleeting sense of disbelief. Thelma had left a monstrous brassiere hanging over the towel warmer just outside Nora's shower door. Good god, was Thelma staying here? She'd apparently hand-laundered the garment, which featured stiff, oversize lace cones sufficiently reinforced and buttressed to support the weight of two torpedoes. Nora was appalled at the casual appropriation of her space, though why she bothered to react at all was a question worth examining.

Carefully, she surveyed the room. There were signs of Thelma everywhere. If Nora had hoped for evidence, here it was. She looked down at the silver tray that rested on her countertop, feeling her lips purse as she picked up her hairbrush now threaded with Thelma's dye-coarsened red hair. She opened one drawer after another. Thelma had helped herself to a little bit of everything. Cold creams, Q-tips, cotton balls, expensive colognes. Nora made a point of keeping track of what she used in this house and what she needed to replace. She could have recited, item by item, the exact status and placement of her toiletries.

She checked the cabinet under the sink. Thelma must not have expected anyone else to examine the contents of the wastebasket, where she'd tossed the paper wrapper and lollipop stick from a tampon she'd inserted. Cheery news, that. At least the sow wasn't pregnant. The cleaning ladies came on Monday. Thelma must have intended to remove all traces of her stay by then.

Nora went straight to her walk-in closet and flung open the double doors. To the left, there was a climate-controlled closet-within-a-closet where she kept her cocktail dresses and her full-length gowns. The room was intended for fur coats, but since Nora owned none, she used the space for her wardrobe of designer creations, elegant classics by Jean Dessès, John Cavanagh, Givenchy, and Balenciaga. She'd put together her collection by patiently scouring estate sales and vintage clothing stores. The dresses had been bargains when she bought them, picked over and ignored in favor of what was trendy at the time. Now the interest in early Christian Dior and Coco Chanel had created a secondary market where prices were through the roof. A few of the gowns were too large for her now—the size 6's, 8's, and 10's she'd worn before the weight came off. She'd considered having them altered but felt that resizing would affect the integrity of the design.

She slid dress after dress aside, working her way down the line. When she found the white strapless Gucci, she removed it, still on its hanger, and inspected it carefully. Some of the beading had come loose, crystals and sequins missing, and there was now a tiny split in the seam where Thelma's fat ass had stressed the threads until they popped. She held the fabric to her nose, picking up the lingering musk of Thelma's perspiration. Of course, she'd been nervous. She'd co-opted Nora's husband. She'd helped herself to Nora's clothes, her jewelry, and anything else she fancied. Thelma was impersonating a woman of class, and she'd gone through a major bout of flop sweat because she knew what a fake she was. For the first time, Nora felt rage and she leveled it at Channing. How had he tolerated this trollop, this corpulent interloper, stepping into her shoes?

She returned the Gucci to the hanging rod. She could see now that Thelma had been trying on a number of her cocktail dresses, perhaps debating which of them to wear that night. Two she'd rejected, tossing them over the back of the velvet slipper chair. She must have realized she had no prayer of squeezing into the 4's. Instead, she pulled out Nora's three Hararis, one of which she hadn't yet had occasion to wear. Nora could picture the scene. While Thelma pondered her choices, she'd hung them on the retractable caddy Nora used for clothes when they first came back from the dry cleaners. The Hararis were more forgiving than the more form-fitting of Nora's clothes, diaphanous layers of silk, in pale smoky blues and coffee tones, overlaid with gray. Each ensemble consisted of multiple pieces: a body slip, a vest that flowed from the shoulder to an irregular hem below. The separates were interchangeable, meant to be worn in varied combinations. There was something sensuous about the way the fabric settled against the skin, transparent in places so that the body was both disguised and revealed. Maybe Thelma thought her sagging, cellulite-ridden arm flaps would look especially fetching in such a getup.

Nora removed six hangers from the rod and folded the dresses across her left arm. She removed another handful and laid them on top of the first. She carried them downstairs and out to the car, loading first the trunk and then the backseat. The gowns were surprisingly heavy, well constructed, many of them so densely embellished with crystals and beads that the weight of them was palpable. It took her six trips before she'd successfully stripped her closet of all her evening wear: full-length gowns, cocktail dresses, the entire collection of haute couture fashions in every shape and size. The provenance didn't matter. Nora removed every garment that might have been at all suitable for the dinner dance that night.

It cheered her enormously to imagine the sequence of events. Thelma and Channing would leave the office early, maybe 5:00 instead of the usual 7:00 P.M. The drive home would take an hour or more at the height of the rush hour traffic, which would be particularly heavy along Pacific Coast Highway. By the time they arrived at the house, it would be 6:00 or 6:30, and all the nearby dress shops would be closed. Maybe they'd have a drink before getting dressed. Maybe they'd make love and then take a shower together. Eventually Thelma would turn her porcine attention to what she'd be wearing that night. Buoyed at the prospects, she'd fling open the double doors to the closet. Right away, she'd realize something was wrong. Baffled, she'd open the climate-controlled closet-within-a-closet, which was virtually empty. Thelma, the buxom, lumbering, pot-bellied slob, would find herself with nothing to wear. Not a stitch. She'd shriek and Channing would come running, but what could either of them do? He'd be as horrified as she was. Someone had entered the house and walked off with thousands and thousands of dollars' worth of formal wear. What would he tell Nora? And how would he appease the wailing Thelma, whose evening was ruined? Her crappy little condominium was in Inglewood, thirty miles south-east, not far from the Los Angeles International Airport, so even if (by some miracle) she had something adequate at home, she'd never make it in time. The dinner dance was being held at the Millennium Biltmore in downtown L.A., forty-nine miles away, distances it would be hopeless to navigate at that hour.

Nora would have given anything to see the look on Thelma's face. Neither she nor Channing could lay the issue at Nora's feet even if they figured it out. What would they chide her for? Removing her own clothes from the premises to prevent Thelma from squeezing her way into them the way she'd squeezed her way into the rest of Nora's life?

Nora locked the house and went out to the car. She looked at the clock on the dashboard, noting that it was only 3:56. The traffic north to Montebello might be slow, but she'd be home by 7:00 at the very latest. Plenty of time to dress and meet Belinda and her sister at the concert hall. How perfect was that?

# 11

Once Marvin left, I set up a file for Audrey Vance. Ordinarily, I'd have had Marvin sign a boilerplate contract, specifying what he'd hired me to do and agreeing to my rates. In this matter, we were operating on a handshake and my assignment was open-ended. He wrote me a check for fifteen hundred dollars as a retainer, against which I'd bill. If my charges exceeded the total, he had the option of authorizing additional expenses. Much would depend on how effective I'd been. I made a copy of his check, tucked it in the file folder, and set the check itself aside to be deposited.

In essence, I was doing a background investigation on a dead woman. In terms of our attitudes, he and I were at odds. I thought he was in denial, resisting the truth about Audrey when it didn't tally with his hopes. I had my suspicions, but I understood his hanging on to his belief in her innocence. He didn't want to think he'd been played for a fool. I was convinced she was a professional crook and he'd been duped. I simply hadn't proved it yet. At the same time, I was irritated with him for being too stubborn to admit he'd fallen in love with a skunk. I've done the same thing myself, so if you want to consider the underlying motivation, you might say I was acting in his behalf as a way of taking care of myself. Psychobabble 101. In the past, when I was embroiled with rogues, I'd been as blind as he was and just as intractable. Here, I had a chance to take action instead of sitting around in a stew of misery. Anger is about power. Tears are about weakness. Guess which category I prefer?

I put a call through to Cheney Phillips at the STPD. Cheney was a fabulous resource and usually generous with information. I thought I'd start with him and work forward from there. Lieutenant Becker picked up the call and told me Cheney'd just gone out for lunch. Lunch? I checked my watch, trying to figure out where the morning had gone. It was clear I'd have to go hunting for him. I knew his favorite haunts—three restaurants in a four-block radius, within walking distance of the police department. Since my office was in the area, the trek couldn't have been easier. I tried the Bistro first, the closest of the three eateries. I struck out there and struck out again at the Sundial Café. My efforts finally paid off at the Palm Garden, which was located in a downtown arcade, replete with art galleries and jewelry stores, leather shops, high-end luggage and travel goods, along with a boutique that sold trendy clothing made of hemp. The palm trees, for which the restaurant was named, survived in large square gray boxes, responding to their cramped conditions by sending out air roots that crept over the edges like worms. Really appetizing if you were sitting next to one.

Cheney was at a table on the patio, accompanied by Sergeant Detective Leonard Priddy, whom I hadn't seen for years. Len Priddy had been a friend of my first ex-husband, Mickey Magruder, who'd been killed two years earlier. I'd met and married Mickey when I was twenty-one years old. He was fifteen years my senior and working for the Santa Teresa PD. He left the department under a cloud, as they say, accused of police brutality in the beating death of an ex-convict.

On the advice of his attorney, he resigned long before he went to trial. Eventually, he was cleared in criminal court, but not before his reputation had sustained major damage. Our marriage, shaky from the start, imploded for largely unrelated reasons. Nonetheless, Priddy had seen my leaving Mickey as my abandoning him when he needed me most. He'd never said as much but on the rare occasions when our paths crossed, he made clear his contempt. Whether his attitude toward me had softened was anybody's guess.

I'd heard plenty about him because his career had taken a similar left-hand turn after a shooting incident in which a fellow officer had been killed in the course of a drug raid gone sour. Len Priddy was a maverick to begin with, written up on more than one occasion for violations of department policy. Twice he'd been the subject of a citizen's complaint. During the months-long Internal Affairs investigation, he was suspended with pay. IA finally concluded the shooting was accidental. He'd salvaged his standing with his colleagues, but his career had stalled out. It was nothing you could put your finger on. Rumor had it, if he took an exam, hoping for advancement, his grades weren't quite good enough and his annual reviews, while acceptable, were never sufficient to rectify the blow to his good name.

Mickey swore he was a stand-up guy, someone you could count on in a fight. I had no reason to doubt him. In those days, there was a posse of cops known as the Priddy Committee—Len's boys, rowdy, rough, and given to busting heads when they thought they could get away with it. Mickey was one of them. That was the era of the Dirty Harry movies, and cops, despite protests to the contrary, took a secret satisfaction in the lawlessness of the Clint Eastwood character. The department had changed radically over the years, and while Priddy had hung on, he hadn't been promoted since. Most cops in his position would have moved on to other work, but Len came from a long line of police officers, and he was too identified with the job to do anything else.

In Priddy's company, Cheney seemed to take on a different coloration. Or maybe my perception was affected by my knowledge of Priddy's notoriety. Whatever the case, I was tempted to avoid the pair, postponing the conversation with Cheney until later. On the other hand, I'd searched him out in hopes of getting the lowdown on Audrey Vance, and it seemed cowardly to veer off when he was only fifteen feet away.

Cheney spotted me as I approached and stood up by way of greeting. Priddy glanced in my direction and then diverted his gaze. He made a faint show of acknowledgment and then became absorbed in the packet of sugar he was tapping into his iced tea.

Cheney and I had once had what is euphemistically referred to as a "fling," meaning a short-lived dalliance without any lasting effect. We were now studiously polite, behaving as though we'd never trifled with each other when we were both hyperconscious of the once-fiery exchange. He said, "Hey, Kinsey. How's it going? You know Len?"

"From way back. Good to see you." I didn't offer to shake hands with him and Len didn't bother to rise from his chair.

Priddy said, "I didn't realize you were still around." As though my past ten years as a PI had completely slipped his mind.

"Still hangin' in there," I replied.

Cheney pulled a chair back. "Have a seat. You want to join us for lunch? We're waiting for Len's girlfriend so we haven't ordered yet."

"Thanks, but I'm here to ask a couple of questions that shouldn't take long. I'm sure you have things to talk about."

Cheney took his seat again and I perched on the edge of the chair he'd offered just to put myself at eye level with the two men.

"So what's up?" he asked.

"I'm curious about Audrey Vance, the woman who—"

"We know who she is," Priddy cut in. "What's the nature of your interest?"

"Ah. Well, as it happens I was a witness to the shoplifting incident that resulted in her arrest."

Priddy said, "Good news. I caught that. I'm working vice these days. Cold Spring Bridge is county so the sheriff's department is looking into her death. You have questions about that, you ought to talk to them. I'm sure you have a lot of good friends out there."

"Scads," I said. Maybe I was being paranoid, but to me the comment suggested that as long as I'd screwed Cheney for information, I'd doubtless screwed the entire sheriff's department as well. "I'm actually more interested in whether she'd ever been picked up before." I glanced at Cheney, but Priddy had decided the subject belonged to him.

He said, "For shoplifting? Oh, yeah. Big-time. That one's been around the track. Different names, of course. Alice Vincent. Ardeth Vick. She also used the last name Vest. I can't remember the first on that one. Ann? Adele? Some A name."

"Really. Was this petit or grand theft?"

"Grand and I'd say five times at least. She had some shit-ass attorney busy filing six kinds of paperwork. He'd have her plead down and take reduced jail sentence plus community service. First two times she got off scot-free. That was nickel-and-dime stuff and charges were dismissed. Did alcohol rehab or some such. What a pile of crap that was. Last time, the judge wised up and threw her in jail. Score one for our side." He paused, clicking his tongue to mimic the sound of a baseball being hit, followed by an auditory rendition of cheers from the crowd. "If these people did serious jail time from the get-go, it would cut down on the repeats. How else are they going to learn?"

"There's more," Cheney said. "Friday, when the female jail officer had her strip, it turned out she was wearing booster gear—pockets in her underwear stuffed with more items than she had in her shopping bag. Major haul. We're talking two, three thousand dollars' worth, which makes it grand theft again."

"Were you surprised to hear she jumped?"

Priddy addressed his response to Cheney, as though the two had been discussing the subject before I arrived, debating the relative merits of sudden death versus the judicial system. "Ask me, it's a courtesy, her going off that bridge. Saves the taxpayers a chunk of change and spares the rest of us the aggravation. Besides which, jumping, you don't leave a big ugly mess for someone else to clean up."

"Any question of foul play?"

Priddy's gaze slid over to mine. "Sheriff's homicide detectives will approach it that way, sure. Protect evidence at the scene in case shenanigans come to light. She got off parole about six months ago and now here she comes again, facing another stretch. She's engaged to some guy and there goes that life. Talk about depressing. I'd have hopped the rail myself."

He shook loose the ice in his glass and upended it, letting a cube drop into his mouth. The crunching of ice sounded like a horse chewing on its bit.

Cheney said, "They're running a toxi panel, but we won't get results for three to four weeks. Meantime, the coroner says there's nothing to suggest she was manhandled. He'll probably release the body in another few days."

I looked at him with puzzlement. "He's already released the body, hasn't he?"

"Nope."

"I went to the visitation. There was a casket and two floral wreaths. You mean she wasn't actually *in* there?"

"She's still out at the morgue. I wasn't at the post—Becker took that—but I know the body's being held, pending blood and urine."

"Why would they have an empty coffin?"

"You'd have to ask her fiancé," Priddy said.

"I guess I will."

"Sorry to be a hard-ass, but the kindhearted Mr. Striker had no idea what he was messing with when he took up with her." Priddy looked up and I followed his gaze. A young woman in her late twenties was working her way across the patio. Ever the gentleman, Cheney rose from his seat as she approached. When she reached the table, she gave him a quick hug and then leaned over and gave Len a kiss on the cheek. She was tall and slim, with an olive complexion and dark hair to her waist. She wore tight jeans and high-heel boots. I couldn't imagine what she saw in Len. He didn't seem inclined to introduce us so Cheney did the honors.

"This is Len's girlfriend, Abbie Upshaw," he said. "Kinsey Millhone."

We shook hands. "Nice meeting you," I said.

Cheney held her chair for her and she sat down. Len caught the waitress's eye and lifted a menu. I took it as a not-so-subtle suggestion that I should be on my way and I was happy to oblige.

I stopped off at a nearby deli and bought myself a tuna salad sandwich and Fritos, then returned to the office where I ate at my desk. While the information was fresh in my mind, I took out a pack of three-by-five index cards and jotted down the tidbits I'd picked up, including the name of Len's girlfriend. The whole point of making notes is to be thorough about the details since it's impossible to know in the moment which facts will be useful and which will not. I put the cards in my shoulder bag. I was tempted to gallop back to Marvin and drop the revelations at his feet like a golden retriever with a dead bird, but I didn't want to add to his burden just yet. He hadn't made his peace with the notion of Audrey shoplifting on *one* occasion, let alone having been convicted five times previously.

Modesty compels me to take only *partial* credit for being on target with my guess about her criminal history. A crime like shoplifting is more often a pattern than a one-shot deal. Whether the urge stems from necessity or impulse, that first success creates a natural temptation to try again. The fact that she'd been caught before should have cautioned her to brush up on her sleight-of-hand skills. Or maybe she'd been picked up only five times out of five hundred tries, in which case she was doing a damn fine job. At least until the previous Friday when she'd botched it royally.

I finished lunch, crumpled up the sandwich wrapping, and tossed it in the trash. I folded down the top of the cellophane bag with a generous helping of leftover Fritos and secured it with a paper clip. I slid them into my desk's bottom drawer, saving them for a snack in case I felt peckish later in the afternoon. I heard the door in my outer office open and close. For a brief moment, I thought it might be Marvin and I looked up expectantly. No such luck. The woman who appeared in my doorway was Diana Alvarez, a reporter who worked for the local paper. While I'm not famous for my friendliness and charm, there aren't many people whom I truly detest. She was at the top of my list. I'd met her in the course of the investigation I'd closed out the week before. Diana's brother Michael had hired me to find two guys he'd suddenly remembered from an incident that occurred when he was six. The particulars don't pertain so I'll skip right over to the relevant part. Michael was highly suggestible, given to bending the truth. In his teens, he'd accused his family of hideous forms of sexual molestation after a shrink administered truth serum and regressed him to an earlier age. Turned out to be hogwash and Michael eventually recanted, but not before the family was destroyed. His sister, Diana—also known as Dee—was still bitter and did everything she could to undermine his credibility, even in death.

I took in the sight of her, reveling in my distaste. Seeing someone you dislike is almost as much fun as reading a really bad work of fiction. It's possible to experience a perverse sense of satisfaction on every clunky page.

Diana was officious, superior, and aggressive. On top of that, I didn't like the clothes she wore—though I'll admit I'd adopted her habit of wearing black tights on the rare occasion when I wore a skirt. Today's ensemble was a perky red-and-black plaid jumper with a red V-neck T-shirt under it. I repressed a tiny spark of appreciation.

I said, "Hello, Diana. I didn't think I'd see you so soon."

"A surprise to me as well."

"I'm sorry about Michael's death."

"It's just like the Bible says: you reap what you sow. I know that sounds cold, but what else would you expect after what he did to us?"

I let the comment pass. "I thought I'd see something in the paper about his funeral."

"There won't be one. We've decided against. If we change our minds, I'll be happy to contact you."

She sat down without invitation, tucking her skirt under her in a manner meant to minimize wrinkles. She put her purse on the desk while she settled herself. The first time she came to my office, she'd carried a clutch not much bigger than a pack of cigarettes. This bag was substantially bigger.

Fully settled, she said, "I'm not here to talk about Michael. I'm here to talk about something else."

I said, "Be my guest."

"I went to the services for Audrey Vance. I saw your name in the guest book, but I didn't see you."

"I left early."

"The reason I bring it up is I pitched a story to my editor about the people who've gone off the Cold Spring Bridge, starting with Audrey and working back to 1964 when the bridge was completed."

Her tone suggested she'd composed the lead in her head so she could try it out on me. My gaze strayed to the purse still sitting on my desk. Did the clasp harbor a teensy-weensy microphone attached to a recorder picking up every word we said? She hadn't taken out her spiral-bound notebook, but she was clearly in reporter mode. "How did you know Audrey?" she asked.

"I didn't. I went to the funeral home with a friend, who was there to pay his respects."

"So your friend was a friend of hers?"

"I don't want to talk about this."

She steadied a look on me, one brow rising slightly. "Really. And why is that? Is there something going on?"

"The woman died. I never met her. Sorry I can't help you turn her miserable demise into a feature-length article."

"Oh, please. You can drop the pious tone. I'm not in it for the sentiment. This is work. I understand there's a question about whether or not she jumped. If you think I'm exploiting her death, you're missing the bigger picture."

"Let's just say this. I'm not a good source. You should try someone else."

"I did. I spoke to her fiancé. He says he hired you to investigate."

"Then I'm sure you understand why I can't comment."

"I don't know why not when he's the one who suggested I talk to you."

"I thought it was because you saw my name in the guest book and couldn't wait to chat."

Her smile was thin. "I'm sure you're as interested as I am in finding out what happened to the poor woman. I thought we could team up."

"Team *up*? As in what?"

"Sharing information. You scratch my back and I'll scratch yours."

"Uh, no. I think not."

"What if it was murder?"

"Then you can get the inside dope from the cops. In the meantime, don't you have a string of suicides to research?"

"I'm not your enemy."

I said nothing. I swiveled in my swivel chair, which made a satisfying squeak. In the silence department, I could outlast her, which she must have realized.

She put the strap of her purse over her shoulder. "I'd heard you were difficult, but I had no idea."

"Well, now you know."

The minute she was gone I picked up the phone and called Marvin. He was in a chatty mood. I was not.

"Excuse me for cutting in," I said, "but did you send Diana Alvarez over here to talk to me?"

"Sure. Nice gal. I figured it would help if we had someone like her on our team. She says newspaper coverage can make a big difference. 'Huge' is what she said. You know, getting the word out to the public something fishy's going on. She said it would encourage people to come forward. Somebody might have seen something without realizing what it was. She suggested I offer a reward."

I suppressed the urge to bang my head on the desk. "Marvin, I've dealt with her before . . ."

"I know. She told me. Her brother was murdered so she's sympathetic to the situation."

"She's as sympathetic as a piranha gnawing on your leg."

He laughed. "Good line. I like that. So how'd you do with her? I thought the two of you could brainstorm and come up with a gameplan, maybe develop a few leads."

"She's a bitch. I don't talk to her about anything."

"Oh. Well, it's your call, but you're making a mistake. She could do us some good."

"Then why don't *you* talk to her. Or better yet, she can talk to the police. These are two of the three suggestions I have for her. The third I won't repeat."

"You sound testy."

"I *am* testy," I said. "Is there anything else?"

"Actually, there is. I've been thinking about this shoplifting stuff and I don't see that much to get upset about. Sure, Audrey might have lifted a couple of items. I'm willing to concede the point, but so what? It's not like I approve, but in the greater scheme of things, it's not that big a deal, right? I'm not whitewashing her actions. All I'm saying is shoplifting's not the same as knocking off banks."

"Oh, really. Well, maybe I can put it in perspective," I said. "Audrey wasn't operating on her own. You're disregarding what I told you before, which is that I saw her working with another woman. Trust me when I tell you, there are others involved. These people are highly organized. They make a regular circuit, moving from town to town, stealing anything that isn't nailed down."

"I can do without the lecture."

"No, you can't. Has anyone ever given you the formula for calculating losses due to retail theft? I learned this years ago at the academy so I may be fuzzy on the math, but what it boils down to is this: the profit margin on each of those pairs of pajamas she stole is roughly five percent.

"This is after subtracting the cost of the goods, salaries, operating expenses, rent, utilities, and taxes. Which means that out of the $199.95 retail price, the store makes $9.99, which we'll round off to ten bucks just to keep it simple, okay?"

"Sure. I can see that."

"If you look at the numbers, this means that for every pair of silk pajamas stolen, Nordstrom's has to make *twenty additional* sales to break even on the loss of that one. Audrey stole two pairs. Are you following?"

"So far."

"Good, because this is like a thought problem in elementary school, only you have to multiply by thousands because that's how many shoplifters are out there year after year. And who do you think pays for the losses in the end? *We* do, because the cost gets passed on. The only difference between Audrey's crime and the guy who robs banks is that she didn't use a gun!"

Then I banged down the phone.

# 12

Henry had encouraged me to park in his driveway while he was out of town. Without his lighted kitchen window to greet me, it felt like the energy had been sucked out of the entire neighborhood. I let myself in to his place. The first thing I did was to put his oven on preheat, just for the scent of warm spices. I did my walkabout in a haze of caramelized sugar and cinnamon, turning on lights where necessary. I checked the kitchen, laundry room, and both baths to make sure pipes hadn't burst and a gas leak wasn't threatening to blow the place sky-high. Bedrooms were clear, no broken windows and no signs of forced entry. I took messages off the answering machine, making sure he wasn't missing anything critical. I went on to water his plants, first sticking a finger down into the potting soil to make sure I wasn't overdoing it. Sometimes I think routine is everything in life. The weekend would never come and when it did, it would seem endless. My only hope was to retreat to Rosie's Tavern as often as possible. I fully expected

Marvin to fire me for insolence, but so what? It would save me the annoyance of dealing with Diana Alvarez.

I turned off the oven, doused the lights, and locked up. I stopped in at my place long enough to turn on table lamps and avail myself of the facilities. Then I walked to Rosie's, where I ordered a glass of Chardonnay and a bite to eat. Dinner wasn't the worst example I've had of Rosie's cooking, but it was a fair approximation. In the dazzling rotation of dishes in her madcap cuisine, she presents me with a corker on an average of once a month.

I chatted with William, gave my compliments to the chef, said a brief hello to a couple of people I knew, and scurried out the door. By the time I let myself into my place, it was 7:00. I'd managed to kill an hour. Big whoopee-do. This was April. It wouldn't be full dark until close to nine, so leaving lights on for myself was evidence of my optimism, thinking I could while away an entire evening with one glass of wine and a plate of pork and sauerkraut. Fortunately, my message light was blinking and I fell on the play button like it might provide communication from outer space.

Marvin said, "Hey, Kinsey. This is Marvin." In the background I could hear the clatter of dishes, the clinking of glasses, and more laughter than was probably warranted by the conversation under way. He had to be calling from the *Cheers*-type bar where he'd met Audrey. There was a sudden surge of guffaws. I had to squint and press a hand against one ear to pick up his end of the call.

"I've been thinking about what you said and I understand where you're coming from. You don't want this Alvarez woman messing with your investigation, which is understandable. We're talking about professional integrity and I admire that. Your point about shoplifting versus a bank heist, well, I get that too. This is the first I've ever been exposed to any kind of crime and it's hard to put it all in context. Whyn't you call me and we'll talk. I still want you to drive up to Audrey's place in San Luis Obispo. Get back to me when you can."

Well, that sucked. How was I supposed to hang on to righteous anger when he'd totally surrendered? It would be politic to head over to the bar and have a heart-to-heart with the man . . . and more important, with Audrey's friends. Problem was, no one had mentioned the name of the place. All I knew was that it was somewhere in Marvin's neighborhood. I pulled out the telephone book and looked him up, and for once scored a hit. Often the phone book is a waste of time, but not in this case. I made a note of his address, which was on the far side of town, just at the big bend on State Street before it becomes Holloway. I debated a change of clothes but decided against it. I looked fine as I was. Jeans, boots, and a turtleneck. I was looking for a neighborhood bar, not a pickup joint. I shrugged into a denim jacket, slung my bag over one shoulder, and went out to my car.

Marvin lived in an area of middle-class homes, small houses on small lots with architecture typical of the '40s and '50s. I slowed, absorbing the flavor of the neighborhood. Exteriors were stucco or frame, roofs made of aged red tile or an asphalt material fashioned to resemble shake. I could see the care with which property owners maintained their parcels. Most kept their lawns mowed, the hedges clipped, and their wooden shutters painted. While the homes weren't large or lavish, I could see the appeal to someone like Audrey, whose other stops in life had included at least one state prison and a few local jails. Moving in with him, she must have thought she'd died and gone to heaven.

I circled back to State Street and turned right, rolling past a short stretch of businesses, most of which were closed. Streetlights shone bleakly on a barbershop, a darkened hardware store, a Thai restaurant, and a hair salon. I remembered a small bar along here somewhere because I'd seen it in passing.

I went around the block and spotted it on my return. I'd missed it the first time because the signage was poor. The name of the bar, Down the Hatch, was painted on the front of the narrow yellow building, which was modestly illuminated. The point was apparently not to attract new patrons, but to cosset the loyal, long-term clientele. The door stood open, revealing a comforting darkness within, relieved by a blue-neon beer sign on the back wall. I parked on the nearest side street and approached on foot. I picked up the smell of cigarette smoke from a hundred yards away. A haze of tar-and-nicotine residue hovered in the doorway like a curtain one had to pass through to gain entry. This meant a trip to the cleaners where I'd picked up my denim jacket the day before. I deserved far more money than I was being paid.

Once inside, I was assailed by odors of beer, bourbon, and sour dish towels. Two tall clear-glass cylinders with glass lids had been set side by side at the near end of the bar, one holding a murky liquid, brandy perhaps, in which peaches or apricots had been submerged. The other was half filled with pineapple rings and maraschino cherries. The heady scent of fermentation lent an aura of Christmas to the atmosphere. As in many bars, there were assorted television sets mounted across the room, no two tuned to the same channel. One choice was an old black-and-white gangster movie with lots of guys in fedoras toting tommy guns. Option two was a boxing match, and three was a night baseball game probably being played in the Midwest. Rounding out the selection was a home-improvement show in case you were unsure how to use a miter box.

Marvin stood at the bar, where guys were layered two deep, crowded against the knees of drinkers who'd staked out the black leather bar stools. Marvin wore charcoal dress pants and a sport coat over an open-collared polo shirt. He had a martini glass in one hand and in his other a lighted cigarette. His gaze flicked to me, veered off, and returned. He smiled and raised his glass.

"Hey, guys, look who's here. This is that private detective I was telling you about."

His coterie of stalwart drinkers turned as one, five pairs of eyes fixed on mine, some more focused than others. There were introductions all around. I made a quick study of the women, easy since there were only two of them. Geneva Beauchamp was in her late fifties, heavyset, with shoulder-length gray hair, bangs cut severely across her forehead. The other woman, Earldeen Rothenberger, was tall, thin, and round-shouldered, with a long neck, slightly undercut chin, and a nose that might have benefited from the gentle adjustments of a plastic surgeon. I had to chide myself. These days when so many women have undergone correction, refinement, and reconstruction, you have to admire those who accept what they were given at birth.

The men were more difficult to sort out, primarily because there were three of them, and the names came so rapidly I hardly had time to separate them. Clyde Leffler to my immediate left was clean-shaven with a sparse gray pompadour, bony shoulders, and a sunken chest, accentuated by a green V-neck acrylic sweater, which he wore with jeans and running shoes. Buster Somebody, his physical opposite, had a big chest, heavy arms, and a bushy black mustache. The third fellow, Doyle North, had probably been handsome in his twenties, but he hadn't aged well. The fourth fellow of the sixsome had gone off "to see a man about a dog." He'd be back shortly and Marvin said he'd introduce him.

I said, "Don't worry about it. I'm never going to remember who's who anyway." I leaned closer to Marvin so I could make myself heard. "I didn't know you smoked."

"I don't except occasionally when I drink. Speaking of which, can I buy you one?"

"No, thanks. I'm a working girl. I have to keep my wits about me."

"Come on. A little something. A glass of white wine?"

I declined, but the words were lost in a momentary outcry of excitement and dismay. I looked up in time to catch a replay of the last few seconds of a prize fight in which one fellow hit the other so hard, you could see his jaw dislocate. Marvin was already inching toward the waitress, who was picking up a tray of drinks at the far end of the bar. I saw him lean in and say something to which she nodded before heading to a table. Marvin made his way back, holding his drink aloft to avoid an errant elbow knocking into it. His cigarette he also held above the fray lest he sear small holes in the clothing of those he sidled past.

When he reached me, he gave the bartender the high sign, and I watched the man amble over to our end of the bar. Raising his voice, Marvin said, "This is Ollie Hatch. He owns the place. Ollie, this is Kinsey. Anything she wants, she gets."

"My pleasure," Ollie said. He reached across the bar and the two of us shook hands.

Marvin turned to me. "You have business cards?"

"I do." I searched the depths of my shoulder bag and came up with the little metal case in which I carry my cards. I gave him six and he held them up, saying, "Listen, gang. You think of anything that might be useful, Ollie's got a bunch of Kinsey's cards. She'd appreciate any help she can get."

This did not generate an outpouring of pertinent information, but perhaps the timing was off. He passed the cards across the bar to the owner and then took my arm and steered us to one side. The noise level made it impossible to converse. If he lifted his voice and I tilted my head, I could still pick up only disjointed portions of what he said. "Apologize again for that business with the newspaper gal. Guess I got carried away . . ."

"She set you up. She's done it to me too."

"Say again?" Marvin put a finger behind the flange of one ear, pressing the rim forward as though to capture more sound.

I was about to raise my voice and repeat myself when I decided what I'd said wasn't worth the effort. I pointed at the door and he pointed quizzically at his chest. I nodded and moved toward the exit with Marvin close behind. I more or less fell through the open door. The fresh air was so chill and clean, it felt like I'd stepped into a refrigerator. The noise level dropped to a blessed hush.

I said, "I don't know how you stand it in there. You can't hear a thing."

"You get used to it. Crazy bunch. We call the place the Hatch.

We're Hatchlings. Most of them have been coming here for years. Place is open seven days a week. Tonight was rowdy for some reason. Lot of times it's dead. You take it as it comes."

He glanced down. "Hey now, the waitress never brought your drink. Hang on and let me see if I can catch her . . ."

"I'm not here to drink. I'm hoping to pick up the key to Audrey's house in San Luis. I've got time in the morning to make the round-trip drive."

"Yeah, well that's just it. I don't have a key. All I have is the address, which I don't remember offhand. You have a minute to stop by? I live a block from here."

"I don't want you cutting your evening short."

"Don't worry about it. I'm here three, four nights a week as it is, so it's not like I'm in danger of missing anything fun."

"Such as what," I asked.

"Oh, you know. Sometimes Earldeen topples backward off her bar stool, but she usually doesn't hurt herself. You have a car?"

"Parked around the corner. Don't you want to settle your bill first?"

"Nah. I keep a running tab and pay at the end of the month."

We walked the half block to my car and I ferried him from there to his house, which was literally one block away. I parked out front and followed him up the walk, waiting while he sorted through his ring of keys and unlocked the front door. He reached around the frame and switched on the overhead lights. He went in first and made a quick circuit through the living room, turning on table lamps. The living room and dining L were both tidy and there was no reason to believe the rest of the house was any different.

I said, "So tidy."

"Place was a mess before Audrey moved in. She talked me into a cleaning lady, which I never bothered with. I figured it was me on my own and what difference did it make? She set me straight on that score."

"Women tend to do that."

"Not my wife. Margaret wasn't much of a housekeeper. She was more the creative type. She was a daydreamer. Most of the time she walked around in a fog. She just didn't see the chaos. She saw what she meant to do with it, but hadn't gotten around to yet. Kitchen looked like a bomb hit it, but in her mind's eye she was getting everything under control. Company showed up, she'd shove dirty dishes and all the bric-a-brac in the oven to get it out of sight. Then she'd forget and preheat the oven and the place would fill with smoke and the alarm would go off. What did I know? My mother was the same way so I thought that was normal."

While he talked, he crossed to a small rolltop desk and opened the middle drawer in a bank of cubbyholes. He took out a notepad and leafed through it until he found what he was looking for. "Address is 805 Wood Lane. A piece of mail showed up here for her and I made a note. I guess in case I wanted to send flowers or something. What a laugh." He ripped off the leaf and handed it to me. "Audrey mentioned her landlady lived right next door so maybe you can get a key from her."

"Worth a try," I said. "Something I need to ask you. I have a friend who's a cop, and he told me Audrey's body was still at the coroner's office. So what was with the coffin if she wasn't in there?"

"Mr. Sharonson provided one if I promised to have her buried in it once the body was released. It just seemed fitting, you know? Someone dies, you have a visitation. You think that was bad?"

"Of course not. It just took me by surprise."

"Sorry if it seemed dishonest. I wanted to do right by her."

"I understand," I said. "While I'm here, would you mind my taking a look at her things?"

"You can do that. Sure. Doesn't amount to much. The desk was hers. My office is in the second bedroom. I cleared two drawers of a chest of drawers in the master. In the bathroom, she's got the usual shampoo, deodorant, that kind of thing."

"Let's start there."

"You want me to hang around or make myself scarce?"

"Come with me. That way, if anything comes up, I can ask questions while I search."

He showed me into the bathroom off the master bedroom. "Margaret and I remodeled fifteen years ago. Tore out a wall here and opened these two bedrooms to form a master suite. Doesn't look like much compared to new houses these days, but we were happy. We did a bump out in the kitchen to make like a breakfast nook and then added a screened-in porch."

I made what I hoped were appropriate responses while I sorted through the medicine cabinet and the vanity drawers she'd been allotted. He was right about her medications—no prescriptions at all. Sixty-three years old, you'd think she'd be into hormone-replacement therapy or thyroid medication, pills for high blood pressure or elevated cholesterol levels. Her personal hygiene products were just what you'd expect. Nothing exotic. I'd have been happy to see a tube of Mary Kay lipstick, just for the chance to track it back to the local rep.

"The police still have her purse," he said apropos of nothing.

"Doesn't surprise me. Too bad she didn't take prescription meds. We might have tracked down her doctor and learned a thing or two."

When he saw that I'd run out of drawers to tackle, he said, "Bedroom's this way."

I followed him into the bedroom where he pointed out the drawers she used. When I opened the first, I was greeted by a soft cloud of fragrance—lilac, gardenia, and something else.

Marvin took a step back. "Whoa . . ."

"What?"

"That's the White Shoulders I gave her on our six-month anniversary. It was like her signature perfume." He shook his head once and his eyes flooded with tears.

"Are you okay?"

He gave his eyes a quick swipe. "Took me by surprise is all."

"You can wait for me in the other room if it's easier."

"No need."

I went back to my search. Audrey's tidiness extended to her lingerie. In both drawers, she was using fabric-covered boxes to store her neatly folded underpants, bras, and panty hose. I felt my way through the items without discovering anything. I pulled the drawers all the way out and checked for papers or other items taped under them or on the back. Zip.

I crossed to the closet and opened the door. There were rods for double hanging, cubbyholes, shelf dividers, wire baskets, and cedar-lined shelves tucked away behind clear Lucite doors. Her wardrobe struck me as skimpy for a working woman. Two suits, two skirts, and a jacket. Of course, this was California, and work clothes were more casual and relaxed than in other places.

Marvin's side of the closet was as organized as hers. I said, "You guys are something else. She must have had a closet company come in and do this."

"Matter of fact, she did."

I removed stacks of folded sweaters, felt along the seams for anything hidden. I checked the pockets in her slacks and jackets, opened shoe boxes, and rooted through the laundry hamper. There was nothing of interest.

I returned to the small desk in the living room, where I sat down and worked my way through the drawers he'd cleared for her. No address book, no month-at-a-glance calendar, no appointment book. It was possible her route was preset and she had no need to make penciled reminders to herself. But what about the ordinary day-to-day transactions? Everyone has to-do lists, scraps of paper, scratch pads with scribbled notes. There was none of that here. Which meant what? If Audrey had decided to kill herself, she might have systematically deleted anything of a personal nature. I wasn't sure why she'd be that secretive unless she was paranoid about anything connected to her shoplifting extravaganzas. She'd been working with a younger woman.

If the two were linked to a larger retail-theft ring, even a fragment of information might be telling. So maybe the other woman was the one who kept track of their activities.

The flip side of the issue was just as troubling. What if she hadn't killed herself? If she'd been murdered, she probably didn't have warning and therefore she'd have had no opportunity to erase personal or professional references. Did she tidy up after herself as she went along? I had to credit her with a job well done. So far, she was invisible.

I sat in her desk chair and pondered the situation. Marvin had been good about keeping his comments to a minimum. I turned and looked at him. "When it came to business travel, what was the pattern?"

"She was usually gone three days a week."

"The same three days or did it vary?"

"It was pretty much the same. She'd be gone Wednesday, Thursday, Friday, and every other Saturday. With outside sales, you usually have a regular route for customers you visit or stores you service. Plus, you make a certain number of cold calls, developing new contacts."

"Was she in town last Friday when she was ordinarily gone?"

"I have no idea. She said she'd be away the usual three days. She worked from home on Monday and Tuesday and then took off, saying she'd be back first thing Saturday morning."

"In time for her regular hair appointment."

"Right. That and the real estate agent."

I changed my focus. "Did she have hobbies? It may sound irrelevant, but I'm looking for any kind of crack in the wall."

"No hobbies. No exercise program, no sports, and she didn't cook. She used to make jokes about what a rube she was in the kitchen. If I didn't do the cooking myself, we went to restaurants, did takeout, or ordered in. She liked anything that could be delivered. Lot of times we ate at the Hatch, which has a limited menu of bar food—burgers and fries, nachos, chili, and these premade burritos you can heat in the microwave."

I was already thinking about whizzing back over to the Hatch to catch a bite to eat before the kitchen closed for the night. I returned my focus to the job at hand. "Where did she do her banking?"

"No idea. I never saw her write a check."

"Did she cover her share of the living expenses?"

"Sure, but she paid me in cash."

"No checking account?"

"Not as far as I know. She might have had a checkbook in her purse, but the cops still have that and I doubt they'd provide us an inventory."

"Did she pitch in on groceries?"

"When she was in town. I covered the household because my name's on the mortgage and I have to pay water and electric whether she's here or not."

"What about when you went out to dinner?"

"I'm old-school. I don't believe a lady should pay. If I invited her for a meal, it was my treat."

"Did she explain her reliance on cash? Seems quirky to me."

"She said she got into debt at one point, overdrawing her account, and the only way she could curb her spending was to switch to all cash."

"What about credit card statements?"

"No cards."

"Not even a credit card for gas when she was on the road?"

"Not that I ever saw."

"How about telephone bills? Surely, she made business calls on days she worked from home."

He considered the question. "You're right. I should have thought of that myself. I'll pull the phone bills for the months she was living here and mark any numbers I don't recognize."

"Don't worry about it until I've checked the house in San Luis. That might be a gold mine of information."

"Anything else I can be doing?"

"You could put a notice in the newspapers—the *Dispatch*, the *San Francisco Chronicle*, the *San Luis Obispo Tribune*, and the Chicago papers. "Seeking information about Audrey Vance . . ." Use my phone number in case we get crank calls, which are all too common in these situations."

"And if no one comes forward?"

"Well, if the house in San Luis doesn't net more than this, I'd say we were up shit creek."

"But overall, this is good, right? I mean, so far, you haven't uncovered any evidence she was a master criminal."

"Ah. Funny you should say that. I forgot to mention my talk with the vice detective. Audrey's been convicted of grand theft on at least five prior occasions, which suggests she was into retail theft up to her pretty little neck."

"Saints preserve us," he said, which was a phrase I hadn't heard in years.

# 13

The drive from Santa Teresa to San Luis Obispo took an hour and forty-five minutes. I was on the road by 8:00 A.M., which put me in S.L.O. at 9:45 on the nose. The late-April weather was sunny and cool with a breeze blowing flirtatiously through the trees along the side of the road. Traffic was light. The winter months had generated sufficient rainfall to transform the low rolling hills from the usual honey and gold hues to a vibrant green. San Luis Obispo is the county seat, the home of Mission San Luis Obispo de Tolosa, the fifth in the string of twenty-one missions that dot the California coast from San Diego de Alcala, at the southernmost point, to San Francisco Solana de Sonoma, to the north. The charm of the town was completely lost on me. I'm single-minded when it comes to the hunt and I was interested in what I might find in Audrey's house. The fact that I didn't have a key in my possession only added to the fun. Maybe I'd have the opportunity to use the key picks Pinky had given me.

I left the 101 at Marsh Street, cleared the off-ramp, and pulled over to the curb. I'd tossed a city map on the passenger seat beside me and now I spent a few minutes getting my bearings. I was looking for Wood Lane, which the street index indicated was somewhere on the grid designated as J-8. I followed the coordinates, taking the dog-leg from Marsh to Broad Street, one of the main arteries through town. Closer to the airport in the southeastern section of the city, Broad became Edna Road. Wood Lane was an offshoot as delicate as an eyelash and just about that long.

The area was mixed use, industrial and agricultural. I could imagine a city planner or a developer many years before with vision enough to realize the land would be more valuable vacant than given over to subdivisions. A few single-family dwellings had cropped up in what was otherwise a flat countryside. Aside from the fields under cultivation for spring planting, the landscape was hard-packed dirt, sparse vegetation, and the occasional fence. Here and there I could see an outcropping of boulders as big as sandstone sedans. In the absence of trees, the wind swept across the bare acreage, throwing up eddies of dust.

Wood Lane was a cul-de-sac with two small frame houses at the end. The ranch-style house on the right was set in the middle of a well-kept lawn. The driveway was blacktopped and lined with white stones. The address there was 803, which I took to be her landlady's house. Audrey's driveway consisted of two dirt ruts with a stretch of dead grass between. At the end of the drive there was a single-car garage with a small shed attached. I parked and picked my way down the rough drive, taking note of the overgrown shrubs surrounding the house on three sides. The overhead garage door looked ancient, but it yielded without a fuss. The interior was empty and smelled of hot dust. The floor was concrete, marked by a black patch in the center where a vehicle had leaked oil. I leaned down and touched the surface of the spill, which was still sticky. The adjacent shed contained two bags of bark mulch the rats had chewed through.

I returned to the front porch and climbed the stairs. The white paint on the one-story cottage had turned chalky with age. The windows sported injured-looking venetian blinds, hanging crookedly from their mounts. A mailbox was nailed to one side of the front door. I did a quick check and came up with two pieces of mail, both addressed to Audrey Vance. As she was dead and I was unobserved, I opened both envelopes. The first was a preapproved credit card offer from a company that looked forward to serving her financial needs. The second was a response to an inquiry about rental property in Perdido, twenty-five miles to the south of us in Santa Teresa. It was a form letter sent in response to an application she'd filled out in which she'd neglected to complete certain items that were required for proper processing. There followed several X's in parentheses, indicating that she needed to supply the address and telephone number of her employer, her job title, and the number of years in that position. Also, the name and contact number for her current landlord along with her reasons for leaving. *"Regretfully, we have nothing available at this time. We have, however, placed your letter in our files and if at any point in the future one of our tenants should give notice, we'll be happy to get in touch."*

I shoved the two letters into the outer compartment of my shoulder bag. The credit card offer I'd toss at the first opportunity. The form letter from the property-management company I'd look at again. It was possible that on further reflection I'd see a way to make use of it, though I wasn't quite sure how. Which left me with the physical premises. On the off chance the door was unlocked, I tried the knob. Nope.

While I was at it, I went around to the rear and tried the back door with the same result. I returned to the front yard and studied the sparsely traveled road. Audrey was a party animal. Yet here she was, miles from the nearest bar and the nearest convenience store. What was the point? If she'd needed to spend two nights a month in San Luis Obispo, why not camp out at the nearest Motel 6? I couldn't imagine why she'd elect to rent such an isolated place unless she was up to no good.

I looked over at the house next door, which was separated from

Audrey's by a sagging wire fence. Everything in Audrey's yard was dead, but I could see signs of a newly planted garden on the neighbor's side of the fence. Behind the house, a woman with a laundry basket was pinning freshly washed linens on a clothesline. The sheets flapped and snapped, sounding like the beating of wings as they tossed in the wind.

I crossed to the fence and waited to catch her eye. She was in her forties, wearing a cotton housedress with an apron over it. Her bare legs were sturdy and the muscles in her arms had been defined by hard work. When she noticed me, I waved and gestured her closer. She put a handful of clothespins in her apron pocket and approached the fence. "Are you looking for Audrey?"

"Not exactly. I don't know if you're aware of it, but she died this past Sunday."

"I was about to say the same thing to you. I read about it in the local paper."

"You're her landlady?"

"She rented the house from my husband and me," she said, with caution.

"I'm Kinsey Millhone. I'm a private detective." I reached into my shoulder bag and extracted a business card, which I passed to her. I could see her take in the information at a glance.

She said, "Vivian Hewitt. I thought you might be the police."

"Not me. Audrey was engaged to a friend of mine. Questions have come up in the wake of her death and he's hired me to fill in the blanks."

"Questions of what sort?"

"For one thing, she told him she had two grown kids living in San Francisco. He has no way to reach them. If nothing else, he'd like to let them know what happened. He thought she might have kept an address book up here among her personal effects."

"I can understand his concern. Is there something else?"

"Basically, he's wondering just how big a fool he was. Some of what she told him turns out to be false. She also omitted a couple of crucial details."

"Such as what?"

"She'd been convicted of grand theft and served time in prison. Grand theft means she was picked up with merchandise worth more than four hundred dollars. Six months ago, she finally got off parole. Then, Friday of last week, she was arrested again. We hoped you'd be willing to open the house so I can have a look. You're welcome to accompany me, if you're worried this isn't on the up-and-up."

She studied me briefly. "Wait here and I'll fetch the key."

I returned to the front porch and tried peering in the windows while Vivian Hewitt was gone. The slats in the venetian blinds were set so all I saw were thin slices of the floor, not that informative as these things go. A few minutes later, she returned with a big ring of keys. I watched her sort through the collection until she found one marked with a dot of red nail polish. She inserted it in the lock. The key refused to turn. Frowning, she pulled the key from the lock and tried it again.

"Well, I don't know what's wrong. This is a duplicate of the one I gave her."

"Mind if I have a look?"

She handed me the key. I checked the manufacturer's stamp and then leaned forward and examined the lock itself. "This says Schlage. The key is a National."

"She changed the locks?"

"She must have."

"Well, she never said a word to me."

"Audrey's full of surprises. I have ways of getting us in there if you don't object."

"I don't want my windows broken or the door kicked down."

"Absolutely not."

We circled the house to the rear and tried the same key again. Not surprisingly, that lock had been swapped out as well.

"You have a problem with my picking this?"

"Help yourself. I've never seen it done."

I took out my trusty leather zip case and removed the custom-made picks Pinky Ford had fashioned for me. Pinky had confessed that he sometimes constructed picks with complicated-looking bends and twists when in reality the only two items required were a tension wrench and a length of flat wire, bent at the tip. A bobby pin or a paper clip would do the same job. I removed the tension wrench from the case and inserted it into the lock, applying a gentle pressure while I eased the feeler pick to the back of the lock. The trick was to wiggle the pick as I pulled it out, easing it past the pins. With luck, the pick would toggle each pin in turn until it cleared the shear line. Once all the pins were up, the lock would pop open as though of its own accord. I have an electric lock pick that does the job in half the time, but I usually don't have it with me. It's a felony offense if you're caught carrying burglar tools.

During my initial instruction, Pinky had dismantled a number of different lock mechanisms to demonstrate the technique. After that he said it was a matter of developing the proper touch, which differed from person to person. Like any other skill, practice made perfect. There was a period when I was adept, but it had been a while since I'd had occasion to pick a lock, so the task required patience. Vivian watched with interest and I wouldn't have put it past her to try it herself once I was gone. One minute became two and just when I was about to despair, the pins gave way. The door swung inward and we were at liberty to tour the place.

"That was handy," she remarked.

"You bet."

In a circumstance such as this, I like to be systematic, starting at the front door and working my way back. Vivian was a step behind me as I turned to survey the space. "Have you been here recently?"

"Not since she moved in."

The interior was a simple box, divided into four squares: living room, kitchen, bedroom, and a combination mudroom, bath, and laundry room. The living room contained a collection of mismatched furniture: chairs, two end tables, a couch, a sewing machine, and a credenza with a faux marble top, all pushed to the outside walls. All the drawers and cabinets were empty. On one of the tables there was an old-fashioned Princess phone. I picked up the handset and listened for a dial tone. The line was dead.

"How long was she a tenant?"

"A little over two years."

"You put an ad in the paper?"

"We tried that but had no response, so we staked a For Rent sign in the yard, and she came knocking on my door, asking to see the place. My husband and I bought these two properties at the same time, thinking one of our kids would move in. When that didn't work out, we decided to offer it for rent so we'd have money coming in. This end of town, we don't get many prospects so I was happy to show her around. I told her we'd waive the cleaning fee as long as she didn't have pets."

"Did she fill out a rental agreement?"

"No need. She paid me cash, six months in advance. Took out her wallet, counted the bills, and put them in my hand."

"You must have been delighted."

"I was. Most of all, I liked the idea of someone living close by. We only have the one car and I was hoping she'd drive me into town now and then. I didn't realize how seldom she'd be home, though 'home' is probably not the right term. She traveled a lot and only wanted the use of the place when she was in the area."

"How often was that?"

"Every other Saturday."

In the absence of a dining room, the living room had been called into service, the center taken up with a harvest table big enough to seat ten. The room smelled of a pine-scented cleaning product. I leaned closer to the tabletop, peering at a slant so the light washed over the surface. No smudges and no fingerprints. That was interesting. I flicked a switch and the overhead light came on. I got down on my hands and knees and did an eyeball scan of the floor. By the table leg I found a three-inch T-shaped length of clear plastic, not much thicker than a thread. I held it up so Vivian could see. "Know what this is?"

"Looks like a piece of plastic used to secure the price tags on items of clothing."

"Exactly," I said. I put it in my pocket. Under the table leg, I found a second one that I added to the first.

I continued to search, quizzing her as questions occurred to me. The kitchen was immaculate. Counters and windowsills were spotless. Marvin had said Audrey was a neatnik, but when had she had time to scrub the place down? The refrigerator was empty except for the standard items: Tabasco sauce, mustard, ketchup, olives, and mayonnaise, which were stashed in the door. The stove top had been scoured with an S.O.S pad, judging from the residue of blue foam and a few stray fibers of steel wool. The flip-top trash can was lined with a brown paper bag. At the bottom I found a crusty cleaning rag, gray with dirt and smelling of the same pine scent that permeated the rest of the house. Under the rag I found remnants of two S.O.S pads reduced to nubs. I'm sometimes a whiz when it comes to clues.

"Did she have visitors?" I asked.

"I'm sure she did. Twice a month I saw a van pull in a short time after she arrived. She'd go around and open the garage and have the driver pull into the garage. If visitors went in and out the back door, I wouldn't have seen them from my house. There was also a white panel truck over there at the same time."

"Quite a crowd," I said.

"Nights she was here and the lights were on, she made a point of closing the venetian blinds."

"Guess she didn't want you peeping in."

"No danger of that. Rafe and I are usually in bed by ten. She was a night owl. Sometimes I'd see lights burning into the wee hours. I don't sleep well, which means I'm up two or three times."

"Do you remember when was she here last?"

"I'd say Sunday or Monday night, but that can't be right. According to the paper, she was found Sunday afternoon so I must be mistaken."

A survey of the under-the-counter cabinets revealed a stack of big cast-iron skillets and cheap six-quart saucepans. In the upper cabinets there were numerous tumblers and two sets of melamine dinnerware. One drawer was packed with a jumble of kitchen utensils and another held assorted flatware. There was no dishwasher and no disposal, but I found an adequate supply of dish soap in a squirt bottle under the sink. While the shelves in the reach-in pantry were bare, numerous sticky circles on the otherwise clean surface suggested the recent presence of industrial-sized canned goods. For a woman who didn't cook or entertain, Audrey had been prepared to feed the multitudes.

"What happened when the first six months' rent were up?"

"She stopped by one afternoon and paid for the next six."

"Always in cash?"

She nodded. "I suppose I should have asked her about it, but it really wasn't any of my business. At least I didn't have to worry about a check not clearing."

"Didn't you wonder why she carried so much cash?"

"I can guess what you're getting at. You think she might have been dealing drugs. I read the papers like everyone else and I know about meth labs and marijuana farms. If I'd thought she was doing something illegal, I'd have called the police."

"Good for you. Sometimes people get so busy minding their own business, they forget to do what's right."

I went into the bedroom, which was crudely outfitted with a full-size mattress, two pillows, and a pile of blankets neatly folded at the foot of the bed. The closet was empty, not even one wire hanger left on the rod. I closed my eyes and drew in a breath. The lingering scent of White Shoulders cologne was unmistakable.

I made two more circuits of the room, talking to Vivian over my shoulder. "Let me know if you see something I've missed."

By then, the idea of finding her address book seemed laughable since there were no personal items at all. I was satisfied I'd seen everything, though I hadn't dug up the dead flower beds or tapped my way around the walls in search of secret panels.

I scribbled Marvin's address on the back of a second card. "This is her fiancé's address. If mail comes for her, could you forward it to him?"

"I don't see why not."

"You want me to lock up?"

"No point. I'll have the locks changed as soon as I can get someone out. No telling who else has a key."

She walked me out to my car.

I said, "I appreciate your being so nice about this."

"I don't want to protect the woman if what she did was against the law. I'll admit I was a bit uneasy, which is why I kept an eye on her. I couldn't put my finger on what was wrong, and when it came right down to it, I didn't have anything concrete to report."

"Understood. You can't call the police because someone's drawing the blinds," I said. "When your husband comes home, would you ask if he has anything to add?"

"I'll ask, but he won't be much help. I was the one who dealt with Audrey. She was a nice woman, by the way. I thought her schedule was odd, but aside from that, I had no quarrel with her."

"My client's in the same boat," I said. "If you think of anything else, would you give me a call? My office number's on my card and my home phone's on the back."

"Of course. I hope you'll let me know what you learn."

"I'll do that, and thanks for your help."

I returned to my car and fired up the engine. I pulled out of the cul-de-sac and turned right on Edna Road. I kept an eye on the rearview mirror, and once I was out of sight of the house, I pulled onto to the berm and took the pack of index cards from my shoulder bag. I wrote down what I'd learned, which didn't amount to much. Audrey

Vance was a cipher and as such, she was getting on my nerves. When I finished making notes, I put the car in gear and returned to the 101, arriving in Santa Teresa at 1:05. While the trip felt like a waste of time, I didn't write it off altogether. Sometimes coming up with nothing is a form of information in itself.

I stopped by Marvin's on my way through town, hoping he'd be home. He answered my knock with a paper napkin tucked under his chin. He removed the napkin and crumpled it in one hand. "This is a nice surprise. I didn't expect to see you so soon."

"I'm interrupting your lunch."

"Not at all. Come on in."

"I wondered if you'd had a chance to scare up the old phone bills."

"I pulled the file. Have you had lunch?"

"I'll grab something on my way back to the office."

"You should have a bite to eat. I made a big pot of soup. Chicken noodle with lots of fresh vegetables thrown in. I vary the soup from week to week depending on what looks good at the farmer's market. We can talk in the kitchen."

"A man of talent," I remarked.

"I'd reserve judgment if I were you."

I waited while he closed the front door, then followed him into the kitchen with its bright yellow breakfast nook. He turned the gas up under the six-quart stockpot and took a bowl from the cabinet. "Have a seat. You want something to drink?"

"Tap water's fine."

"I'll take care of it. You sit and relax."

He put ice in a glass and filled it at the kitchen sink. He took out a paper napkin and a soup spoon, then ladled soup into a bowl, which he carried gingerly from the stove with a shy smile. He seemed happy to have company. In the center of the table he'd put a jumble of wildflowers in a jar, and I had the sudden sense of what a nurturing man he was. I felt badly about Audrey's deceit. He deserved better.

The soup was rich and dense. "This is wonderful," I said.

"Thanks. It's a specialty of mine, just about the only one I have."

"Well, it's a good one," I said. "Do you bake?"

"Biscuits, but that's it."

"I'll have to introduce you to my landlord, Henry. He's William's younger brother. I suspect the two of you would have lots to talk about."

When I'd eaten, Marvin insisted that I sit while he washed the dishes and set them in the rack.

I filled him in on my visit to Audrey's house in San Luis. "You could have made the trip yourself," I said. "I know you were worried about the impact, but there were no surprises. The place was bare."

"Was it nice?"

"Nice? No, it was a dump. Small wonder Audrey liked living with you."

"What about an address book? Any sign of it?"

"There was nothing personal at all."

"That seems odd," he said. "Hang on a minute and I'll go get the phone bills."

He left the kitchen and returned moments later with a file folder that he placed on the table in front of me. "I hope you don't mind but I went over them myself. This past month, she made two calls to Los Angeles; three to Corpus Christi, Texas; and one to Miami, Florida. Same thing in January and February. If there were other calls, they must have been in the 805 area code."

"Too bad." I ran an eye down the list of numbers. Marvin had put a checkmark beside calls he ascribed to her. "Have you tried calling these?" I asked.

"I thought I'd leave it to you. I'm not that good at thinking on my feet. I get rattled and no telling what I'd blurt out. You want to use my phone?"

"Sure. As long as I'm here."

"Have at it," he said, indicating the wall-mounted phone.

I stood and reached for the handset, tucking it between my shoulder and my ear. I held the phone bill with my thumb close to the first mark he'd made. I punched in the number in the 213 area code. After three rings, I was treated to an ear-splitting screech, followed by a mechanical voice telling me the number was a disconnect: *"If you feel you have received this recording in error, please hang up, check the number, and dial again."*

"Disconnect," I said.

I tried the number again with the same result. The second Los Angeles number was also no longer in service. I dutifully tried a second time to be sure I was dialing correctly. Same dead end. "This is informative," I said. I zeroed in on the Miami call and punched in those numbers. When the screeching began again, I held out the handset so Marvin could hear. The number in Corpus Christi rang twenty-two times by my count but no one answered. I hung up and sat down again, putting my chin in my hand.

"So now what?" he asked.

"I'm not sure. Let me think about it for a minute."

He shrugged. "The way I see it, we've got nothing."

"Shhh!"

"Sorry."

Marvin returned to his seat. He was on the verge of saying something else, but I held up a hand like an auditory traffic cop. In my mind, I was running through index cards in rapid succession. We still had no address book and no appointment calendar. The numbers she'd called in the past few months were useless at this point. If I'd had access to Polk directories for Corpus Christi or Miami, I might have been able to backtrack from the phone numbers to the relevant street addresses. Checking those addresses, even if I had them, would have meant making the trip myself or hiring private investigators in Texas and Florida to cover the job for me. Both options were expensive and might not have netted us anything. If the phones had been shut down, the target locations had probably been shut down as well.

This is what I knew: Audrey had reason to spend the night in San Luis Obispo on an average of twice a month. During her stays, she made use of a house in an isolated area where, with the exception of her neighbor, her privacy was guaranteed. What she did in that house entailed the use of a table big enough to seat ten, a pantry full of oversize canned goods, and skillets and saucepans sufficient to feed any number of visitors. Vivian Hewitt said she'd seen a van and a white panel truck pull into Audrey's drive from time to time, but she'd never seen anyone going into Audrey's house. This suggested that her visitors came and went by way of the back door, which wasn't visible from her neighbor's vantage point. Vivian had also told me that on nights when the lights were on late, Audrey made a point of closing her venetian blinds.

I'd thought at first Audrey was the one busy covering her tracks. The problem was she'd been dead since Sunday, and I didn't see how she could have done such a thorough job in the brief period between her arrest and her going off the bridge. This was Thursday and the house in San Luis had been stripped of personal items and all of the surfaces wiped down. When had she found the time? Vivian Hewitt claimed someone had been there Sunday or Monday night. Clearly, it wasn't Audrey.

I looked down at the phone bill. Of four phone numbers she'd called, three had been disconnected. Someone was sweeping up in the wake of her death, shutting down all the links, eradicating evidence. The only thing I'd spied with my little eye were the two snippets of clear plastic. I met Marvin's gaze.

He said, "What?"

"I did find these." I held up a finger, alerting him to my find while I slid a hand into my pocket and pulled out the two clear plastic stems. "What do these look like to you?"

"The little doodads they use to secure price tags to clothes in department stores."

"Right. You know what I think was going on? Twice a month Audrey met with her crew and they sat around the table clipping tags out of all the garments they'd stolen. I don't know what happened to the goods afterward or what happened to the crew, but once she died, someone got busy dismantling the operation."

"So now what?"

"I think I started in the wrong place. There's no point investigating Audrey. She's gone. It's the younger woman we need. I'm still mad at myself for not catching her license plate."

"Yeah, too bad you don't have a time machine. You could whiz back to the parking garage and take another look."

I felt a small mental jolt. My mouth didn't actually drop open, but that was the sensation I experienced. "Oh, wow. Thanks for saying that. I just came up with an idea."

# 14

## DANTE

Late Thursday afternoon Dante finally caught up with his brother. When he left the office, Tomasso and Hubert were waiting in the parking garage, the limousine idling. As he emerged from the elevator, Cappi came around the corner, apparently on his way up. Dante saw him first and he was already in motion when Cappi realized what was coming down. He stumbled backward, arms flailing as he tried to put himself beyond Dante's reach. He pivoted and he'd made it four steps when Dante tackled him from behind, both men going down with a grunt. Dante scrambled to right himself and grabbed Cappi by the front of the shirt. He hauled him to his feet in one move and jammed him against the wall. Both were breathing hard, Cappi trying to loosen Dante's grip. Dante had fifty pounds on his younger brother and even with the age difference, he was in far better shape.

Dante's breath came hoarsely as he tightened his hold, twisting one hand over the other so Cappi's shirt collar formed a ligature. He could hear a momentary singing in Cappi's throat and then there wasn't air enough for any sound at all. Dante had lost touch with his rage and, consequently, had lost touch with his power. The feeling was familiar, immediate, and all-encompassing. He poured all of his energy into his hands until Cappi's eyes bulged, his face engorged and hot pink. Sweat seeped through his pores, and Dante was happy.

His bodyguard, Hubert, had appeared at his shoulder. He'd stopped in his tracks, taking in the situation. He did a quick scan of the area to assure himself no pedestrians were close enough to see what was going on. If anyone noticed, one look at the three-hundred-pound bodyguard would have discouraged intervention. That was Hubert's job, discouraging others from interfering with his boss no matter what he did.

Dante knew if he'd chosen to go on until Cappi's legs folded and he sank as dead weight, Hubert would have shrugged and had Tomasso get out of the limo so they could load the body in the trunk. Dante knew he would have done it without a word of reproof. The simple presence of the man restored his self-control. Dante loosened his stranglehold, giving Cappi access to air. He kept his face close to Cappi's, even though the kid's nose was running and his breath was tainted with fear. "Listen, you dumb fuck! Do you have any idea how much damage you've done?"

Cappi grasped his brother's wrist and pried his fingers away from his throat. Dante released him suddenly, shoving him hard against the wall. Cappi bent over and sucked in air, shaking his head. "She agreed to a deal. She was rolling over on us."

Dante leaned close. "You don't pull shit like that, you asshole. Audrey wouldn't turn on me. Never."

"Wrong. You're wrong." Cappi kept a hand on his throat, close to weeping. "They came down on her. They scared the shit out of her and she caved."

"Who did?"

"Some cop. I don't know his name. All I know is she broke down and agreed to tell 'em everything. She'd have done it right then only her boyfriend came through with the bail so they had to let her go. She'd set up a meeting with the DA first thing Monday."

"You're full of shit. You don't step in, you don't take it on yourself. Nothing. Not anything. You get that?"

"Pop backed me. I told him and he said do what needed to be done."

Dante hesitated. "What are you talking about? You told Pop?"

"I did. Ask him. I got word and I went straight to him. He said take care of it. You weren't here and someone had to shut the bitch down."

"Pop said?"

"I swear. I wouldn't have done it without him. What the hell were we supposed to do? She'd have ratted us out."

"You do anything like that again, I'll kick you to death. Now keep away from me." Dante pushed Cappi toward the elevator, kicking him hard in the ass as a fare-thee-well.

In the limo, he leaned back against the seat and closed his eyes. The smack-down was pointless. Dante knew his brother would run straight to Pop and whine about mistreatment. What felt good in the moment would just come back and bite him in the butt. His only hope was to get to his father before Cappi did, a matter of who could tattle first. Absurd for a man his age. He put the incident out of his mind. He had other issues to worry about.

He'd had lunch with his sister Talia that day and he'd broached the subject of Lola. "I've been thinking I'd ask her to marry me."

"Well, that's a cheery prospect."

"I can do without the sarcasm. I'm telling you because you're one of the few people I trust."

"Sorry. I thought you were joking."

"I'm not. We've been talking about it and it's not such a bad idea."

"I don't get it. It's been eight years. Why marry her now?"

"She wants a kid."

"She wants a *child*?"

"What's wrong with that?"

Talia laughed.

Dante closed his eyes, shaking his head. "Don't do this. Don't turn this into a fight. Say what you want. That's why I brought it up. Just don't be a bitch about it."

"Fine. You're right. Let me take a deep breath and we'll start again. Nothing accusatory. I'll ask questions, okay?"

"Fine."

"How's she going to handle a pregnancy?"

"Like every other woman, I guess."

"Not like other women. She's a head case. I don't mean this as criticism. I'm stating a fact. She's obsessed with her body and nutty about her weight. That's why she smokes. To keep the pounds off."

"She says she'll quit. She's also cut back on alcohol. Glass of wine a day and that's it."

"Because she's worried about the calories, which is why she does drugs."

"She doesn't *do* drugs. Would you listen to yourself? She's dead set against drugs."

"Except for appetite suppressants. Have you looked at her lately? She's skeletal. She has an eating disorder."

"She *had* an eating disorder, but that's done. She saw Dr. Friedken for a year and she's fine."

"He's not 'doctor' anything. He's not even a licensed clinical psychologist. He's a psychic nutritionist. A quack."

"He helped her. She's better. She eats like a normal person."

"And then goes in the bathroom and sticks a finger down her throat. Pregnant women get fat. It's a fact of life. She'll go off the deep end."

"Not all pregnant women get fat. You didn't."

"I gained forty pounds!" Talia reached out and gripped his hand. "Dante, you know I love you more than life itself, so please let me speak from the heart. Lola's a narcissist. She's moody and insecure. All she thinks about is herself. How could she possibly make room for a child?"

They changed the subject at that point since neither of them trusted themselves to go on. The question she'd posed was a bothersome one that he was still pondering.

He caught his father after dinner when he was sitting out on the verandah, smoking a cigar. Dante had always associated the smell of cigar smoke with Pop. There was a time when Lorenzo Senior had smoked in the house. He considered this his due. The living room drapes and the upholstered furniture had been saturated with smoke, the ceiling pale gold with nicotine, windows clouded with the residue. When Dante moved his father into the big house, he insisted Pop confine his smoking to one of the outdoor patios.

The old man was eighty-three and far less imposing than he'd been in the days when Dante was routinely pounded to a pulp. The punches and kicks were meant to keep him in line, or so his father said. Now he couldn't get over how small his father was, like a miniature adult, his cheeks lined and sunken, his nose and ears out of proportion to the size of his face. His hairline had receded in the shape of a heart, a V of gray in the middle of his forehead with a balding arc on either side.

Dante sat down facing him. "You heard about Audrey?"

"I hope you're not here to complain."

"Matter of fact, I am. I can't have Cappi pulling shit like that."

"Hey, bub. You were gone. He came to me with a problem. His solution made sense. He knew you'd never go for it. You're too busy playing boss man and pissing on his shoes. Besides which you're off on some mountain and no one could get hold of you."

"They have phone service in Canada. You could have called anytime."

"Says you. Someone had to step up to the plate."

"Pop, I've known Audrey years. She wouldn't have turned on us. I can guarantee."

"That's not what Cappi heard. Word on the grapevine, she was rolling over on us. I told him to take care of it."

Pop and Cappi had used the same phrase, "rolling over on us."

Dante wasn't sure who'd come up with it first. "I don't get where you're coming from. You tell him to take care of it and he goes out and whacks a valuable employee. That doesn't seem right. Does it seem right to you?"

"That might have been a bad call. I won't argue the point. You delegate responsibility, you can't come along after and second-guess what went down."

"I didn't delegate anything. You did that. I can't have you undermining my authority."

"What authority? Anything you have, I gave you."

"That's right. I run the operation. He doesn't know the first thing about business."

"So you teach him."

"I've tried! He has the attention span of a gnat."

"He says you're condescending. He says you belittle him."

"That's bullshit."

"Don't argue the point with me. I'm just telling you what he says."

"And I'm telling you, he's not cut out for this. I promote from within the company based on merit and seniority. He's sitting on a felony conviction. How does *that* look?"

"You've been accused of a thing or two yourself."

"All the more reason to keep the lid on."

"You're the strong one. You've had all the advantages. Your brother wasn't as lucky."

Dante tried to bite back his response. Anytime his father was losing an argument, he shifted to this old saw. Dante couldn't help himself this time. He said, "He wasn't as lucky about what?"

"Your mother ran off and left him."

"Jesus. You know what? She ran off and left me too. I don't see you cutting me any slack. Just the opposite. I gotta carry Cappi on my back whether I like it or not."

"Now that's the kind of selfish attitude I'm talking about. He can't help what happened to him. He was a little kid. What she did crushed his spirit. He's never gotten over it. So he's touchy, you know, because she ripped his heart out. He's had a tough row to hoe, which you were spared."

"*I* was spared? News to me. How so?"

"You never said a word about her. Name one question you ever came to me with after she walked out. Every day Cappi asked for her and every day he bawled his eyes out. You never shed a tear."

"Because you told me to buck up."

"That's right. Twelve years old, it's time to get a grip. You knew when she left, it had nothing to do with you. Cappi was four and what's he supposed to think? One minute she's there, the next minute she's gone. He's never been the same."

"I have four sisters who turned out all right. How come they're okay but not him? And what about me?"

"Even then, you knew better. Women are like that. About the time you think you can count on 'em, they take off without a word. She didn't even leave a note."

"So Cappi's a loser and everything goes back to that? He gets a free ride off that one event? I should be so lucky."

"You watch your mouth. You be careful what you wish for."

"Forget it." Dante got up. He had to get away from the old man before he blew his stack.

His father stirred with agitation, his tone peevish. "Where's Amo?"

Dante stared down at him, caught off-guard. "Amo?"

"I haven't seen him since breakfast. He wants me to take him shooting. I said we'd go up to the firing range and get in some target practice."

"Amo's been dead forty years."

"He's upstairs. I told him to find Donatello and come down here, the both of them."

Dante hesitated. "I thought you said Donatello didn't like to shoot."

"He'll get used to it. Make a man out of him. You know him. Wherever his brother goes, he's right behind."

Dante said, "Sure, Pop. If I see either one of them, I'll let 'em know you're waiting."

"And tell 'em I don't have all day. Damn inconsiderate if you ask me . . ."

Dante went into the library and poured himself a bourbon. Maybe the slip was momentary. His father was sometimes confused, especially late in the day. He'd forget a conversation they'd had fifteen minutes before. Dante had written it off, thinking the mental stumbling was a side effect of his being tired or out of sorts. It was possible he'd suffered a small stroke. Dante would have to find a pretext for bringing a doctor in to check him out. His father had no tolerance for sickness or infirmity. He'd never admit he might be subject to weakness of any kind.

Dante carried his drink into the kitchen, where Sophie was cleaning up the dinner dishes, loading plates into the machine.

"You seen Lola?"

"An hour ago. She was in workout clothes, heading for the gym."

"Great."

Dante went down to the basement level. One of the appeals of the house had been the elaborate underground rooms. Not many California homes had basements. Digging twenty-five feet down was a nightmare of rocks large and small, sandstone boulders sunk in heavy clay soil that cost a fortune to remove. This house had been built in 1927 by a guy who made his money in the stock market and held on to it through the Crash. The house was solid and gave Dante a sense of safety and permanence.

He came up the stairs into the pool house. He knew Lola was on the treadmill because the sound on the TV had been jacked up to account for the grinding noise of the moving platform and the thumping of athletic shoes. He paused in the corridor, watching her through the half-open door. It had been a mistake confiding in Talia. He might have gone his whole life without opening himself up to her candor and her acid tongue. He'd done it because he knew she'd play straight and shoot from the hip. He thought he'd blocked Talia's comments, but she'd changed his perception in twenty-five words or less. He could already feel the difference, how Lola had looked this morning, sprawled across the bed in sleep, and how she looked now. She wore makeup when she worked out even knowing she was alone. She still had the same dark eyes, lined with charcoal and looking enormous in her narrow face. She still had the mane of dark hair. It was straggly at the moment because she was sweating heavily, but he didn't mind that. What he saw, thanks to Talia's remarks, was how tiny she'd become. Her shoulders were narrow, her head incongruously balanced on a neck as thin as a pipe. She looked like one of those elongated creatures who steps out of a spacecraft, moving languidly through mist and smoke, oddly familiar and at the same time not of this world.

When she caught sight of him, she muted the sound but continued to run. She was wearing sweatpants and an oversize long-sleeve T-shirt with the cuffs turned back to expose wrists that were all bone, fingers strung together with tendons that lay along the tops of her hands like piano wire.

He said, "Hey. Come on. Pack it in for tonight. You look pooped."

She checked the readout on the machine. "Five more minutes and then I'll quit."

She popped the mute button again and the sound blared as she ran on. While he waited he puttered around the place. The room was twenty feet by twenty, lined with mirrors and fitted out with weight-lifting equipment, two treadmills, a recumbent bike, and an upright stationary bike. How many hours a day did she spend in here?

When her time was up, the machine put her through a five-minute cooldown and then she finally shut it off. He handed her a towel, which she pressed against her face. When she blotted the sweat that trickled down her neck a peachy beige foundation came off on the towel. He put an arm across her shoulders and walked her to the door, shutting off light switches as they passed.

Lola put an arm around his waist. "So what'd Talia say?"

"About what?"

"Come on, Dante. You know what."

"She wasn't thrilled."

"Of course not. She thinks I'm neurotic, temperamental, and self-centered. I'm sure she thinks I'd suck as a wife and suck even worse as a mom."

"She didn't say that."

"Would you stop trying to protect me? I'm a big girl so spell it out. I want to know what she said."

Dante sorted through Talia's objections and picked one. "She wondered about the weight gain. She thought a pregnancy would be hard on you."

"And?"

"She might have a point. I worry about you."

"I know you do and you're a sweet guy. You can tell her the baby's a nonissue. I haven't had a period for a year. She'll be tickled to death."

"Let's not talk about that now. We have time once you get healthy again."

"Ha."

"You know there's help out there if you're interested."

She leaned her head against his shoulder, matching her step to his. "That's what I love about you. You never give up hope. You think if you keep at it long enough, everything will turn out all right."

"You don't see it that way?"

"Here's my view: I think this relationship has run its course. I'm releasing you from any sense of obligation because that's the only thing keeping you here. The rest has been gone for a long time."

Dante squeezed her shoulder, but he had no reply. There was a time when the remark would have cut him to the core. Now his thoughts reverted to Nora with a flicker of joy.

. . .

He drove Cappi to the Allied Distributors warehouse in Colgate to the shipping and receiving department. Pop had acquired the brick-and-frame complex in the days when he was running booze. Dante had adapted the structure for his purposes, expanding the square footage by incorporating a prefab steel addition across the front. The mechanicals were below ground, a largely unfinished area that Pop had always referred to as the catacombs. Dante suspected there were actually more than a few bodies buried there. He'd take a flashlight down and explore the space from time to time, occasionally coming across dusty cases of whiskey and gin tucked away in the odd corner.

As the two walked from the parking lot to the loading dock, Dante filled him in on the basics. "Audrey was a trotter, the middleman between the whips and the baggers. She covered the tricounties, coordinating the central coast operation with San Francisco and points north. Ordinarily, she wouldn't have been on the scene, but one of our pickers was arrested on a bad check charge and she was filling in. You tossed her off the bridge and the entire circuit was thrown into disarray. We're still scrambling for coverage."

"How was I supposed to know?"

"Cut the whining. I'm done hassling you on that score. You fucked up big-time. You should've asked, but we'll leave it at that. I'm trying to get you to understand how the system works. That's what you're so hot to hear about, right?"

"Well, yeah. If you want me to be useful."

"All right. So the trotters pay the pickers for a day's work, usually runs about three grand in cash. The goods are called 'the crop' or 'the bale,' sometimes 'the bag.' Workers we call 'crop dusters' strip tags and remove identifying marks. They meet every couple of weeks."

"Where?"

"Couple of places we rent. There's a regular route we call 'the tour.' The guys who drive it, we call 'cabbies.' Don't worry about job titles. I know it's a lot to take in. It's a tight fit. Take out any one of the players and you got a problem on your hands."

"How many people are we talking about?"

"Enough. We make sure each crew knows as little as possible about the other crews so if there's a breakdown, no one's in a position to expose the rest. Eventually, the crop comes off the circuit and lands here for distribution."

"To where?"

"That depends. San Pedro. Corpus Christi. Miami. At every point along the way, the crop's passing through the hands of people I know I can trust. Doesn't always work that way here. This is the current trouble spot. We've been hit twice. Last week, someone walked off with a pallet of pharmaceuticals. Now we're short cartons of infant formula. I can't even get a count on that. I thought it was a clerical error, someone puts a decimal in the wrong place and it throws everything off. This's not a paper loss."

"Somebody's stealing from *us*? You gotta be kidding."

"We don't recruit help from vacation Bible schools. Point is, we have to limit access to the loading docks. This is the area where we're most vulnerable. Guys come out for a smoke and end up hanging around. It doesn't look like they're doing much, but they've got no business being here. We're initiating new oversight procedures, which is where you come in."

Cappi's tone of voice took on an edge. "And you want me to do what, stand here with a clipboard, counting widgets and making sure everybody has a hall pass?"

"If you want to look at it like that, yes. Once a shipment's inside the building, somebody has to reconcile the goods with the manifest—"

"What's with the lingo? What the fuck is a 'manifest'?"

"A list of goods. Same as an invoice, an itemized account of what's been shipped to us and where it goes next. In the meantime, we hold everything here until it's ready to be moved."

"Why didn't you say so in the first place? I can't learn anything with you lecturing me. You yap, yap, yap, and what goes in one ear goes out the other. I can't retain if I don't see it written down. Like I learn with my eyes. I need facts and figures so I can understand how all the pieces fit. You know what I'm saying? The pipeline. Accounts payable and stuff like that."

"I have bookkeepers for that end of the business. I need you here."

"Yeah, but you haven't really said where these shipments are coming from or where they go. I know it's Allied Distributors, but I don't have a clue what we distribute. Baby food? That don't make sense."

"Doesn't have to make sense to you. It makes sense to me."

"But where are all the records kept? Has to be written down someplace. You don't carry this stuff in your head. Something happens to you, then what?"

"Why the sudden curiosity? Years we've been doing this and you never gave a shit."

"Fuck you. Pop said it was time I learned. I'm here doing the best I can and you criticize me for not showing interest before?"

"It's a legitimate question. Sorry if I seem skeptical, but what do you expect?"

"What kind of shit is that? You either trust me or you don't."

"I don't."

"You accusing me of something?"

"Why so defensive?"

"I'm not defensive. All I'm asking is how you run an operation this size without somebody writes it down."

Dante dropped his gaze, working to control his temper. If Cappi was pressing for the information, he'd get information. Dante said, "Okay, fuck it. I'll tell you how. You see that computer terminal over there?"

To the right, just inside the door that led into the warehouse proper, there was an unmanned desk with a computer keyboard and monitor, the CPU tucked into the kneehole space. Dante could see Cappi's gaze shift to the darkened computer screen.

"What, that thing?"

"That 'thing' as you refer to it is a remote terminal with access from the house and the office downtown. In the wall behind, there are dedicated lines laid in. It may not look like much but that's the brains of the business. It's how we keep track. We got backup on backup. Password changes from week to week, and the hard drive is purged every Thursday at noon. Clean slate. The only dollar figures left look legitimate."

"You wipe out everything? How can you do that?"

"To all appearances, yes. If files are subpoenaed, they got nothing on us."

"I thought files stayed in the machine even when it looks like it's erased."

"Since when do you know shit about computers?"

"Hey, I hear stuff like everybody else. I thought the FBI had experts."

"So do we."

"What if there's a goof?"

"Like what?"

"I don't know. Power outage, something like that. Computer freezes up before a purge is complete."

"Then we're screwed. Any other questions?"

Cappi said, "I'm cool."

"Good. Now maybe we can move on to the problem at hand. This is the hole needs patching. I'd like to know who's bleeding us, but more important, I want to put a stop to it."

"Why me? What if I don't want to stand out here in a coverall like some stupid-ass warehouse goon?"

Dante smiled, wishing he could punch his brother's lights out. "You have an attitude problem, you know that?"

"This is chicken shit. Pop said bring me in. What you're doing here is keeping me out."

"This is in. Where you're standing right now. You want more, you can earn it like I did."

He left Cappi on the loading dock while he went up the metal stairs to the mezzanine level, where operations was housed in five offices behind a wall of waist-high windows. From there he could see much of the warehouse operation—guys on forklifts, speeding along the narrow corridors between two-story-high storage bays, guys engaged in private conversations, unaware that he was watching. His office here was crude, the basics, no refinement whatever. Dante didn't have a view of the loading dock, but he'd mounted security cameras in strategic locations.

Cappi was trouble. He'd been out of prison for six months, his release dependent on his having a job. Previously he'd worked construction as a heavy-equipment operator, making good money until he was fired for drinking on the job. His response had been to climb back on the bulldozer and plow into the construction trailer, destroying the trailer and all its contents, and narrowly missing the job-site supervisor, who was injured by flying debris. Along with a laundry list of property crimes, he'd been charged with aggravated assault, assault with a deadly weapon, and attempted murder, which was how he'd ended up in Soledad.

Pop wanted him brought into the business, so Dante had put him on the payroll. Cappi reported this to his parole officer without mentioning he'd never shown up for work. He told Pop he needed time to get reacquainted with his wife and kids. What kept him busy was honing his pool skills in the family room of his house in Colgate. In public, he was careful to avoid bars, firearms, and the company of known criminals. At home, he went through two six-packs of beer a day and popped his wife in the face if she complained. After a month of this, Dante had finally insisted that Cappi show up for work, a move he now regretted.

In the absence of an intercom, Dante hollered for his secretary in the outer office. "Bernice? Could you come in here please?"

"In a minute. I got stuff to finish first."

Dante shook his head. The girl was nineteen. He'd hired her four months before and she already had his number. He sorted through the papers on his desk until Bernice appeared in the door. She was tall and lanky with a big wad of frizzy blond hair she wore in a ponytail. She came to work in jeans and running shoes, which was fine with him. The low-cut top he could have done without. Weren't women these days taught anything about modesty?

"What?" she said.

"You know my brother?"

"I look like an idiot? Everybody knows Cappi. He's crazy as a loon."

"I'd like you to keep an eye on him. He's new to the concept of work for pay. I don't think he's got the hang of it yet."

"I charge extra to babysit," she said.

"How about spying?"

That idea seemed more appealing to her. "You want regular reports?"

"That would be nice," he said. "Meanwhile, get Dade O'Hagan on the line. His number's in there." He pushed the Rolodex in her direction and watched as she worked her way through.

"O'Hagan, like the mayor?"

"Ex-mayor. You're behind the times. This is old business. I'm calling in a marker if it's any of your concern."

She smiled. "Hot stuff."

"You bet."

# 15

I left Marvin's house at 2:15 with a promise to keep him posted on my progress. I was feeling more optimistic. Marvin's mention of time travel had sparked a train of thought. I too had regretted I couldn't go back to relive those moments in the parking garage when I'd blown the opportunity to pick up the plate number on the black sedan. The nice man who'd come to my aid had suggested I notify mall security and file a report. At the time, I'd been distracted by my outrage, my throbbing shin, and my badly scraped palm. With Marvin's offhand remark, it dawned on me that I did have a way to go back in time and review events. I knew the woman in charge of mall security.

Maria Gutierrez had been the beat officer assigned to my neighborhood some six years before. On the last case I'd worked, I'd crossed paths with her former partner, Gerald Pettigrew, who was now in charge of the K-9 unit at the Santa Teresa Police Department. Maria's name hadn't come up in conversation, but she'd been on my mind.

Some months before, I'd found myself standing behind her in the checkout line at the supermarket. She looked familiar, but she wasn't in uniform and I didn't make the connection. She'd been quicker at the recognition. She greeted me by name and identified herself. As we inched our way closer to the register, we played a quick game of catch-up. I filled her in on my life, Henry's whereabouts, and my last encounter with Lieutenant Dolan, whom she knew from the police department. She told me she'd resigned from the PD in order to take a job in the private sector. That's when she'd given me her business card.

I stopped by my office and sorted through the pile of business cards I routinely toss in my bottom drawer. After a bit of digging I found hers, and I was just about to call when I noticed the light blinking on my answering machine. I punched play.

"Hello, Kinsey. This is Diana Alvarez. Please don't hang up. I need to talk to you about the article I'm writing. I'm offering you the opportunity to clarify the facts and add any comments you might have. Otherwise, it's going in as is. My number is . . ."

I didn't bother to make a note.

I checked the phone number on Maria's business card and called her instead. I told her what had occurred and asked if I could have a look at security tapes for April 22. I thought she might be wary. Security measures are considered proprietary and, therefore, not to be disseminated to the general public. Information leaks are more likely to serve the criminal element than the law-abiding citizen, so it's better for all of us if crooks are kept in the dark about how the traps are set. Apparently, the fact that I was a PI and already known to her constituted a waiver. I gave her my guarantee that the information would remain confidential. She said she had a meeting at 3:00, but if I could make it to her office before then, she'd be happy to help. Two minutes later, I was in my car and on my way. Screw Diana Alvarez.

I found a parking spot at the Nordstrom's end of the underground structure at Passages Shopping Plaza. I bypassed the escalator and took the stairs up a level, where the retail storefronts had been designed to resemble an old Spanish town. The narrow shoulder-to-shoulder buildings varied in height. Most were stucco with the occasional picturesque chunk of plaster missing to expose the faux brick underneath. Some boasted pricey second- and third-floor offices, with shutters at the windows and flower boxes on the sills.

Along the wide central plaza corridor there were boutique restaurants with outdoor tables, benches for weary shoppers, and kiosks selling sunglasses, junk jewelry, and women's hairpieces. At the midpoint, a stage had been constructed where musicians played for summer tourists. I went up a wide set of red-tiled stairs to the second floor. To my right there was an auditorium available to local theater groups for stage productions. The mall business offices were located down a hall to the left.

Maria was waiting at the desk when I walked in.

"You're a doll to do this," I said.

"No problem. The police circulated the information to all the store managers and cc'd us so we'd know what was going on. Included with the bulletin was Audrey Vance's mug shot."

"Did you recognize her?"

"Not me, but I heard a salesgirl at Victoria's Secret saw her the same day. Apparently, she's a regular customer and nobody had any idea she was stealing from them. They're doing an inventory check now to see how badly they were hit."

"I thought these gangs originated in South America."

"Those are the worst. They can sweep through and clear a tabletop in the blink of an eye. They blast into town and they're gone again just that quick."

"How does it work? They have to be highly organized, but I don't understand how they operate."

"You start with the worker bees, who go out and steal the merchandise. Sometimes they're given a regular shopping list, products the fence knows he can sell. For instance, there's a big traffic in Gillette razor blades, Tylenol, Excedrin, pregnancy tests, diabetic test strips.

I've heard Oil of Olay products are a hot ticket as well. The list goes on and on and changes all the time."

"You mentioned Victoria's Secret."

"Sure. Think how many bras you can fit in a shopping bag. Same with panty hose. It's much tougher to steal bulky items like men's cologne sets or VCRs. You can't jam a TV down the front of your pants."

"But where does the fence lay off the goods?"

"Swap meets are a good bet, thrift stores—places like that. A lot is shipped out of the country."

"Are these rings run by the mob?"

"Not in the old-fashioned sense of the word. If the business was mob-run, you'd have a widespread network that might be vulnerable to infiltration. These crews are connected loosely, if they're connected at all, which makes apprehension and prosecution a pain in the butt. In each city, the setup is different, depending on how many people have been brought in and what kind of fencing operation is up and running in any given area."

"I remember the good old days when I was a rookie, shoplifters were amateurs."

"Not anymore. We still have the dabblers and wannabes, teenagers sneaking record albums into their backpacks, thinking they can get away with it. Kids are the least of our worries. Though if you ask me, we ought to go after them and nail them." She waved a hand, impatient with the subject. "Don't get me started. Come on back and let's take a look at what we've got."

"You still like the new job?"

"I love it," she said over her shoulder.

I followed her down a short hall to an office outfitted with closed-circuit television cameras massed together in an alcove. There were ten monitors mounted in proximity, all working independently. A young man in civilian clothes sat in a swivel chair, remote control in hand, following the live images as they flipped from view to view. The two of us stood and watched.

Depending on the angle, I could just about guess where each camera was mounted, though, in truth, I'd never noticed them before. Both entrances and both exits of the parking garage were covered. There were an additional six cameras anchored at the second-floor level, each one focused on a different line of sight. I followed one shopper from the time she entered the mall off State Street until she turned left into the main avenue and disappeared from sight. Another camera picked her up as she proceeded down the wide walk toward Macy's and went into the store. None of the pedestrians seemed to have any idea they were being watched.

"These work off coaxial cables," Maria said. "All of the cameras operate at the same time. By swapping out cassettes, we can capture images twenty-four hours a day over the course of a month. Unless we have reason to keep a cassette, we tape over what we've done. Eventually the tapes get worn or the CCTV heads get dirty, and the images end up fuzzy and not much use. After I talked to you, I pulled the cassette from last Friday."

She turned to her desk and picked up four cassettes. "There's a VCR next door."

We went into the next office, which was plainly furnished and looked like it was called into service on occasions when a mall executive was in town and needed temporary space. She pulled up a straight chair for me while she took the swivel chair behind the desk and rolled it closer to the set. The VCR was wired to a small black-and-white television that looked like something right out of the 1960s, the screen small and the housing enormous. She checked the date on the first cassette and slid it into the machine. "You said between five thirty and six fifteen?"

"Roughly. It was five twenty-six when I looked at my watch. That's when I first saw Audrey slide the pj's into her bag. She was the older of the two women working the lingerie department. By the time the loss-prevention officer was called and the whole scene played out, I'd say it was closer to five forty-five," I said. "I could be off. Time gets distorted when you're caught up in these things. At the time, everything went by in a blur and that's why I missed the plate number. I was so astonished at what happened I didn't register much else."

"I know the feeling. On the one hand you're hyperaware and at the same time you blank out the details."

"Amen. I couldn't for the life of me go back and reconstruct the incident."

"Don't I know," she said. "A foot chase you swear took fifteen minutes turns out to be half that. Sometimes it works the other way."

With a remote, she fast-forwarded. Date and time stamps sailed along in the upper right-hand corner. It was like watching an old-time movie, people walking herky jerky, cars zooming by so quickly they seemed to leave a trail of afterimages. I was amazed at how much the eye could pick up from that fleeting series of pictures. When she reached April 22, she slowed the stream of images to a more stately pace.

I pointed and said, "There."

Maria hit the pause button and rewound the tape.

The black Mercedes sedan, which was halfway up the ramp, reversed itself and disappeared from sight. She advanced the film by degrees. The car reappeared and I saw the younger woman hand a ticket to the parking attendant, who ran it into her machine. The attendant verified the time stamp, put the ticket to one side, and waved her on. The younger woman looked left and smiled, smug and self-satisfied. That much I remembered. As the sedan continued up the ramp, Maria paused the tape again, freezing the shot of the rear bumper. The license frame was in view but the plate had been removed.

"Now you know why you missed it," she said.

"What shitty luck. I thought if I picked up the plate number, someone at the PD might run it for me."

Maria said, "Let's look at it again."

She caught the Mercedes on its way up the ramp. It came to a halt with a flick of her remote and disappeared from sight, reversing down the ramp. We watched it as though it were the slow-motion photo finish of a horse race. "Check the license plate frame," she said. "Top says, 'Keep honking . . .' Bottom says, 'I'm reloading.'"

She squinted and tilted her head. "What's that on the right side of the bumper?"

As the car came up the ramp, she stopped the picture midframe. There was a bumper sticker affixed to the right-hand side. I got up and peered more closely, but the picture seemed to dissolve. Both Maria and I backed up halfway across the width of the office space.

She smiled. "That should help."

"Can you read that?" I asked.

"Sure. You ought to get your eyes checked. Says, 'My daughter is on the honor roll at Climping Academy.'"

"Oh, wow. That's great!"

"Right. All you have to do now is find the car."

"I've tackled tougher jobs in my day."

"I'll bet. Keep me posted. I want to hear how this turns out."

Running surveillance is an exercise in ingenuity. As a rule, sitting in a parked car for an extended period generates public uneasiness, especially in a school zone where parents are fretful about abductions, kidnap for ransom, and other forms of child-oriented mischief. Horton Ravine is a natural habitat for wealthy people with expensive tastes. There might be a hundred black Mercedes sedans passing back and forth through the front and rear gates. With roughly eight hundred private homes spread over eighteen hundred acres, my only hope of spotting the car was to find an observation post and wait.

After a quick drive through the area, I decided the obvious location was at the foot of the private drive leading up the hill to Climping Academy. I had to take into consideration that the woman's bumper sticker might be out of date. Her daughter might have already graduated from Climping. She might have dropped out or transferred to another school. Even if she were currently enrolled, her dad might be in charge of dropoff and pickup, using another vehicle altogether.

Meanwhile, I had to come up with a reasonable explanation for my presence on the road where I intended to keep watch. For short stints, the appearance of car trouble will sometimes work. With the hood up, a puzzled look on my face, and my owner's manual in hand, I can stall for an hour unless a Good Samaritan comes to my aid. This happens with annoying frequency when I'm least desirous of the help.

Devious creature that I am, an idea occurred to me almost instantly. I left Horton Ravine and took the 101 to a strip mall in Colgate, where I'd seen a large craft mart two doors down from an office-supply store. In the latter, I bought a handheld tally counter, a device that advances one number with each click of a button. At the craft shop, I bought two pieces of heavy-duty poster board, thirty-six inches square, and ten packets of self-adhesive black alphabet letters, with a bonus packet of most-often-used vowels and consonants.

I went home with my packages and set to work on my kitchen counter. With the poster board and stick-on alphabet, I fashioned a sandwich-board sign, hinged at the top, with the same message visible on both the front flap and the back. When I finished the job, I leaned the sign against the wall and climbed the spiral stairs. I sorted through the hanging clothes in my closet and took out my generic uniform, an outfit I'd designed myself and had made many years before. The pants and matching shirt were constructed of a sturdy, no-nonsense dark blue twill, complete with brass buttons, epaulettes, and belt loops through which I can thread a wide black leather belt. On each sleeve I'd sewn a round patch with SANTA TERESA SERVICES embroidered in gold. In the center of the patch there was a vaguely governmental emblem. If I wore clunky black lace-up oxfords and carried a clipboard, I could easily pass for a city or county employee.

I hung the uniform on a peg, ready for my next day's work. It was almost 5:00 by then, time, I thought, to check in with Henry back in

Michigan. I hadn't talked to him since Monday, and I felt a twinge of guilt that poor Nell and her broken hip hadn't even crossed my mind. I sat down at my desk and punched in the Michigan number, mentally composing a summary of what had transpired over the past couple of days. The number rang five times and just when I thought the machine would kick in, Henry's brother Charlie picked up. "Pitts. This is Charlie. You'll have to speak up. I'm deaf as a post."

I raised my voice. "Charlie? This is Kinsey. Out in California."

"Who?"

"KINSEY. HENRY'S CALIFORNIA NEIGHBOR. IS HE THERE?"

"Who?"

"HENRY."

"Oh. Hang on."

I could hear muffled conversation and then Henry took the handset, saying, "This is Henry."

Once we sorted out who was who, Henry brought me up to speed on Nell's condition. "She's fine. She's tough as nails and never a word of complaint." He said she'd be in a residential rehab facility for another ten days. They'd come up with a pain-management plan to help her tolerate the physical therapy sessions twice a day. Meanwhile, Henry, Charlie, and Lewis spent the better part of the day with her, playing board games to keep her mind off her infirmity. As soon as she mastered her walker, she'd be allowed to come home. "How's your shin?" he asked.

I pulled up the leg of my jeans and had a look, as though he could see it as well. "More blue than purple and my palm's just about healed."

"Well, that's good. Everything else okay?"

I filled him in on the latest developments, including Marvin Striker's hiring me to look into Audrey's death, my trip to San Luis Obispo, and my theory about her involvement in organized retail crime.

Henry was properly sympathetic, mystified, and outraged depending on what part of the story I was telling him, and he asked enough pertinent questions to fill in the blanks. "I'd offer to help, but there's not much I can do at this remove," he said.

"Actually, there is. I need to borrow your station wagon for a day or two."

"No problem. You know where I keep the keys."

On we went in this fashion and when we finally said our good-byes, I realized we'd been on the phone for forty-five minutes.

As usual, I was starving to death, so I grabbed my shoulder bag and a jacket, locked my door, and trotted up the street to Rosie's. Claudia Rines was sitting at a table near the door. She had a drink in front of her, grapefruit juice by the look of it, probably laced with vodka.

I said, "Hey, how are you?"

"Fine. I feel like I haven't talked to you in weeks."

"It's been five days, but I know what you mean. You're meeting Drew?"

"As soon as he takes his break. Are you up for a drink?"

"I'd love one, but just until he arrives. I don't want to horn in on your dinner plans. Is that vodka and grapefruit juice?"

"It is. William brought in fresh-squeezed juice just for me. You ought to try it."

"Hang on," I said. We both turned to catch William's eye. Claudia held her drink up, indicating she needed a refill. I pointed to myself and held up two fingers. He nodded and leaned down to open the small refrigerator under the bar.

I turned back to Claudia. "So what's up?"

"Too bad you weren't here sooner. You just missed a friend of yours."

"Sorry to hear that. Who?"

"Diana somebody. She works for the local paper."

"You're kidding me. When was this?"

"I don't know, maybe fifteen minutes ago. She came in shortly after I did and introduced herself. She said she didn't want to be a bother, but she had a few questions about my encounter with Audrey Vance."

"How did she know who you were?"

"I thought you told her."

"I never said a word."

"That's odd. She knew I worked at Nordstrom's and she knew I was there when Audrey was arrested. She said she was fact-checking a few items her editor wanted confirmed. I just assumed she'd spoken to you first and was filling in the holes."

"No way. She showed up at my office on Wednesday, wanting to be all buddy-buddy. I don't talk to her about anything because I know how she operates. She'll extract all kinds of information while swearing up and down your comments are off the record."

"She said that just now, literally word for word. I told her I couldn't discuss Nordstrom's business. Mr. Koslo takes a dim view of reporters. He's also paranoid about getting involved in the middle of a lawsuit. Not that there is one."

"So what'd you tell her?"

"Nothing. I referred her to him. That seemed to annoy her, but I couldn't see putting my job at risk, even if she's a friend of yours."

"She's not a friend. I swear. I can't stand the woman. She's a pushy, calculating bitch." I gave her a summary of her relationship to Michael Sutton and how that disaster had played out.

"What's her interest in Audrey?" Claudia asked.

"She heard about Audrey's suicide and now she wants to write an article about all the people who've taken headers off the Cold Spring Bridge. She went to Audrey's visitation and saw my name in the guest register. Then she wheedled her way into Marvin's good graces and he made the mistake of sending her to me. I had a fit when I realized what was going on. He's since repented, I'm happy to report."

"Oh, lord. She sounds like trouble. I had no idea."

I looked up to see William approaching the table with my vodka and grapefruit juice in one hand and hers in the other. I said, "Thanks. This looks great."

"I hope you enjoy it," he said and then returned to the bar.

Claudia and I resumed our conversation, though there wasn't much more to say on the subject. She was relieved to hear she hadn't caused offense by refusing to discuss Audrey Vance with my good friend Diana Alvarez, and I was relieved she'd kept her mouth shut for reasons of her own.

In the interest of work, I skipped my run the next morning. I ate a bowl of Cheerios, then showered and donned my uniform à la Santa Teresa Services. Shoulder bag in tow, I put my sandwich-board sign in Henry's station wagon and backed out of the garage. The school day at Climping Academy started at 8:00. By 7:30 I was parked on the berm at the bottom of the drive with my sign, which read:

**This Vehicle Count is part of an Environmental Impact Study and represents your tax dollars at work. We thank you for your cooperation and apologize for any inconvenience. Drive safely!**

I stood on the side of the road in my uniform, tally counter in hand, clicking off cars as they passed. On the plus side of the ledger, my shin felt better, still bruised I knew, but not throbbing. On the minus side was a visitor. Five minutes after I set up shop, a Horton Ravine patrol car rolled by and pulled over to the side of the road. The driver got out and ambled in my direction. He was wearing dark trousers and a white short-sleeve shirt. I didn't think he was a "real" policeman. He might have been a cop wannabe, but he wasn't driving a black-and-white, he had no badge, and he wasn't wearing a regulation uniform for either the STPD or the sheriff's department. In addition, he wasn't carrying a handgun, a night stick, or a heavy-duty flashlight, which might serve as a weapon if I needed to be subdued. I was engrossed in my car count so I couldn't give him my undivided attention.

Blond, midthirties, trim, with a pleasant demeanor. He took out a pen and pad and prepared to take notes or write a ticket, I wasn't sure which. "Good morning. How are you?" he asked.

"I'm fine, thanks. How about yourself?"

"Good. May I ask what this is about?"

"Sure. I'm doing a vehicle count for the county."

There was a brief delay while he processed my reply. "Are you aware this is a private road?"

"Absolutely. No doubt about it, but as long as there's public access, it goes into my report."

Mentally, he was going through his checklist. "You have a permit?"

"For this? I was told I didn't need one to do a road-use analysis."

"May I see some identification?"

"I have my driver's license in my shoulder bag. I'll be happy to show it to you if you can wait until there's a break in traffic."

He watched as two cars came through the main entrance. One turned up the drive to the school and the other continued on into Horton Ravine. *Click. Click.* I counted both. At the first gap in passing cars, I reached through the open window and picked up my bag from the passenger seat. He waited patiently while I paused to count a car. I took out my wallet, flipped it open, and offered it to him. He took it and jotted down my name, driver's license number, and home address in his notebook.

I said, "That's Millhone with two L's. Lotta people leave out that second L." His name, I noticed, was B. Allen. "The car belongs to my landlord. He said I could use his today because mine's in the shop. The registration's in the glove compartment, if you want to have a look. You'll see that my address and his are one house number apart."

"That's not necessary," he said. He handed me my license and turned to watch cars approaching.

One car passed and I dutifully clicked. He'd already fallen into the rhythm of these intermittent interruptions.

He looked back at me. "I don't see an EPA badge."

"Don't have one yet. This is the first time I've been asked to do this.

The Department of Transportation conducts an annual survey and I was tapped for it this time. Lucky me."

"How long do you anticipate being here?"

"A day and a half, max. I tally an hour in the morning and another in the afternoon unless I'm sent somewhere else. You never know with these clowns."

I held up a finger, saying "Hang on," while I clicked off another car turning up the drive to Climping. "Sorry about that. We forward statistics to Sacramento and that's the end of it as far as I know. Typical governmental boondoggle, but the pay's good."

He pondered the proposition. It must have been clear I wasn't breaking the law. Finally, he said, "Well. Just so you don't interfere with traffic."

"I'll be out of your hair as soon as possible."

"I'll let you go on about your business. Have a nice day."

"You too. I appreciate your courtesy."

"Sure thing."

I was so busy maintaining the fiction that I nearly missed the Mercedes. Out of the corner of my eye, I saw a black sedan speeding up the hill toward Climping, a young girl at the wheel. I couldn't read the bumper sticker, but it was pasted in the right spot and worth a closer look.

# 16

I waited until the Horton Ravine patrol car had pulled away. It was five minutes to eight and the cavalcade of arriving students had slowed to a trickle. I stayed at my post until 8:15 and then picked up my sign and tossed it into the backseat of the station wagon. Then I drove up the hill to Climping Academy and sailed into the parking lot. I cruised the rows of BMWs, Mercedes, and Volvos, and finally spotted the black sedan. The lot was full and I was forced to park in a slot intended for the vice principal. I left my engine running while I doubled back on foot. The girl had locked the car, which forestalled my rooting through the glove compartment for the registration and proof of insurance. I wrote down the license number, which was actually a vanity plate that read HOT CHIK. The frame on the plate was a match for the one Maria had pointed out as she wound and rewound the CCTV tape.

Now that I'd found the car, I had two choices. If I drove to the nearest pay phone, I could call Cheney Phillips and ask him to run the plate through his work computer. This would net me the name and address of the registered owner in a relatively short period of time. Strictly speaking, however, it's against department policy, perhaps even illegal, to tap into the system for personal reasons. I was also acutely aware of Len Priddy's presence in all of this. If I called Cheney, he'd want to know why I needed the information. The minute I told him I was on the track of Audrey's shoplifting partner, he'd expect to be brought up to speed. Whatever I told him, even if I were vague and evasive, would go straight to Len Priddy, who was working the shoplifting angle for the Santa Teresa Police Department. While I know it's very, *very* naughty to withhold information from law enforcement, I thought it wise to leave Cheney out of the equation and, thus, reduce the chances of Len Priddy getting wind of my pursuit.

My other option was to wait until school was out and tail the girl when she left. I wasn't crazy about the idea of lurking on campus until classes were dismissed. I certainly couldn't leave my car where it was. The vice principal was bound to show up and how could I explain my poaching her spot? I decided to take off and return closer to the time when classes ended for the day. If the girl ducked out early, I'd be screwed. I could always come back in the morning and count cars again, but I wasn't sure how far I could push my EPA charade. Faux officer B. Allen might consult the Horton Ravine rule book, bone up on the regulations, and chase me off if he saw me again.

I surveyed my immediate surroundings. Tall hedges separated the parking lot from the administration building, with its second- and third-floor classrooms. No faces in the windows. No sign of a campus security guard. No students arriving late. I hunkered by the rear passenger side of the Mercedes and let the air out of the tire. I then went around and deflated the tire on the driver's side. I figured when school was out and my honor roll student discovered the two flats, she'd call the automobile club or a parent to come pick her up. In either case, the delay would allow me a clear field. All the other students and faculty would be gone, and I could linger near the entrance to Horton Ravine until my quarry appeared.

I returned to my car and went home. I left Henry's station wagon in the drive and let myself into my studio. I changed out of my uniform, which I hung in the closet, and substituted jeans. On my way out the door, I picked up the morning paper and shoved it in the outside pocket of my shoulder bag. Once at the office, I let myself in and gathered up the mail from the day before. I put on a pot of coffee. I had bolted down a quick bowl of cereal that morning before I left for Horton Ravine, but I hadn't had my coffee or a chance to catch up on the news. While the coffee brewed, I took my leftover Fritos from the bottom drawer of my desk and put them in my bag. When I returned to my vigil in Horton Ravine, waiting for the girl to leave school, I'd have them with me to munch on.

Satisfied with my preparations, I settled at my desk and opened the paper. The first article that caught my eye, front page, left-hand column, had been filed under Diana Alvarez's byline.

**Police Launch Inquiry into Suicide Victim's Link to Organized Crime**

In the space of one sentence, I could see she'd abandoned the usual reporter imperatives—who, what, when, where, and how—and jacked up the tone for maximum emotional appeal.

*The April 24 suicide of Audrey Vance, 63, was first thought to be the unfortunate consequence of her arrest on shoplifting charges two days before. Her fiancé, Marvin Striker, was shocked when the police arrived at his door to inform him that her body had been recovered from treacherous terrain off Highway 154. Santa Teresa County Sheriff's K-9 unit and a search-and-rescue team were summoned to the scene when a passing motorist, Ethan Anderson, of Lompoc, noticed the victim's car parked near the bridge. When he stopped to investigate, he found the vehicle unlocked with the keys in the ignition. A woman's handbag and high heels had been neatly placed on the front seat. "I knew right then we had a problem on our hands," Anderson said. Queried about a suicide note, authorities indicated later there was none.*

*Striker, while vehemently refuting the notion that his bride-to-be would intentionally harm herself, admitted she'd reacted with extreme emotional distress to recent events. Vance, who died Sunday after a fall from the Cold Spring Bridge, had been apprehended April 22 at Nordstrom department store after a local private investigator, Kinsey Millhone, witnessed the theft of several hundred dollars' worth of lingerie and reported the incident to sales clerk Claudia Rines. According to reports, Rines, who declined to be interviewed for this article, notified Nordstrom's loss-prevention officer, Charles Koslo, who detained the alleged shoplifter in the mall after electronically tagged goods concealed in a shopping bag tripped an alarm. Vance was subsequently taken into custody and charged with grand theft.*

*Letitia Jackson, public relations officer for the Santa Teresa Police Department, confirmed a report that a physical search of Vance by custodial officers revealed the presence of specially designed undergarments, known as booster gear, in which additional stolen merchandise had been hidden. Pressed for a response, Koslo said he wasn't at liberty to comment because he hadn't read the police report and wasn't a party to all the facts in the case. "We extend heartfelt condolences to her loved ones," Koslo was quoted as saying.*

*Marvin Striker, 65, who was newly engaged to Ms. Vance, has asserted repeatedly that his fiancéé would never have taken her own life. "Audrey was the last person in the world who'd consider such a step." Asked to speculate whether her death was accidental or the result of foul play, Striker said, "That's what I intend to find out." Striker contacted Millhone, of Millhone Investigations, after a mutual acquaintance told him of her connection to the shoplifting incident. It was Millhone who suggested that Vance might be part of an organized retail crime ring operating in Santa Teresa and surrounding counties.*

*When questioned, Santa Teresa Vice Detective Leonard Priddy said his department was looking into the allegation. "As far as I know, there's no truth to the rumor, which from our perspective appears to be purely fanciful." Priddy said a full-scale investigation was under way but that he was confident no evidence of gang activity would surface. Millhone did not return repeated phone calls requesting comment.*

*Vance is the eighteenth Santa Teresa County resident to plunge to her death. Caltrans representative Wilson Carter called the loss of lives resulting from individuals jumping from the 400-foot-high bridge a "regrettable and entirely preventable tragedy." Statistical studies show that barriers erected on comparable structures contribute significantly to the reduction in suicide attempts. Carter further stated, "The long-term emotional and financial toll as a direct result of suicide offers a compelling argument for the construction of such a barrier, which has long been under discussion by state and county officials."*

*A bereaved Striker expressed the hope that his loss, however painful, might spur renewed interest in the project. In the meantime, the probe into the circumstances surrounding Vance's death suggests few if any answers to the sad and troubling questions generated by her fall from a bridge where so many have ended their lives in despair and isolation.*

My entire body was engulfed in heat. Diana Alvarez had slanted the truth, insinuating actions and attitudes I had no way to refute. It didn't surprise me she'd talked to a Santa Teresa Police Department vice detective. The fact that it was Len Priddy was just my bad luck, unless she'd somehow picked up on his disdain for me. His use of the terms "allegation" and "purely fanciful" in the same sentence suggested I was deluded. It was obvious he considered me a buffoon. She'd also implied that Claudia and I were deliberately ducking her inquiries into a sensitive matter of importance to the community at large.

The woman was dangerous. I hadn't understood before the power of her position. She could present the so-called facts in any light she wanted, using neutral-sounding language to drive her point home. How many times had I read similar accounts and taken the contents at face value? The gospel according to Diana Alvarez was anything she wanted the public to believe. She was sticking it up my nose because she knew I had no way to fight back. She hadn't defamed me and nothing she'd said had been libelous. Taking issue with her would only make me appear defensive, which would further her views.

I got up and walked back to the kitchenette. I poured myself a cup of coffee. I had to hold the mug with two hands to keep the surface steady. I carried the coffee back to my desk, wondering how soon my phone would start to ring. What I was graced with instead was a visit from Marvin Striker, who had a copy of the paper tucked under one arm.

He looked as dapper as ever. Even in the midst of fuming, I had to admire the conservative dress code to which he adhered. No jeans and flannel shirts for him. He wore dark slacks, a muted sport coat, a white dress shirt, and a gray wool tie. His shoes were polished and he smelled of aftershave. In an earlier age, he would have been known as a dandy, or a swell, or a man about town.

He noticed the paper lying on my desk, which saved him beating around the bush. "I see you read the article, same as me. So what did you think?"

"You come off looking a lot better than I do, that's for sure," I said. "I told you she was a troublemaker."

I gestured him into a chair.

He sat down, posture erect, his hands on his knees. "I'm not sure I'd call her a troublemaker. Granted, she's got a different point of view, but that doesn't mean she's wrong. Like she says, she's looking at the bigger picture. I already got two calls this morning, wanting me to sign a petition in support of the suicide-prevention barrier."

"Oh, come on, Marvin. That's a smokescreen. She's using the issue to stick it up my nose. She doesn't like it that I won't jump when she says jump."

He stirred uneasily. "I can see you're taking this personally, which is a mistake in my opinion. I understand you don't like criticism. None of us want to be held up to public scrutiny, so I don't fault you for that."

I waited. He made no response. I said, "Finish the sentence. You don't fault me for that so what *do* you fault me for?"

"Well, you know . . . that vice detective didn't exactly endorse your point of view. About Audrey and this gang stuff."

"Because he's just like Diana Alvarez, thrilled at the chance to cast me in a bad light."

"Why would he do that?"

I waved the question aside. "It's not worth getting into. It's ancient history. I won't claim he hates me. That would be an exaggeration. Let's just say he dislikes me and the feeling's mutual."

"I gathered as much. I mean, I wasn't sure how well you knew the guy, but he didn't come across as a big fan of yours."

"He was a friend of my ex-husband's, who was also a cop. Believe me, there's no love lost between us. I think he's a creep."

Marvin's right knee began a subtle jumping that he stilled with one hand. "Yes, well, that's an item I thought we should cover while we're at it. You don't like Diana Alvarez and now it turns out you don't like the vice detective. No offense, but it sounds like they don't like you either."

"Of course they don't. That's the point I just made."

"Which presents me with a problem. The newspaper gal I don't care about so much as this vice cop, what's his name."

"Priddy."

"Right. If you'll remember our initial conversation, you said I should hire you because they considered you a professional. Now it looks like that's not true."

"He doesn't consider me a professional at any rate," I said.

"So that has me wondering."

"About what?"

"If you're the best person for the job. I thought we could kick the subject back and forth between us. I'm curious what you have to say for yourself."

"I've said my piece. You want to fire me, fire me."

"I never said anything about firing you," he said, aggrieved.

"I thought I'd save you some time. No need to dance around the subject. You want me gone, I'm gone."

"Don't be in such a rush. Thing is, I don't question your qualifications or your sincerity. It's just the police don't believe there's anything to this business about a shoplifting gang. You have to admit it sounds farfetched, which I've said all along."

"I'm not going to argue. You know why? Because it would sound self-serving, like I'm promoting my theory to protect my job. You're the boss. You can believe anything you want. Audrey was an angel, falsely arrested, and falsely charged. She didn't throw herself off the bridge, she tripped and fell."

"Now you're twisting my words. I accept Audrey stole things. I already gave you that the last time we talked. It's this notion there was more going on, like this big conspiracy. The cop isn't buying it and he should know, don't you think?"

"Marvin, she had *hundreds* of dollars' worth of stolen items in her underwear, which was specifically designed for just that purpose. Shoplifting wasn't a hobby. She was a pro."

"That doesn't mean she was part of an organized ring. The cop pretty much said the whole idea was bogus."

"Len Priddy would scoff at anything I said. You have no idea how contemptuous he is of me."

"That's what I'm saying. You go forward, he's not going to cooperate, which means you and the cops are working at cross-purposes."

"What do you want to do? Just give me the bottom line here and let's get on with it."

He shrugged, apparently not wanting to be pinned down without agonizing first. This was Marvin's version of playing fair. "I thought we should toss around some possibilities, like maybe you could confine your questions to how she died and leave the other part to the police."

"If you think her death was a homicide, the sheriff's department is in a better position to investigate than I am. They'll bend over backward finding out what went on. I'm coming at events from the other end, trying to figure out what she was involved in and whether that got her killed."

He shook his head. "Doesn't feel right to me."

"It doesn't feel right to me either."

"There's gotta be a compromise. We split the difference, as it were, so you get what you want and I do too."

"This is a business arrangement. Compromise doesn't come into it. I think it's cleaner and more honest if we part company. No harm, no foul. You go your way and I go mine. We shake hands and walk away."

"I have a lot of respect for you."

"Uh-hun. Right."

"No, I mean it. So how about this? Go ahead and work off the money I paid you and then we'll talk. That way, I don't come off looking like I'm disloyal or a cheapskate."

"You're not a cheapskate. Don't be ridiculous. Who said that?"

"Diana mentioned maybe I was reluctant to cut ties because you might not give my retainer back and I didn't want to be out the bucks."

"Why don't we leave her out of it, okay? Because here's the issue as far as I'm concerned. I don't think you should pay me when you're so clearly convinced I've got my head up my ass. If you think I'm on the wrong track, it's a waste of your money and my time to go on with this. It's a vote of no confidence."

"I have confidence in you, just not the tack you're taking. Problem is, you could turn out to be right and then how would it look if I, you know, terminated your employment?"

"I can't help how you look to other people. I can appreciate the bind you're in and I'm letting you off the hook."

"Then why do I feel bad? I don't like feeling bad."

"Fine. If it makes you feel bad, you don't have to make the decision right now. Take your time. Whatever you want, I'll be cool with it. We can't keep going around and around like this."

"In that case, I gotta go back to my original proposition. How about you work off the dough I paid you up front? You can spend your time any way you want. You don't even have to itemize where you went or what you did. Your prerogative entirely. Money runs out, we'll talk just like this and you can tell me what you found."

"You don't have to humor me."

"No, no. That's not where I'm coming from. I'm fine with this," he said. "How much time have you put in so far?"

"I have no idea. I'd have to go back and calculate."

"Then figure it out and whatever time you have left, use as you see fit. We have a deal?"

I stared at him for a moment. I didn't like any of it, but I didn't want Diana Alvarez and Len Priddy lording it over me.

I said, "Sure."

We fumbled the conversation to a close and left the conflict with neither one of us at peace. The whole complexion of the game had changed. On the surface, it looked the same. I had the younger woman in my sights. Another half a day and I'd know where she lived and from that I could find out who she was. Sooner or later, she'd tip her hand. Inevitably, I'd reach a point where I'd be operating on my own dime. But so what? Even if I ended up with egg on my face, there are worse things than that. The little cynical voice in me piped up, saying, "Oh, yeah? Name one."

Aloud, I said, "Letting the bad guys win."

At 2:45 I parked just outside the entrance to Horton Ravine, angling the station wagon so the long drive up to Climping Academy was in plain view. I couldn't imagine a tow truck driver opting to remove the disabled Mercedes through the rear entrance to the Ravine, but I was prepared to follow him either way. In the meantime, since I wasn't actually *in* Horton Ravine, I was beyond the jurisdiction of the proto-cop. He'd been nice enough on our first encounter, but I didn't want to push my luck. I shut down my engine and removed a map of California from the glove compartment. I opened the map fully and laid it across the steering wheel, hoping I looked like a tourist who'd pulled off the road to get her bearings. I turned on the radio, tuning in to a station that played hit songs twenty-four hours a day. I listened to two Michael Jackson cuts and then Whitney Houston's "Where Do Broken Hearts Go." The DJ announced she'd just knocked Billy Ocean out of the number one spot. I didn't know if this was good news or bad.

At 3:00 the cars began their exodus, pouring down the hill from Climping, one luxury vehicle after another. When I was in high school, I'd used public transportation. Aunt Gin had a fifteen-year-old Oldsmobile that she used to get back and forth to work. In those days, teenagers had no rights and no sense of entitlement. We knew we were second-class citizens, entirely at the mercy of adults. There were kids who had their own cars, but it wasn't the norm. The rest of us knew better than to bitch. I pictured this crop of youngsters, not spoiled so much as unaware of how fortunate they were.

Three thirty came and went, and just when I was getting worried, a tow truck approached from my left, passed me, and headed up the hill. In my mind's eye, I could see the parking lot, which would be largely deserted by now. The damsel in distress would be easy to spot. The driver would pull up in the empty lane and get out of his truck. The girl would explain the problem while gesturing at the tires. I could picture him hunkering down to have a look, quickly realizing, as she must have, that human mischief was at the root. I'd left the two valve caps on the pavement, one sitting neatly beside each flat tire. She was bound to have spotted them, and if she'd complained about being the victim of a prank, the driver had probably brought along a portable air compressor. It would be a simple matter then of his inflating one tire at a time and screwing the valve caps back into place. This would take no more than three minutes, maybe four taking into account the back-and-forth of polite conversation.

I checked my watch, fired up my engine, and turned off the radio. I looked up as though cued and said, "Ah!" because there came the tow truck, turning right at the foot of the hill. The Mercedes followed. Though I knew the upscale private school drew students from all over the city, I'd assumed the girl lived somewhere in Horton Ravine. However, instead of turning left and heading into the heart of the Ravine, she took a right as well. I kept my face averted, making a serious study of the map still open in front of me. She didn't know me from Adam, but on the off chance we crossed paths in the future, I didn't want her making the connection. The tow truck passed me, slowed at the intersection, and took a right. She was two car lengths behind. I was already folding up the map, which I left on the passenger seat. As soon as she'd cleared the intersection, I checked for oncoming traffic, made an illegal U-turn, and followed her.

The tow truck continued on across the freeway overpass. The Mercedes moved into the right lane. The girl took the 101 on-ramp and merged with the stream of speeding cars heading south. I slowed, adjusting my speed to allow another car between us. Traffic was light and it wasn't difficult keeping up with her. She stayed in the right-hand lane and passed the off-ramp at Little Pony Road. She got off on the Missile Street exit and kept to the left in preparation for a turn. The car between us sped on. We were both caught at the stoplight at the bottom of the ramp. I could see her adjust the rearview mirror and reapply her lipstick. When the light changed, it took her a moment to register the fact. I was patient, not wanting to call attention to myself with even a quick toot of my horn.

She turned left and kept to surface streets, which meant we encountered a stop sign or a stoplight at just about every intersection. I stayed three car lengths behind her. She didn't seem aware of me, and why would she? There was no reason for her to fret about an old station wagon. I watched her shake her shoulders and bounce on the seat. She lifted her right arm, fingers snapping in time to music audible only to her. I flipped on my radio again, picking up the same pop music station I'd listened to before. I didn't recognize the female vocalist, but the girl's car dancing was perfectly synchronized with the song.

She turned left on Santa Teresa Street, drove three blocks, and then turned right on Juniper Lane, which was an abbreviated half block long. Ten yards before reaching the corner, I pulled over to the curb in front of a small green stucco house that fronted on Santa Teresa Street. I shut down the engine and got out, trying to behave as though I were in no particular hurry. There were newspapers piled up on the front porch steps and the letter box bulged with mail. I blessed the householder for being away and at the same time faulted him for not having someone cover the house for him while he was gone. Burglars were now at liberty to break in and help themselves to his coin collection and his wife's silverware.

I cut across the yard on the diagonal, happy I didn't have to worry about witnesses. An oversize weeping willow occupied one corner of the lot. Four-foot hedges grew along the edge of the property as far as a detached two-car garage with an apron of concrete in front sufficient to allow guest parking for two.

I peered over the neatly trimmed shrubs. There were only three houses on the far side of Juniper Lane. The centerpiece was a two-story mock Tudor, with a one-story ranch-style house on the left and a one-story board-and-batten cottage on the right. The Mercedes was idling at the entrance to the Tudor. As I watched, the wide wrought-iron gate slid open with a screech of metal on metal, and the black Mercedes sedan turned into the drive. Through the wrought-iron fence I saw the middle of three garage doors rumble up. The girl pulled in and a moment later, the gate slid shut again, squealing as it had before.

I reversed my steps and returned to the car. I unearthed pen and paper from my shoulder bag. I looked to my right and made a note of the street number on the green stucco house where I'd parked. I turned the key in the ignition, put the car in gear, and proceeded to the corner. I turned right and drove at a sedate two miles an hour as was appropriate on a residential street of such short duration. As I passed, I scribbled down house numbers for the three houses on the left: 200, 210, and 216. On the right-hand side of the street there were four houses, respectively numbered 209, 213, 215, and 221. At the end of the block, I turned right and drove to the parking garage adjacent to the public library.

# 17

I took a seat at my favorite table in the reference room at the public library. I'd plucked the *Santa Teresa City Directory* from the shelf and I worked my way through, running my finger down the page. In the section I'd turned to, streets were listed alphabetically. For each street, the house numbers were arranged in an orderly progression. Opposite each number, the name and occupation of the householder was given, with the spouse's name in parentheses. In a separate section, residents were listed in alphabetical order by name, this time including a phone number as well as the address. By flipping from section to section, crisscrossing, so to speak, one could pick up more information than you'd think.

In my notebook, I jotted down the names of the occupants I was interested in, including those of the mock Tudor, the neighbors on either side, and the families across the street. I also looked up the owner of the green stucco house that fronted on Santa Teresa Street at the corner of Juniper Lane. This is what constitutes happiness in my life—the garnering of facts. The younger woman, Audrey's accomplice, was Georgia Prestwick. I now knew her address and her phone number, which I would probably never have occasion to use. Her husband's name was Dan. His occupation was "retired." If I wanted to know what he'd done before retirement, I could track through past city directories until I caught him in the act. From a different source, I knew the Prestwicks had a daughter, who was an honor roll student at Climping Academy.

The owner of the green stucco house was Ned Dornan, whose wife's name was Jean. He worked for the city planning commission, though the directory didn't specify in what capacity. I left the library, retrieved my car, and went home. It was 4:30 by then and my day wasn't even close to being done. I sat down at my desk. My answering machine was blinking merrily. Apparently I had any number of messages and I was guessing all of them were related to the article in the paper. I didn't have the patience to listen to the blah, blah, blah. I'd be hearing from people I hadn't spoken to in years and why did I owe them an explanation? I opened my bottom drawer and hauled out the phone book. I paged through until I found the all-purpose number for the City of Santa Teresa. I punched in the number and when the operator picked up, I asked to be connected to the city planning offices. When a woman answered in that department, I asked to speak to Mr. Dornan. She said he was out of the office and wouldn't be back until Monday, May 2. She offered to redirect my call. I thanked her and declined, saying I'd call again.

I went up the spiral stairs and cleared the top of the footlocker I use as a bedside table, setting the reading lamp, the alarm clock, and a stack of books on the floor. I lifted the lid, took out my 35mm single-lens reflex camera, inserted fresh batteries, and set it aside along with two rolls of film. Then I closed the lid and rearranged the items, pausing to dust the top with a sock I pulled out of the clothes hamper.

I was, I confess, flying by the seat of my pants, but I had reasonable hopes of zeroing in on the woman who'd aided and abetted Audrey's shoplifting jaunt. There was no way I could risk a face-to-face encounter. While she'd shown no sign of recognizing me when we passed each other in the Nordstrom's ladies' lounge, she had most certainly known who I was in the moment when she tried to run me down. If I wanted to find out how she operated, I'd better be prepared to wait.

I went out to the Mustang, a 1970 Grabber Blue speed monster that I'd bought to replace the VW I'd driven for years. I'll admit the car was a mistake. It was too conspicuous and it netted me the sort of attention ill favored by those in my line of work. I was more than ready to off-load the beast if a decent offer came along. I unlocked the door on the passenger side, opened the glove compartment, and removed my binoculars. I also hauled my briefcase from the backseat and checked to make sure my Heckler & Koch was still present and accounted for, along with an ample supply of ammunition. I didn't intend to shoot anyone, but I felt more secure knowing the weapon was close at hand. I moved both briefcase and gun to my trunk, which I locked (a wise decision, as it turned out).

I carried the binoculars to Henry's station wagon and set them on the floor near the driver's seat. In the backseat, I found the folded windshield screen Henry used to deflect the hot sun during protracted parking stints. Some weeks before, he'd cut holes in the cardboard so I could spy on a nasty customer I'd met on an earlier case. I put the cardboard screen on the floor on the passenger side.

Back in my studio, I sat down at my desk again and punched in the phone number for the green stucco house. The phone rang five times and then the machine picked up. A mechanical voice said, *"No one is here to receive your call. Please try again at a later time. Thank you."* Ned and Jean were apparently on vacation.

Humming, I made myself a peanut butter and pickle sandwich, which I cut on the diagonal, wrapped in waxed paper, and placed in a brown paper bag. I took a wash rag from the linen closet, wet it, and squeezed most of the moisture out, tucking it into a Ziploc storage bag that I placed in my shoulder bag. This was so I could tidy up after I ate. I'm ever so dainty when I'm out in the field. I was thrilled to discover that the Fritos I'd tucked in there earlier were more or less intact. I filled a thermos with hot coffee and set that beside my brown bag lunch. I found my clipboard and tucked a legal pad under the clip. Then I added two paperbacks, my denim jacket, my camera and film, a baseball cap, and a dark long-sleeve shirt to the pile. This was as much trouble as leaving town for a week.

I made a pit stop, knowing it might be hours before I'd have another opportunity. On the way back to Juniper Lane, I stopped at the market and picked up a bag of Pepperidge Farm cookies, Milanos being essential for surveillance work. Without them, I'd just end up feeling sorry for myself.

I parked on Santa Teresa Street, donned my baseball cap, locked the car, and did a quick survey of the neighborhood. I walked the long block northwest along Santa Teresa until it dead-ended into Orchard Road. Around that corner and two blocks to the left, Orchard intersected State Street. Where I stood, the street made a sweeping bend to the right, hugging the walled boundaries of a convent. By following the curve on foot, I reached the far end of Juniper Lane. I was looking for a spot that would allow me to keep the Tudor in my visual field without generating curiosity about my presence. The same strictures applied here as they had in Horton Ravine. Anyone sitting in a parked car for more than a few minutes generates uncomfortable questions. I walked along Juniper Lane, paying particular attention to the parking area provided by the absentee owner of the green stucco house. To the left of the garage, he'd carved out a space wide enough to accommodate a pickup truck or a recreational vehicle, neither of which were there. Instead, I was looking at a U of chicken-wire fence laden with morning glory vines.

I returned to my car, fired it up, and took a right on Santa Teresa Street, which I followed as far as Juniper Lane, turning right as I had a short time earlier. The question I asked myself was this: what would happen if I backed into this perfect spot and the owner returned? It seemed unlikely. As nearly as I could ascertain, the Dornans were out of town. He wasn't due at work until Monday, which didn't rule out the possibility that he'd show up early in order to enjoy a weekend at home. If so, how would I explain myself?

Clueless. I had no idea.

I pulled forward a good six feet beyond the spot and proceeded to back in, a maneuver that took a bit of doing since the station wagon felt like a boat and I wasn't familiar with the turning radius. I pulled forward again, lining myself up properly, and then eased backward as far as the fence, which shivered when my rear bumper made contact. I rolled down the window and then shut off the engine. I popped open the windshield screen and slid it into place. I was now sheltered between the fence on my right and the garage on my left. The cardboard screen cut the daylight by half, creating quite the cozy effect. I leaned forward over the steering wheel and peered the through holes in the cardboard at the Tudor across the way. The electrified wrought-iron gate was no more than fifty feet in front of me. I could see the entire facade of the house and a portion of the three-car garage. If Georgia Prestwick emerged in her Mercedes or in any other vehicle, I'd not only have a clear view, I'd be in position to follow if she turned in either direction. I checked my watch. It was 5:45. I picked up my clipboard and made a note of the time, which made me believe I was doing something worthwhile instead of wasting my time.

I'd brought along my index cards and I studied them as though preparing for a test. A week had passed since Audrey was arrested, jailed, and released on bail. If she were alive and kept to her routine, tomorrow would have been her Saturday in San Luis Obispo, doing whatever she did in that house with the crew that was ferried in by van. They had to have been clipping tags from stolen merchandise, maybe sorting and packing items for redistribution. Why else would so many people assemble and disassemble every other week? The system was probably designed so that Audrey's death, or the loss of any of the intermediaries, wouldn't cripple the operation. There had to be a backup plan in place, at least until someone could be found to fill her shoes and a new hierarchy could be established.

Audrey and Georgia had worked as a team and there were doubtless other sticky-fingered pairs also making the rounds. Somewhere along the line, there had to be a fence, as well as someone in charge of moving the goods. If I remembered correctly from my days in uniform and from what Maria said, certain items, like infant formula, beauty products, smoking-cessation patches, and diet supplements, would be shipped overseas to countries willing to pay inflated prices for such goods. Other items would be sold at swap meets and flea markets. I wondered what Georgia would be doing now that Audrey was out of the picture. I didn't believe the van would arrive at Audrey's this week as it had in the past. The house had been stripped and sanitized. All the fingerprints had been wiped clean, and I assumed Vivian Hewitt had changed the locks, which would put the place out of commission any which way you looked at it. A new location had probably been set up so the job could go on as before.

I finished my Fritos and ate a cookie to keep up my strength. Twenty minutes later, I poured myself some coffee from my thermos. I figured once it got dark, if my bladder required relief, I could slip out of the car, proceed to the vine-covered fence at the rear, and squat. In the meantime, I didn't dare turn on the radio or do anything else that might call attention to my hidey-hole. I picked up the first of the two paperback novels and read through the acknowledgments, hoping to come across the name of someone I knew. This was a first novel and the writer thanked a hundred people individually and profusely. I was already worried this was as good as the book was going to get.

Ordinarily, I'd have been thrilled with having the time to read, but I felt jumpy and tense. I set the paperback aside and ate my sandwich, well aware that I was running through my food supplies at too quick a pace. I took out my wet wash rag and wiped my hands. It wasn't even dark and I had hours to go. My plan was to follow Georgia if she left the house in the next five hours. If there was no activity, I'd wait until the house was dark and everyone was tucked in for the night, and then I'd go home for a few hours' sleep. I picked up my book again and turned to page 1.

I didn't realize I'd fallen asleep until a police officer tapped on my car window with his flashlight, which jump-started my heart and nearly made me wet my pants. The cardboard screen was still in place, blocking my windshield so I couldn't actually see out. I could hear the sound of a car idling and I assumed it was his patrol car. Around the edges of the cardboard screen, I could see flashes of red and blue, a Morse code of dots and dashes that spelled out *you-are-so-screwed*. I glanced at my watch and saw that it was just past midnight and pitch black outside. Except for the flashing lights, of course, which would probably alert everyone in the neighborhood that some kind of trouble was going down. I turned the key one notch in the ignition and lowered the window, saying, "Hi. How're you?"

"You're parked on private property. Are you aware of it?"

My mind was blank. How could I not be aware of it? I didn't live here. I flashed on my alternatives—telling lies, fibbing, making stuff up, or telling the truth—and decided on the latter. Under the circumstances, lying was only going to make life more complicated and I didn't want to risk it. "I'm a private investigator and I'm running a surveillance on the woman who lives in the house across the street."

He remained expressionless and kept his tone neutral. "Have you had anything to drink in the past two hours?"

"No, sir."

"No wine, beer, cocktails of any kind?"

"Honestly." I put my hand over my heart as though reciting the Pledge of Allegiance.

Unconvinced, he held up his flashlight, directing the beam into the backseat and the front, ostensibly looking for empty wine, beer, or whiskey bottles, weapons, illicit substances, or other evidence of bad behavior. I knew for a fact the flashlight was equipped to pick up traces of alcohol. Good luck to him. I had no outstanding wants or warrants, and if he insisted on a Breathalyzer test, I was going to blow a zero, which he must have realized when his tricky flashlight failed to detect even one particle of ethanol per gazillion. If he put me through a field sobriety test, I'd pass with flying colors unless he asked me to recite the alphabet backward. I've been meaning to practice that just in case, but so far I haven't gotten around to it.

"Ma'am, I'm going to have to ask you to step out of the car."

"Sure." I released the power locks and opened the car door. There was a second officer, standing in the street beside the patrol car, radio to his mouth, probably calling in the license plate number. Aside from my occasional (very minor) violations of the law, I consider myself a model citizen, easily intimidated by police officers when I know I'm in the wrong. I was guilty of trespassing and also in violation of municipal codes unknown to me, but very well known to the police. I was glad I hadn't added public urination to my list of sins. I was also glad I didn't have my handgun in my briefcase anywhere within range.

Once I was out of the car, the officer said, "Would you turn around and face forward, put your hands out, and lean against the car?"

He couldn't have been more polite. I did as instructed and was subjected to a brisk but thoroughly professional pat-down. I wanted to volunteer the fact that I had no weapon, but I knew that would sound suspicious when he was already on red alert. Stops like this can turn deadly without warning or provocation. For all he knew, I was a parolee in violation of section such-and-such. I might have been a fugitive with a felony warrant out against me.

"May I see your license and registration?"

"I'll have to reach into the glove compartment. Is that all right? My wallet's in my shoulder bag."

He gestured his assent. This was the second time in twenty-four hours I'd been asked to provide identification. I slid into the driver's seat and reached across to the glove compartment. Henry was meticulous about things of this sort, so I knew I could lay hands on the current paperwork, including proof of insurance. I found both and offered them to the officer. "The car belongs to my landlord," I said. "He's out of town and said I could drive the car in his absence to keep the battery from going dead." I didn't like talking to him from a seated position, but I wasn't keen to exit the car again unless instructed to do so. Here are some handy little tips for those of you who don't want to fall victim to deadly officer shootings: Do as you're told. Don't talk back. Don't be rude or belligerent. Don't try to escape. Don't get back in your car and try to run over the nice officer performing the traffic stop. If you should be so foolhardy as to attempt any of the above, don't complain later of your injuries and do not file suit.

I wanted to make sure he was watching me extract my wallet from my bag so he wouldn't think I was about to pull out a little two-shot Derringer. I removed my driver's license and a photocopy of my private investigator's license from my wallet and handed them to the officer. He read the information on both and gave me a look, which I took as a form of encouragement—all of us law-enforcement types being in this together. His name tag said P. MARTINEZ, though he didn't appear to be Hispanic. I wondered if *wondering* if he was Hispanic was a form of racism, but I thought not.

He walked over to the patrol car and conferred with the other officer. I took advantage of his absence to get out of the car again. The two walked back in my direction. Of course, there were no introductions. P. Martinez was tall and a bit on the hefty side, midforties, fully decked out in all the regulation paraphernalia: badge, belt, holstered gun, night stick, flashlight, keys, radio. He was a one-man army, prepared for just about anything. His partner, D. Charpentier, appeared to be in his fifties and similarly arrayed with an arsenal of crime-stopping gear. On a guy, there's something sexy about all that shit. On a female officer, it only creates the illusion of being overweight. It's amazing to me that any woman would volunteer for such a look.

Officer Martinez said, "You want to tell him what you just told me?"

"The long version or the short?"

"Take your time," he said.

"I'm running a surveillance on the woman across the street. Her name is Georgia Prestwick. Last Friday, I was a witness to a shoplifting incident at Nordstrom's that involved a woman named Audrey Vance, who's since gone off the Cold Spring Bridge. All of this must have come up at one of your briefings." I looked for a spark of recognition at the mention of Audrey's name, but both were too professional to display facial feedback. At least I had their full attention. "Audrey was taken into custody, though I'm sorry to say I don't know the name of the arresting officer. Georgia Prestwick was working with Audrey Vance, and she took advantage of the diversion to exit the store. I went after her and when she realized I was following her, she tried to run me down."

All of this sounded preposterous in summary, but I'd launched into the account and I thought I'd best continue.

Officer Charpentier still held my driver's license and copy of my PI license, and he seemed to make a study of both while I went on in this vein, dropping Maria Gutierrez's name into the mix in case either gentleman was acquainted with her.

Winding up, I said, "At any rate, I think Ms. Prestwick is tied to a larger organization. I hope you're not going to tell me she's the one who called 9-1-1."

The two officers exchanged a covert look, and I knew right then they'd read the article in the paper in which Diana Alvarez had bandied my name about. I may not have been drinking, but they had it on good authority that their fellow officer Len Priddy thought I was a crackpot.

Officer Martinez returned my two licenses. "No one called. We've been coming by twice a day, doing house checks for the property owner while he's out of town. My partner's the one who spotted you. Technically, we could cite you on the trespass, but we're going to let that one go as long as you move on."

"Thank you. I appreciate it."

I glanced at the facade of the Tudor across the street. There were no lights visible, but that didn't mean someone wasn't looking out an upstairs window, attracted by the flash of police lights that were lighting up the night like a mortar attack. It was going to look better anyway if I left as I'd been asked to do. If the Prestwicks were peeking out, let them think I was drunk or a vagrant living in my car. That's what our police presence is supposed to do, make our neighborhoods safe from the likes of me.

I got into my car. I removed the cardboard screen from the windshield and tossed it in the backseat. The two officers returned to their unit and got in, their two car doors slamming in quick succession. They waited until I pulled out and then followed me for a good eight blocks, assuring themselves that I wouldn't circle back and park where I had before. When they turned off, I waved and drove home. I couldn't believe cops were so distrustful.

# 18

# NORA

Channing arrived in Montebello Saturday afternoon. He'd called from Malibu ostensibly to let her know he was on his way. She suspected his true intention was to test the waters on the home front, angling to see if his cover had been blown. She'd made a point of being pleasant on the phone, playing the conversation at exactly the right pitch, her manner easy and light. Certainly, there was none of the tension and fury he must have anticipated. As the exchange went on, she could hear him relax, relief seeping into his tone. She glossed over the particulars of how she'd spent her Wednesday afternoon, laying in just enough detail to make it convincing. She knew how anxious he'd be to avoid discovery. His feelings for Thelma were running high and he'd be determined to hold on to her. Eventually, he'd tire of her, but for now his affair provided all the thrills and suspense of a spy novel.

Nora heard his tires crunching in the gravel courtyard. She went downstairs, breathing deeply, like an actress getting into her role.

Wednesday night was accounted for. The symphony had run ninety minutes. Afterward, she and Belinda and Nan had a bite to eat at a bistro across the street. Nora had picked up the check so Channing could see it for himself when the Visa bill came in. Lest he harbor any doubt, she'd tossed her concert program on the kitchen counter as though by oversight. Now all she had to do was explain the missing clothes.

Channing came into the kitchen from the garage, where he'd parked his car. He'd stopped at the mailbox and picked up the day's delivery, so he was already separating the magazines from the catalogs. He put both stacks on the kitchen counter and glanced at the program in passing. "Mahler's Sixth. I didn't know you were a fan."

Nora smiled as she lifted her face so he could kiss her cheek. "Nan's idea. She read a biography that suggested he stole the melodic line from a piano duet by Weber. There was also this whole big brouhaha about whether the scherzo should precede or follow the andante. I know it sounds tedious, but it was fun knowing what went on behind the scenes."

"I'm glad you enjoyed it."

"I did. Very much so. Sissy and Jess were there, but I didn't have a chance to talk to either one of them. What about you? How was your evening?"

"I changed my mind about going. When it came right down to it, I wasn't in the mood."

"Really? You seemed so set on being there."

"I had a hard day at work and I couldn't bear the idea of getting into a tux. On the way home, I stopped at Tony's and picked up an order of ribs."

"Bad boy. If I'd known you were going to play hooky, I'd have made a point of joining you. What happened to your table for ten?"

"I guess there were two empty seats instead of one."

She smiled. "Oh, well. The money went for a good cause so I suppose it doesn't matter."

"We have something on for tonight?"

"Dinner with the Hellers at Nine Palms."

"What time?"

"Six thirty for drinks. Dinner reservation's at seven, but Mitchell said he'd seat us whenever we were ready."

"Good. Sounds like fun."

Nora took the teakettle from the stove and carried it to the sink, filling it from the filtered-water tap. "Did you notice all my formal wear was gone?"

She could see the caution rise in him. "I just got here."

"Not here. Malibu."

He opened a piece of mail and glanced at the contents. "Went right by me," he said. "What's the story?"

"I had Mrs. Stumbo drive down Wednesday and bring everything back. I would have called to tell you, but I'd talked to you once and I didn't want to bother you again."

"You're not a bother when you call."

"Thank you. That's sweet, but I don't like being a pest when it's not important. At any rate, when I realized I wouldn't be coming down last week, I asked her to take care of it. She dropped the whole carload at the cleaners so at least that's out of the way."

"I don't understand. Did I miss something here?"

"Spring cleaning. A closet purge. I've had some of those gowns for years, and half of them don't fit. I'll keep the best ones, and any I don't want I'll donate to the Fashion Institute."

She put the kettle on the stove and turned on the burner. "Would you like a cup of tea?"

"I'm fine. What if an occasion comes up?"

"I guess I'll just have to go shopping. You know what a chore that is," she said, smiling.

"Might require a trip to New York," he said, matching her tone.

"Exactly."

. . .

Dinner at the club was pleasant. The place had an old-fashioned fusty air about it, like the home of a rich maiden aunt. The once grand furniture was upholstered in a peach brocade that had seen better days. The couches and chairs were arranged in conversational groupings. Some of the cushions were lumpy and the arms were frayed in places, but an upgrade would require a membership assessment, which would set off endless disagreements and endless complaints. The club was largely given over to couples in their seventies and eighties, whose homes had appreciated in value while their retirement income had dwindled, subject to the whims of the economy. The so-called younger members were in their fifties and sixties, better off financially perhaps but destined for the same fate. Old friends would start dropping off one by one and in the end, they'd be grateful to spend an evening with the few tottering acquaintances who were left.

Robert and Gretchen were their usual ten minutes late. The delay was so consistent, she wondered why they couldn't manage to be on time. The four of them hadn't seen one another since the Christmas holidays, so they caught up over drinks. Their relationship was amicable but superficial. All four were ardent Republicans, which meant any talk of politics was quickly addressed as they were all in agreement. Nora had met the Hellers in Los Angeles shortly before she and Channing were married. Robert was a plastic surgeon who'd been felled by a heart attack ten years earlier. He was fifty-two at the time, and from that point on had cut his practice back to two days a week. Gretchen was his first and only wife, also in her early sixties, but with the years artfully erased. She had big green eyes, white-blond hair, and flawless skin. Her boobs were fake, but not conspicuously so.

The Hellers were the first to buy in Montebello—a six-thousand-square-foot French Normandy house at Nine Palms, which in addition to the golf course offered one-acre parcels in a gated community with like-minded souls. Robert was a dumpling of a man, half a head shorter than Gretchen, bald, and apple-shaped. The two so plainly adored each other that Nora was often envious. Tonight she was especially grateful for their company because it kept the flow of conversation light and inconsequential. Nora managed to remain gracious while keeping her distance from her husband. At moments, she saw his gaze settle on her quizzically, as though he sensed the difference in her without being able to put his finger on it. She knew he wouldn't ask for fear she'd tell him something he didn't want to know.

They moved from drinks in the parlor to the dining room where they ordered their second round of drinks, menus open in front of them. There was a set selection of entrées at surprisingly reasonable prices. Where else could you order Salisbury steak or beef Stroganoff for $7.95, with a salad and two sides? These were foods from the 1950s, nothing trendy, spicy, or ethnic. Nora was debating between the pan-seared petrale sole and the roast chicken and mashed potatoes when Gretchen leaned toward Robert and placed a hand on his sleeve. "Oh my god. You won't believe who just walked in."

Nora was sitting with her back to the entrance so she had no idea who Gretchen was referring to. Robert glanced discreetly to the side and said, "Shit."

Two men passed the table in the wake of the maître d' who was leading the way. The first Nora knew by sight though she didn't remember his name. The second was Lorenzo Dante. She dropped her gaze, feeling the warmth rise to her cheeks. Despite his claim he might be there, he was the last person in the world she had actually expected to see at Nine Palms. She'd put the meeting with him out of her mind, refusing to think about the awkward transaction with the ring. She'd returned the ring to her jewelry box, wishing she hadn't been so adamant in her refusal of the seventy-five thousand dollars. She should have taken it.

Nora leaned forward. "Who is he?"

Under her breath, Gretchen said, "Lorenzo Dante's son. They call him Dante." Then she mouthed, "He's Mafia."

Robert picked up on the comment and responded with impatience. "Good god, Gretchen. He's not Mafia. Where did you get that idea?"

"The equivalent," she said. "You told me so yourself."

"I did no such thing. I said I did business with him once upon a time. I said he was a tough customer."

"You said worse than that and you know it," she replied.

The maître d' seated the two men at a corner table, and Nora found Dante facing her, visible just over Channing's shoulder. The juxtaposition was an odd one, Channing's slim elegance in contrast to Dante's more substantial build. Channing's hair was white, clipped close on the sides with a short rough on top. His brows were almost invisible and his face was narrow. Dante was silver-haired and his complexion was a warmer tone. Dark brows, gray mustache, deeply dimpled cheeks. With his features lined up against Channing's, she could see how pinched her husband looked. Maybe the strain of his secret life was taking its toll. Nora had always thought Channing was good-looking, but she wondered about that now. His face was drained of color and he looked like he'd lost weight. The waiter appeared at the table and they ordered their meal and a bottle of Kistler Chardonnay.

She felt herself detach, a state that was becoming all too frequent with her of late. Whatever Robert's business with Dante, he clearly didn't want to talk about it now. Gretchen would have enlightened her, given half a chance. In their social set, gossip was a sport. There was no "fact of the matter," only rumor and innuendo. Points were awarded for anything juicy, regardless of the truth content. This was what she knew of Dante, that he'd come to her defense. This was what she also knew, that he'd offered her a way out.

She tuned in to Robert's conversation with Channing and heard him propose lunch and a round of golf.

"You have a tee time?"

"Don't need one on Sundays. The course won't be crowded. We can walk on anytime we like."

Channing caught Nora's eye. "Is that okay with you?"

"Fine."

The talk shifted to Robert's last round of golf. He'd played Pebble Beach the weekend before, and the two men discussed the course. Neither she nor Gretchen played golf, which meant the two men could hold forth while nothing was expected of them. The salads arrived and the topic of conversation shifted again, this time to the cruise to the Far East the Hellers were taking at the end of June. They compared notes about cruise lines, and Nora was able to keep up her end of the conversation without effort. Once she disconnected, everything was so much easier.

Channing poured her another glass of wine. He smiled when their eyes met, but there was no emotional content. She missed the early days of their romance. Thelma was now the recipient of all that she had cherished in him. If she were honest about it, she'd acknowledge how little of herself she'd given Channing in the past few years. The disconnect wasn't the direct result of his affair, it was habitual to her.

The petrale sole turned out to be a mistake. White and flavorless, lying in a pool of butter. Nora picked her way through the meal, and in the lull between the entrée and dessert, she excused herself and headed for the ladies' lounge. She went about her business, ran a comb through her hair, reapplied her lipstick. She'd felt so clever disguising her feelings from Channing, making sure he had no inkling of where she was or what she knew. But in pretending not to care, she'd actually ceased to care. Reviving her old feelings for him seemed to be out of her control.

As she emerged from the ladies' lounge, she saw Dante coming down the corridor. She felt a jolt—tension or apprehension, she wasn't sure which. He wore a pale gray suit and a dark gray dress shirt with a black tie. The combination gave him the look of a gangster, which he was either unaware of or didn't care to hide. She knew he'd timed his leaving the table to coincide with her return.

She said, "What are you doing here?" Somehow the question seemed accusatory, which wasn't her intent.

"I told you I'd be here. I'm having dinner with a friend."

"I thought you were just making conversation."

"I was. You left the office, I decided I better have a look at the guy lucky enough to be married to you. I don't think he appreciates what he has."

She dropped her gaze. "I have to get back."

"Why don't you have a drink with me tomorrow, just the two of us?"

"I don't drink."

"You had wine with dinner. We should talk."

"About what?"

"How you ended up married to a bum."

"He's not a bum."

"Yes, he is. You just haven't seen it yet. I know his type. He looks good on the surface, but underneath, he's a royal shit."

Nora felt the heat rise in her cheeks. "My friend says you're Mafia."

He smiled. "Flattering, but false. I'm connected in other ways."

"You're a thug."

He smiled. "Now you've got it. A bona fide badass," he said. "Give me an hour of your time tomorrow. That's not too much to ask."

"I can't."

"There's a place out on State Street called Down the Hatch. You can look it up in the phone book. It's a dive. You won't see anyone you know."

"Channing and I have plans."

"So cancel 'em. One o'clock. The place will be deserted."

"Why would I agree?"

"I want to sit someplace quiet and dark so I can look at you."

"That's not a good idea."

"I'd say lunch, but then you'd think it was a date and that, I know, you'd refuse."

"No, thank you."

"Think about it."

She started to protest and he put a finger on her lips. His touch was brief but startlingly intimate. "Excuse me," she said and moved away.

When Nora returned to the table, Channing was talking about leg-hold traps. She was confused that such a subject had come up. As she took her seat, she said, "Leg-hold traps? Where did that come from?"

Gretchen said, "Your gardener's complaining about the coyotes."

Nora realized Mr. Ishiguro had told Channing about the coyote scat he'd showed her Wednesday when she was at the house. Since she'd told him she'd sent Mrs. Stumbo, she had to play dumb. Even if Mr. Ishiguro had mentioned her being there, his English was so fractured that Channing wouldn't get the reference. "What about the coyotes?" she asked.

Channing's gesture was impatient. "They've invaded the property. They're crapping everywhere. Mr. Ishiguro says he's seen the male leap that six-foot wall between us and the Fergusons'. Karen's two cats disappeared this past week. I told you about that."

"She shouldn't have left them out. You said yourself how irresponsible it was."

"You're missing the point. They're getting bolder by the minute. Once they lose their fear of humans, they're really dangerous. Mr. Ishiguro suggested traps and I said fine."

"Why would you let him use leg-hold traps? Those are horrible. They can snap an animal's leg in two. If the poor things don't bleed to death, they're in excruciating pain. Why would you agree to something so barbaric? Those coyotes have never bothered us."

"They're predators. They'll eat anything. Birds, garbage, carrion. You name it."

Gretchen said, "I'll tell you something gruesome. A friend of ours had her little shih tzu dragged off and eviscerated. She was standing right there. The poor dog all bloody and screaming. She said it was the worst thing that's ever happened to her. She went out and bought a shotgun and she keeps it by the back door. She won't go out in the yard now unless she's armed."

"That's ridiculous," Nora said.

Gretchen said, "I beg to differ. Even where we are, you can hear them howling after dark. Sounds like a pack of wild Indians about to attack. It gives me the willies."

"I better keep my pistol loaded," Channing said with a smile. "If the traps don't work, I can pick them off from the deck."

"You have a *pistol*?" Gretchen asked.

"Of course."

"Well, aren't you the wily one. I had no idea."

"Stop it," Nora snapped. "If that man sets leg-hold traps, I'm firing him."

"Well, you better be quick about it. He picked the traps up yesterday and he's using chicken carcasses for bait."

"Won't work," Robert said. "They're too smart. Even the faintest whiff of humans, a coyote won't come anywhere close."

Nora snatched her bag and got up. "I'm going out to the car. You want to talk about this shit, you can do it without me."

On the way home, Channing made an attempt to jolly her out of her mood. "It was a joke," he said.

"There's nothing funny about suffering."

"What's wrong with you?"

"Jesus, Channing, nothing's *wrong*. Coyotes were here long before we were. We're the ones encroaching on their territory, not the other way around. Why don't you just leave them in peace?"

"So now you're an environmentalist?"

"Don't be snide. It's unbecoming."

"Well, you don't have to sound so fucking righteous. I mean, give me a break."

"Don't push it off on me."

"Fine. I'm just telling you the Hellers were offended you made such a scene."

She leaned her head back against the seat. "Who cares about them?"

"What do you care about?"

"I've lost track."

They made love that night, which was strange, given the strain between them. She initiated the sex, fueled by fury and despair. The reality of Channing with Thelma was like a dark aphrodisiac. If the woman was competition, then let her compete with this. She straddled him, pounding away as though riding him until the pleasure peaked between them, harsh and raw. He flipped her over on her back, dragging her to the edge of the bed and lifting her hips while he drove into her again, his legs braced. There was a barely suppressed violence in the encounter, something savage in the way they went at each other, and if what she felt wasn't love, at least it was a feeling of *some* kind, intense and immediate.

Afterward, they lay together, winded, and when he turned his head and looked at her, she knew he was present. In his face, she could see the Channing she'd loved once upon a time, the Channing who'd loved her even while her heart was broken and she was half dead, emotion drained out of her, leaving only dust. She felt tears welling and she turned over onto her side so he couldn't see her face. She might have regained her composure if he hadn't seemed so kind. He said, "Are you okay?"

She shook her head. She turned onto her back and covered her eyes, feeling the tears seep into her hair. There was no holding back. She felt herself dissolve, and she wept as she had as a child when pain and disappointment were at their sharpest. She wept as she had as an adult when she'd been dealt a blow so bitter there was no coming back. She allowed him to comfort her, which she hadn't done in months. She remembered how sweet he'd been and how patient. "Oh, god. It all seems so hopeless," she said. She tucked the sheet under her arms and pulled herself up into a sitting position, her arms wrapped around her knees.

"Not so. Not hopeless at all."

He stroked her hair, which was tangled and wet from tears and from the sweat of their lovemaking.

She reached over to snatch a tissue from the bed table and blew her nose. "Don't look at me. I'm hideous. My face is all swollen and my eyes feel like ping-pong balls."

His smile was lazy in the half-light shining in from the street. "Where have you been? I've missed you."

"I know I've been distant, but sometimes I can't help myself. It's just so much easier to zone out and shut down."

"But you always come back to me. I look up and there you are," he said. "Come here." He opened his arms and she stretched out beside him, tucked into the crook of his shoulder. He was a spare man, narrow through the chest, and his skin felt two degrees cooler than hers. He smelled of sex and sweat and something sweet.

She spoke into the hollow of his throat. "What about you, Channing? Where have you been?"

"No place important. Go to sleep."

# 19

Saturday morning, 6:00 A.M., I was back at my post. I'd managed four hours of sleep, after which I showered, dressed, and headed to the upper east side of town. En route, I stopped at McDonald's and picked up a large coffee, an orange juice, and an Egg McMuffin. Before long, the coffee and OJ would send me in search of a public restroom, but I had to risk it for the moment. In times past, during surveillance work, I've used a tennis ball can for urinary emergencies. This was unsatisfactory. For women, strategy is problematic when it comes to body functions. Aim and positioning are more art than science, and I'd been wondering, of late, if a Rubbermaid food container wouldn't be superior. Wide mouth, with an airtight lid. I was still running the pros and cons on the notion.

When I pulled around the corner onto Juniper Lane, I parked on the same side of the street as the Prestwicks' mock Tudor house. I stationed myself fifty feet away from the driveway, which kept me just outside their visual range. Or such was my hope. It was still dark out and as I settled in to wait, I saw headlights swing around the corner from Santa Teresa Street. A car approached, moving at a crawl. I slouched down on my spine, peering out at the street under the lower edge of the screen. Even with the screen in place, I knew I'd be visible if someone passing turned to look directly at me.

I saw a newspaper fly out of the car window. I heard a *thwop* when it landed and then the car moved on. At the next house down, a second paper sailed out and into the yard. When the driver turned the corner at the end of the block, I got out and scurried around the side of the green stucco house. I plucked a plastic-wrapped newspaper from the steps and scurried back. In the car again, I removed the plastic sleeve and placed it on the passenger seat beside my camera and my clipboard. I made a note of the time in the interest of record keeping. There was no real imperative for me to do so. In theory, I was working off the hours Marvin had paid for, but he'd told me I could use the time any way that suited me without accounting to him. At this point, I was in it for the pleasure of the game, though I couldn't afford to do so indefinitely. I had a business to run and bills to pay, matters I wasn't at liberty to ignore.

When it was light out, I read the paper, occasionally peering through the holes Henry'd cut in the screen. Not that there was anything to see. I searched for a Diana Alvarez byline, but she'd apparently fired off her best shot. There were already six letters to the editor commenting on the subject of the proposed suicide barrier, half in favor and half against. Everybody was indignant about the opinions and points of view that didn't line up with their own.

For the next three hours, I watched the neighborhood come to life. A jogger trotted into view on Santa Teresa Street, moving left to right. Three women walked their dogs, moving in the opposite direction. Two guys bicycled past in skintight bicycle shorts and what were surely shaved legs. It served no purpose to think about how bored I was. I went through my index cards, which I'd just about memorized.

Surveillance is not for the fainthearted or for those dependent on external stimulation.

For a brief period, I filled in what I could of the crossword puzzle in the local paper, a version Henry disdains as too simpleminded. He likes thorny puzzles based on common sayings spelled backward, or puzzles where all the answers have a tricky common link—birds of a feather, for instance, or famous last words. I got stuck on 2 Down: "Patron deity of Ur." What kind of person knows shit like that? It made me feel dumb and uninformed.

Idly, I registered a shriek of metal on metal and when I looked up, I realized the Prestwicks' front gate was sliding open. The black Mercedes eased out of the driveway and into the street. I squinted through the hole in the cardboard screen and caught a flash of blond as the driver turned right. Mother or daughter, I wasn't sure which. As she slowed at the corner and took a second right onto Santa Teresa Street, I turned the key in the ignition. I snatched the screen off the windshield and tossed it over the seat. I headed after her at a modest rate of speed, hoping not to call attention to myself.

At the corner, I nosed the station wagon forward and caught the dull red glow of two taillights a block down on my right. She'd reached the T at Orchard Road and stopped for two cars that were speeding around the bend. She turned left toward State Street. I gunned it to the end of the block and took the same left she had. The Mercedes waited at the four-way stop, allowing cross traffic to pass. She turned right. I goosed it again and reached the four-way stop moments after she had. I turned right, straining for sight of her.

This end of State Street became livelier as it bore west. After a string of apartment buildings and condominiums, the area was given over to small storefront businesses. At the next light, a supermarket on the left anchored a strip mall that didn't have much else to recommend it. In another three blocks, I'd pass Down the Hatch, where I'd met Marvin three nights before.

I expected the Mercedes to keep moving, but her left-hand turn signal began to blink. When the light changed, she turned onto the side street that bordered the supermarket parking lot. Commercial establishments in this part of town seemed to go from "Grand Opening" to "Liquidation Sale, Everything Must Go" without much in between. I kept well back as I followed her into the parking lot. She proceeded to the far aisle and came to a stop in front of a large metal donation bin, painted white with an oversize heart outlined in red. The lid of her Mercedes trunk popped up.

I reached for my camera, focused, and started clicking off pictures. I captured her image as she got out and left the car idling while she went around to the rear. I was happy to note this was Georgia and not her daughter. She hauled out two bulging black plastic garbage bags and dumped them in the bin. She must have done a closet cleaning, which I was due for myself. She slid back under the steering wheel and circled the parking lot until she found a spot. She went into the supermarket without a backward glance. I set my camera aside. I didn't believe her actions were crime related, but it's good to be alert and even better to keep in practice.

I found a parking spot two aisles away, locked my car, and followed her into the store. It was a sunny Saturday morning, and I figured I had just as much right as she did to go grocery shopping. She had no reason to think she'd run into me. Having bested me, she'd probably dismissed me from memory. The store was crowded and there were any number of areas where I could loiter if necessary, casually reading the nutritional content of whatever foodstuffs were close by. I walked the width of the store, glancing down each aisle in turn. By the time I saw Georgia, she was in the produce department, squeezing avocados. I left the store by the nearest exit. It was just shy of 10:00, so the other stores in the mall were still closed.

A few minutes later, she emerged with her cart. I turned and made an earnest study of the nearest storefront, which turned out to be Santa Teresa Prosthetics and Orthotics. There wasn't much to see as (perhaps) the owners had thought better of creating a window display made up entirely of false feet. Out of the corner of my eye, I watched Georgia load groceries into her car. While her attention was occupied, I returned to the station wagon. I was hoping I wouldn't have to trail after her for an entire roster of Saturday chores. I was willing to tag along, but even a vehicle as nondescript as Henry's would warrant notice with repeated sightings.

She pulled out of the lot and turned left on State Street, moving toward the La Cuesta Shopping Plaza. I felt my interest perk up, thinking she might go into Robinson's and launch a madcap shoplifting spree. Instead, she drove into the mall parking lot along the back side of a row of shops and pulled up to another white donation bin that bore a big heart outlined in red. The lot was filling rapidly and I pulled into the nearest available spot within range of her. I reached for my camera and snapped photos of her as she popped open her trunk, walked around to the rear, and removed two more bulging black garbage bags that she dropped into the bin. Whatever the name of the charity, the bins were identical, and I couldn't figure out why she needed two. Surely there wasn't a limit on how much used clothing one could contribute at one time. I waited while she returned to her car and pulled out of the lot. I was more interested in what she'd dumped than where she intended to go next.

The minute she was out of sight, I grabbed my camera and proceeded to the bin. HELPING HEARTS, HEALING HANDS was written in curlicue letters around the border of the heart. I took two photographs of the logo. No address and no phone number. There wasn't even a disclaimer forbidding idlers from helping themselves to all the secondhand shoes, clothing, and assorted household items. I was on the verge of lifting the lid so I could see what was in the plastic bags when a white panel truck approached and pulled up at the curb. HELPING HEARTS, HEALING HANDS was writ large on the side.

Casually, I moved away from the bin and walked toward the entrance to the mall. I resisted the urge to turn around to see what was going on behind me. I rounded the corner into one of the side avenues and then peered back at the panel truck. The driver had propped up the bin's lid with one hand while he removed first one and then the other garbage bag and set them on the walk beside him. He dropped the lid with a bang and carried both bags to the back of his truck. He tossed them in and slammed the rear doors. I withdrew from his line of sight. Shortly after that, I heard the driver's-side door slam shut with a muted bang.

I kept my camera at the ready, and when the truck crossed my line of vision, moving toward the exit, I stepped out onto the walkway and took pictures of the back end. There was no license plate. I made a beeline for my car, but by the time I started the engine and pulled out, the panel truck had merged with passing traffic and disappeared.

I doubted the charity was legitimate. The name itself was so saccharine, it almost had to be a cover for a racket of some kind. At least it gave me a lead. In California, any organization claiming nonprofit status has to file articles of incorporation, listing the corporation's address, the name and address of a "registered agent," and the names of the directors. This was all part of the public record, available to anyone. I closed my eyes and patted my chest, mimicking a heartbeat. How much better could it get? One quick moment of payoff for all the hours I'd put in.

If I was right, Georgia's job was to collect stolen merchandise and drop the goods in donation bins for retrieval by her cohorts. Audrey's landlady had mentioned the presence of a white panel truck on the occasions when Audrey was staying in her little rented house. I was guessing the driver was responsible for collecting the bags and delivering them to San Luis Obispo. In the past, Audrey had worked every other weekend. Her death had doubtless disrupted the routine, but maybe the gang was back in the swing and ready to carry on. It was possible my conclusion was wrong, but I couldn't think of another explanation that made quite as much sense. I put my surveillance on hold. I'd have to test my suspicions, but meanwhile, I didn't want my cover blown.

I drove back into town and made another stop at the public library and proceeded to the reference department, where I checked both the current phone book and the current city directory for Helping Hearts, Healing Hands. No listing under "Charities." Nothing under "Social Service Organizations," "Women's Shelters," "Churches," or "Rescue Missions." I wasn't surprised. I had other avenues to explore, but this was Saturday morning, which meant that all the usual sources—the Hall of Records, the courthouse, the tax assessor's office—would be closed. I'd be back in business Monday morning, but for now I was out of luck.

On the way home, I did a supermarket run for essentials and then spent a few minutes putting groceries away. I started a load of laundry and would have gone on in this thrilling vein—scrubbing toilets, vacuuming—if not for the ringing of my telephone. I picked up and found Vivian Hewitt on the line.

I said, "Hey, Vivian. How are you?"

"I'm fine, thanks. I hope you don't mind my calling you at home, but something's come up. Did I catch you at a bad time?"

"Not at all. What's happening?"

"I did something I shouldn't have and now I don't know how to make it right."

"Wow, I'm all ears," I said.

"You're going to think I'm awful."

"Would you just get on with it?"

"I will, but you won't like it."

"Vivian . . ."

"Friday morning, Rafe left on a fishing trip and he won't be back until Sunday night."

"I see."

"I'm just telling you why he's not here to help me sort this out. Yesterday when I went over to Audrey's to meet the locksmith, a delivery truck pulled in. Someone overnighted a package to Audrey and the driver needed a signature. When I said she wasn't there, he asked if I'd sign for it and I agreed."

I said, "Ah."

"I don't know what got into me. It was one of those situations where an opportunity presented itself and I took advantage. Now I'm thinking what I did was wrong."

"You know, I'm not exactly the person to consult when it comes to tricky ethical issues. I'd have done the same thing in your shoes."

"But what am I supposed to do now? I feel so guilty. Rafe would have a fit if he knew."

"It's no big deal. Why don't you call the company and tell them you made a mistake? Have them come pick up the package and return it to the sender."

"I thought of that myself. The problem is I didn't pay attention to the name of the courier so I have no idea who to call."

"Isn't there a label that gives the name?"

"Nothing," she said.

"What about the locksmith? You think he'd remember?"

"He was changing the lock on the back door, so he didn't see the truck."

"Did you look in the yellow pages?"

"I did, but none of the names looked familiar. That's the reason I called. I could open the package, but I didn't want to do anything without talking to you first in case you wanted to be on hand."

"Go ahead and open it. There's no point in my driving up if it's trivial. Are we talking about a box or a padded envelope?"

"A box, a big one, and sealed with so much packing tape it might as well be waterproof. Hold on a minute. I'm putting the phone down so I can tackle this. I can't tell you how relieved I am you didn't condemn what I did."

"I'm happy to offer absolution if it makes you feel better," I said.

I listened to a stretch of Vivian breathing and making remarks to herself, a running account of her progress, accompanied by the sound of paper tearing. "Okay, got the wrapping off. Oh, rats. The box is taped shut around the edges. Let me get a kitchen knife."

A silence while she labored and then she said, "Oh."

"'Oh,' meaning what?"

"I've never seen so much cash in my life."

"I'll be right there."

I pushed the speed limit and an hour and a half later, I rang the bell and she opened the door, her face pale and drawn. She peered at the street behind me and hurried me in. She closed the door and leaned her back against it, saying, "Things just got worse."

"What now?"

She moved to the living room windows and lowered the shades. "After we hung up, I assembled my embroidery supplies. I have my stitching group at three and my cousin is picking me up a few minutes before. I wanted to have everything ready."

I made a rolling gesture with one hand, hoping she'd get to the point.

"Next thing I knew, someone knocked on my door."

"Why am I thinking *Uh-oh*? Was this the courier?"

She shook her head. "He didn't say so, but he implied he was. He said a package had been delivered erroneously and he'd come to pick it up."

"Erroneously? He actually said that?"

"He did and it seemed like an odd choice of words. Aside from the fact he wasn't wearing a uniform, I couldn't see handing over all that cash to a man I'd never laid eyes on. It didn't seem right."

"So far, so good. I can't wait to hear what you did."

"I told him I didn't have it. I said I notified the company a package was delivered to the wrong address and they picked it up half an hour before."

"And he believed you?"

"I suppose. He didn't seem happy, but there wasn't much he could do."

"Ah. So he didn't know you'd opened it."

"He might have. The box was sitting right there."

I looked over at the dining room table, which was clearly visible from where I stood. She'd placed the lid upside down on the box to conceal the cash, but the wrapping paper was in plain sight. I crossed to the table and set the lid to one side. I stared at the money with the same admiration and disbelief she'd expressed on the phone. I nudged the brown paper wrapping, turning it over with the kitchen knife she'd used to cut the tape. The return address was a post office box in Santa Monica. I copied the number into my notebook and returned to a study of the cash. "How much do you think we're looking at?"

"No telling, but I don't think we should touch anything."

"Hey, I'm with you. I don't want my fingerprints showing up on this thing. Bad enough you handled the package before we knew what it was."

The box was roughly twelve by twelve by twelve, packed with bundles of bills, the uppermost of which were hundreds.

Vivian said, "What do you think we should do?"

"Turn it over to the police."

"And say what? Isn't it against the law to intercept someone else's mail?"

"Good point. It's federal. I've done it lots of times but never netted anything like this. On the other hand, anyone who claimed the cash would have some serious explaining to do."

"What about me? I can't claim I just happened to come across it on Audrey's porch, because the driver knows I signed for it and he put it in my hands."

"You'll just have to level with them."

"*I* will? Why not you?"

"Look at the logic here. Audrey's dead. You're her landlady, so it's not out of line for you to pick up her mail, especially when you know she was charged with a crime. Isn't that why you took the package in the first place?"

"Sort of. It was an impulse—a bad one, as I'd be the first to admit."

"You did them a service. The police can use the return address to trace the package back to its origin."

"This is making me nervous. I still don't see why you can't take care of it."

"Nope. Don't think so," I said.

I was already picturing myself showing up in Cheney Phillips's office with the contraband cash, which was most assuredly connected to Audrey's shoplifting, which meant that Len Priddy would be apprised of it, which meant I'd be subject to the scrutiny of a man who didn't like me to begin with. At the same time, withholding evidence of this magnitude probably constituted a crime far worse than mail tampering.

"What other options do we have?" she asked.

"Beats the hell out of me," I said. "Situations like this, it's better to do what's right and take the heat. I'm not going to haul the money home and hide it under my bed."

"I don't suppose you could handle it without bringing my name into it. I don't want Rafe to find out."

"Sorry."

"Well, shit," she said, which seemed so out of character I laughed.

We took my car since Rafe had taken theirs. The only compromise I could think of was to deliver the cash to the San Luis Obispo County Sheriff's Department instead of the city police. This had certain built-in advantages. The sheriff's department and the Santa Teresa Police Department were separate jurisdictions. With luck, it would take time for one law-enforcement agency to communicate with the other. I didn't think there was any rivalry between the two, but there was probably a pecking order and the usual bureaucratic bullshit standing in the way. The longer it took for Len Priddy to get wind of the cash, the happier I'd be.

We said little on the drive over, each of us contemplating the possible repercussions—she from Rafe and I from Sergeant Priddy. We presented ourselves as model citizens, the equivalent of Good Samaritans turning in a wallet full of money found on the street. The deputy at the desk made a phone call and the matter was redirected to a Sergeant Detective Turner, who came out to the counter. We signed in and were given self-adhesive passes that we stuck to our shirts. He escorted us through the inner offices to his cubicle. Once seated, I launched into an explanation of how we'd come by the cash. Vivian nodded frequently but managed to remain silent, lest anything she said could and would be used against her in a court of law.

Once I got into the spirit of the tale, I was even so forthcoming as to fill them in on Audrey's arrest and subsequent death leap. I made no mention of Sergeant Priddy as the detective investigating the shoplifting incident. They could figure that out for themselves. I did explain Marvin's hiring me and my enlisting Vivian's assistance in searching Audrey's place. We did a bit of hand-waving when it came to the issue of how she'd ended up with the package, though it actually made perfect sense. If the cash was connected to a criminal enterprise, better to turn it over to the authorities than see it fall into the wrong hands. Even the investigator we spoke to didn't seem to think we'd done anything wrong. If we were dishonest, we could have filled our own coffers and no one would have been the wiser.

It occurred to me to suggest Sergeant Detective Turner count the cash before we let it out of our sight, but I didn't want to insult the man. Since we were busy persuading him of our honorable intentions, it didn't seem wise to question his. The package was booked into evidence and whisked away to Property, where it would sit on a shelf until somebody decided what to do next.

When we finally left the station and drove back to Vivian's house, we were feeling sweaty with guilt even though what we'd done was honest and aboveboard. It was 2:00 by then, and I was eager to hit the road. I followed her to the kitchen, where she filled an electric kettle with water and plugged it in.

"Thank goodness that's over with. Do you have time to join me in a cup of tea?"

"I should be getting back. Would you mind if I took a quick look at your phone book?"

She removed the phone book from a kitchen drawer close to the wall-mounted phone. "What are you looking for?"

"A charity called Helping Hearts, Healing Hands. Ever heard of it?"

"Doesn't ring a bell."

I started with the yellow pages, checking for social service agencies. I tried the white pages as well and bombed out on both. "They've got a couple of donation bins in Santa Teresa, but the organization isn't listed. I thought it might be headquartered here."

"What's the relevance to Audrey?"

"Sorry. I should have brought you up to speed." I told her how I'd identified Georgia Prestwick and ended up following her that morning. The story was almost as long and boring as the surveillance itself. "I remembered your mentioning a white panel truck parked next door on the nights Audrey worked late."

"Absolutely. It was always there when she was in town."

"If you see it again would you let me know? I snapped a couple of photos as it was speeding away. I also took a shot of the logo on the bin. Once I get the film developed, I'll let you take a look. It would be great if you recognized either one."

It was 2:20 when I finally turned onto the southbound 101. I maintained a sedate sixty miles an hour. It was a gorgeous afternoon with perfect road conditions, and I used the drive time to assess my discoveries to date. I was happy with the progress I'd made. I wasn't certain how Marvin would feel or whether he'd be willing to underwrite my continued investigation. I'd have to have a long chat with him before I did anything else.

As is so often the case in life, I pictured myself in a holding pattern, like an airplane circling a field. I knew where I'd been and I had a sense of where I'd land. All I needed was clearance from the tower. In hindsight, I see how complacent I was, lulled by a feeling of accomplishment. If I'd been alert and kept an eye on the rearview mirror, I might have spotted the pale blue sedan that had fallen in behind me as I left Vivian's house.

# 20

I left the freeway at Capillo and kept to surface streets as I worked my way through town to the lower part of State. When I passed the pawnshop I'd visited with Pinky, I turned right at the corner and parked on the side street. I walked the half block to State and went into Santa Teresa Jewelry and Loan. As far as I could tell, everything was exactly the same, from the paintings mounted on the wall to the guitars strung together in a line to the glass cases filled with watches and rings. Now I wondered if there was any turnover at all. Perhaps when we're forced to forfeit what we own, we lose any sentimental associations. Perhaps pawning our valuables frees us in the same way a house fire destroys not only our worldly goods, but our attachment to what's gone.

June was at the register when I entered the shop, and she looked up as I approached. She'd re-dyed her hair since I'd seen her last. Gone was the wide ribbon of gray roots she'd shown the week before. Her eyeglasses were also different. This pair was framed in lime green and seemed better suited to her wavy red-gold locks.

I said, "Hi, June. Kinsey Millhone. I came in with Pinky Ford when he reclaimed his wife's engagement ring."

She fixed me with a shrewd look. "You're the private detective."

"I'm impressed. I didn't think you'd remember."

"I saw your name in the paper after that woman went off the bridge. The way I read it, the reporter had it in for you."

"Thanks for saying so. I thought I was being paranoid."

"Not a bit of it. She made it sound like you were just plain uncooperative."

"And 'fanciful.' Don't forget that."

"The vice detective was the one who threw that in. He's a piece of work. I've had dealings with him before and didn't much care for the man. I couldn't believe he'd pooh-pooh the idea of organized retail theft. He knows better or why would he be in here chatting with me?"

"Probably following up."

"About time," she said. "Too bad he was so arrogant or I'd have given him an earful."

"Try me. I could use the education."

"What in particular?"

"Well, I know professional thieves are out there—Audrey Vance being one. I'm trying to get a line on where they set up shop. They have to have places to lay off merchandise."

"You bet. With stolen property, there's always a fence. Nothing comes through us, in case you're wondering."

I smiled. "It did cross my mind."

"It's a common misconception. People think pawnshops are a magnet for stolen goods, but nothing could be further from the truth. We're strictly regulated. By law, we are required to get a photo ID, a thumbprint, and a detailed description, including serial numbers, for every item we take in. We forward the information to the police department so they can check it against reported thefts. It works the other way too.

If they're investigating a burglary, they notify us so we're aware of what's in circulation."

"So how does it work? Someone has to be on the buying end or the market would dry up."

"Depends on the goods. Articles of clothing are stripped of store labels and moved out of the area. Same thing with items like athletic shoes. Who wants to pay full price if you can get the same thing for half? There's a big market for brand-name goods overseas. Here too for that matter."

"Someone suggested swap meets."

"Sure, and there are other unregulated vendors—secondhand stores, flea markets, garage sales. You could even take a look at the classified ads in the local paper. The reason most off-market items are taken out of one community and circulated somewhere else is because it's smart to put as much distance as possible between the source and the final sale. You don't want someone recognizing a garment they just saw on the rack at Robinson's."

"Makes sense," I said. "What do you know about the fences in town?"

She shook her head. "Can't help you there."

"But surely, word gets around."

"You'd think. Problem is, you make a statement to that effect and you're risking a lawsuit. These days, criminals have better lawyers than the rest of us."

"That's the truth," I said. I took out a business card and gave it to her, jotting my home number on the back. I was so free with that number, I might as well print it on the front with my office number. "If you think of anything else, would you give me a call?"

"Not a problem," she said. "Nice seeing you again."

"Same here. You might see me again if I need additional help. I appreciate your time." I reached across the counter and shook hands with her.

"One correction," she said as I turned to go.

I looked back at her.

"You asked me what I *know* about fences. You didn't ask me what I suspect."

The consignment shop June suggested would be of interest was on Chapel in the middle of a run of storefronts I'd seen on countless occasions. There was a crappy-looking little fast-food place on the corner with a take-out window that opened onto the sidewalk. A few dispirited wrought-iron tables and chairs were arranged to one side for the sit-down trade. After rigorous inspection, the health department had awarded this establishment a C, which suggested cockroaches and rat turds where you least expected them. I was so hungry I'd have been willing to compromise my already low standards if the place had been open.

I found a parking spot right out in front, a cause for great joy until I realized all the stores were closed for the day. A sign in the window of the consignment shop indicated the business hours were Monday through Friday, 10:00 to 6:00, and Saturdays, 10:00 to 4:00. A quick look at my watch showed I'd missed by twenty minutes.

To the left of the consignment shop there was a store that sold wigs made of fibers that didn't come close to resembling human hair. I've seen Barbie dolls sprouting better tresses in those evenly spaced plugs that always give me the creeps. The wigs, displayed on featureless Styrofoam heads, would have been perfect if you were forced to attend a costume party at gunpoint. Beyond the wig shop, there was an outlet for bawdy underwear, and beyond that an alleyway with a sign pointing to additional parking in the rear. I walked around to the back and had a look.

All I saw were bulging trash cans and empty parking spots. Every space was earmarked for one of the businesses, with the bawdy underwear store claiming the lion's share. Behind the consignment shop there was a stack of battered cardboard boxes broken down and bound with twine. Nothing out of the ordinary as far as I could see, but at least I'd satisfied my curiosity.

I drove home and parked Henry's station wagon in front of his garage beside my Mustang. In the morning, I'd return it to his garage. I did a walkabout in his house. Over the past few days, I'd seen lights winking on and off at burglar-fooling intervals. Living room lamps came on at 4:00 and went off at 9:00 when the bedroom lights came on and then off again at 10:30.

It was almost like having Henry in residence. So far the ruse had worked because no one had broken in. He'd been gone for a week and the very air smelled forlorn. I dampened a sponge and wiped down the kitchen table and the counters, which had picked up a fine haze of dust. Aside from that, all was well. I locked up.

I stopped in my studio briefly, pausing to wash my face. I'd been up for hours, and with the drive to San Luis Obispo and back, I was bushed. I decided on an early supper at Rosie's, followed by an early bedtime. I turned on my desk lamp and flipped on an outside light in anticipation of my return. I locked my door and walked the half block to Rosie's. It was close to five when I arrived, and the only other patrons were a pair of day-drinkers who'd probably been sitting on the same stools since noon. Rosie was tending bar and she poured me a glass of bad wine before retreating to the kitchen, where she was apparently preparing one of her zany Hungarian entrées.

William arrived shortly after I did. He was still carrying his wooden cane with the curved handle, which he would occasionally swing in a half arc. He didn't seem to need it to balance his weight, but it lent him the jaunty air of a man on the move. Judging from his three-piece suit and the shine on his wingtips, I was guessing he'd just returned from a funeral. I expected an outpouring of gossip and information, the sort of inside dope that only an inquisitive chap like William can elicit from total strangers in their hour of grief. Instead, he greeted me with a fistful of pamphlets he'd received from Mr. Sharonson.

"What's this?" I asked when he'd pressed one in my hand.

"Pre-need funeral arrangements. Take a look," he said.

Once I heard the term, I couldn't believe he hadn't thought of it himself. I gave the information a cursory look while he took out a second pamphlet and opened it. "Just listen to this. 'Preplanning a funeral allows you to determine the type of service and disposition you've always dreamed of. You have time to consider important details and to discuss them with your loved ones. Preplanning spares your survivors the uncertainty of last-minute decisions that may or may not be in keeping with your most cherished beliefs.' I can't wait to tell Rosie. She'll be thrilled."

"No, she won't," I said promptly. "Would you listen to yourself? She's bossy. She likes to be in control. If you died, she'd be in her element. She'd have Mr. Sharonson in tears, trying to please and appease her. Surely you don't propose to spoil the moment for her."

He frowned. "That can't be true. Are you sure? Because this says 'Your loved ones can rest assured that the distress of this deeply personal moment has been minimized by your lingering consideration.'"

"Which is the same as taking all the fun out of it for her. Look at it from her perspective. She's opinionated and overbearing. She'd love nothing better than to tangle with Mr. Sharonson over every everlasting detail."

"What if we worked on it together?"

"And spoil the current peace? I thought you and Rosie were getting along so well."

"We are."

"Then why mess it up? Take my word for it. You bring up the topic, Rosie will have a fit."

"But it makes so much sense. You think she'd be pleased."

Rosie used one ample hip to push open the swinging door and emerged from the kitchen with a plate piled with fried potatoes, which she fed to the local drunks in hopes of offsetting the worst effects of alcohol consumption. In one smooth motion, William took the pamphlet from my hand and slid the lot of them into the inner pocket of his suit jacket. Returning, Rosie took one look at him and came to a halt. Her sharp gaze moved from his face to mine.

"Wot?"

He must have guessed that if he said 'Nothing' it would be all over for him. She'd know he was getting into trouble of some kind. I stepped into the gap. "I was just asking what smelled so good. He said you were working on a dinner special, but he wasn't sure what it was called."

"*Kocsonya.* I cook yesterday and is chillink as we speak."

I said, "Ah."

"You puts any five Hungarian womens together and you gonna have argument about who cooks the best *kocsonya*. Makes no mistake. Is me and I give you Rosie's secret family *kocsonya* recipe. Hev a seat and I'll dictate."

I took a chair at the nearest table and dutifully dug into my bag. I pulled out a pen and an envelope, which I noticed was my unpaid electric bill. I put that aside and grabbed my spiral-bound notebook.

Rosie was already impatient to get on with it. "You no writing."

"You haven't said anything yet. I'm getting myself set."

"I'm wait."

"Is this like a regional specialty?"

"Absolutely. Is whatever you say. Years I'm working on my recipe and is finally perfect."

"What did you say it was?"

"*Kocsonya*? Is jell . . . how you say it . . ."

"Jellied pig feet," William supplied.

Wincing, I lifted my pen from the paper. "Uh, you know, Rosie, I'm really not much of a cook."

"I'm telling you wot to do. Exactly wot I say. Okay so you puts in one pig ear, one tail, and one jowl. Plus one fresh pig's knuckle cut in half, plus one pig's foot. I sometimes put two. Slowly bring boil and keep over low fire one hour. Then is adding . . ."

She was going on. I could see her mouth move, but I was wholly distracted by the picture she'd painted of pig parts—not even the good ones—simmering in water. She stopped midsentence and pointed at my paper.

"Put down about froth," she said.

"Frost?"

"Froth. Is skimming froth like gray fat scum. No wonder you can't cook. You no listen."

By the time she finished telling me how tender the feet should be when I put them in a serving dish, my eyes were beginning to cross. When she went on to describe the side dish she was serving—pasta filled with calf's lung—I thought I'd have to put my head down between my knees. Meanwhile, William had backed away from us and he was now busy behind the bar.

Rosie excused herself and returned to the kitchen. This was the only chance I'd have to get away. As I reached for my shoulder bag, she burst back into the bar with a dish of cold jellied pork and a soup bowl filled with what looked like ravioli filled with dark clots. She put the two dishes down in front of me and wiggled in place, hands clasped under her apron. The ravioli was surrounded by a clear broth, and the steam coming off the surface smelled like burning hair.

I stared. "I'm at a loss for words."

"You try. I'm seeing how you like."

What was I to do? I retrieved a modest spoonful of broth. I raised it to my lips and made a slurping sound, saying, "Oh, boy. It's perfect with this wine."

She might have pressed me for more since she favors detailed compliments that abound in adjectives. Happily, a number of patrons had drifted in and Rosie had responsibilities in the kitchen. As soon as the swinging door closed behind her, I picked up my shoulder bag and rescued my wallet from the depths. I left a generous sum of money on the table and eased out the door. Later I'd think of a compelling story to cover my hasty exit. I didn't think imminent upchucking would be considered a compliment. For now, it was enough that I escaped without having to eat anything.

On the street again, I had to control the urge to break into a run. It wasn't fully dark, but the neighborhood was gloomy under trees just beginning to leaf out. I paused at the curb and waited for a car to pass. The car windows were down and the driver had the music turned up so loudly, the car seemed to pulsate. I crossed at the corner and continued the half block to my apartment, walking on the opposite side of the street. A pale blue sedan was idling in Henry's driveway, and as I watched, two men emerged from the backyard and got in, one into the backseat and the other, the passenger-side seat. The driver backed into the street and drove away. The car turned at the corner onto Bay and disappeared.

What were two strangers doing in Henry's backyard? His station wagon was in the drive where I'd parked it. His house lights were on. The lights in my studio were out. I hesitated, heart thumping. When I'd left for supper the sky was still light, but I'd realized I'd be returning home after dark so I'd turned on the desk lamp. I retraced my steps and returned to the intersection where Rosie's Tavern sits. This time, I kept to the side street and continued as far as the alleyway that runs along Henry's rear property line. On more than one occasion, I'd used this approach, which allowed me to slip through the shrubs that envelop the fence behind his garage. By pushing the chicken wire away from the support post, I could slip into the backyard unseen.

I stood in the shadows and watched my back door. The porch light was off. There was no sign of anyone on or near the darkened patio. Henry's kitchen light was off, as it should have been. There was enough ambient glow from the streetlights out front that I could identify the various dark patches in the yard: patio furniture, hose reel, Henry's potted ferns, and a few young trees planted along the walk.

I studied the porthole in my door. I scanned for lights, wondering if perhaps I'd catch the soft gray beam of a flashlight inside. I had every reason to believe the men in the pale blue sedan were gone, but what had they been doing there in the first place? I fumbled in my shoulder bag for my penlight and flicked it on. I leaned close to the lock. There was no sign of forced entry, which was not to say someone hadn't used a set of key picks to get in. At least no one had kicked a big hole in my door or used a boot to bash it off its hinges.

My gun was in my briefcase, locked in the trunk of the Mustang, which was parked in the drive. I would have felt a whole lot braver if I'd had my H&K in hand, but I didn't want to show myself on the street. It seemed a bit melodramatic when I really couldn't be sure the two guys had been inside. Maybe they'd knocked and then left when it became clear no one was home. I removed my key ring and carefully inserted my key in the lock, turning it with care. Through the porthole, all I could see was flat darkness. I pushed the door open and leaned in to flip on the overhead light.

My living room and kitchen were empty. There was no sign of a disturbance. I'd half expected to see drawers pulled out, chairs overturned, and the sofa gutted with a kitchen knife. In movies, that's how it's done. Here, nothing of the sort.

"Hello?" I called.

I turned my gaze to the spiral stairs, listening for sounds. Reason told me there was no one on the premises. I locked the door behind me and walked around the ground floor with the same attention to detail I used when checking Henry's place. There was no obvious evidence anyone had come in while I was out, but the longer I looked, the more indication I had that something was off. The bottom desk drawer was open a marginal half inch. I'm compulsive about closing drawers and cabinet doors, even in someone else's home.

I went up the spiral stairs, pausing at the top to peer over the rail. I crossed to my bed table and studied the arrangement of items on top. The clock, the lamp, and the magazines were there, but not quite as I'd left them, which suggested someone had cleared the lid and looked inside. I opened one drawer after another, and while the contents weren't jumbled, I sensed that someone had searched. I peered into my bathroom, which harbored no hiding places except for the laundry hamper. I was, of course, mindful of the box of cash Vivian and I had delivered to the sheriff's department in San Luis. I was also thinking about the man who'd rung her doorbell inquiring about the package that had been delivered in error.

When the phone rang, I was so startled I jumped, and while I don't believe I shrieked, I may well have yelped. I picked up the handset.

"Kinsey?"

It was Vivian, her tone plaintive. "Is everything all right at your place? Because I just got home from my stitching group and I think someone's been here."

# 21

At this point I should have called the police. Ordinarily, I'm not shy about such things. In this instance, however, I had the following factors working against me: I didn't know the make and model of the pale blue sedan. It was almost dark when I'd spotted the two guys getting into the car, which was half a block away. I couldn't have sworn the two had actually been *in* my place, though I couldn't imagine why else they'd be coming out of Henry's backyard. There were no scratches on my front door lock and no obvious indications that anyone had been inside. I was convinced they'd broken in, but I had no evidence. If they'd searched the studio, they were probably smart enough not to leave fingerprints. So what was there to report? As far as I know, there isn't a provision in the California penal code for the crime of "I believe a man might have put his hand in my underwear drawer."

Assuming I was right and the guys had entered the studio, it was surely with an eye to retrieving the shitload of cash Vivian and I had turned over to law enforcement. There might have been an argument for calling the cops just to "have something on record," as though a police report might pave the way for later action on my part. I knew I wouldn't be filing a claim on my renter's policy because I'm reasonably certain I'm not covered for damages resulting from someone peeking in my freezer, thinking I'd be dumb enough to hide masses of cash next to that ancient package of frozen peas.

In my phone conversation with Vivian, I'd told her to do as she saw fit. I didn't think it was my place to advise her one way or the other. She said she was fine but would call her cousin to come pick her up. She didn't want to be alone in the house, a sentiment I understood. She did say she had a shotgun that her husband had taught her to use to good effect, provided she had the nerve to blow an intruder off his feet. She doubted her ability and I applauded her good sense.

For my part, as soon as I hung up I armed myself with a butcher knife, went out to the Mustang, and fetched the briefcase that contained my Heckler & Koch. After I double-locked my door and made sure the windows were secured, I cleaned and loaded my gun. I left the desk lamp on downstairs and retired to my loft, where I fell asleep on top of the covers fully dressed. Three times I woke to investigate noises I probably hadn't heard.

There's much to be said for sleeping fitfully. The brain, when it isn't swaddled in a happy cocoon of dreams, reverts to other means of amusing itself. Mine reviews all the data it's accumulated during the day and sends me telegrams I wouldn't stop to open if I were awake. The brain functions like a camera, clicking off a steady stream of pictures. Incoming data is automatically sorted so that what's relevant can be stored for future reference and what's irrelevant can be deleted. The problem is that we don't know until much later which images count and which don't. My subconscious nudged me, letting me know I'd seen something that might be more important than I'd thought. The idea would excite me for the moment and I'd make a mental note. Then I'd fall asleep and by the time I woke up again I'd forget what it was.

Sunday morning, I rose early and went out for a three-mile jog. As a rule, this is not something I do on weekends, which I reserve for rest and relaxation. However, in the previous week, I'd skipped the exercise because business required my presence elsewhere. Now it was time to take hold. I did my token thirty-minute jog along the beach, hoping to generate a moment of runner's high. Mostly, my whole body hurt. Parts that had never given me trouble before spoke up to complain. On the plus side, there was the stress reduction and the following insight that popped to mind. I'd reached the end of my run and I'd slowed to a walk to cool down when I remembered the point my subconscious had been trying to make in the dead of night. *Take another look*, whispered she, *at the stack of flattened cardboard boxes behind the consignment shop.*

As soon as I'd showered, dressed, and bolted down a bowl of cereal, I checked my desk drawers for my Swiss Army knife, which I tossed into my shoulder bag. I found my steam iron and put it with my briefcase and gun. I returned to the Mustang and locked both in the trunk. I paused to make a careful study of the street, looking for the blue sedan, which was nowhere in sight. This was not a comfort. If the guys had tailed me from Vivian's house the day before, they were probably smart enough to use more than one vehicle.

I took the 101 to Missile and then turned right on Dave Levine. I cruised past the strip mall where the consignment shop was located. Storefronts were dark as expected on a Sunday morning. At the corner, I turned right and entered the alley that ran behind the row of shops. When I pulled in the parking lot was empty, the trash cans still bulging. I let the Mustang idle while I crossed to the stack of cardboard boxes and used my Swiss Army knife to cut the twine. I flipped through quickly, glancing at each box in turn. Most had been used more than once, the recipient apparently unpacking the contents and using the same boxes for subsequent shipments. This was a frugal move on the part of the business owner and worked to my advantage because in almost every case, a new shipping label had been slapped over the old. As one does when tracing layers of sediment, I could work backward, tracking the boxes from one location to the one before. I loaded the stack in the trunk of my car. Better to dig for information in private instead of standing in a parking lot taking notes.

Downtown Santa Teresa was largely deserted at that hour and traffic was light. Department stores wouldn't open until noon, so I was able to travel the surface streets with some confidence I wasn't being followed. I kept an eye on the rearview mirror, but I didn't see any cars that seemed worrisome. I drove to the office, unloaded the boxes from the trunk, and carried them to the office door, where I let myself in. I filled my iron with water, plugged it in, and moved the lever to steam. Then I sat on the floor cross-legged while I worked my way through the stack of battered boxes.

I kept a record of the addresses as I uncovered them, wondering if a pattern would emerge. Most of the shipping had been done through a carrier I didn't know. I made a note of the name, thinking I'd check with Vivian to see if it was a match for the service that had dropped off the package at Audrey's door. I steamed off label after label, watching the addresses change. It was almost impossible to discern shipping dates. The tracking numbers had been blacked out and sometimes a label had been torn off entirely before another one was pasted on top. On the fifth box, under the top two labels, I found Audrey's name and the rental address in San Luis Obispo. It looked like the boxes were being moved from one California location to another, the preponderance of it a short loop between Santa Teresa and San Luis Obispo. If stolen merchandise left the country, it was probably sent by way of a shipping company. Goods would be stripped, sorted for distribution, and sent on. Once I reached the bottom of the pile, I stood the boxes upright and shoved the flattened cardboard into the space between my file cabinet and the wall.

I locked the office and got back into my car. I pulled the Santa

Teresa County map from my glove compartment, unfolded it, and propped it on the steering wheel. I checked the list of addresses I'd culled. Audrey's in San Luis Obispo I knew. The other two were in Colgate. In the key of streets at the bottom of the map, I found both streets. The first skirted the boundaries of the airport and continued on to the university. The second address was half a mile from the first.

I took the 101 north. Traffic in the southbound lanes was picking up, visitors returning to Los Angeles after a weekend away. By midafternoon, vehicles would be bumper-to-bumper, barely moving. I was mindful of the cars behind me, watching to see if any seemed to replicate my route or appeared more often than was natural. When I took the Fairdale off-ramp, no one left the highway with me. Maybe the guys in the pale blue sedan had been called off once they failed to find the money. No profit in killing me. If I knew the whereabouts of the cash, I'd only be of use to them alive.

I stayed in the left-hand lane and followed the road up and to the left, crossing the highway on the overpass. Off to my right there was a research park, a drive-in theater, a nine-hole municipal course, two motels, three gas stations, and an auto-repair shop. At the intersection, I paused for a red light and then crossed the main thoroughfare, staying on the street leading to the airport. Not surprisingly, this was called Airport Road. While the surrounding terrain wasn't as isolated as the area in San Luis Obispo where Audrey had rented her place, the neighborhood was far from residential. On the left I passed three small frame cottages that were almost certain to be rentals. Who else but tenants would pay good money to live in such a tacky, out-of-the-way location?

When I reached the airport, I did a turnaround and went back for another look at the cottages. The structures were probably meant for the migrant workers who labored for the owner of the adjacent agricultural fields. I hadn't caught house numbers on the first pass, but there was nothing else out here except a post office sorting depot. Approaching from this direction, I could see a run of frame garages at the rear of the three vintage cottages, all of which appeared to be identical. The address on the first was a match for the address on one of the flattened cardboard boxes. There were no parked cars visible and no signs of life. When I reached the driveway between the first two cottages, I slowed and pulled in. No trash cans, no laundry hanging on the line.

I got out of my car, trying to look like someone who had business to conduct. I could feel my anxiety stir, but having committed myself, there was nothing for it but to proceed. The windows were bare and there were no crusty dog bowls in evidence. So far, so good. I went up the back porch steps and peered through the glass in the upper portion of the door. The kitchen was empty of furniture. I knocked nonetheless, thinking it was something I'd have done if I'd had a legitimate reason to be on the premises. Naturally, no one responded. I glanced over at the house next door, which also appeared to be unoccupied. No one was looking out of the window at me. In a rare moment of good sense, I didn't whip out my key picks and let myself in.

Instead, I went around to the front door, where I saw for the first time the substantial padlock affixed to the hasp that had been screwed in place. I cupped my hands and looked in the two front windows. Curled against the glass on the right, there was a For Rent sign. I looked in at an empty living room. I crossed to the window on the left and stared at an empty bedroom. The interior was shabby but tidier than I'd expected. I wondered if a merry little band of thieves had convened here as they had at Audrey's. Boxes had been sent to and from this address, so someone had been in residence these past few months. I wondered if this house, like Audrey's rental in S.L.O., had been stripped after her death.

As long as I was about it, I checked the other two cottages, which were also deserted. As I crossed the yard returning to my car, I spotted a For Sale sign that had been propped on its side, half buried in the weeds. The support post looked as though a car had backed into it and sheared it in half. I made a note of the name and phone number of the real estate office for later reference.

I got in my car and backed out onto the road, returning to the major intersection where I turned left. The second address I'd picked up turned out to be a warehouse on a side road that ended in a cul-de-sac. Beyond its being remote, there was not much else to recommend it. This area would probably be zoned "light industrial," though Colgate supports no heavy manufacturing. The property was surrounded by eight-foot-high fencing and the windows were covered with steel mesh. There was a truck yard at the rear, and closer to the main building, off-street parking for employees. The loading docks were empty and the retractable metal doors were rolled down and secured. The name on the sign read ALLIED DISTRIBUTORS.

This would be a convenient and remote location for distribution of stolen goods, thought I. The purpose of any carefully structured fencing operation is to put distance between the actual thieves and the ultimate dispensation of the merchandise. A company like Allied could put together a confusing mix of lawful and unlawful activities. I couldn't even imagine the accumulation of evidence that would have to be assembled before law enforcement could move in. An illegal operation involving the crossing of state lines creates a jurisdictional nightmare for investigating agencies, which have been known to arrest one another's undercover operatives and informants by mistake. Here long-haul trucks might be used for legitimate purposes and smaller trucks employed for goods that wouldn't stand up to roadside weigh-station inspection.

I returned to the main road and from there to the 101, which took me into town. I went back to my office. The light on my answering machine was blinking, and I felt a flash of irritation because I wanted to get to work and I wasn't in the mood for interruptions. Nonetheless, being a good girl, I pressed the play button. This was the message that awaited me:

"Kinsey, this is Diana. Somebody's come to me with a story I think you should hear. I hope you'll set aside whatever bad feelings you have about me and return this call. Please." Then she recited her number.

To the machine I said, "Oh yeah, sure, Diana. Like I'm going to call you back after what you did to me." Then I hit delete.

I hauled out my Smith-Corona portable typewriter and set it on my desk. I'm usually good about writing reports, always aware that it's best to capture information while it's fresh. If too much time passes, half the details get lost. With any investigation, the small revelations sometimes contribute as much to the whole as the more dramatic discoveries. So far, all Audrey's file contained was a copy of Marvin's check. Time to make amends. I pulled out a sheaf of typing paper with tissue carbons and rolled the first sheet into place. I set my index cards on the desk beside me and began typing up my notes.

When I finished it was close to noon. I was tired. I'm not a skilled typist, though I do better than hunt-and-peck. What I'd struggled with was the job of converting the bare facts into a coherent narrative. Some information was still in outline form with gaps where I hadn't yet filled in the blanks. Aside from the missing links, it seemed clear I was onto something big. I made a neat stack of my typed notes and put one copy in my shoulder bag, along with the index cards, which I secured with a rubber band. I placed the second copy of my report in an unlocked file drawer in a folder labeled GYNECOLOGY & FEMININE HYGIENE ISSUES, subjects I hoped the average thief would find repellant.

Time to talk to Marvin, whose house was less than two miles away. I'd made progress, but I still had to frame my findings so they made sense to him. In essence, I'd been suspended without pay. Now I hoped to persuade him to underwrite the next phase of my investigation. If he wasn't home, there was a good chance he'd be at the Hatch. A serious drinker sees Sunday as just another day of the week, except that it begins with a Bloody Mary and progresses to beer, bourbon, or tequila depending on the company and seasonal sporting events. I was starving as usual and thought I'd stop in at the Hatch for bar grub whether he was there or not.

I made a right turn onto State and drove the half mile to Marvin's neighborhood. I parked and trotted up the walk to his front door. I knocked and waited. Nothing. I knocked again. Still nothing. I peered in the windows along the front of the house and saw no indication that he was home. I returned to my car and drove the additional block to the Hatch, parking on the side street as I had before.

It felt odd to be walking into a bar at such an early hour on a Sunday. Apparently, others felt fine about it because the place was doing a lively business. All four television sets were turned on. The jukebox blared, and there were ten or twelve patrons congregated at the bar where Ollie, the owner, seemed to be making drinks with both hands. The air was already hazy with cigarette smoke, and I could feel my eyes cross at the notion of particulate matter settling on my clothes.

Marvin was among those gathered, talking to one of the two women who were part of his inner circle—Earldeen Somebody-or-Other, if memory served. He toted a bourbon on the rocks as dark as strong iced tea. He put a fresh cigarette between his lips and extended a light to Earldeen before he applied it to his own. I tapped him on the shoulder. He turned and when he realized it was me, his expression downshifted ever so slightly from relaxed to disengaged. "Hey. Look who's here. What's up?"

His tone was flat and that should have been a clue, but it went right over my head. I saw the flicker in his eyes but thought he was embarrassed I'd caught him smoking again. That's how far off track I was.

"I've updated my report," I said. "If you have a second, I'll tell you what I've learned since I saw you last."

"Yeah, well, you caught me in the middle of something, so it might be better if we talk another time," he said. His gaze drifted to one side.

By now it was apparent he was angry about something and I realized I'd have to stop and deal with his pissy mood before I went on.

"What's wrong?"

"I don't think you'd be interested. You don't take kindly to anyone challenging your point of view."

"Come on, Marvin. You're obviously frosted about something. You want to fill me in?"

"Just what I said. It's your way or the highway."

I glanced at Earldeen, who was avidly watching the exchange. She didn't seem perplexed by his attitude, which suggested this was something he'd discussed with her previously.

"Can we go somewhere and talk?"

"This is good enough right here."

"Then tell me what's happened." In my experience, when people like Marvin get mad, it doesn't take much coaxing before they unload.

"I'll be happy to, as long as I'm not on the receiving end of an argument."

"I'm not arguing," I said argumentatively.

"Word on the grapevine has it that an ex-con was seen in the area right about the time Audrey went off the bridge. This is a guy just out of prison with dangerous associates. It's possible she came across information that would have put him away, so he threw her over the rail."

"What information?"

"Sorry, but I can't say. This was told to me in confidence, so you'll have to take my word for it. If you'll remember, she was in jail for a couple of hours before I arrived with the bail. Speculation has it she saw something she wasn't supposed to see."

"Such as what?"

"I already told you I can't get into it. Point is, if she'd blown the whistle on the guy, he'd have gone back in the slammer. Might have been more to it. Cops are not above tampering with evidence. Maybe that's what she got wind of."

"You're saying she was murdered because of something she found out."

"At the station. That's what I just said."

"So she wasn't affiliated with a retail-theft ring."

"Would you quit harping on that? Right from day one, you've exaggerated the whole incident. She pilfered a few items. Big deal."

"What about the booster gear?"

"There's no proof she wore booster gear. That's all part of the attempt to discredit her. Did you see it yourself? I doubt it."

"Of course not. I didn't know Audrey at that point, so how would I know anything about her underwear?"

"Just stick to the facts. Did you or did you not see booster gear? The answer is no. The entire time I knew her, did I ever see this alleged gear? No, again. Just because some cop put it in the police report doesn't make it true."

I stood and stared at him, processing what he'd said. I was about to remind him I hadn't read the police report, but that was beside the point. He'd reverted to whitewashing Audrey's character, but what had caused the shift? I glanced over at Earldeen, who'd propped her chin on her fist, fascinated by the discussion. I wanted to slap her face but thought better of it.

He said, "This is refreshing. For once, you're at a loss for words."

"Because what I'm hearing you say is you now believe Audrey was the victim of a conspiracy that originated with the police."

"Makes a lot more sense to me than *your* theory."

"What prompted your change of heart?"

"There's no change of heart. I said from the get-go she was innocent. So what if she snitched a teddy? For cripes sake, that doesn't make her a hard-core criminal."

I shut my mouth and let him run on.

"You know what your problem is?" he asked. He pointed with his cigarette, which came perilously close to my face. "You want to believe the worst about people. Doesn't matter to you if there's proof or not."

"What are you talking about?"

"You were married to a police officer accused of beating a guy to death, right?"

"I told you about that."

"No, you did not. You mentioned you were married to a cop who was a friend of Detective Priddy's and you said Priddy was a creep. What you *didn't* say was your ex-husband was exonerated. Interesting you elected to leave that part out."

"I don't see the relevance."

"You don't? Well, think about it. You were so sure you were right, you abandoned the guy when he needed you most." He dropped his cigarette on the floor and stepped on it.

"It didn't happen that way," I said.

"You can quibble all you like, but I'm close enough, am I correct?"

"Marvin, you're trying to draw a parallel between my relationship with my ex and my belief in Audrey's guilt. You're saying Mickey was eventually cleared and therefore she will be too. Is that it?"

"Right. And she's dead, same as the guy you were married to." He looked skyward and tapped his chin like a cartoon character. "Hmmm. Let's see. What do these two stories have in common?"

I said, "Those two situations are so different I can't even begin to set you straight."

"Don't be so defensive. I'm just telling you what I was told."

"By Len Priddy."

"I didn't say it was him."

"Of course it was."

He shrugged. "You don't like the guy, that doesn't mean he's trying to do *you* in," he said. "At any rate, I apologize for being rude. I should have asked why you're here. Let me guess. You used up the balance of the retainer and you're hoping to hit me up for more."

"That's true, but the game has changed, hasn't it?" I said mildly. I was keeping my voice low because my rage was rising to a white-hot peak and I didn't dare give vent to it.

"Oh, geez. Now *you're* pissed off. I hope you're not telling me you quit," he said facetiously.

"Quit? No, sweetheart. I'm in this for the long haul whether you pay me or not."

He drew back. "You can't do that. I won't have you meddling in her affairs. Audrey's past is none of your business."

"Sorry to disagree, but this is my job and I'm on it. Too bad you didn't fire me when you had the chance."

# 22

## DANTE

Dante counted laps as he swam, his mouth lifting to the left to take in a breath of air, turning into the water to release. There was little sound beyond the bubbles he breathed out. He was conscious of the strength of his arms as he moved through the water, hands slicing down, pulling through, propelling himself forward. He recited the numbers in his head with each stroke. *Eighteen, eighteen, eighteen* down the length of the pool. *Seventeen, seventeen, seventeen* on the return. It was easy to lose track of where he was and how far he'd come when the water was such a perfect temperature and there was nothing to interrupt the easy flow of energy. The noisy chatter in his head gave way to the simple repetition: arms, legs, inhale, exhale.

The day after his mother left, Pop had drained the pool at the house where they lived, leaving a great empty hole in the ground to remind them of the pleasures she'd taken with her. Rain and falling leaves had rotted together, filling the bottom with black sludge. Dante knew his father had done it out of spite, to deprive them of the solace she'd offered and the confidence she'd instilled. Whatever pain she'd inflicted on her husband, he'd doubled when he'd passed it on to his son. Dante hadn't gone back into the water until he bought this house and had his own pool put in.

The last lap was the best. By then his body was relaxed and his mind was still. After the final few strokes, when he lifted himself out of the water and onto the concrete apron, his limbs felt rubbery and loose. He'd press a towel against his face, flush with the heat the exercise had generated. Where lifting weights pumped his muscles, the swimming stretched him out and kept him long and lean. He'd see Nora in the afternoon, if she decided to come.

By the time he reached the master suite, his body heat had dissipated and he needed a hot shower to offset the chill. Usually on Sunday mornings he didn't shave, but he did so today. Because of Nora, of course. Since he'd first set eyes on her, everything was about Nora. He couldn't identify the draw and he didn't question it. It had never happened to him before and he had no explanation. What difference did it make why he was obsessed? In point of fact, he was.

He peered into the bedroom. Lola was still asleep, buried under the weight of the comforter. She had so little body fat she was cold all the time. During the night, if she snuggled up against him, her skin was as cold as Naugahyde. He eased the dressing room door shut and pulled on his clothes: light pants, a red silk shirt, loafers without socks.

Sophie had Sundays off, so he was alone when he wandered into the kitchen. The counters were gleaming and the stainless steel appliances gave off a silvery light. The coffeepot was preprogrammed and the insulated carafe was full. Sophie had made him a coffee cake that she'd covered in Saran Wrap. He cut a generous slice and ate it with one hand while he poured his coffee with the other. He added milk and carried the mug with him as he moved through the tunnel to his office in the Cottage.

Lola mocked his passion for underground passageways, but he found it satisfying to travel from place to place unseen. She claimed it was his way of returning to the womb, an assertion he found annoying. What did she know about anything? In his mind, it was about the ability to escape. He was a man who always had a way out.

From the Cottage, he crossed the lawn to the guesthouse. The nurse on duty had been looking after his uncle for the past five months. She was close to six feet tall and built like an athlete, all muscle and sinew. Strong features, short cropped blond hair. He'd dated her nine years before, though the relationship was short-lived. Cara was promiscuous by nature and thought nothing of taking up with any man who came along. A woman would do if a guy wasn't available. When she applied for the job, he'd hesitated, wondering if it was wise to have her so close by. Lola's neediness would surface and he'd have to shore her up with constant reassurances. He needn't have worried. Nine years was nine years, and the physical attraction had faded. Cara was competent and she worked hard, and he knew his Uncle Alfredo liked looking at her.

She met him at the door. "He's been waiting for you. He woke up at midnight and wanted company. We played gin rummy and watched television for most of the night. I don't know where he gets the energy."

Dante followed her into the living room, where his Uncle Alfredo was seated by the fireplace, wrapped in a big puffy yellow comforter. April nights were still chilly and the mornings were not much warmer. Dante crossed to the fireplace, leaned down, and kissed the top of his uncle's head. Alfredo grabbed his hand and clung to it laying it up against his cheek.

"You're a good boy, Dante. Let me say that while I have the opportunity."

When he finally let go, Dante pulled up a chair and sat down across from him. "How goes the battle?"

"About like you'd expect. This morning's not so bad."

"Cara says you were up half the night."

"I'm afraid I'll die in my sleep."

"Don't want the Grim Reaper catching you unawares?"

"I intend to put up a fight," Alfredo said. "Your father came to see me yesterday. We had a long talk."

"Let me guess. He thinks I'm too hard on Cappi. He wants me to hand over the bale and let him run the circuit."

"That was the gist of it. Not that I'm siding with Lorenzo, but how's the kid going to learn responsibility if he's never given any? I'm not making a judgment here so don't get on your high horse. I'm just asking."

"The 'kid' as you so aptly refer to him is forty-six years old. I think he's already demonstrated his capacity for growth and maturity," Dante said. "Cappi takes advantage. He wheedles and whines and next thing you know, Pop thinks he's come up with the idea himself."

"No doubt about it. Cappi pays me a visit, I know he's working an angle, maneuvering for support."

"He's not getting it from me. I may make a show of teaching him the system but I'm not going to cut him in on the profits from an operation worth millions. You think that's a good idea, you're nuts."

Alfredo tilted his head, his tone mild. "Here's another way of looking at it. How many years you been saying you want out of the business? This might be your opportunity."

"Doesn't work that way. I'm fifty-four years old. What would I do, go to medical school? Get a law degree? It's too late. Pop expected me to do this and I'm doing it. Now he expects me to turn the biggest chunk of it over to Cappi, who fucks up everything he does. I won't do it."

"How are you going to get around it when he's made up his mind?"

"He can make up his mind about anything he wants. I'm the one in control. Anyway, ask me, he's losing it. He's talking about Amo and Donatello like they're in the next room."

"He's forgetful sometimes. Happens to all of us."

"Not you," Dante said.

"I'm a special case," Alfredo said wryly. "Big problem you got is Lorenzo doesn't always see what Cappi's up to. You should put a stop to it before it gets out of hand."

"How?"

His uncle's face registered distress. "What's the matter with you? You know better. That's not a question you should ever have to ask." Alfredo studied him briefly. "You know what your problem is?"

"I'm sure you'll enlighten me."

"You've gone all dainty on me. There was a time when you'd have taken care of this. No talk, no hesitation."

Dante smiled. "'Dainty.' That's a first."

"You know what I mean. Man in your position can't afford a conscience. It's unbecoming. You don't back away from what's difficult. You do what needs to be done."

"You don't believe we are what we do?"

"Of course. We just have to accept that about ourselves. That we're corrupt, that our sins are mortal. God knows mine lie heavy on my soul."

"And you wish the same torment on me?"

"You know what's right."

"Not what's right. I know what's expedient. I'm trying to rise above it for a change."

Uncle Alfredo shook his head. "Contrary to your nature."

"I'd like to think I'm a better man at this late stage in my life."

"Your brother doesn't share your moral sensibilities, which gives him the upper hand."

"That's how he looks at it, at any rate."

Dante took his own car, a 1988 Maserati, silver with a black leather interior. He arrived at the Hatch at 12:45 and parked his car around the corner. He'd given his chauffeur and his bodyguard the day off, opting instead for a loaded Colt Lightweight Commander that he kept in a special compartment in the driver's-side door. He'd instituted the heavy security measures two years before, when a Colombian gang set up shop in Perdido, twenty-five miles south of Santa Teresa. A crew of ten came to town, six men and four women, using driver's licenses that identified them as Puerto Ricans. They were, in fact, trampling on territory run by a friend of his who was a Puerto Rican by birth and took offense, not only at their encroachment, but at their maligning his country of origin. Since Dante's friend was in prison at the time, he'd volunteered to have his own men step in. They cornered the Colombians in a motel room, where a faulty heater exploded, killing the occupants and blowing off half the roof. After that, the remaining Colombians kept their distance but let it be known they'd settle the score in their own good time. Dante's friend had been felled by a sniper's bullet his first day out of prison, and from that point on Dante insisted on armed household guards and armor-plated transportation.

Entering the Hatch, Dante nodded at Ollie and took a table in view of the door. He wanted a bourbon and water but decided to abstain. Ordering a drink seemed like a cheat, as though seeing Nora again was something he couldn't manage without being fortified with booze. He wasn't sure what he'd do if she didn't show. He was just as anxious at the idea that she *would* show. Then what? He'd told himself to have no expectations, but he did.

There was an impressive gathering of patrons at the bar, faces he'd seen on previous occasions. He hadn't been at the Hatch for months, but nothing had changed. He looked around, seeing the place as Nora would see it, shabby and unappealing. No charm, no character. He'd chosen the spot because, as he'd said to her, there was no danger she'd run into anyone she knew. Those in her social circle had probably never heard of the bar and wouldn't be caught dead there if they had.

His gaze strayed to the door, which stood open, admitting a column of daylight, smoky at the edges, as though a filter had been placed over a camera lens. The haze infused the room with a vintage air, a World War II movie set against a backdrop of loss and death and betrayal. That was a cheerful prospect. He didn't know her at all, had no idea, for instance, whether she was punctual or habitually late. He checked his watch and saw that it was 1:00 straight up. Ten more minutes and he'd either order a drink or get up and leave. She was a happily married lady, or said she was, so why would she meet him here, or anywhere else for that matter? She was elegant. She had class. She was reserved and self-contained. There was something in her face that made him want to weep, that made him long to see her again, whatever the cost.

It was three minutes after one when she appeared in the doorway, blocking the light briefly as she came in. He stood. She saw him and crossed the room. He held a chair for her and she sat down. She wore a white wool suit with a short skirt. The jacket was neatly fitted, and where the lapels met the collar there was a rim of red lace. He nearly reached out and slid a finger down between her breasts.

He said, "I didn't think you'd come."

Her smile was brief. "I doubted it myself." Her gaze flicked from the lighted neon beer sign mounted on the wall to the bar and from there to the cartoon arrow that pointed to the ladies' room.

"I'd offer to buy you a drink, but you're not comfortable."

"Of course not. All this cigarette smoke? By the time I get home, my clothes will stink and I'll have to wash my hair."

"I've got a better idea. Place I want to show you. You'll like it."

"We're going someplace else?"

"Don't be so nervous. Nothing's going to happen to you."

She dropped her gaze. "I have time constraints."

"We're not leaving town," he said. "Let me correct myself. A short distance out of town. Fifteen minutes max."

"What about my car?"

"I'll bring you back. What time do you have to be home?"

"Four."

"Not a problem."

When he got up, she put a restraining hand on his arm. "Drop me at my car and I'll follow you," she said.

He leaned close to her ear, taking in the smell of her hair and the light scent of lilac coming off her skin. "You just want to be in control."

She seemed to shiver at the touch of his breath. "That's what you want, isn't it?"

He stood up and held her chair. "Where are you parked?"

"Around the corner."

"Me too. I'll walk you out the side door. That way you won't have to parade past these yahoos. They've been staring at you."

He took her arm lightly, shielding her from view.

"Where are you taking me?"

"I'm not telling you. This is an experiment in trust."

"Why would I trust you?"

"You already do. Evil as I am, I've got an honest face."

"You're not evil, are you?"

"Not entirely. Then again, I'm not entirely honest."

He saw her to her car, a snappy teal blue Thunderbird in mint condition. Somehow it pleased him. He was parked three cars behind her. He turned the key in the ignition and pulled out. She waited until he'd passed before she pulled out behind him. He led her down surface streets, watching her in his rearview mirror. She kept pace with him. As he drove through each stoplight, he was careful she made it through the intersection as well.

When he reached the 101, he took the southbound on-ramp and continued for a mile. He got off at Paloma Lane, which ran parallel to the freeway on a wide stretch of land that bordered the Pacific Ocean. The railroad had co-opted the right of way some years before, but aside from the thundering of the trains passing twice a day, this was prime real estate. Most houses couldn't be seen from the road, which meant that privacy was guaranteed. The mix of evergreens and eucalyptus cut the sunlight into patches.

He slowed and activated an automated gate of weathered wood. The houses on either side of the property were hidden behind eugenia hedges some thirty feet high. He turned into the driveway and followed it around to the left until it widened to a motor court sufficient for six cars. He parked and got out. He waited until she'd pulled in behind him and parked and then he opened her car door. He offered her a hand and helped her out.

"This is your house?" she asked.

"A weekend place. No one knows it's mine."

As they walked toward the front door, he took out a set of keys. The exterior of the house was board-and-batten, painted yellow, the windows shuttered in white. The roof was standing-seam metal with a low pitch that suggested the architecture of the tropics—Key West or Jamaica. Palms were grouped in the small yard, which was half sand, half grass. The front door swung back and she stepped into the small foyer, pausing to take in the space.

The front wall of the living room was floor-to-ceiling windows. Just outside there was a wide wooden deck enclosed by a board-and-batten barrier wall, waist high, topped with darkly tinted glass panels, which kept the ocean visible while anyone standing on the deck was screened from view. She walked as far as the glass and looked out. The air was fully saturated with the scent of ocean, and Dante watched her close her eyes and inhale.

"You like it?"

She smiled at him. "It's perfect. I love the ocean. I'm a water baby. Pisces."

"Me too. Only I'm Scorpio."

"How long have you had the place?"

"Three days."

"You bought it this week?"

"Lease-purchase agreement. You're my first guest."

"I'm flattered."

"You want to look around? I can give you the tour."

"I'd like that."

The two moved from room to room. His commentary was minimal because the house was small and the spatial designations were self-evident. Kitchen, big master bedroom, one guest room, two baths, living room with a dining area at one end. The place was furnished right down to the bed linens.

She said, "I like buying on impulse. It's fun. I confess I can't imagine doing it on such a scale."

"It was a good deal all around. The guy owns the house owes me money so he's paying off a debt. I called and told him I wanted it and he was happy to oblige. The fifteen thousand a month includes the vig. We close in thirty-six months. A bargain from his perspective."

Nora seemed taken aback. "How much did he *owe* you?"

"A lot. I offered him a discount to sweeten the deal."

"Why would someone have to borrow that much?"

"Cost of living's up. The market's down. The guy's well known in town and he has a front to maintain. His wife has no idea how far in the hole he is."

"Don't they use the house?"

"Not anymore. He told her he sold it."

"Just like that?"

"Sure."

"And her name wasn't on the deed?"

"Her name's not on anything. He's like Channing in that respect."

She hesitated, perhaps reluctant to pursue the point, but curiosity got the better of her. "Meaning what?"

"I'm guessing the Malibu house is in his name."

"He owned it before we met."

"So when you married him he declared it his sole and separate property."

"Of course. I have separate property as well. We've both been married before so it's only right."

"What about the house up here? Your name on the title?"

"Well, no, but he said it was for tax reasons. I can't remember now how he explained it."

"How many times was he divorced before you married him?"

Nora held up two fingers.

"Bet he got taken both times, yes?"

"According to him."

"That's why your name's not on the title. Because he's screwing you in advance."

"Stop that. This is a community-property state. If we divorce, I get half of everything regardless."

"Nora, he's an *attorney*. All his friends are attorneys and if not, they know other attorneys whose sole purpose in life is to keep assets out of the hands of women like you. The tax reasons he referred to? Guys call that the stupid tax—paying through the nose because they haven't played it smart."

"I don't think we should be discussing this. It's inappropriate."

"'Inappropriate.' Well, that's one way to look at it. You want my take? You're a beautiful woman. You're in trouble and you know it. I can see it in your face. The way I read you, there's a reckless streak in you a mile wide. You used to be a wild child and you did as you pleased."

"I thought that's what being young was about."

"My point exactly. This is how we get old. Thinking too much about things we used to do without any thought at all."

"Please don't go on with this."

"Why not?"

"I shouldn't have come here. I made a mistake."

"We're having a conversation. There's nothing wrong with that."

"You know better."

"Yes, I do. I wasn't sure you did. That's the problem with choices.

Eventually you have to decide. Maybe not right this minute, but soon," he said.

"What about you? What do *you* want? You fault me for indecision, but you haven't declared yourself."

"For starters, I'd like to avoid spending the rest of my life in prison."

"Is that a possibility?"

"According to my attorneys. I have four of 'em and they're top guns. I mention their names and trust me, Channing would know who they are."

"What did you do?"

"The question is, what am I *accused* of doing? You want to hear the list?"

"Of course."

"Income tax evasion, filing false returns, failing to report offshore bank accounts and international income. Also, racketeering, conspiracy, money laundering, interstate transportation of stolen property, sale of stolen goods. That about sums it up. Well, mail fraud. I don't think I mentioned that. There might be a few I forgot, but most are variations on a theme."

"No violent crimes?"

"Those charges were filed separately. The ones I mentioned are all under the RICO Act."

"Will you be convicted?"

"Not if I can find a way out. My attorneys tell me the feds will offer a plea bargain, but the terms won't be nice."

"What kind of sentence are you looking at?"

"Forty years. Plus forfeiture of a shitload of property, which really pisses me off."

"Forty years? Well, I'm sorry to hear that. I don't think I'll wait, but I'll miss you."

He laughed. "It hasn't happened yet. The good news is these investigations move forward at the typical government pace. Glacial. It'll take 'em years. In the meantime, there are contingencies in place."

"Well, that's interesting. What contingencies?"

"I've told you enough. The point is, if I opt out, you might consider going with me. There's more than one kind of prison."

"Don't be theatrical."

"I'm stating a fact. Stay married to Channing and you know what you're in for. He'll have a string of affairs that everyone will know about before you do. The best you can hope for is an affair of your own."

"Which is where you come in."

"Why not? I'm not trying to talk you into anything, except maybe taking off with me when the time comes."

"I should go."

"It's not even two o'clock. You don't have to be home until four."

She laughed. "You're bad. If I'm not careful, I'll end up calling my therapist about you."

"You're in therapy?"

"I was. Twice a week for a year."

"Why?"

"I lost a child."

"You want to talk about it?"

"No."

"Did therapy help?"

"No. That's why I quit. I got tired of the sound of my own voice. Grieving is like being ill. You think the entire world revolves around you and it doesn't."

He reached out and stroked her cheek with the back of his hand. "Poor little sparrow."

"Yes. Poor me," she said, but she didn't pull away.

Monday morning, Saul came into Dante's office with a thick packet of papers in hand. "We've got a problem."

Dante was sitting at his desk, toying with a letter opener that he then tossed to one side. He folded his hands in front of him. He was not a happy man and the last thing he needed was another problem. "What."

"Georgia called. She needs to meet with you."

"Why is that a problem? Tell her I'll pick her up at the usual place."

"That's not the problem I was referring to."

"Forget the bad news. You look grimmer than usual and I don't want to hear about it."

Saul was silent.

Aggravated, Dante said, "Fuck you. What?"

"Maybe I can come back later."

Dante made an "out with it" gesture with his hand.

"The payroll was intercepted. That's why Georgia wants to talk to you. Some schmo in Miami didn't get word Audrey was out of the loop so he shipped the cash as usual. Her landlady intercepted the package. The money's gone."

"What do you mean, gone? When was this?"

"Friday."

"And Georgia's just now reporting in? Tell her to get it the fuck back."

"She tried, only now there's a local private eye in the mix. I guess she and the landlady are in it together. Georgia sent guys to both places, here and up there, and there's no trace. Rumor has it they turned it over to the sheriff's department in San Luis Obispo."

"Well, that's terrific," Dante said. "What else?"

"Georgia thinks the PI has been tailing her."

"Georgia's PMSie. Every thirty days, she turns paranoid and thinks someone's after her. Fuckin' drama queen."

"Sounds convincing to me. Maybe you ought to hear it from her."

Dante waved a dismissive hand. "Fine. You got more? Because so far you've only darkened my mood by half. You can do better than that."

"I wondered if you'd given any further thought to Cappi. He's asking too many questions and I don't like his drift."

"I gave him a nugget of information and we'll see what he does with it. I told him we purge business records every Thursday at noon. I made it up on the spot, but what does he know? He's double-dealing, he'll hightail it back to whoever's running him and tattle on us. I figure the feds will show up with search warrants and tear the place apart. Destroy his credibility and then what's he worth?"

"Why would anyone believe a story like that?"

"By the time he blabs, he'll have the facts so fucked up no one will know what to think. They'll come after us on the off chance the asshole's telling the truth."

"Nice to know something's under control."

Dante pointed at the papers Saul had brought in. "What's that?"

Saul put the sheaf on Dante's desk. "The latest pound of pretrial paperwork. You want to go over it?"

"What for? I'm screwed either way. I lie, they got me for perjury. I tell the truth, I'm down the toilet. What am I supposed to do?"

"What's to debate? You lie through your teeth. It's up to them to prove otherwise."

"I don't like the idea of lying under oath. It might seem like splitting hairs, given things I've done in my life, but I've got standards like everyone else."

"Then go to Plan B: get out of the line of fire."

"How can I do that? I step to one side, that leaves you exposed."

"Don't worry about me. I'll be fine. If you're out of the picture, I can plead ignorance and blame it all on you."

"It *is* on me."

"I'll tell Lou Elle it's a go anytime you like."

"Not yet. I've got things I want to take care of first."

"Like what? Everything's in place. We've been working on this for months."

"I know," Dante said, irritably. "I just don't think now's the time."

Cautiously, Saul said, "And why is that?"

"There's this woman I'm seeing."

It took a brief moment for Saul to absorb what he'd said. "What about Lola?"

"That's over. She's still in the house, but she'll be gone before long."

"I had no idea."

"Me neither. She's the one who called it off or I'd still be in there fighting. I thought we were good. I was playing for keeps. Shows how much I know," he said. "Meantime, I met someone else."

"Who?"

"Don't worry about that. The point is, I'm in way over my head."

"You?"

"Who else are we talking about?"

"Since when?"

"Since yesterday."

# 23

First thing Monday morning on my way into the office, I stopped by the Hall of Records and started a paper search, looking for information about Helping Hearts, Healing Hands. If the organization was a charity, it would have to be registered. In the state of California, as in most states I'm sure, any group seeking to obtain tax-exempt status is required to fill out forms, which are filed with the state, accompanied by the requisite filing fees. Whether the entity is a sole proprietorship, a partnership, a limited partnership, or a corporation, the applicant must list the name and address of the organization itself and the name and address of every partner, trustee, or officer.

I tried the registry of charitable trusts, which netted me nothing. I tried looking under nonprofits and reached another dead end. Baffled, I asked the clerk at the desk if she had a suggestion. She suggested I try "Fictitious Business Names," also known as DBAs, short for "Doing Business As." She directed me to another office. DBAs expire after five years, but a refiling is required within thirty days. I thanked her for her help. This time I was in luck, though the answer to the question took me right back to my starting point. Helping Hearts, Healing Hands was owned and operated by Dan Prestwick, husband of the very Georgia I'd been tailing for days.

It wasn't clear what his purpose was in establishing this enterprise, but I assumed he'd acquired the proper licenses and permits, that he'd been assigned a federal tax ID number, and behaved himself in accordance with federal and state regulations in furtherance of his stated goals, whatever those might be. He was supposed to list funds, property, and other assets, but I couldn't see any sign that he'd done so. I was sure people were dumping all manner of household items and used clothing in his donation bins, but I wasn't sure what happened to the goods afterward. He certainly didn't declare the potential value. Maybe he turned around and dumped the same goods into Salvation Army bins or left them at the drop-off point behind the Goodwill shop on Chapel.

Helping Hearts, Healing Hands appeared to be a shell company created to shelter Dan Prestwick from closer scrutiny. My best guess was this so-called charity was a conduit for stolen merchandise. Georgia did some of the journeyman shoplifting and she also had a hand in collecting stolen goods, judging from the bulging plastic bags she'd dumped in two separate bins as I looked on. Apparently, she wasn't involved in the transportation of goods from point to point. My guess was that she off-loaded the stolen items as quickly as possible, passing them along to others in the loop. I couldn't picture the Prestwicks at the top of the heap. More likely they were employed by someone higher up on the food chain. Audrey's calls to Los Angeles, Corpus Christi, and Miami suggested an organization with branches in ports of call across the country. Somewhere along the line, cash had been generated and shipped to the now-deceased Audrey Vance. She probably used the money to pay the workers she'd assembled every other Saturday. Now what?

I left the county building and drove back to Juniper Lane. I parked two doors down from the Prestwicks' house and stared at the narrow slice of driveway I could see. I wasn't officially on surveillance. I needed a place to sit while I sorted myself out and why not in range of two principal players? I took my index cards from the depths of my shoulder bag and made a few notes, discouraged by the paucity of facts. I had lots of good guesses and little evidence.

Now that Marvin Striker and I had parted company, I was on my own. While I liked not having to answer to him, I wouldn't net a nickel for my services. This is a dumb way to run a business, especially when the usual bills came due and I'd find myself short on funds. I have a savings account to cover shortfalls, but I don't fancy dipping into it. Despite my huffy claims to the contrary, I couldn't afford to work for long without pay. The sensible course of action would be to collate the data I'd collected and hand it over to Cheney Phillips. I had no intention of dealing with Len Priddy, but if Cheney wanted to pass on the information, that was up to him.

I caught movement ahead and watched as Georgia emerged from her driveway on foot. She wasn't dressed for exercise unless she leaned toward jogging in a tight skirt, panty hose, and strappy spike-heel shoes. She reached the corner and paused. As I looked on, a long black limousine pulled into view. The back door swung open and she got in, after which the limousine glided out of my line of sight. I fired up the Mustang and drove to the end of the block, where I nosed forward slightly and peered to my right. The limousine had pulled over to the curb and it sat there, engine idling. A very large man in a black suit had stepped out. He stood beside the vehicle, hands neatly folded in front of him while he scanned the immediate area. His gaze came to rest on my car, and I had no choice but to turn left and drive on as though that had been my intent. I didn't even have time to pick up a plate number, which I could see was becoming a habitual failing of mine. Once again, I cursed the Grabber Blue Mustang, which was much too conspicuous. I couldn't even speed around the block and approach from the opposite direction.

I returned to the office, and as I pulled up in front, I saw Pinky Ford sitting on my porch step, a manila envelope in hand. I'd been looking forward to time on my own, but that was apparently not in the cards. When he saw me, he stood up and dusted off the seat of his pants. He wore the usual jeans, this time with a Western-cut shirt, black with silver studs up one side like upholstery tacks. He'd been there for some time judging by the number of dead cigarette butts at his feet. As I approached, he tucked the envelope under one arm and bent down to collect the butts. He held them cupped in one hand while he made a show of rubbing out the ashes with the toe of one boot.

I said, "Hey, Pinky. How are you? I hope you're not here to tell me you hocked something else."

"No, ma'am. I've been good," he said. "About that, at any rate."

I unlocked the door and he followed me in. "I can make a pot of coffee if you like."

"I'm kind of in a hurry."

"You want to have a seat or would that take too long?"

"I can sit," he said.

I pulled the trash can from under my desk and held it out to him, waiting while he deposited his cigarette butts and wiped his hands on his jeans. Personally, I'd have loved a cup of coffee but I postponed the pleasure in the interest of speed and efficiency. He settled on the guest chair and placed the manila envelope on my desk. As I looked over, I saw that the light on my answering machine was winking merrily. "Hang on."

I pressed play and the minute I heard "This is Dia . . ." I punched delete.

Pinky said, "Geez, I can tell you're fond of her."

"Long story," I said. "Is that for me?"

He pushed the envelope forward an inch. "I was hoping you could hang on to it temporarily."

"What is it?"

"Photographs."

"Of?"

"Two different individuals in compromising circumstances. It's better if you don't know the particulars."

"Why is it better? It doesn't sound better to me."

"The subject matter's on the sensitive side. In the first set, someone's reputation and good name are at stake."

"You with another woman?"

"Not me. I don't have a good name or reputation, either one. Besides which, I wouldn't fool around on Dodie. She's explained in some detail what she'd do to me if I strayed."

"What about the other set?"

"Second's more serious. I'd say life-or-death if it didn't sound like I was blowing smoke up your skirt."

"How many photographs altogether? Doesn't matter. I'm just curious," I said.

He thought about that, like the idea hadn't occurred to him before. "I'd say ten."

"You're guessing ten or you've actually counted them?"

"I counted. There's also the negatives. Copies without the negatives aren't worth shit. Destroy one set and all a fellow has to do is print 'em up again."

"Why give them to me?"

He paused to remove a fleck of tobacco from his tongue. "Good question," he said without volunteering a response.

"Pinky, I'm not going to hang on to anything unless you tell me what's going on."

"Understood," he said. He looked up at the ceiling. "Let's see how I can explain and still exercise my fifth-amendment rights."

"Take your time."

He thought for a moment. "I may have picked my way into the premises of a person I believed was in possession of the material in the envelope. I'm not saying I did, but it's possible. It's also possible I'd looked for the items elsewhere and when they didn't come to light, I deduced their whereabouts."

"Why get involved in the first place?"

"I wanted to eliminate the threat to a friend of mine. In the process, these other pictures came to light and that's what's put me in a bind. Big-time."

"Doesn't that suggest that anyone *holding* the photographs would be in trouble if *someone else* figured it out?"

"Why would anyone suspect you?"

"What if you were followed? There could be a guy parked down the block with binoculars trained on my door. You come in with the envelope. You leave without it. The bad guys aren't stupid. I don't care who they are, they're going to figure it out."

He shifted in his chair, apparently discomfited by the idea. The look he turned on me was shrewd. "You could give me another manila envelope to carry with me when I leave."

I squinted. "You know what? This really doesn't sound like a good plan to me. You know I'd help if I could, but you've dug yourself a hole and I don't want to fall into it with you."

This was not the response he was looking for. "How about I leave the photos for one day?"

"How do I know you'll come back for them?"

"Because I got a good use for them, but not right away. This is just for safekeeping. One day." He held up one finger to dramatize the time frame like the number 1 was somehow ambiguous.

"I know you better than that. You'll do what's expedient and I'll be stuck."

"Promise I'll come back for them. I swear."

"I don't understand why one day will make a difference."

"I'm setting up a meeting for tomorrow afternoon. I'm in a jam and the photos are my get-out-of-jail-free card, but only if I get them to the relevant party. Meantime, you can put the envelope in your safe and forget it's there."

"What makes you think I have a safe?"

The look he gave me was pained, like it was obvious. "I'll pick 'em up by noon tomorrow and that's the last you'll hear."

I wanted to slam my fingers in the pencil drawer, which in the end would have been less painful than his proposal. "Please don't ask me to do this."

"I *am* asking you. I'm desperate." He managed to look solemn and plaintive and helpless and dependent.

I stared at him. Jailbirds are so often like this, I thought. In prison or out, they wheedle and manipulate. Maybe they can't help it. They chain themselves to the proverbial railroad tracks knowing good souls, like me, will gallop to the rescue. When I do as predicted, guess who ends up under the train?

Everything in me cried out in protest. How many times have I said yes in situations like this with disastrous results? How many times have I fallen for just such a pitch? The purpose of intuition is to warn us when the wolf arrives at the door dressed as Little Red Riding Hood. I opened my mouth, not even certain what would come out. "Something about this doesn't feel right to me," I said. "Actually, none of it feels right."

"You're the only friend I have."

"Stop that. There has to be somebody else."

He shrugged, refusing to look me in the eye. "Let's hope. Otherwise, I'm in a world of hurt."

I sat there wondering which was worse: making the wrong decision and having a load of shit rain down on my head, or avoiding calamity and feeling overwhelmed with guilt. That was the moment that nearly did me in. I teetered on the brink and finally shook my head. "I can't. I'm sorry, but if I agree, I'll regret it."

He stood up and I followed suit. When he reached across the desk to shake my hand, he managed to convey a sense of finality. "I don't want you to feel bad for turning me down. I shouldn't have put you in this position."

"I hope you figure it out."

"Me too. Meanwhile, I appreciate your time. You take care now. I can let myself out."

"Will you keep in touch?"

"If possible," he said.

We exchanged awkward good-byes and then he left my inner office, moving toward the outside door. I truly wondered if I'd ever see him again. I returned to the office window and looked out. It took a few seconds before he appeared in my field of vision. I should have known he was up to something, but I didn't think anything of it at the time. I leaned my head against the glass, watching as he disappeared down the street. I half expected to hear gunfire or the squeal of tires as a license-plate-free vehicle accelerated and ran over him.

I sank into my swivel chair and experienced the full weight of my remorse. Next time he asked for anything—if he lived long enough—I'd say yes no matter what. This was one of those "little did I know" moments, though I wasn't aware of it at the time. I don't know how long I might have sat there berating myself, but I had another visitor.

I heard a tap on the outside door, which then opened and closed. I got up and crossed to the door, peering around the frame to find out who'd come in. Marvin's bar buddy, Earldeen, was in the process of taking off her coat. It crossed my mind he might have sent her to apologize, being too cowardly and too embarrassed to do so himself.

I said, "Hey, Earldeen. I didn't expect to see you."

She held up one of the business cards I'd left at the Hatch. "Lucky Ollie had this or I wouldn't have known where you were."

"Come on in," I said. "You want me to hang that up?"

"This is fine," she said. She laid her coat over the back of one of the guest chairs while she took a seat in the other. She was easily a head taller than me and she'd probably fallen into the habit of bad posture as a teen in hopes of looking the same height as everyone else. The scent of bourbon hovered in the air around her, though she was sober as far as I could tell.

I returned to my desk and sat down. "Is there some way I can be of help?"

"More like I'm here to help you. Something came up I thought you ought to know about."

"I can hardly wait."

"Well, after you left the Hatch yesterday, this fellow came in. I hadn't seen him for a while, but he knew Audrey pretty well, because the two of them used to have these long heart-to-heart talks. This was a year ago, before she and Marvin started stepping out together. I haven't seen him since. I thought he must be an ex-husband or an old boyfriend, someone she didn't want Marvin to know about."

"And was that the case?"

"At the time, I wasn't sure, but I'll admit I was curious. He's a good-looking guy. Midfifties, tall, with curly gray hair, and these big old brown eyes. He and Audrey always had their heads together and when I asked who he was, she brushed the question aside. They were a bad match in my opinion. She was a good ten years older than him and, no disrespect intended, he was much too handsome for the likes of her. I know that sounds terrible, but it's the truth."

"Did he come in looking for her yesterday?"

Earldeen shook her head. "He was meeting someone else. This was a woman who didn't have any business in a place like the Hatch. She was more the country-club type, if you know what I mean."

"Close enough," I said. "What happened?"

"Nothing much. They chatted for a minute or two and then he ushered her out the side door and that was the last I saw of them."

"Why tell me?"

"Well, that's just it. Back when this was going on, I asked Ollie who he was and he told me his name is Lorenzo Dante. Have you heard of him?"

"I don't think so."

"He goes by the name Dante so nobody gets him mixed up with his dad, Lorenzo Dante Senior. Ollie says he's a gangster."

"The father or the son?"

"Both. I guess the father's retired. Of course, I don't travel in those circles, but I hear this fellow has a hand in a number of shady dealings."

"Such as what?"

"Well, he's a loan shark for one thing. He also owns an import-export warehouse out in Colgate called Allied Distributors. I have a hunch Audrey worked for him."

My heart had started to thump because I'd seen that same warehouse the day before. "Why didn't you tell me this a week ago? I've been busting my butt trying to figure out what she was up to. This would have been a big help."

"I got sidetracked, I guess. I was so upset thinking she killed herself, it didn't occur to me her death might be connected to her boss. It wasn't until I saw him yesterday, the penny dropped."

"Does Marvin know?"

"Let's put it this way. I told him straight out, but that doesn't mean he got the message. He doesn't want to hear Audrey was working for a crook. He thinks she's a saint and he won't listen to anything else."

"That's the same charge he leveled at me."

"Oh, I know. It's called projection. I see it all the time at the Hatch. You accuse someone else of having traits you refuse to acknowledge in yourself," she said. "Don't look so shocked. I got a college education back in the day. I majored in psychology with a minor in fine arts."

"Sorry. I'm just trying to take this in. You'd think Marvin would be thrilled. He's convinced she was murdered and this supports the claim, don't you think?"

"Well, I don't know about that," Earldeen said. "Audrey and this Dante fellow were thick as thieves, if you'll pardon the pun. She worked hard. She was always on the road and she made a ton of money. To me, that's the mark of success. Why would he kill her when she was so good at what she did?"

"Maybe she got too big for her britches and threatened to take over."

"I guess it's possible. You heard what Marvin said. Somebody talked him into the notion she was tossed off the bridge because she knew too much. The question is what?"

"Beats me," I said. I considered the implications. Based on the sketchy facts I had in my possession, I had no clue what she might have discovered.

Earldeen fidgeted. "What do you think I should do?"

"Well, if I were you, I'd go to the police."

"I tried that. Before I came here, I went down to the police department and asked to speak to someone about Audrey's death. The fellow at the desk made a call and said Sergeant Priddy would be right out. I said never mind and hightailed it out of there as fast as I could. I don't like how his name keeps coming up. Anyway, I just hope Marvin doesn't find out I was here or he'll chew me a new one."

# 24

After Earldeen left, I went over my notes again. I'd never felt quite so enamored of my index cards. They were like the pieces of a puzzle that would fall into place once I understood what I was looking at. I shuffled the cards and laid them out on my desk. I could arrange the facts in any order I liked, but the bits and pieces would come together only when I perceived their true relationships. The process kept my thinking loose, so I didn't get too invested in having the narrative line up the way I thought it should. For the moment, I was without direction, but instead of being discouraged, I saw this as an opportunity to stop and take note. It was like standing in a slow-moving stream with information flowing over and around me. I could turn in any direction and survey my surroundings while I debated where to cast my line.

I turned up the card on which I'd noted the name of the real estate office offering the ramshackle cottages for sale, a company called Providential Properties. It would be interesting, thought I, to find out who the tenant had been and for what period of time. I pulled out the phone book and looked up the real estate office in the yellow pages. There was only one address listed, that being in Colgate, California, which suggested this wasn't a multinational company with branches in London, Paris, and Hong Kong. A chat with the realtor would be nice, and better in person than by phone.

I stopped for gas and a trip to the ladies' room before I got on the 101, which gave me time to think about a cover story. Why would I be inquiring about run-down real estate? In my jeans and turtleneck, I looked shabby enough. I'd never bought property, even in pretense, and I had no idea how one went about it. What if I were asked for my home address, occupation, and my place of employment? I decided to make that part up if and when it came to it. For all I knew, Providential Properties, like Helping Hearts, Healing Hands, was a figment of someone's imagination.

I found the office in a line of businesses on the main street that ran through Colgate. I passed the place, did a quick scan, and then parked down the block. Outside the office, I paused to look at the window display showing photographs of the properties available. Most appeared to be commercial, and I noticed then that the small print on the company sign said OFFICE, INDUSTRIAL, RETAIL, AND INVESTMENT PROPERTIES. It wasn't until I'd put my hand on the knob that I spotted a paper clock and a note dangling from a suction cup affixed to the inside of the glass. BACK IN TEN MINUTES. The clock hands had been set to 11:00. My watch said 11:45. I turned and checked for pedestrians up and down the sidewalk, thinking the returning agent might be in sight. While there were any number of people out and about, none was heading in my direction. I wasn't sure whether to wait or give it up altogether.

I went into the shoe-repair shop next door, which smelled divinely of leather, glue, paste shoe polish, and machinery. The fellow working behind the counter was restitching the strap on a knapsack. He was in his seventies and looked up at me over the half rims of his bifocals, his curly white hair brushing his shoulders.

I said, "Do you have any idea when the realtor next door might return? The sign on the door says ten minutes, but that was forty-five minutes ago."

"She went home. She does that sometimes when business is slow."

"Really. I wonder why she didn't just close up shop and be done with it?"

"She hates to turn away a client. Lot of people come in here looking for her. I'll give you her business card. If you leave a message on her answering machine, she'll call you back."

This would mean a second trip out, which annoyed me no end, but I couldn't see an alternative. "I guess that'll have to do."

He got up and crossed to the counter where he opened a drawer and fumbled among the contents before handing me a card decorated with smudged fingerprints.

As I thanked him, my gaze dropped to the agent's name. Felicia Stringfield. I said, "Felicia?"

"Do you know her?"

"I believe I've heard the name," I said. "Does she handle residential properties?"

"If she's given the opportunity. She's not one to refuse a request."

"Well, that's good," I said. "I'll give her a call and maybe stop by again if she's going to be in."

"You want to leave your name and phone number?"

"Don't worry about that. I'll get back to her. Thanks."

I returned to my car and dug out my index cards. I removed the rubber band and rifled through them rapidly until I came to the notes I'd taken after my first meeting with Marvin. Felicia was the first name of the agent who was set to show Marvin and Audrey houses for sale on the day she disappeared. There could be a whole subset of agents named Felicia, but I doubted it. I would have loved confirmation, but I really didn't want to talk to Marvin at this point. If the agent was the same, it couldn't be a coincidence that she was offering cottages for sale or rent at an address that was tied to the consignment shop.

I closed my eyes, running the facts down in my mind. I couldn't see a junction where all the points converged. I sensed the contours of the theft ring and I knew some of the players by name. I also knew how (but not what) they moved between locations. The problem was I had no authority to act. At best, I could make a citizen's arrest, but I'd never set much store by the concept. If I managed to collar a crook, what would prevent his simply laughing it off and walking away? The minute I laid a hand on him, he'd respond with charges of assault. I'm a small-town private investigator. Bringing down an organization like this was the job of law enforcement.

I found the nearest pay phone and called Cheney Phillips's direct line. When he picked up, he seemed to recognize my voice but I identified myself nonetheless. "Can I talk to you?"

He said, "Sure. I've got time this afternoon if you want to stop by. What's good for you?"

"Not your office," I said.

He was silent briefly. "Okay. Then where?"

"What about the Shack at Ludlow Beach?"

"Great. We can have lunch. My treat. See you there in twenty minutes."

I hadn't called him looking for a lunch date, but the minute he mentioned it, I realized I was starving so why not? I'd chosen the location because it was off the beaten path, a tourist spot as opposed to a restaurant frequented by local residents. The place was bound to be somebody's favorite, but it wasn't popular with cops. The Shack was right on the beach, sheltered from the view of passing cars by a large parking lot. Blue-and-white-striped awnings shaded the deck where the tables were set out. Once upon a time, I'd come close to being killed in the big trash bin outside. This counts as nostalgia for someone like me.

I found a table for two in the corner on the far side and sat facing the entrance. When Cheney appeared, I lifted my hand to attract his attention. He threaded his way between the tables, and when he reached me he gave me the obligatory buss on the cheek before he pulled out a chair and sat down. He was in chinos, a white dress shirt, and a sueded silk sport coat the color of wild brown bunnies. Cheney came from money and while he'd declined to go into his father's banking business, a trust fund allowed him to dress with impeccable taste. He favored earth tones, colors that reminded me of nature's softer side, in sensual fabrics I wanted to reach out and touch. He also smelled better than almost any man I've known, some combination of soap, shampoo, after-shave, and body chemistry. There were moments I remembered from our short-lived affair and I had to resist the temptation to sexualize my contact with him.

We chatted and then ordered and then ate. As hungry as I'd been, I scarcely paid attention to the meal. I was anxious and I could feel myself stalling, not wanting to launch into my spiel. I don't know if I was afraid he wouldn't take me seriously or that he'd judge the facts too thin to act upon.

Cheney finally pushed the point. "What's on your mind?"

I reached into my shoulder bag, took out my report, and placed it facedown on the table. "I've put together some information that should probably go to Len, but I can't bring myself to deal with him. You know how he feels about me after what happened to Mickey. He'd dismiss anything I said, but he might pay attention if it came from you."

"Give me the gist."

"Organized retail theft. I wouldn't have known anything about it if it hadn't been for Audrey's death . . ."

I'd been engrossed in the subject for days and I laid it out for him in an orderly progression. I watched his expression alter as I worked my way through events from the beginning to the current moment. Cheney's a smart guy, and so I knew I didn't have to spell out the broader picture when I was already providing the specifics. At the end of my summary, he held out his hand for the report. I gave it to him and watched him leaf through the pages. Once or twice he looked at me in sharp surprise, which I confess I took as a compliment.

When he finished reading, he said, "How'd you come up with the connection to the consignment shop?"

"I was chatting with someone about fencing operations. The name came out of our conversation." I told him about the boxes I'd picked up and the shipping labels.

He was momentarily quiet and not making eye contact, which didn't bode well. He seemed to be filtering the information through a framework different from mine.

"What's the matter?" I asked.

"Sorry. You caught me by surprise. I didn't realize what you were up to."

*"What I was up to?"*

"I didn't know you were so interested in Audrey Vance."

"I don't know why not. I told you Marvin Striker hired me to look into her past. That's what I was asking about the day I ran into you and Len having lunch. What's going on?"

"Nothing you could have known about."

"What, like there's already an investigation under way?"

"All I can tell you is you're treading on sensitive ground and I suggest you back off."

"Well, if it's any comfort to you, I've come to a dead end," I said. "If I knew what to do at this point, I wouldn't be here. This is your bailiwick, not mine."

"True, and I appreciate what you've accomplished. Now promise me you'll let it drop."

I said, "Ah. So I must be on track or you wouldn't be clamming up."

"This is not your concern. I don't mean to be hard-nosed, but I know how you operate. You get on the scent of something and it's hard to pull you off. I'm not faulting you on that score or any other."

"Imagine my relief," I said.

He looked down at the report. "You have copies or is this it?"

"Why do you ask?"

"Because I might need to confiscate the material for a period of time. I don't want the information floating around."

"You're kidding."

The look he gave me was utterly without mirth, so I thought it best to abandon my jocular tone.

I leaned toward him and lowered my voice. "Jesus, Cheney. If I was stepping in a pile of shit, why didn't you say so at the time?"

"My fault entirely. I should have warned you."

"Of what?"

"Just let it go, okay? I know you mean well . . ."

"I don't understand what's at stake. I don't want to make trouble. You know me better than that, so what's the deal?"

"You're putting a CI in jeopardy."

"How so? I don't know anything about a confidential informant. This is all news to me."

He studied me briefly. "I'll tell you this if you swear you won't breathe a word of it to anyone."

"I swear."

"The retail-theft ring is only one part of the equation. Priddy's under investigation as well. The informant's working both sides of the street. Len thinks he's milking the guy for information, but the CI is reporting back to us and feeding him lines while we build our case. His testimony will be critical. Priddy's a slippery customer. In all these years, no one's been able to nail him."

"Oh, I hear you," I said. "I'd love nothing better than to see him brought down."

"Leave that to us. Len's got cop friends who'd do anything for him. We know some of them, but not all, so walk a wide path around him. You can trust me but don't talk to anyone else." He took out his wallet and extracted a twenty and a ten and put it under his plate.

"Lunch didn't cost that much," I said.

"I like to leave a good tip so here's one: bury the topic until I tell you it's okay. I'll send someone around to pick up any other copies of this you have on hand." He folded the report and slid it into the inside pocket of his sport coat.

Driving back to the office, I deconstructed the conversation, separating the elements for review. It was obvious the police department was running an investigation that paralleled mine, the two intersecting at more than one point. I wasn't sure where they were in the process, but they had to be focused on the same operation I'd been looking at, though doubtless at a more sophisticated and comprehensive level. There was probably a task force in place, several agencies pooling their resources as they gathered intelligence. Cheney's revelation both thrilled and troubled me. I didn't expect him to bare all. These days, the legal system is so finely calibrated that a breach in security or a violation of procedure can spell disaster. As a rule, I keep my nose out of police business, though it's not always easy. I do tend to fixate on a problem and worry it to death. Here, what I loved more than snooping was the idea of Len Priddy being exposed for what he was. Cheney's warning had come too late to steer me off the subject of retail theft, but I intended to heed his caution about Len. What disturbed me was knowing just enough to feel I might be vulnerable.

As I turned onto my block, I noticed a dark green Chevrolet parked in my usual place at the curb. I didn't think much about it since parking is at such a premium. It's first-come, first-served, and I'm often forced to hunt for the next available spot. I found a length of curb where my front bumper encroached on a private driveway, but only by three feet. At the end of the day, if I was lucky, I'd escape without a ticket.

Coming up the walk, I stopped short of the front steps, alerted by the fact that the door was open when I knew I'd locked up when I left. I took four paces to the side and peered in the window, where I could see Len Priddy doing a finger-walk through my files. I tried to think how I'd behave with him if Cheney hadn't warned me. Len already knew there was no love lost between us, but beyond our mutual dislike, I'd never had reason to be afraid of him. Now I was. I went into the outer office and when I appeared in the doorway, he didn't even seem embarrassed at being caught in the act.

I said, "You mind if I ask what you're doing?"

He turned. "Sorry. You weren't here when I arrived so I let myself in. Is that a problem?" He had tossed any number of file folders on the floor, not because it was necessary, but to illustrate his contempt.

"That depends on what you want."

I moved toward my desk, keeping as much distance between the two of us as I could muster. Glancing down, I could see he'd made a point of leaving my desk drawers ajar so I'd know he'd been through them as well. I made no comment.

He said, "Relax. This is nothing official. I thought it was time for us to chat." He removed a file folder and slid the drawer shut. He tossed the folder on the desk and then settled in my swivel chair, tilted back, propping his feet against the edge. He reached for the folder and pulled out the single sheet of paper, the photocopy of Marvin's check. Cleverly, I'd filed the written report on Audrey elsewhere, so he had no way to determine what I knew.

He shook his head in disapproval. "Looks like you haven't come up with anything on Audrey Vance, which surprises me. I thought you were a crack investigator and you've got bupkes. You take Marvin's money, the least you could do is give him something in return."

Rapidly, I scrolled through the possible responses, trying to figure out how best to protect myself. "I haven't started on it yet. I have a case that took precedence," I said. The lie slipped out so easily, I didn't think he caught the hesitation before I answered him.

"Then you ought to give his money back."

"Good plan. I'll have a chat with him and see if he feels the same."

"He does. He's no longer in the market for your services."

"Thanks for the heads-up," I said. The game playing annoyed me, but it was better for him to think he had the upper hand. I didn't want to antagonize him. No sass. No wisecracks. "If you tell me why you're here, maybe I can help."

"I'm in no hurry. How about yourself? You have pressing business to conduct?" He peered closely at my empty calendar. "It doesn't look like it."

He tossed Audrey's file on the desk and got up. He put his hands in his trouser pockets and looked out the window at the street. By turning his back, he was showing me how sure he was of himself. He was a big man and seeing him in silhouette, I was unnerved by his bulk. Like many middle-aged men, he'd gained weight, twenty-five to thirty pounds by the look of him. In his case, most of it was muscle mass. He and Mickey had lifted weights together in the early days, a routine he'd apparently kept up. He seemed indifferent to any action I might take, but I knew better.

He turned around to look at me, leaning a hip on the windowsill. "We have a mutual friend, who came to see you earlier."

"I've been out."

"Before you left for lunch."

He had to be referring to Pinky or Earldeen, and I was nominating Pinky. In a flash, I knew he was after the photographs. As quickly as it occurred to me, I suppressed the thought, cautious he'd pick up on my mental process. Many sociopaths, like Len, seem able to read minds, a skill that doubtless results from the in-built paranoia that motivates so much of what they do. I said, "I'm not sure who you mean."

"Your pal, Pierpont."

"Pierpont?" The name meant nothing. I shook my head.

"Pinky."

"His real name is Pierpont?"

"That's what his jacket says. He has a long criminal history as I'm sure you're aware."

"I know he's been in jail. Are you looking for him?"

"Not him. A manila envelope. I believe he left it with you."

Len was either featured in one set of photographs or protecting the person who was. If the photos were of Len, I couldn't imagine how he'd been compromised. Pinky viewed the pictures as his trump card, so what was that about?

I said, "You've got it wrong. He asked me to hang on to the envelope and I refused."

He smiled. "Good try, but I don't think so."

"It's true. He wouldn't tell me what was in the envelope so I said I couldn't help. He took it with him when he left."

"Not so. He walked out empty-handed. I was watching."

What had Pinky done? I remembered the brief lag time between his leaving my inner office and his appearance on the street. The only thing I could think of was that he'd hidden the envelope under his shirt or down the front of his pants. I was the one who'd suggested he might be under surveillance, so I'd unwittingly engineered my current difficulty, which was to persuade Len the envelope wasn't in my possession.

I put my hands in the air, as though at gunpoint. "I don't have it. Honest. You've already searched my file cabinets and the desk drawers, so you know it's not there. Check my shoulder bag if you want."

I set my bag on the desk. He didn't want to appear too interested, so he took his time, casually pawing through the miscellany. Wallet, makeup bag, a few over-the-counter meds, keys, spiral-bound notebook, which he stopped and leafed through before tossing it aside. I was fearful he'd spot the index cards and confiscate the lot of them, but he was focused on the image of an eight-by-ten envelope and disregarded anything that didn't match that description. I could feel the tension seep into my bones. I was reacting to Len the way I'd react to a street thug or a belligerent drunk, someone capable of violence if provoked. I didn't believe he'd attack me because an assault would leave him vulnerable to charges. There were no wants and warrants out against me, and he had no way to justify getting physical.

"Where's the safe?" he asked.

I pointed at the floor to one side of the room. My safe was concealed under a section of my bubble-gum-pink wall-to-wall carpeting. He gestured impatiently, indicating I was to hop to, and I complied. I knew there was no manila envelope, so what was it to me? He crossed the room and stood over me while I pulled the carpet back and exposed the safe to view. I hated his knowing where it was, but it was better to appear cooperative. I got down on one knee and dialed in the combination. When the door swung open, he was forced to assume the same kneeling posture so he could empty the contents. I glanced at the door, realizing if I intended to bolt, this would be the time to do it. I kept the impulse in check, believing it was wiser to let the situation play out. The safe held nothing of interest: insurance policies, bank information, and the modest amount of cash I like to keep on hand.

That's when I noticed he'd ripped the phone cord out of the wall and smashed the housing until it cracked in half. There was something about the savagery that scared me senseless. Too late, I realized I'd adopted the mind-set of a kidnap victim, thinking everything would be all right as long as I did as I was told. This notion was foolish on the face of it. It's always better to scream, run, or fight back. No one knew he was here. My bungalow is the only occupied structure on this side of the street. If he decided I was holding out on him, whether it was true or not, he could handcuff me, throw me in the trunk of his car, and pound the shit out of me in private until I gave him what he wanted. The fact that I didn't have the photographs wasn't relevant and would only net me more punishment.

He was still pulling papers out of my safe when I made a break for the outside door. The problem was I'd been standing stiffly at attention and I couldn't move fast enough. Even as I took the first two steps, I felt like I was weighted in place. He was on me before I'd gone six feet. I couldn't believe a man his size could act so quickly. He grabbed me by the shirt and hauled me backward off my feet, hooking an arm around my neck before I could marshal a defense. I knew the choke hold from my days as a rookie. This was called a lateral vascular neck restraint, or blood choke. With the crook of his elbow over the midpoint of my neck, all he had to do was increase the pressure, using his free hand for leverage. If I tried to turn around, it would only escalate the force of the hold. The pressure on my carotid arteries and jugular veins would result in hypoxia that would render me unconscious in seconds. Most police departments prohibit the use of the carotid hold unless an officer is threatened with death or serious injury. Len Priddy was from the old school, coming up through the ranks while the blood choke was still considered fair play. He was a full head taller and weighed a good hundred pounds more than I did.

I couldn't make a sound. I clung to his arm, holding on with both hands as though I might actually ease his grip when I knew the effort would be futile. The pain was excruciating and I was starved for oxygen.

Len had his mouth up against my ear, his voice low. "I know how to finish you off without leaving a mark on you. Complain about me and I'll hurt you so bad it'll put you out of commission for the rest of your life. I'm coming down on you hard for your own damn good. Audrey Vance is none of your business, you get that? Anything you hear about, you keep shut. Whatever you see, you'd best look the other way. I find out you have those photographs, I will come back and kill you. Make no mistake about it. If you tell anyone else about this, the same penalty applies. Is that clear?"

I couldn't even nod. Next thing I knew he'd shoved me to the floor and backed off, breathing hard himself. I was down on my hands and knees, sucking air into my lungs. I put a hand against my throat, where the sensation of compression and restriction was still vivid. I leaned my forehead on the carpet and put my arms over my head, gasping for breath. I knew he was standing over me. I thought he'd punch me or kick me, but he probably didn't dare risk bruising me or cracking my ribs. Dimly, I was aware of his walking away. I heard the outer office door open and shut. I crawled after him and locked the door in his wake. It wasn't until I heard his car start and pull away that I started to shake.

# 25

I rolled over on my back and lay on the floor until my heartbeat had slowed and the blood no longer pounded in my ears. I sat up, doing a canvas of my physical and emotional state. Swallowing was painful and my confidence was shaken. Beyond that, I wasn't injured, but I was badly frightened. Now that the immediate threat had passed, I needed to pull myself together. I turned and stared at my office floor, which was littered with the papers Len had pulled from the safe. File folders and reports had been dumped from the file cabinets and lay scattered about. I wanted nothing more than to spend the next few minutes cleaning up the mess. Getting to my feet first would be a big help. My emotions were all over the place, and tidying my surroundings was the way I soothed myself in times of stress. For the moment, I'd have to forgo indulging my inner Cinderella because Pinky had priority. I didn't believe Len would kill me (unless he could be sure the deed wouldn't be traced back to him). Pinky was the obvious target. He was a low-level criminal with prison associates who probably already represented a risk to his health and safety. If he died, no one would think much about it. Why he imagined he could outwit someone like Len was a mystery. I used a guest chair to pull myself upright and went into the bathroom, where I stretched the rim of my turtleneck so I could examine my poor abused flesh. Len was right when he boasted he hadn't left a mark.

I picked up my broken telephone and tossed the hull in the trash. Fortunately, I still had the previous instrument I'd owned. I went into the kitchenette and opened and closed closet doors until I found it. It was an old black rotary phone, powdered with dust. I wiped it down with a towel and took it back to the office, where I plugged it into the old jack. I picked up the handset, reassured by the dial tone. I needed to contact Pinky and tell him what was going on.

I was acutely aware of Len's warning to keep away from matters related to Audrey Vance, but Pinky and the photographs were another matter—weren't they? I knew that if Len caught up with Pinky, he was dead meat. I had to make sure I got to him first. I wondered if Pinky had any idea the jeopardy he was in. He'd talked about using the photographs to get out of a jam, but trying to outsmart Len was trouble of a greater magnitude.

I sat down at my desk and checked my address book for Pinky's phone number. I seldom had occasion to call him, and for all I knew, the contact number I had was long out of date. I put the end of my index finger in the first hole, in which the number 9 appeared. I moved the dial to the right as far as the finger set and released it, thinking how odd it was to have to wait until the metal circle with the little holes in it rotated all the way back before hooking my finger into the next number in the sequence. Seemed to take forever. Lo and behold, the line rang. I listened, counting. At fifteen, I gave up hope and put the handset back in the cradle. I had no idea if he was actually home and too clever to answer the phone, or if he'd gone into hiding, as any sensible fugitive would do. I didn't even know if the number was still his. I was going to have to drive over to his place and check it out.

I left the disorder where it was and locked the office door behind me. Before I got in the Mustang, I went around and opened the trunk and took the H&K out of my briefcase. I didn't have a concealed carry permit but I wasn't going to leave myself unprotected. There was a fellow waxing his car in the driveway between my bungalow and the one next door. I wasn't aware a new tenant had moved in, but what did I know? He'd set a bucket and some rags to one side, and he was applying paste wax to the front fenders and hood of a black Jeep. A hose lay on the sidewalk, snaking out from between the buildings. He paid no attention to me, but I was careful nonetheless to slide the gun into my shoulder bag before I stepped into view. I got into the car and tucked the gun under the front seat before I turned the key in the ignition and pulled away from the curb.

My run-in with Len played in my head like an endless loop of film. I lived those moments over and over, but regardless of how many times I reviewed the encounter, it ended the same way. Self-preservation being what it is, I wouldn't have handled myself any differently, but I wondered if there were options that hadn't occurred to me. My neck still felt like it was caught in a noose. I kept putting a hand against my throat as though to assure myself of my ability to breathe.

I cut over to Chapel and took a right, driving the eight blocks to Paseo Street, where Pinky and Dodie lived. I didn't think I'd been followed, because why would Len bother? He knew where Pinky lived or if he didn't, it would be a simple matter to pull up the data on his computer. I wondered if he had me in his sights, playing out enough rope to see if I'd make a beeline for Pinky. But if Len had known where he was, he wouldn't have had to jump me for the whereabouts of the manila envelope. I checked my rearview mirror, but there was no sign of an approaching car or idlers on the street.

Gamely, I parked, got out of my car, and crossed the street. The front windows in both halves of the duplex were dark. I had no idea which was theirs, but I would soon find out. It was 1:50, sunshine, temperatures in the midseventies, the scent of honeysuckle in the air. The breeze was playful, making it hard to believe there was anything going on that wasn't purely recreational in nature. But here I was looking for a goofball who thought he was smart enough to pull a fast one on a bad cop. This was probably the same skewed reasoning that got him thrown back in prison every time he got out. It was just my bad luck I liked the guy, but that might have been what Len was counting on when he cut me loose.

The name above the doorbell on the left was Ford, and on the right, McWherter. I rang the Fords' bell and waited. If I were Dodie or Pinky, I wouldn't open the door to anyone. I turned and scanned the street first in one direction and then the other. I didn't see anyone sitting in a parked car, no one slipping furtively through the bushes.

I leaned my head close to the door and knocked. "Dodie? Are you in there? It's Kinsey, a friend of Pinky's."

I waited.

Finally, I heard a muffled "Show me."

I recognized Dodie's voice, so I moved over to the living room window that was blocked by drawn drapes. Dodie made a small opening between the panels and stared out at me. A moment later, I heard her turn the deadbolt and slide the chain back on its track. She opened the door a crack and I sidled in. I stood to one side as she reversed the locking process. If Len Priddy decided to come after her, all the locks in the world wouldn't do any good. He'd bash in the front window and that would be the end of that. I didn't mention the likelihood, thinking there was no point in scaring her when she was already scared to death.

In the living room to my right, the television set was on with the sound turned down. She put a finger to her lips and then gestured toward the back of the house. We tiptoed down the hall and into the kitchen, during which time I had the opportunity to register the changes in her. She'd been transformed by the weight loss. Pinky had told me she'd dropped sixty pounds and the difference was amazing. Her bright blue eyes had always been her best feature. Now she had a better color on her hair, a better cut, and better makeup as a result of her new occupation. She'd also improved her wardrobe. The outfit she wore—long-sleeve V-neck sweater, well-tailored slacks, and expensive high heels—gave her the elongated look of a fashion model, though Pinky was right about her tush.

When we reached the kitchen, I whispered, "You look great."

"Thanks," she whispered back.

"Why are we whispering?"

She held up a finger and wagged it, like I wasn't supposed to ask. She grabbed a pen and a copy of the newspaper and wrote a note in the margin that said, "Bugged."

Under her breath, she said, "You must be looking for Pinky. What's he done now?"

"He's pissed off a cop named Len Priddy, which is not a good idea."

"Oh, him," she murmured. "He stopped by a while ago and I said Pinky'd gone to see you."

I closed my eyes, suppressing a shriek. No wonder Len had showed up. He'd already spied on Pinky at my office that morning and now she'd steered him right back.

"What's the matter?" she asked.

"Don't worry about it," I said. "You know anything about the photographs he stole?"

She blinked. "Photographs?"

I waited, hoping she'd cough up what she knew. "Dodie, you gotta trust me. So far, I'm operating in the dark. I can't help him unless I know what's going on."

"Promise you won't tell."

I wanted to roll my eyes. Instead, I crossed my heart with my index finger, swearing fealty for life.

She put a hand across her mouth to shield what she said lest someone looking on from a distance might be skilled in reading lips. As we were indoors, I didn't see the necessity. I was forced to lean close to hear her since she was already whispering. "There were pictures of me. Mug shots from that time I was picked up for soliciting. Also, the mug shots and police reports from the drunk and disorderly arrest. That cop knows I work for Glorious Womanhood, and if my regional manager finds out I've been in jail, I'll lose my job. She's already pissed off that I'm beating her sales."

"Len's blackmailing you?"

"Not exactly. He's using the photographs to keep Pinky in line, making sure he reports all the talk on the street."

"Pinky's a confidential informant?"

"I suppose. Anyway, he's destroyed all the stuff on me, so he says Len can go screw himself."

"Unless Len uses his computer to call up your criminal history and print it out again."

"Oh."

"That aside, I still don't get it. From what Pinky told me, there was a second set of photographs he thought he could use to get himself out of trouble. You know the story there?"

"I do, but he doesn't know I know so you have to promise you won't ever let on."

"I'm already under oath here," I said.

She wagged a finger at me again and then opened the back door and pulled me out onto the porch. "He borrowed money from a loan shark named Lorenzo Dante and payment's come due."

"How much?" Her paranoia was contagious and I couldn't bring myself to use a normal tone of voice.

"Two thousand dollars. He's been trying to get the money together, but no luck. He sold his car and pawned the Rolex that came into his possession from an unnamed source. He also hocked my engagement ring, but then got cold feet."

I thought back to our first meeting, remembering the band of white on his wrist where he'd once worn his watch. It dawned on me then his car hadn't been in the repair shop at all. By the time he came to me for help, he'd already sold it.

She looked at me anxiously. "I don't suppose you could lend him the money. He'd pay you back." She paused and then, in the interest of full disclosure, added, "Eventually." She had the good grace to blush.

I was offended she'd try dinging me for the bucks, but it's tough to convey outrage when you're whispering. "He already *owes* me two hundred and twenty-five bucks, which is how he got your engagement ring out of hock."

She squinted at me in disbelief. "He took two hundred dollars for a ring worth three grand?"

"Let's not worry about that now. What makes the second set of pictures so valuable?"

"I'm not sure. I do know that cop wants to get his hands on 'em."

"Tell me about it," I said drily. "Where's Pinky now?"

"He said it was better if I didn't know. He said if you came around looking for him you'd figure it out."

"Oh, great. Did he say anything else?"

"Not a word."

I thought about it briefly but couldn't think how else to quiz her on the subject of Pinky's whereabouts. "I think it'd be smart if you laid low yourself. You have a place you can go?"

She fixed her big blue eyes on me. I thought she'd seriously overdone the mascara until I realized her lashes were false. "I'm completely on my own."

"Oh, come on. There must be *some* place."

She reduced her whisper to a point that only animals could hear.

I leaned close.

"What about your apartment?" she said. "No one would think to look for me there."

I said, "Ah. Well, that's a tricky proposition. Len's already pissed off. He threatened to kill me less than an hour ago. I'm risking life and limb just talking to you. I put you up at my place, no telling what he'd do. You must have family or friends."

She shook her head. "Pinky's all I got. Anything happened to him, I don't know what I'd do."

"I'm sure he'll be fine."

"What about me? What am I supposed to do?"

"Just don't open the door. Someone knocks hard, call 9-1-1."

"I'd rather come to your place. We wouldn't be a bother."

"'We'?"

"Me and Cutie-pie, the cat. I can't leave him here all by himself."

I looked around but there was no sign of the beast. What was with these people? She was just like Pinky, trying to maneuver me into doing her a favor that would put me in the soup. Having said no once, however, I found this round easier. "Sorry, but it's out of the question. I'd be happy to drop you at a motel."

"Oh no, hon. Motel won't take a cat like him. For one thing, he sprays, and if he gets mad, which he does about half the time, he pees in the middle of the bed. So I guess I'm stuck."

"You'll think of something," I said, having no idea what.

As she walked me down the hall to the front of the house, she pointed at the television set in the living room. She did a charade of listening devices and a transmitter and a receiver. Or at least I think that's what it amounted to. I nodded, and when we reached the door, she said, "Well, it was nice of you to stop by. If I ever hear from Pinky again, I'll let you know."

Her tone, while ostensibly normal, had a singsong quality that wouldn't have fooled anyone with an ear to the wall.

"Thanks and good luck," I said.

Whispering again, she said, "You sure we can't stay with you?"

"Did I mention my allergies? Put me in a room with a cat and I blow up like a puffer fish. I had to be hospitalized just last month."

"Too bad," she said. "I could have done you a makeover. You could really use the help."

Once back in my car, I cut over three blocks and turned right onto State Street, then pulled into a small parking lot where an Asian food market and an acupuncturist had set up shop side by side. I found an empty slot and sat there thinking about Pinky and where he might be. From what Dodie said, he was confident I'd figure it out. Which meant what? The only haunt of Pinky's I knew about was the Santa Teresa Jewelry and Loan. Oh. I fired up the Mustang and drove into town. I reached lower State and cruised past the pawnshop, and when I turned at the corner, I saw Len Priddy's dark green Chevrolet parked at the curb. Clearly, June had company and I'd have to postpone our conversation. I kept on going, a shiver of cold running up my spine.

I returned to the office, thinking I'd call her after a decent interval had passed. In the meantime, I'd use the time to tidy up. I picked up folder after folder, reuniting them with their contents and returning them to the drawers. After fifteen minutes I took a break. I'd never had my morning coffee. I'd offered Pinky a cup, but he'd declined, citing the hurry he was in. After that I'd been distracted by Earldeen's visit, lunch with Cheney, and my surprise visit from Len. I went down the hall to my kitchenette, picked up the coffeepot, and turned on the water. There was a hissing, pop, and spurt that made me jump half out of my skin, but no water. What the heck was that about? I remembered then that the water department had notified me of the eight-hour shut-off. I'd forgotten that I'd intended to work from home and nearly wept when I thought of all the trouble I could have avoided if I hadn't come in.

I abandoned the idea of coffee and went back to my desk. I looked at my watch. It had been a good thirty minutes since I'd driven past the pawnshop. Surely Len was gone. I hauled the phone book from the bottom drawer. Once I found the listing for the pawnshop, I made a note and dialed the first three digits. I don't know what stayed my hand. Only that I hesitated. This is how I experience the Aha! moment on the occasions when they occur. In the back of my mind, I carried the imprint of Dodie's whispering because she believed her place was bugged. I'd apparently juxtaposed that worry with the recollection of the fellow waxing his car in the driveway that runs between my bungalow and the one next door. It seemed curious at the time but not alarming. What lingered was the image of the hose. As far as I knew, no one had moved in, so who was the guy? More important, how had he managed to wash and wax his car with the water turned off?

I got up and peered out the window. He was long gone and I didn't see any unfamiliar cars parked on the block. I took the penlight from my shoulder bag and instead of using the front door, I let myself out the back and moved between the two bungalows. I wasn't sure what I was looking for. While there was still ample daylight, the space was in shadow. I scanned the roofline for wires. I shone a light into the crawl space under the building. I reached the faucet where the hose had been neatly recoiled. Above the spigot was the window that looked into one end of my kitchenette. I looked down. In the wall, there was an aluminum mount with something affixed to it by means of a wing-nut. I hunkered and let the light play over the device. The pickup unit was a vibration-sensing contact mike of the sort I'd seen at the local electronics store. A hole had been drilled through the siding and the mike installed between the studs. The amplifier, transmitter, and recorder were concealed in a wall-mounted box that looked like something a utility company would insist on your using and then charge extra for. This type of surveillance equipment was limited, but it was cheap and easy to acquire. I didn't think Len was concerned about the legalities. Whatever intelligence he gathered wouldn't be used in a court of law. It was intended for his ears only.

I returned to the office and crawled along the baseboard on my hands and knees. The technician (doubtless a cop in Len's personal posse) had miscalculated the depth of the wall, and I could see a tiny point in the drywall where the probe had come close to breaking through. My first impulse was to go back and rip out the wires, or at the very least, find a way to short the connection. I considered my options and decided it was better to leave it where it was so that Len would imagine he had access to my private conversations.

I gave myself the rest of the day off. I couldn't work in circumstances where everything I said might be monitored. This meant phone conversations would be impossible and any walk-in clients—few and far between as they were—would have to be removed to a separate location to discuss their business. This would not make a good impression. With the water off, I couldn't flush the toilet or wash my hands. Aside from that, I still felt like crap, and since I wasn't being paid for the pain and suffering, I decided to bag it. Once home, I searched my apartment for bugs and when fully convinced the place was clean, I went to Rosie's, where I drank bad wine and ate a Hungarian dish I couldn't pronounce. This was getting on my nerves and I wondered if I'd have to find another place to hang out. Nah, probably not.

By morning, I felt restored. I took Len's threat seriously enough that I decided to avoid the topic of Audrey Vance from that point forward. I should probably have been ashamed of my cowardice, but I was not. I resolved to mind my own business as Cheney Phillips had cautioned me. This determination lasted the whole of the drive to the office. I wasn't sure what to do about the bug in my wall, but I knew I'd figure it out. I parked in a generous spot and patted myself on the back for my good fortune. I was on my way up the front steps when a car came around the corner and pulled into the spot behind mine. Diana Alvarez got out. At the sight of her, I jumped as though I'd touched a live electrical wire. I thought about fleeing, but she'd wedged her nifty white Corvette into the space behind my Mustang, parking so close to my rear fender that I couldn't have pulled away from the curb without inching forward and back, shifting from drive to reverse fifteen times, which would have been humiliating for someone bent on escape. I was also inhibited by the fact that she had a young woman with her. Perhaps, not content to aggravate the life out of me herself, she'd brought along a cub reporter for training purposes.

Diana wore an adorable dark brown A-line skirt and matching vest that looked great with her blunt-cut brown hair and tortoiseshell glasses. I was dying to ask where she got the outfit, but I didn't want to get into any girlish exchanges lest she imagine I liked her. She held her left hand in an upright position, much as a dog owner would in signaling "Stay." I checked her right hand to see if I'd get a doggie treat for my obedience. "I know you don't want to talk to me, but hear me out. It's important," she said.

I didn't trust myself to speak so I shut my mouth.

"This is Melissa Mendenhall. She read the article about Audrey and has information that casts her death in a whole new light."

All I could think about was the spike mike sticking out of the exterior wall of my bungalow not twenty feet away. I knew it was geared to pick up conversations within the office walls, but at the mere mention of Audrey's name, I could feel a damp spot form across my lower back. Len had warned me Audrey was off-limits unless I wanted my life shortened by some years. While I didn't take the threat that seriously, I'd developed an appreciation for the man's ability to inflict pain.

I said, "This isn't any of my business. Marvin fired me."

"I talked to him about that and he's beginning to repent," she said. "I promise you'll want to hear what she has to say."

I gave this four seconds' worth of consideration and then said, "Not here. If you want to have a conversation, let's get off the street."

She said, "Fine."

There was no way the three of us could squeeze into the Corvette unless Melissa sat on my lap. My two-door coupe wasn't much roomier, but at least I'd be in the driver's seat in the literal sense of the word.

I unlocked the Mustang and we sorted ourselves out, me getting under the wheel and Diana hunched over, edging awkwardly around the passenger-side seat and into the rear, which was barely big enough for grocery bags. Melissa was a tiny slip of a thing, small dark eyes, wispy dark hair in what they used to call a pixie cut. Kids nowadays wouldn't know the term, but the effect was the same, short and brushed forward around her face. She should have consulted Diana about her wardrobe. Even I would have done better than the oversize T-shirt and jeans that were inches too short.

I turned to the two of them. "So what's up?"

"I'll go first," Diana said with a quick look at Melissa.

"Sure."

"Melissa contacted me at the paper. She hadn't heard about Audrey's dive off the bridge until she read the article last Thursday. The minute she saw it she went to the police, because her boyfriend died exactly the same way two years ago. She thought they'd want to pursue the connection, so she gave them all the relevant information. She hasn't heard from them since."

I said, "That's not unusual. An inquiry like that takes time."

"The guy stonewalled her right there. She thought he'd follow up, but he won't return her calls."

"Who'd she talk to?"

"That's just it. Sergeant Priddy . . ."

Melissa said, "The fuckhead. He was horrible. He treated me like shit."

She looked too dainty and feminine to use such foul language. This, of course, elevated her in my opinion, and I hoped she was just warming up. People are all the time wanking on me about my potty mouth, so I like being able to point out someone worse.

"Tell her what you told me," Diana said to her.

Our proximity discouraged conversation face-to-face. Melissa had delivered her remarks to my front windshield, and Diana was leaning forward avidly, with her head between us like a dog eager for a Sunday drive. This was the second time I'd referred to dogs and Diana in the same breath and I apologized silently to mutts everywhere.

"My boyfriend committed suicide two years ago, or so I thought. I was devastated. I had no idea anything was wrong, so I couldn't come to grips with what he'd done. I knew Phillip had gambling debts, but he was basically an optimist and talked like he was getting his shit together. Next thing I knew, he jumped off the side of a parking garage . . ."

"Binion's in Vegas. Sixth floor," Diana said, always one for the telling detail.

Melissa went on. "What struck me about Diana's article was the business about the woman's high heels and handbag side by side on the front seat of her car and the absence of a note. Phillip's wallet and his shoes were arranged just like that in his Porsche and he didn't leave a note either."

Diana said, "Now she's convinced he didn't kill himself and here we are with Marvin who feels the same way."

I thought the analogy was thin but I wanted to hear the rest of it. "The police in Vegas must have investigated your boyfriend's death."

"They blew me off," Melissa said. "All I wanted was someone to look into it and tell me if he did it on purpose or not. I didn't really believe it, but I figured that was just me in denial. Like maybe he was in over his head and this was his only way out."

Diana said, "She got her tires slashed."

"I was getting to that," Melissa said sharply.

"Sorry."

"Phillip had been to Vegas three times in three weeks and lost a bundle playing poker, or so the detective said. It still didn't sit right because his parents are loaded and they'd have come to his rescue if he was in *that* much trouble. I explained all this and the cops shut me down. I wasn't happy about it, but I knew they heard stories like this all the time and I didn't expect special treatment. Then the vandalism started. I got my tires slashed, my apartment broken into, and all my ski gear stolen."

"You needed ski gear in Vegas?" I asked.

"No, no. I was working in Vail, which is where I went after college, just for something to do. Phillip used to come up and visit every couple of months. We both loved to ski and it was easy to work all year long because it's so beautiful up there. A lot of people come in the summer as well."

"Can I say something?" Diana asked.

I pointed at Diana, as though calling on her.

She said, "A friend of hers—this was someone who worked at one of the Vegas casinos—told Melissa she must have stepped on some toes because she had the same thing happen to her when she complained about this goon who roughed her up one time. Guy's name was Cappi Dante. He just got out of prison on a conviction for assault. His family lives here in town. His older brother's a loan shark. You might have heard of him, Lorenzo Dante? This is junior, not senior, though I understand the dad was just as bad in his day."

Dodie had just mentioned Lorenzo Dante, the loan shark from whom Pinky had borrowed two grand. "I know the name but I've never met the man."

"Melissa found out Phillip borrowed ten grand from him and that's what he lost at poker shortly before he died."

"Or was killed," Melissa corrected.

"Are you telling me this loan shark's reach stretched from Vegas to Vail?"

"Look. All I know is what happened when I made a stink. I'd heard Dante's name and I thought the Vegas police should be told. Then the problems started and I took my cue. I packed up my stuff and came back to Santa Teresa because my parents are here and I really felt I needed to hang out someplace safe. Now I'm living with them and working as a nanny, so my name doesn't appear in public records, like telephone and utility hookups."

"And you explained this to Sergeant Priddy?"

"Every word of it. I told him Audrey's suicide and Phillip's were identical and I thought they should contact the Las Vegas police about reopening the case to see if there was a link to Lorenzo Dante here."

"Police don't always appreciate being told their business," I remarked.

Diana said, "Now she's scared. She thinks she saw Sergeant Priddy drive past her parents' house, like he wants her to know *he* knows where she lives."

"The car was dark green, but I couldn't tell you what kind."

"So what do you think?" Diana asked, in a rare concession that I might have something to contribute.

"I don't know what to think, but here's my take on it: You made a mistake going to the Santa Teresa police. Len Priddy works vice and he's handling the shoplifting angle of Audrey's case. The Santa Teresa County Sheriff's homicide detectives are the ones in charge of the death investigation. You should drive out to Colgate and tell them."

"You think they'll take her seriously?"

"Well, I know for sure they won't drive past her house, scaring her out of her wits."

# 26

## NORA

Dante had given her a key to the beach house. In her mind's eye she was already there, waiting for him to appear. In reality, Channing had postponed his return to L.A. until Tuesday morning, which nearly drove her insane. She'd managed to get in a quick call to Dante's private line, where she left a message indicating she couldn't see him that day. Monday went on forever, so dull and flat she wondered how she'd endured before Dante came along. Tuesday morning, she and Channing ate breakfast together, their conversation pleasant and inconsequential. The entire time she thought about Dante. It was almost as though he were sitting at the table with them, and she wondered if Thelma was present as well. She pondered the complexities of the human heart, cunning, opaque, unknowable, and impervious to judgment. What one did in the world at large might be condemned, but thoughts and feelings and daydreams were protected by the simple expedient of silence. How easy it was to deceive Channing, whose inner state was as unavailable to her as hers was to him. How many times had they sat at this same table, conducting the ordinary business of life? Courtesy served as an artful disguise that veiled the more profound dialogue of fantasy and desire. Toast, coffee, talk of her appointment in Santa Monica later in the day. She told Channing she'd set up a meeting with her broker to review her portfolio. He urged her to stop by the office and she demurred, citing a round of errands. The exchange was perfunctory. She'd never understood Channing so well or liked him so little, but at least her infidelity had evened the score. Maybe one day she'd tell him. She hadn't decided yet. She walked with him to the door and they kissed briefly. She took care to give no indication of her impatience to have him gone or the giddiness she felt at what was to come. The minute he was out of the house, she put on her sweats and walking shoes and drove to the house on Paloma Lane.

She left her car in the motor court at the beach house and tramped through the soft sand to the hard pack. She did her four miles on the beach, timing herself since she had no way to measure distances. Beach access was blocked in places, which forced her into detours that took her up a set of steep wooden stairs built into the hillside and through two gated communities otherwise closed to the public. She emerged on the two-lane road that passed in front of the Edgewater Hotel, pausing to allow two cars to pass. The first turned into the driveway leading to the hotel entrance. The second came to a stop. She heard a horn toot and looked over as the driver rolled down her window.

"I thought I recognized you," the woman said, with what passed for gaiety. "What are you doing in this neck of the woods?"

Imelda Malcolm lived two doors away from the Vogelsangs' Montebello house. She was in her early sixties and bird thin, with sparse hair dyed a tawny shade. She pushed her sunglasses up on her head and her washed-out gray eyes were sharp. Imelda walked the neighborhood streets, and Nora had learned to avoid the woman by varying her time and route so their paths wouldn't cross. Imelda was a vicious gossip, unapologetic about her rumormongering. Nora had joined her a few times just after they moved to town and noted that even in the open air, Imelda's comments were made under her breath, as though the intimacies she passed along weren't meant to be overheard. It gave Nora the uncomfortable sense that she was supporting Imelda's malevolence.

"I like the occasional change of scene," Nora said. "How about you?"

Imelda made a face. "I told Polly I'd sport her to a facial. You know Rex filed for Chapter 13 or maybe it was Chapter 7, I forget which. Talk about a low blow."

"I heard. That's too bad."

"Horrible," Imelda said. "Polly says she can't bear to walk into the club, and not just because they're so far in arrears. I'm sure Mitchell will find a way to let them know they're not welcome anymore, though he has too much class to make a scene. She says the women aren't actually cutting her, but the pity is more than she can stand. Have you seen her lately?"

"Not since New Year's."

"Oh, my god. She looks *awful*. Don't tell anyone I said so, but I promise you she's aged fifteen years. And she didn't look that good to begin with, if you'll pardon the observation."

"I'm sure they'll weather the storm," Nora said. She glanced at her watch and Imelda picked up on the hint.

"I won't keep you," she said. "I'm glad I ran into you. I was going to call you about bridge tomorrow afternoon. Mittie's doing pre-op appointments for the work she's having done, and I thought with Channing gone, you'd have time on your hands."

"Won't work," Nora said promptly. "I have to be in L.A. I'm just waiting for a call back from our accountant to set a time. Besides, I haven't played for months. I'd make a miserable partner for anyone."

"Don't be silly. This is four tables. Lunch and lots of wine so no one takes it seriously. We're playing again on Friday, so I'll put your name down."

"I'll have to check my calendar and get back to you."

"My house. Eleven thirty. We're usually done by three."

She did a little finger wave, rolled up her window, and glided away.

Nora closed her eyes, so irritated with the woman she could hardly move. She loathed presumption. She loathed the sort of female aggression Imelda wielded as a matter of course. As soon as she reached the beach house, she'd call and leave a message on Imelda's answering machine saying she'd forgotten a prior engagement. So sorry. Kiss, kiss. Maybe another time. Imelda would know she was lying, but what could she do? Nora continued to the seawall and picked her way down the battered concrete stairs that put her back on the beach. If Imelda ever got wind of Nora's relationship with Dante, she'd have a field day.

In truth, she was embarrassed she'd slept with the man. What was the matter with her that she'd succumbed so easily? She knew there was anger at Channing buried in the act. What distressed her was the truth about herself embedded in her decision. Apparently, she didn't require longevity or trust or the sanctity of marriage. All she needed was the opportunity and there she was, flinging off her clothes in a white-hot flash of desire. Granted, Dante was spectacular, giving and tireless and loving and complimentary—the latter being another source of dismay. Remembering certain things he'd said to her, she felt easily gulled, a woman so shallow that the slightest praise had her flat on her back with her legs in the air. Had Thelma surrendered as easily? Good wine, a few superficial strokes, and she'd hopped in the sack without regard to Channing's marital status. Now Nora had tossed aside loyalty and fidelity, and while she was ashamed of her behavior, she was also unrepentant. The recollection made her shiver and the shivering made her smile.

By 10:00, she was showered and lying naked on a double chaise longue on the deck at the beach house, protected from view by the half wall and the darkly tinted glass windbreak above. The sun felt extraordinary on her skin. She sensed the tension draining out of her, and without even meaning to she fell asleep.

She was wakened by a rustling and opened her eyes to see Dante, also naked, sitting on the chaise next to hers. He had her handbag at his feet and her passport in his hand.

"What are you doing?" she asked.

"Memorizing the number on your passport. I can do that when I put my mind to it. It's like taking a picture."

"Where'd you get my passport?"

"It was in your bag. Why keep it with you, are you going someplace?"

"I picked it up at the bank the other day and forgot to leave it at the house. Why are you going through my handbag?"

"It seemed rude to ask how old you are so I thought I'd see for myself."

She smiled. "My age is no secret."

"Now it's not. March 15th. The Ides," he said. "Here's something you probably don't know: The Ides refers to the 15th of March, May, July, and October. Refers to the 13th of all other months. My birthday's November 13th, so that's the Ides, just like yours."

"Meaning what?"

"Nothing. I just think it's interesting," he said.

He returned the passport and moved forward until he was kneeling on the deck. He placed his mouth on her breast. She made an involuntarily sound, low in her throat, as the heat opened her at the core. The two of them moved into their lovemaking with an ease that suggested they'd been together for years. There was an intensity she couldn't remember ever experiencing, and she gave up all sense of herself, responding with a tenderness that matched his.

Afterward they showered together and then wrapped themselves in terry cloth bath sheets and returned to the deck. Dante had brought a bottle of Champagne and two crystal flutes, and they toasted their own joy. It felt wicked to sip Champagne at this hour of the day. "Almost forgot," Dante said. He got up and went into the bedroom, returning moments later with a handful of travel brochures he dropped into her lap.

"What are these?"

"The Maldives. That's where I'm going when the time comes. Maybe the Philippines, I haven't decided yet. I brought brochures for both because I thought you might like to see them." He sat down on the edge of the chaise and loosened his towel.

She opened the first brochure, which showed photographs of the Maldives, teal and aquamarine waters with islands like stepping-stones spread out across the sea. She sent him a curious look, wondering how serious he was. "I thought you were under indictment. They're not going to let you go out of the country."

"Just because they won't *let* me doesn't mean I won't go."

"Aren't they holding your passport?"

"I've got another."

"What if they intercept you at the airport?"

"They can't intercept me if they don't know. I've got a fortune in offshore bank accounts. I've been planning this for years."

She held up the brochures. "Why the Maldives? I don't even know where they are."

"The Indian Ocean, two hundred and fifty miles southwest of India. Temperatures run between seventy and ninety-one year round. They don't have extradition treaties with the U.S. There are other choices—Ethiopia or Iran, if you'd prefer. You like Botswana, I'll throw it in for laughs."

"What in the world would you do with yourself?"

"I don't know. Rest. Read. Eat. Drink. Make love to you. Study the language."

"Which is what?"

"Don't know yet. I'll find out when I get there. I'll have Lou Elle call you with the details, but only if you're coming with me. Otherwise, the less you know, the better."

"You think *I'd* go?"

"Why not? There's nothing keeping you here. All you need with you is an overnight case. I'll take care of the rest."

"Let's talk about something else."

"No problem. I understand you need time to consider. I'm laying it out so you know what we're dealing with."

"You know I'm not going."

"I don't know that and neither do you."

She sat up, pulling the towel around her. "Don't turn this into something it's not."

"What is it 'not'?"

"It's not deep or complex or even very significant. It's a way to spend the morning when I'm not getting my hair done."

"So I'm just a trivial screw?"

"I never said you were trivial."

"But I'm just some guy you're screwing. It doesn't mean anything more to you?"

"That's correct."

"You're lying."

"Yes, I'm lying. Let's just leave it at that." She knotted the towel in front and got up.

He grabbed her hand. "Don't go. Don't walk away from me. Sit."

"There's no point in talking about a future when we don't have one."

"Listen to me. Would you just listen? Don't hide from me. Don't hold back. Maybe you're right. Maybe this is just a fling, but that's not what it feels like to me. If this is all we have, then let's be honest with each other. Can't we do that?"

She looked down at him. His was a face she loved, but she couldn't tell him that. He tugged at her hand and she sat down beside him.

He lifted her hand and put her fingers against his lips. "Nora, whatever happens—whether you go with me or not—you've gotta get out of that marriage. Maybe that's what I am to you, a midwife, delivering you from him."

"We've been through a lot together. You don't throw away a life because it's rough now and then. History counts for something."

"No, it doesn't. You think being in a bad relationship for a long time makes it worthwhile? It doesn't. It's more time wasted. Fourteen years of misery is fourteen too many."

"Channing and I have had good years. I don't cut and run."

"What about your ex? You don't think divorce is a form of running away?"

"We didn't divorce. He died."

"Of what?"

"A fluke; a heart anomaly he'd had since birth, something the doctors missed. He was a banker. He had a great job. He was thirty-six years old with no idea whatsoever he was living on borrowed time. I thought life was perfect. We had each other, we had our boy. We also had a hefty mortgage and a lot of credit card debt. What we didn't have was life insurance, so when he dropped dead, I was left without a dime. I was thirty-four years old and I'd never held a job. I was in a panic, desperate for someone to take care of me. I met Channing six months later and by the time Tripp had been gone a year, I was married to him. My son was eleven. Channing's twin girls were thirteen."

Dante squinted at her. "What did you say?"

"About what?"

"Did you say 'Tripp'?"

"Yes."

"You were married to Tripp Lanahan?"

"I've mentioned him before."

"You never said his name. I had no idea."

"Well, now you know," she said. She glanced at him. The color had drained from his face and he was staring at her. "What's wrong?"

"Nothing."

"You're white as a sheet."

He shook his head briefly, as though to ward off a ringing in his ears. "We did business once. He approved the loan when I was buying my house. No other banker in town would touch me because of what I did for a living."

She smiled. "He was a good judge of human nature and he wasn't afraid to bend the rules."

Dante hung his head. He'd said the same thing about Tripp in referring to him. He ran a hand down his face, pulling his features out of alignment.

She put her arm around him and gave him a squeeze. "I have to go. I told Channing I had a meeting with my broker in Santa Monica. It sounded like a lie when I said it, but it turns out to be the case. Are you okay? You look like you've seen a ghost."

"I'm fine." He put his hand over hers without quite meeting her eyes.

She tilted her head and leaned against him. "Will I see you tomorrow?"

"I'll call and let you know. You drive safely."

"I will."

The meeting with her broker was brief. He was in his early seventies, lean and humorless. He'd managed her portfolio for twenty years, so long he thought of it as his own. When she told him she was cashing in her stocks, he seemed confused. "Which ones?"

"All of them."

"May I ask why?"

"I don't like what the market's doing. I want out."

He was silent for a moment, and she could see him struggle to frame his response. "I can appreciate your concern, but this isn't the time to bail out. I'd have to advise against anything so precipitant. It's not smart."

"Fine. You've advised me. You can transfer the money to my Wells Fargo account in Santa Teresa. Minus your commission, of course."

"Perhaps you're having problems," he said, too proper to ask outright.

"Perhaps, but not of the sort you imagine."

"Because you know you can talk to me if there's anything amiss. I'm in your camp."

"I appreciate your loyalty."

"Is this coming from Channing?"

"Please, Mark. Just do what I've asked. Put in the sell orders and let me know when everything's cleared."

In the car, driving north along Pacific Coast Highway from Santa Monica, she lowered the window and let her hair blow around her face. She hadn't realized her intention until she spoke of it aloud. She liked the idea of having all that cash on hand . . . should the need arise. She wasn't thinking about what might happen in the coming weeks. She wasn't thinking of packing or of meeting Dante at the airport or of getting on a plane. All those actions lay beyond the realm of propriety, personal dignity, and common sense. But what if, at the last minute, she should change her mind? What if what seemed so impossible right now became imperative to her sense of herself? She needed to be prepared should the need arise. That's how she thought of it. *Should the need arise*. That notion was the motivation for her stopping by the bank to empty her safe-deposit box before she'd left for Santa Monica that morning. It was the reason she'd kept her passport with her this past week, relieved the expiration date was still six years hence. *Should the need arise* had her counting the cash she had on hand, tucking her good jewelry in her handbag. If she didn't go anywhere—which she probably wouldn't—then what had she really lost? The cash would go back in the bank and she'd use the money she'd netted from the sale of her stocks to buy into the market again.

Turning right off PCH, she began the long, twisted ascent to the house. Set against a wide, pale blue sky, she could see four enormous birds circling, wings outstretched, silver flight feathers visible as they rode the thermal currents. If there were ever an act she envied, it would be the graceful gliding of such birds, soaring without effort, sailing on the wind, the land spread out beneath them as they lifted and wheeled. It would be quiet up there, peaceful, and the ocean would go on for miles.

She kept an eye on them, wondering what had drawn them to the mountain. As the road wound upward, she realized they were larger than she'd first thought, turkey vultures by the look of them, with six-foot wingspans. She'd seen them up close on occasion, tearing at carcasses on the road, their featherless heads and necks red and scaly-looking. They had a reputation for being gentle and efficient, nature's humble servants cleaning up carrion. Being bald, they could plunge their heads deep inside a carcass to get at the rich inner meat.

She turned into the driveway and left her car on the parking pad. She'd expected to see Mr. Ishiguro's pickup truck with its cargo of rakes and brooms. The housecleaning crew had come and gone. She saw the bulging bags of trash they'd discarded in their wake. The vultures were directly overhead, like fast-moving clouds that blotted the sunlight. One vulture had settled on top of a garbage can, and he fixed her with a look, his posture hunched and cunning. The vulture hissed at her and launched itself laboriously, with a noisy flap of its wings. She opened the lid of the garbage can and recoiled from the stench and the swarm of flies. Mr. Ishiguro had discarded a rotting chicken carcass. Nora banged down the lid, hand against her mouth as though to shield herself from the repulsive clot of flesh.

Channing said he'd bait the leg-hold traps with chicken carcasses, but how many had he set? Taped to the glass in the back door, she found an envelope that contained the receipts for three traps Mr. Ishiguro had purchased. The chicken carcasses he must have acquired without charge. She unlocked the back door and tossed her handbag and the envelope on the counter. She flipped off her sandals and found a pair of running shoes she pulled on without socks. She grabbed two pieces of firewood and went out the back door again. She pushed through the gate in the retaining wall and set off along the fire path, her gaze raking the landscape for signs of a trap. She found the first in a tangle of brush that Mr. Ishiguro had apparently used to disguise the heavy iron jaws of the device. The carcass was still there, and she used one piece of firewood to trip the mechanism. The jaw snapped shut and broke the four-inch-thick branch in half, sending the pieces flying past her face. Nora jumped, shrieking, and then set off again, nimbly avoiding the paddle cactus that threatened her on all sides. She found nothing more on that narrow dirt lane, and when she reached an intersecting path, she eased down along the incline, hoping she wouldn't fall.

Two big vultures had settled on the ground like sentinels, guarding their find. The male coyote had been caught in the second trap. Aside from the birds, she might not have noticed him except for the female trotting nervously back and forth across the path below her. Mr. Ishiguro had concealed the trap in a soft mound of dry grass. The coyote lay on his side, panting. There was no way of knowing how long he'd been there. His left hind leg was broken, the jagged bone end protruding. The ground around him was dark with blood. She stood stock still, not wanting to frighten the animal into a renewed attempt to escape. He rested. After a minute, he lifted his head again and twisted sideways to lick the wound. His suffering had to be acute, but he made no sound. His dull gaze settled on her with indifference. What was she to him when he was battling for his life?

The hillside was hot, the air dusty with the little eddies of wind that picked up now and then. Nora turned on her heel and went back to the house. She was fearful and weeping, desperate to do something to end the animal's suffering. She went upstairs. She opened the bed table on Channing's side and took out his gun. He'd showed her how to load and fire the High Standard pistol with its push-button barrel take-down. The rear sight was stationary and micro-adjustable for elevation and wind. He'd been reluctant to buy the gun but he'd done so at her insistence. She was there in the house alone on too many occasions to be left without a way to defend herself. She checked to see that it was loaded. The gun weighed fifty-two ounces and she had to hold it with both hands as she went downstairs and out the back door.

The female coyote had circled within range of her mate. She sat some distance away, in his line of sight, whining to herself. The male was diminished by pain. He lunged and thrust with his lean body, scrabbling for purchase against the weight of the trap. He looked at Nora. She could almost swear the coyote knew what she was about to do. In the depths of his yellow eyes, a spark of recognition flashed between them, her acknowledgment of his suffering and his acceptance of the bond. She had the power to free him and there was only one way out. He was too wild a creature to allow her to get close enough to release him, even if she had a way to do so. The vultures flapped upward and circled above, eyeing her with interest.

She wept. She couldn't bear to look at him, but she refused to look away. That this amazing beast had fallen, that he'd been subjected to such cruelty was unthinkable, but there he lay, exhausted, his breathing shallow. To delay his death meant extending his agony. If she had no way to spare him, then she couldn't spare herself. She fired. One bullet and he was gone. The female watched incuriously as Nora sank to the ground close to the male. His mate turned and trotted down the trail and out of sight. She'd return to her pups. She'd go out hunting alone. She'd teach them to hunt as well, venturing into civilized territory if that was the only way to find food. She'd show them the sources of water. If rabbits and squirrels and moles were scarce, she'd show them where to find insects, how to run down, topple, and disembowel house cats inadvertently left outside at night. She'd do the job that was left to her in the only way she knew, driven by instinct.

Nora returned to the house, holding the gun at her side. There was a black sedan parked next to her Thunderbird, and as she approached, two gentlemen in suits emerged and greeted her politely. There was nothing threatening about them, but she disliked them on sight. Both were clean-cut, one in his fifties, the other midthirties. The younger man said, "Mrs. Vogelsang?"

He handed her a business card. "I'm Special Agent Driscoll and this is my partner, Special Agent Montaldo. We're FBI. I wonder if we might talk to you."

"About what?"

"Lorenzo Dante."

She blinked at the two of them, making up her mind, and then went into the house without a word. The two men followed her in.

# 27

I waited until midafternoon to drive past the pawnshop. This time, there was no sign of Len's car. I went around the corner and parked in the pay lot, where I left my Grabber Blue Mustang between two pickup trucks. June spotted me as soon as I walked in and her expression went blank.

I said, "Hi, June. How are you?"

"Fine."

"Something's come up and I'm looking for Pinky. I thought you might know where he went."

"No clue."

"That's too bad. I talked to Dodie and she told me he was here."

"I don't know where she got that idea."

"Come on, June. You're lying and I know you're lying, which is almost as good as telling the truth. I don't know the details about Pinky's so-called plan, but the scheme is probably too harebrained to be worth his life."

June stared at me with the helpless expression of someone watching a movie where she knows the ending isn't good. Len must have done a number on her like the one he'd done on me. She was tense and I wasn't sure how I was going to get through to her.

I tried again. "Look, I know Sergeant Priddy was in here yesterday because I saw his car parked out front. Trust me, whatever he's telling you is bullshit. You know the man's a turd."

She licked her lips and then dried the corners with two fingers. "He says there's a bench warrant out. Pinky's wanted for questioning and if I don't turn him in, I'll be charged with aiding and abetting."

"There's no bench warrant," I scoffed. "What are you talking about? He's got it in for Pinky because he stole a set of photographs. Don't ask who he stole 'em from because I don't know that part. Len Priddy wants them back and came close to choking me to death because he thought I was holding out on him. He's probably threatened you with worse."

Her voice was low. "He came to my house this morning before I left for work. He pushed his way in and tore the place apart."

"Looking for the photographs."

"Probably," she said. "I told him I'd call the cops if he didn't get the hell out. He left and I thought that might be the end of it, but then he stopped again here demanding to search the shop. I'd already talked to my boss and he said not without a warrant, so now Sergeant Priddy's gone off to get one. Door opened just now, I thought it was him."

"A warrant based on what? He's yanking your chain. It's a fishing expedition, pure and simple. How's he going to find a judge who'll sign off on that? He has to show probable cause."

"He said he was almost sure he'd get an anonymous phone tip."

"He's bullshitting."

"Maybe so, but what if he's not?"

"I take it Pinky's here."

She didn't nod but she dropped her eyes, conceding the point. "I was thinking once it got dark, I'd put him in the trunk of my car and take him someplace else. What do you suggest?"

I shook my head. "Bad idea. Len's probably planted someone to keep an eye on you, so it's better if you stay put."

"What about you? He says it's just for tonight."

"Len'll be watching me the way he's watching you. He knows darn well Pinky's on the premises, so he'll anticipate any attempt to get him out of here and into a car. Doesn't matter whose. They'll make a traffic stop using some excuse and that'll be the end of it."

"We have to do something."

"I'm taking off. The longer I stay, the more it's going to look like we're hatching a scheme."

"You're *leaving* me?"

"Briefly. I have an idea and if it works, you'll see me sooner than you think. Just don't make a move until I get back."

"Okay."

Once I was out of the shop, I proceeded to the corner at a leisurely pace. I was operating on the assumption that anyone watching would note my departure and then be forced to choose whether to follow me or stick with June. I turned right onto the side street, but instead of returning to my car, I continued walking until I reached Chapel. If Len had assigned a vehicle surveillance, the focus would probably be on the Grabber Blue Mustang. As long as that stayed where it was, I thought I might move with some degree of freedom. I crossed Chapel and went up to the next intersection, which put me in the same block as the consignment store.

I went in. The woman at the counter looked up and greeted me warmly, a practice meant to discourage shoplifters, who prefer to go unnoticed. I circled the store, browsing through racks of garments, with a particular eye to coats. The temperatures in Santa Teresa sink into the forties and fifties at night, and while heavy outerwear is uncommon, there's always a demand for something lightweight. I checked a couple of price tags and felt myself blanch. This was secondhand clothing, which I assumed was synonymous with "cheap." Not so here. I tried to picture my last credit card statement, wondering if I had the wherewithal to charge the five or six hundred bucks the shop was asking. I'm a stickler for paying off my monthly balance if I charge at all, but I couldn't remember what my limit was. Had to be close to ten grand. I stopped and thought about the situation. I had good reason to believe the shop was tied to an organized retail-theft ring, which meant the woman who ran the place was a scofflaw. So why was I searching my conscience when she was the cheater? She appeared to my right.

"Can I help you with something in particular?"

"I'm looking for a winter coat. Is this all you have?"

"Let me check in the back. I have a few items that came in I haven't had a chance to ring into the system."

She disappeared into the rear of the store and returned moments later with two coats on hangers. One was a double-breasted camel-hair coat for $395, plus change. The other, a full-length black shearling for a nifty $500.

"That one," I said, pointing to the camel hair.

"Very nice. Let's see how it fits."

She helped me slip my arms into the sleeves and then she adjusted the coat at the shoulder until it sat properly. She directed me to the wall-mounted mirror nearby, and I modeled the coat, taking a look at myself from the rear. It actually looked pretty good. "Kind of pricey, isn't it?"

"This is from Lord and Taylor. It retailed originally for fifteen hundred dollars."

"Oh. Well, I guess I better snap it up," I said.

I waited while she rang up the sale. The charge went through without a blip. I signed the slip and tucked my copy of the receipt in my jeans pocket, wondering if it was an expense I could write off. I allowed her to swaddle the coat in tissue paper before she placed it into a shopping bag.

I thanked her and left, making a quick right-hand turn into the wig shop next door, where I selected a head of shoulder-length blond hair for $29.95. I pulled it on, slicking my hair under the edges of the wig and out of sight. I stared at myself in the mirror, bemused by the woman looking back at me.

The salesclerk was male and clearly had opinions about what was suitable for someone who looked as clueless as I did. "Maybe something closer to your natural shade," he said.

"I like this. It's perfect." While it was already hot and scratchy, I was smitten with the image of myself as a blonde.

"I'm not a fan of synthetics, if you don't mind my saying so. I'd recommend real hair. We have hand- or machine-tied cranial prostheses with nonslip cap construction."

"This is for a costume party. It's a joke."

He was wise enough to keep additional remarks to himself, but his disappointment was palpable.

The transaction took longer than I thought was absolutely necessary, but it gave me a chance to pull out the coat and shrug myself into it. I put my shoulder bag in the twine-handled shopping bag, knowing that from a distance, my shoulder bag was as much a visual cue to my identity as my clothing.

"Nice coat," he said as he handed me my change.

"Lord and Taylor."

"I can tell."

The short walk back to the pawnshop gave me the opportunity to scour the area for surveillance measures. While I didn't see anything that seemed out of place, that was no guarantee Len hadn't made the relevant arrangements. At the same time, I didn't believe he had an unlimited number of pals willing to volunteer their services regardless of the story he told.

When I reentered the pawnshop, June was busy with a customer but looked up. She wasn't fooled by my disguise but it wasn't meant to deceive her. As soon as she was free she gestured me over. The two guys working with her must have been aware what we were up to because neither paid much attention when she ushered me into the rear.

Pinky was holed up in a combination broom closet and bathroom where a toilet and small sink shared space with mops, a bucket on wheels, and storage shelves filled top to bottom with recently hocked power tools and small home appliances. The air smelled like motor oil and an air freshener that didn't even come close to freshening the air. A black-and-white television monitor on one side of the vanity displayed a view of the shop out front. As soon as Pinky realized it was me, he flashed me a big goofy grin, probably thinking June had talked me into helping him where he had failed. He took my hand in his and patted it. "Thank you."

I wanted to point out I hadn't done anything yet, but I had another matter on my mind. "What are you doing here? I thought you'd set up a meeting with some guy to hand over the photographs. Wasn't that the plan?"

"That's just it. I been trying to get in touch with the fellow, but his office doesn't know where he is. June let me go out to the counter twice to use the phone, but then she put her foot down. She's worried Len'll come in or one of his guys will spot me through the window. Anyways, the guy's receptionist has been nice about it and says if I tell her where I am, she'll send someone to pick me up as soon as he arrives."

I said, "Really. Well, that's accommodating. What's she think is going on?"

"Beats me. I didn't tell her nothing." He tapped his head to show he was using his brains. "So, now what do we do?"

"Transform you into a girl and get you out of here." I turned to June. "I need you to call a taxi. Tell the dispatcher the pickup's a blond woman in a camel-hair coat who'll be on Hidalgo at the side entrance to the Butler Hotel."

"How soon?"

"Ten minutes. And tell the cabbie to wait in case it takes longer than we think."

"I'll leave you two alone," June said as she moved away.

I made Pinky perch on the toilet lid while I took the wig from my head and secured it to his. He didn't look that bad as a blonde, though his wide shoulders and swarthy complexion gave him the look of a middle-aged Miami transvestite. Once he slipped into the camel-hair coat, most of his tattoos disappeared. I thought he'd pass muster from afar. With luck, he'd be able to walk the half block, slip in the hotel's front entrance, and out the side door.

I wrote Rosie's address on the back of the receipt from the wig shop and gave him thirty bucks in cash. "I'll call and tell her you're coming. She'll keep you out of sight until I get home. It won't be until after dark so don't get antsy on me. Any questions?"

"Can you call Dodie and tell her I'm okay? I know she's worried about me."

"That can wait. I talked to her a while ago and she's fine."

"She'll feel better if she hears my voice."

"Listen to me. Are you *listening*? Do *not* call her. She thinks the house is bugged and she may well be right. A phone conversation would be picked up."

"I wouldn't say where I was."

"What if your home line has a trap on it?"

"Wouldn't matter. I'd be quick. I could use a special code to let her know I'm safe."

"How can you concoct a code without talking to her first?"

"I could ask about the parrot, which she knows we don't have. I could say, 'Is the parrot fine?' and like that."

"Pinky, please don't make life any more complicated than it is. This is all beside the point. Dodie told me about the mug shots of her. Where'd you put the second set of photographs?"

He parted the front of his shirt slightly, and I could see a portion of the manila envelope. "I'm not letting go of this until I hand it over."

"Good plan."

Shyly, he patted the sides of the blond wig. "How do I look?"

"Adorable," I said. "Here's the drill. I'm going to stroll out the front door and go around the corner to the parking lot where I'll pick up my car. You wait five or six minutes and then leave and head in the opposite direction. You know where the Butler is?"

"Sure. It's up on the corner."

"Perfect. You take the cab to Rosie's and stay put. Her husband will bring you to my place after dark. Are we clear?"

"I guess."

"All right. Once I leave, you wait . . ."

"I got it already. Five minutes and I hoof it up to the Butler."

"Don't hoof it. Stroll. See you later."

June let me borrow the phone and I called Rosie's. William answered and when I explained what we were doing, he said he'd be happy to help. I told him to stick Pinky in a booth with his back to the door. I'd be grateful if Rosie agreed to feed him supper, though I did caution him with regard to alcohol, as I wasn't sure about Pinky's tolerance. As soon as it was fully dark, William was to walk Pinky to Henry's house, using the alleyway that runs along his rear property line. I figured a nice-looking elderly couple out and about at that hour wouldn't attract much notice.

I retrieved my car and headed for home. My route was straightforward, though I did stop briefly at the supermarket to pick up milk and toilet paper. I hoped to give any surveillance types the impression that I was dull-witted and unsuspecting. I still hadn't identified a tail, but it was a safe bet one was there. When I finally pulled into Henry's driveway, I left the Mustang parked in front of the garage doors. I let myself into the studio and turned on the lights. I closed the lower bank of shutters in the living room and went up the spiral stairs to the bedroom, where I turned on additional lights. When I came downstairs again, I spent a few minutes crawling along the baseboards again, looking for a listening device. The studio was still clean, at least as far as I could tell. I turned on the television set, sound slightly higher than I liked it in case anyone was there to overhear. I turned off the outside lights as though I were in for the night and then eased out the door again and crossed the patio to Henry's house.

The lights in the front rooms were on timers, but the kitchen wasn't part of the circuit. I left the room in darkness, using my penlight to do my usual walkabout, making sure all was well. Then I used his phone to place a call to him in Michigan. While it didn't appear Len had bugged my studio, I thought Henry's phone was clean. I asked about Nell and he filled me in on her condition, which was much improved. After that, I brought him up to date on my falling out with Marvin, the recording device on my office phone, and the problem I had with Pinky on my hands. I didn't need to justify my request to park him at Henry's for the night. I swore I'd call him again in the morning and fill him in on anything that transpired from that point on.

Darkness had settled over the neighborhood by then. I sat on Henry's back step to wait. Ten minutes later, I heard a rustling in the shrubbery along the alleyway. If you pushed the chicken wire fence until it bowed, it was possible to slip through the gap. I got up and crossed to the side of the garage. When Pinky pushed through, it was a simple matter to usher him into Henry's kitchen. I had to pray William wouldn't go back to Rosie's and blab the whole scheme to anyone who came in looking for a drink.

I locked the door behind us and led Pinky into the inner sanctum of Henry's hallway. I closed the doors leading to the bedrooms, the living room, and the kitchen, and finally turned to him. He looked like he was having the time of his life, which I found irritating. He was surveying the hallway, probably hoping there was something to steal. "This is your place? I remembered it different."

"It belongs to a friend of mine who's out of town. You can stay here tonight, but you have to promise you won't go into any of the other rooms. There are timers on the lights so they'll be going off and on. People in the neighborhood know Henry's gone, so if you're moving around, someone might notice and call the cops, thinking there's been a break-in."

"Hey, right. Cops are the last thing we need."

"That's correct. Can you behave yourself?"

"Oh, sure, but I gotta tell you, I'm so hungry, I could eat my own arm. I been in the pawnshop all day and the only thing June had handy was a box of Milk Duds that made my teeth hurt."

"Rosie was supposed to give you supper."

"She did, but you should've seen it. I didn't even know what it was. Little gristle bits in sauce. I pretended to eat and enjoy myself, but I have a delicate stomach and it was all I could do to keep from hurling chunks. Your friend have anything I could eat?"

"Hold on and I'll check."

I went through Henry's kitchen cabinets in search of food. I knew all the perishables were gone because he'd given them to me. I found a box of Cheerios, but no milk. He did have a bottle of cold Coke and a small can of V-8. He also had a can of cashews, a packet of graham crackers, and some peanut butter. I considered the Jack Daniel's, which Pinky could probably use, but decided not to tempt fate. I took out a tray and placed the items on it along with a paper napkin and some flatware. I wouldn't have minded such a feast myself, but opted against keeping Pinky company. I took the tray into the inner hall and set it down for him. He popped open the Coke and chugged about half. While he was slapping peanut butter between graham crackers, I went into the bathroom and closed the blinds.

Coming out, I said, "You can use the bathroom if you leave the light off. Do you swear?"

Mouth full, Pinky nodded and held two fingers to his temple as though taking a Boy Scout oath. I've done the same thing myself and know how little it means.

He swallowed and then used his finger to clear the peanut butter from his teeth. "Can I trouble you for a blanket and pillow?"

"Fine." The man was exasperating, but I'd signed on of my own free will and didn't feel I had a right to complain. I opened the door to the hall closet, where Henry keeps his linens. I pulled out a pillow, a wool blanket, and a big puffy comforter. "You can put down a couple of big bath towels if the floor gets too hard."

"Thanks. This'll do nice."

I pointed at him sternly. "Behave."

"I'm not *doing* anything."

I returned to my studio. I would have loved getting into my robe and slippers, but my day wasn't over yet. Closer to bedtime, I'd pay Pinky another visit to make sure all was well. He struck me as a man with a limited imagination, which meant that entertaining himself might prove strenuous.

For dinner, I made myself a hot hard-boiled egg sandwich with mayo and put it on a paper plate. Then I poured myself a glass of Cakebread Chardonnay and picked up the *Santa Teresa Dispatch*, still folded for delivery. I settled on the couch, opened the paper, and munched my sandwich while I read the news. It was the first chance I'd had to relax since I'd left home that morning. The obituaries were unremarkable and world news was standard: war in six different places on the planet, a train wreck, a mine collapse, and an infant born to a woman who was sixty-two years old. The Dow was down, the NASDAQ up, or it might have been the other way around.

The only item of note—and this made me sit up straight—was a squib on page 6 in a section that listed brief reports of local crime. This was the daily summary of chicaneries too minor to warrant full-on reporting. Most were simple: a car had been jacked up and the tires removed; a wallet had been snatched from a woman on lower State Street. What caught my eye was a wee paragraph that indicated that a homeowner, returning after a weekend away, discovered someone had broken into her house and removed a fire safe, previously bolted to the closet floor. Abigail Upshaw, age twenty-six, estimated her losses (which included jewelry, cash, silverware, and assorted items of sentimental value) at approximately three thousand dollars.

Ah. Abbie Upshaw was Len Priddy's girlfriend, and I thought it safe to assume Pinky was the one who'd burgled the place. According to what he'd told me, he'd gone in search of the damning photographs of Dodie, which he must have thought Len was hiding at his place. That jaunt was fruitless so Pinky had turned his attention to the girlfriend. I still had no idea who was featured in the second set of photographs or what made them so priceless as barter, but maybe I'd find out in due course.

Almost subliminally, I heard the squeaking of my front gate and I looked up from the paper. The arrow on my inner sensor whipped into the red zone. I set the paper aside and went to the front door, where I flipped on the porch light and looked out through the porthole. Marvin Striker appeared on my doorstep, looking impish and ill at ease.

I opened the door. "What are you doing here?"

"I need to talk to you."

"How'd you know where I lived?"

"I asked Diana Alvarez. She knows everything. You might keep that in mind in case something comes up. May I come in?"

"Why not?" I said. I stepped aside, allowing him to enter.

"Mind if I sit down?"

I gestured at the seating in my wee living room. His choices were the sofabed or one of my two royal blue director's chairs. He choose one chair and I sat down in the other, which caused both our canvas seats to make embarrassing noises.

I wasn't feeling cranky with the man, but I didn't think I should act like we were still the same good buddies we'd been before he'd tried to fire my ass. "What can I do for you?"

"I owe you an apology."

"Really."

He reached into his inner suit-coat pocket and pulled out a windowed envelope with a yellow strip across the bottom. The return address in the upper left-hand corner of the envelope was the Wells Fargo Bank in San Luis Obispo, complete with a tiny stagecoach. I took the envelope and read the name of the recipient. Audrey Vance. The yellow strip indicated a change of address from the little house in San Luis to Marvin's in Santa Teresa. Vivian Hewitt had apparently filled out a form at the post office, forwarding Audrey's mail to him as I'd asked her to do. He'd already torn open the envelope.

I said, "May I look?"

"That's why I brought it. Help yourself."

The statement was subdivided into numerous blocks of information, some in bold print, including phone numbers available for those who wanted to conduct a conversation in English, Spanish, or Chinese. Other nationalities were screwed. There were also columns giving dollar figures for total assets, total liabilities, available credit, interest, dividends, and other income. All of Audrey's transactions had been itemized, deposits going back to the first of the year. To date, she had $4,000,944.44 in her account. No withdrawals. I was impressed by how quickly the minimal interest on four million added up.

"I don't think she got that much money managing wholesale accounts," he remarked.

"Probably not."

"I wondered if you'd consider taking up your investigation where you left off?"

"Well, now, Marvin, that presents a problem, and I'll tell you what it is. Your good friend and confidant Len Priddy threatened to hurt me very badly if I pursued the case."

A flicker of a smile played across his mouth as though he was waiting for the punch line to a joke. "What do you mean, he *threatened* you?"

"He said he'd kill me."

"But not literally. He didn't actually say the words . . ."

"He did."

Out of the corner of my eye, I saw a wash of light slide across the windows looking out on the street. I'd closed the lower set of shutters, which were hinged and had a little stick in the middle that adjusted the slats at an up slant, a down slant, or completely closed. The bottom bank was fully closed, but I'd left the uppers open. A car had come to a stop outside, double-parked by my reckoning since I could hear the engine idle.

While Marvin and I explored the subtleties of language, I was wondering if a brick was going to come flying through the glass. Perhaps a Molotov cocktail refuting Marvin's point about my misunderstanding Len's comment, which Marvin swore was made in jest. I assured him of the seriousness of Len's intent and moved on to my definition of common sense, which was to cease and desist behavior that might result in bodily harm. He derided my being so easily intimidated whereas I felt the promise of death was sufficient to dash any residual bravery on my part. It was when I caught the tiny squeak of my gate that I excused myself, saying, "Would you excuse me?"

"No problem."

I left him sitting in my living room while I grabbed Henry's key and headed out the door and across the patio to his place. The timer in his living room caused the lights to wink off and two seconds later, his bedroom light winked on. This was intended to persuade folks that he was in residence and on his way to bed. I let myself into the darkened kitchen and crossed the room in three long strides. I opened the door to the hall. "Pinky?"

His picnic tray was pushed to one side and I noticed he'd eaten everything. He hadn't yet made up his homely pallet on the floor. Instead, he'd pulled the telephone from the kitchen into the hall, stretching the spiral cord to its full extension. This permitted him to close the hall door and thus keep himself judiciously confined to the inner recesses of Henry's house. The bathroom door was shut. I knocked, not wanting to surprise him if he was settled on the toilet with his trousers down around his ankles.

I leaned my head against the door. "Pinky, are you in there?"

I opened the door to an empty bathroom. I turned and took two steps, reaching for the knob on the door between the hall and the darkened living room. This allowed me a clear view through the front windows where a taxi cab was pulling away, a brightly lighted yellow blur against the dark outside, as it moved out of my view. The passenger silhouetted in the rear seat looked very much like Pinky to me.

# 28

I backed the Mustang out of the driveway, shifted from reverse into drive, and peeled out with a screech of tires that sounded like I'd just run over a cat. Marvin stood on the street and watched me with disbelief. I'd hustled him out of my studio with only the briefest of excuses. Poor, sweet man. He'd come, hat in hand, humbling himself in order to persuade me to go back on the job, but I was anxious about Pinky's disappearance and I couldn't afford to stop and renegotiate. By my calculation, Pinky had a five-minute head start on me, and I'd have been willing to bet he was heading for home. Dodie couldn't have called *him* because she didn't know where he was. If the two had been in contact, he'd have had to call her. Given the total population of the Earth at that time, there were other possibilities. He might have contacted any one of the millions of other human beings who were stretched around the globe, but since he'd been so insistent on touching base with her, my supposition made sense. Why he'd called a cab and dashed off without telling me, I hoped to find out when I caught up with him. Whatever his motivation, he must have believed I wouldn't buy into it and therefore he hadn't wanted to risk informing me.

My apartment near the beach was approximately twelve blocks from Pinky's duplex on Paseo, a mile and a half at most. The speed limit on most residential streets was thirty-five miles an hour. I didn't want to think about stop signs and red lights and other automotive impediments that would slow my progress. I kept a heavy foot on the gas pedal, checking cross streets for approaching vehicles before I sailed through each intersection. I didn't run any red lights but I came close. I was acutely tuned to the risk of black-and-whites in the area, being not that far away from the police department.

I headed north on Chapel, which at that hour didn't have much traffic, so I was making good time. I didn't see the problem until I was right up on it, preparing to turn left on Paseo. A barrier had been erected. A row of orange cones was neatly set out in front of six sections of portable fence, replete with a sign that said ROAD CLOSED TO THROUGH TRAFFIC. I debated an act of civil disobedience. Instead, I continued up Chapel, thinking to turn left at the next cross street, which was also blocked. This felt like a cruel hoax, but was more likely part of a public-works rehabilitation project relegated to off-hours instead of a plot cooked up specifically to inconvenience me. At the next block up, the street was open but marked one-way, the arrow urging me most emphatically to the right when I wanted to turn left. I said to hell with it and turned left anyway, driving the wrong way down a one-way street. At the back of my mind, I was aware that I wasn't exactly stone-cold sober. Less than an hour before, I'd had a glass of wine—six ounces by my guess, but possibly eight—with my sandwich. At my height and body weight, I was flirting with the legal limit for blood alcohol content. I was probably under the .08 threshold, but if a cop stopped me for a moving violation, I might well be required to go through a whole song-and-dance routine. Even if I wasn't compelled to submit breath or body fluids, a traffic ticket would take more time than I could spare.

I accelerated as far as Dave Levine Street, turned left, drove two blocks, and then turned left again on Paseo. There was a sleek new yellow Cadillac parked near the corner, with a bumper sticker that read I OWN THIS GLORIOUS CAR THANKS TO GLORIOUS WOMANHOOD. On the driver's-side door, there was a golden figure of a woman with her arms upraised, surrounded by a shower of shooting stars. I found a convenient parking space along an unoccupied length of red-painted curb. I did a masterly job of parallel parking, obscuring the fire hydrant. I shut down the engine, and as I got out of the car, I hesitated. I went through a quick debate about taking my H&K. Pinky's departure had generated a sense of urgency, but perhaps only in my fevered imagination. There was no reason to think a gun battle would ensue, so I left mine in the Mustang under the driver's seat. I opened the trunk and shrugged into the windbreaker I keep on hand and then left my unwieldy shoulder bag locked inside. I tucked my keys into my jeans pocket and crossed the street to the duplex.

I could see lights on upstairs in the McWherters' apartment on the right. The Fords' living room also showed lights on the ground floor to the left. The drapes were partially drawn, but I spotted Pinky sitting in an easy chair. Dodie sat on the couch to his right, largely blocked by the window hangings. The lights of the television flickered dully across their faces. If seeing Dodie was so important, I couldn't understand why he looked so sulky. With his high cheekbones and swarthy complexion, his face appeared to be carved out of wood. I rang the bell and moments later he opened the door.

"Why'd you run off without telling me?"

"I was in a hurry," he said.

"Well, clearly. Mind if I come in?"

"Might as well." He stepped away from the door.

The foyer was about the size of a bath towel with the living room opening directly to the right. There was a fire in the fireplace, but the logs were fake and the flames appeared from an evenly spaced row of holes in the gas pipe under the grate. The logs were fabricated from a product that mimicked both the outer bark and the raw look of freshly hewn oak, but there was none of the pop and crackle of a live fire and no homely smell of wood smoke. Hard to believe a fire like that had much to offer in the way of warmth. Not that either Pinky or Dodie cared. His attention was fixed on the fellow with a gun pressed against the back of Dodie's head. It looked like the guy had dragged in a chair from the dining room, and he sat behind the sofa, using the back of it to steady his hand.

The gun was a semiautomatic, but I didn't have a clue about the manufacturer. For me, guns and cars fall into the same general category—some identifiable on sight, but many only meaningful by reason of their capacity to maim and kill. What I noticed about this gun was the large frame and the satin chrome finish on the barrel, which also featured a curlicue flourish of leaves engraved along the length. The caliber didn't matter much because with the front sight pressed hard up against Dodie's skull, she couldn't have survived the trigger pull in any event.

She rolled an eye in my direction without moving her head. She was convinced the place was bugged, and she was probably holding out hope the conversation was being monitored, with the possibility of help on the way. I suspected if there was a bug at all, it was connected to a voice-activated tape recorder that would be left unattended until the tape ran out. I shifted my gaze and focused on the gunman. He was in his midforties with a thatch of dark blond hair that stuck up in places. He had two days' worth of whiskers and a nose that angled slightly to the right. His lips were open as though breathing through his mouth was the preferred method for taking in air. Running shoes, jeans, synthetic shirt fabric looking formless and cheap. I might have considered him handsome if he hadn't looked so dumb. Smart guys you can reason with. This mope was dangerous. His eyes flicked from Pinky to me. "Who's this?"

"Friend of mine."

"I'm Kinsey. Nice meeting you. Sorry to barge in," I said.

"This is Cappi Dante," Pinky said, to complete the formalities.

I remembered Cappi's name from my conversation with Diana Alvarez and Melissa Mendenhall. His brother was the local loan shark who might or might not have played a part in Melissa's boyfriend's death. According to her account, Cappi had roughed up a friend of hers, and there was hell to pay when her friend complained to the Vegas police. Nice.

"When I called home earlier, he was already here, holding her at gunpoint. That's why I called the cab and tore out of there without telling you."

Cappi said, "Get her over here so I can watch you pat her down."

"I left my gun in the car," I said.

"Says you." He gestured impatiently.

Pinky and I moved into range and the goon kept a close watch while I turned sideways and lifted my arms, allowing Pinky to run his hands down my sides and along the legs of my jeans. "She's not armed," he said.

"I told you so," I said.

"Shut your smart-ass mouth and keep your hands up where I can see them," Cappi said.

I complied, not wanting to annoy the man more than I already had. Pinky returned to the easy chair and took a seat while I stood with my palms turned up as though checking for rain. "Mind if I ask what's going on?"

Cappi said, "I came to pick up a set of photographs." He shifted his attention to Pinky. "You want to get on with it?"

Pinky unbuttoned the front of his shirt, extracted the manila envelope, and held it out to him. "These are Len's, you know. He's not going to appreciate any interference from you."

"Pass 'em over to your friend. We'll let her do the honors as long as she's here."

I took the envelope. Cappi gestured with the gun, motioning me to the fireplace.

I crossed the room. "I'm supposed to burn these?"

"Very good," he said.

"It'll go faster if I take 'em out and do them one by one," I said. Having been threatened with death over the self-same photographs, I was curious to see what all the fuss was about.

Cappi thought for a moment, perhaps wondering if there was trickery afoot. I was a good fifteen feet away from him, and he must have realized my options were limited. There were no fireplace tools and nothing that might double as a weapon. "Suit yourself," he said.

I tore open the flap and removed the photographs, taking care not to display overt curiosity. The prints were eight-by-tens, in glossy black-and-white. The first showed Len Priddy and Cappi sitting in a parked car. It was a night scene and the picture was taken with a zoom lens from across the street. The light wasn't fabulous, but the closeup left no doubt who it was. I held the print to the fire and the corner began to curl. Dodie's gaze was averted and Pinky's expression was bleak. I tilted the picture to allow the flames to climb along the edge. When it was fully engulfed, I dropped it on top of the fake logs, where it continued to burn. I took the next print and subjected it to the same treatment. Len and Cappi were photographed from roughly the same angle at different locations, but the gist was the same. I focused on the job, guiding the flames as the fire chewed and digested the images. Judging from Cappi's selection of tasteless shirts, he and Len met on six occasions.

While I worked my way through, I thought back to Cheney Phillips's comment about my putting a confidential informant at risk. Dodie'd told me Len was using the mug shots of *her* to ensure that Pinky continued to funnel street rumors in his direction. If this second set of photographs was valuable, it probably meant Len was using them to keep Cappi in line as well. Len himself had nothing to fear from the images. The name of a CI is a closely guarded matter, and if his relationship with Cappi came to light, he could write it off as police business, which it probably was. On the other hand, I had to assume that if Dante found out his brother was having conversations with a vice detective, Cappi would be dead.

"Now the negatives," Cappi said when the prints had been reduced to ash.

I removed the strips of negatives and held them to the blaze. The film flared and disappeared, leaving an acrid odor in the air. Once the photographs and negatives had been destroyed, I didn't think the three of us would be in jeopardy. Cappi was currently on parole, already in serious violation because of the firearm he was waving around. Why would he add to his troubles? He had nothing to gain and everything to lose if he used the gun against us. We were no threat to him. Even if we blabbed about the photographs, the proof was gone. I maintained a cautious silence nonetheless, not wanting to set him off.

He glanced at me, saying, "Kick the ashes around and make sure nothing's left."

I used the toe of my boot to nudge the residue of burned photographic paper. One sheet had retained its soft rectangular shape, and I could have sworn the shadowy image remained, Len and Cappi, features blurred and nearly indistinct. The fragments separated and tumbled soundlessly around the logs.

Cappi got up and tucked the gun in the waist of his jeans at the small of his back. Now that the evidence had been reduced to soot, he seemed relaxed, ready to get on with his evening's entertainment. "You folks sit tight and I'll be on my way. I appreciate your cooperation," he said, showing what an affable fellow he was. He must have seen the movies featuring crooks with good manners.

Dodie wept. She had a hand across her eyes, the tears coursing down her cheeks. She remained motionless, carefully suppressing any audible sobs. Cappi proffered his good-nights and ambled to the door. He had a thug's sense of dignity to uphold, and he didn't want to leave us with the impression he was fleeing the scene. He must have been as relieved as I was that his mission had gone smoothly. Pinky hadn't moved a muscle and I was holding my breath, conscious the situation wouldn't be resolved until Cappi was in his car and driving away. He opened the front door and went out, closing it behind him with an insolent smile.

Pinky screamed, "Son of a bitch!"

He was instantly on his feet. He tore out of the living room and into the hall where he yanked open the closet door and hauled items off the shelf in a tumble until he had his gun in hand. He checked the load and smacked the magazine into place while he ran to the door and flung it open, screaming Cappi's name. I was right behind him, trying desperately to keep him under control. Cappi was halfway across the street, and when he turned, Pinky snapped off three shots, the muzzle kicking up each time. I heard a high-pitched shriek, but it was the sound of outrage instead of pain. Cappi hadn't been hit but he was shocked at Pinky's audacity. He was apparently unaccustomed to being a target and the reality made him sound as shrill as a girl. He pulled the gun from the small of his back and fired twice before he turned and raced away down the street, elbows pumping, his running shoes thumping on the pavement. A moment later, I heard his car door slam and the engine catch. In his haste, he banged into the car in front of him before he cleared the space and took off.

Pinky was panting, his own breathing hoarse with rage and adrenaline. I looked back at Dodie, thinking she'd flattened herself on the floor so she could use the easy chair for cover. Then I saw the blood. One of Cappi's rounds had ripped through the frame wall, which slowed the trajectory of the bullet but not by much. It was my turn to shriek with surprise, but the sound was reduced to one of simple disbelief. Pinky froze, taking in the sight of her. He couldn't seem to grasp her condition from the evidence in front of him. As with me, it was the blood that finally registered.

He scrambled to her side and turned her over onto her back. She'd caught the bullet in her chest on the right-hand side. It looked like her clavicle was shattered and blood oozed dully from the wound. Pinky pressed both his hands over the area and his face turned up to mine in helplessness and horror. I skittered out of the room and headed down the hall to the kitchen, where I snatched the handset from the wall-mounted phone and hit 9-1-1. When the dispatcher picked up, I gave her the bare bones—the nature of the emergency and the location where the shooting had taken place. I put a hand over the mouthpiece and called to Pinky. "Hey, Pinky. What's your street address?"

He hollered out the number, which I conveyed to her.

The dispatcher was methodical, repeating her questions in a matter-of-fact fashion until she was satisfied with the information I'd provided. In the background, I could hear a second dispatcher take another call. The woman I was talking to broke off long enough to initiate the emergency response, launching aid and assistance.

When I returned to the living room, the first thing I spotted was Pinky's gun lying on the floor. With an ambulance on the way to the shooting scene, that was the last thing we needed to be dealing with. I picked up the gun and went out to the hall, where the floor was still littered with the stuff he'd tossed out in his haste to find his weapon. I didn't have the time or inclination to tidy up, so I did the next best thing, which was to return to the living room and stash the gun under a couch cushion. Pinky saw me doing it, but neither of us wanted to worry about searching for a better hiding place.

St. Terry's was less than four blocks away, which worked in our favor. I knelt beside Pinky and we did what we could for Dodie, whose chest was heaving. She was already trembling from shock and blood loss. I'm not sure she had any idea what had happened, but her complexion was pasty and her system was reacting with a series of shudders. I patted and coaxed and reassured her while Pinky babbled whatever comfort and encouragement came to mind. It was the language of alarm and stress, hysteria kept under control by sheer necessity. In that one instant, everything had gone wrong. With the photographs burned, I thought the worst had passed, but it had only begun.

I watched Dodie with a curious sense of detachment. She was conscious, and while she had no way to assess her situation, she knew she was in trouble. I believe that in such circumstances a victim can decide whether to choose life or to let it go. Whatever the severity of her wound, we could talk her into staying with us if she accepted what we said, which was she was fine, she was okay, that she'd make it, help was coming, that she was doing great, that we were with her. It was a litany of life-affirming promises, a pledge that she was safe, that she'd be whole again, fully mended, and without pain. She was teetering on the brink, the abyss opening up before her. I watched her look down into the dark hole of death and then her eyes rolled back into her head. I gave her hand a shake. She opened her eyes again and looked from my face to Pinky's. A message passed between them, silent and intent. If he was capable of calling her back, I knew he was doing so. The question was whether she was capable of responding to his plea.

I heard sirens and moments later saw lights flashing beyond the living room windows. I left Pinky with Dodie and went to the door, waving my arms as though that might hurry them along. The miracle of emergency personnel is the calm response to situations that would otherwise disintegrate into chaos. There were four of them, all men and younger than seemed possible, a team of children with all the optimism of skill and training, four strong boys rising to the occasion. I could see Dodie taking in the sight of their faces, caring and kind. Even Pinky seemed soothed as they tended to the immediate first-aid measures. Pulse, blood pressure. One put in an IV line and another administered oxygen. The four of them wrapped her in blankets and lifted her onto the gurney. It was a practiced and smoothly coordinated effort, and she seemed to give up her confusion and surrender to their care as though reduced to infancy.

As soon as she was out the door, I put an arm around Pinky's shoulder, which was both solid and oddly bony, a small man in a protective armor of muscle. As we emerged from the house, I noticed that his next-door neighbors had turned off their lights, not wanting to be roped in. I walked Pinky to my car and let him in on the passenger side. I made sure he was reaching for his seat belt so I wouldn't slam his fingers in the door. I went around to my side and slid in under the wheel. I turned the key in the ignition, put the car in drive, and eased away from the curb. I thought I was speeding, but the car seemed to move at a crawl as I covered the distance from Pinky's apartment to the hospital. There was no conversation between us, though I reached for his hand at one point and squeezed.

The ambulance had reached the ER ahead of us. I dropped Pinky at the door and told him I'd find parking. Dodie's gurney disappeared through the sliding doors in a rolling flutter of white coats. She'd been swallowed up, leaving him behind. By the time I pulled into the nearby lot and scavenged the closest possible parking spot, my composure was fading and my heart had started to thunder. I grabbed my bag from the trunk and then jogged the half block back. The reception area was bright with overhead lights, and the waiting room was empty. Pinky was sitting in a glass cubicle with a woman in civilian clothing who was typing information onto a form, filling in the blanks as Pinky provided answers.

I took a seat, keeping an eye on the two until she'd finished with him. He looked miserable as he left the cubicle and plodded to the front door. I followed, watching as he sank to the steps outside with his head between his knees. I sat down beside him and we waited. It felt like two in the morning, but when I looked at my watch, it was only 8:35. This was a Tuesday night, and I was guessing the emergency-room personnel had been enjoying a respite from the usual weekend onslaught of the injured and half dead. I pictured cuts and bloody noses and allergic reactions, food poisoning, heart attacks, broken bones. Also, the host of minor illnesses that by rights should have been relegated to the nearest clinic the next day. We were lucky Dodie wasn't having to compete for attention. Wherever they'd taken her, I knew she was in good hands. I got up and went inside, where the aide, a young black guy in scrubs, was sitting at the desk.

I said, "Hi. I'm wondering if you can tell us anything about Dodie

Ford, who was brought in by ambulance a few minutes ago. Her husband's been filling out the paperwork and I know he'd appreciate word."

"I can check." He got up and crossed to the double doors that opened onto the medical bays in back. The glimpse I caught of the interior showed two empty gurneys with the curtains pushed back along the tracks laid in the ceiling. There was medical apparatus at the ready, but no sign of nurses or doctors, and no sense of hubbub. The aide closed the door behind him and returned in less than a minute.

"They're taking her up to surgery. The doctor will be out in a bit. Sorry I can't tell you more. I'm telling you what they told me."

I went outside and gave Pinky the paltry information I'd been given. I was wearing my windbreaker, but the fabric was light and I might as well have done without. He'd gone through four cigarettes, lighting each from the one he was about to stub out. I said, "Why don't we go inside? I'm about to freeze to death out here."

"They won't let me smoke in there."

I didn't have the energy to argue and I didn't want him sitting by himself. I resumed my seat, tucking my hands between my knees for warmth. Beside me, he sighed and hung his head, shaking it back and forth. "My fault. Shit, shit, shit. This is all my fault. I shoulda left well enough alone."

"Pinky, don't get into that. It's not going to help."

"But why'd I go after him? That's what I'm asking myself. It was over and done and if I'dda kept my cool, he'd have been gone."

"You want to talk about it? Fine. If it's going to make you feel any better, I'm listening."

"I don't want to talk about it. Anything happens to her, I'm going to kill that prick. Swear to god I am."

"Dodie's in good hands."

He turned and looked at me. "How am I going to pay for her care? You should've heard what the lady in there was asking me. And what was I supposed to say? We got no insurance, no credit, no savings, nothing in the checking account. Dodie's hurt bad and we're racking up thousands in medical bills. She hasn't been here an hour and I'm already in the poorhouse. She's bound to be laid up, which means no income from her. I'm an ex-con. I can't get a job for shit. And look at all the other bills we got. How will those get paid?"

"I'm sure there's some form of financial assistance through the county," I said.

"I don't want handouts! Me and her are proud. We're not deadbeats, we've just been down on our luck, and now we're totally sunk . . ."

I kept my mouth shut and let him ramble. Dodie's fate was unknown. He didn't dare assume she'd live and he couldn't own up to the fact that she might just as easily die. He was superstitious enough to avoid talk about either possibility lest he tip the scales. Instead, he focused on the financial upheaval, which he was equally ill equipped to deal with. He must have felt safer thinking about the bills he'd be facing, which were at least concrete and more nearly in his control than Dodie's perilous state. I crossed my arms, hunching over to keep warm, thinking he could just as easily give vent to his worries in the hospital waiting room. He never once mentioned running out on his obligations, but his fretting was self-perpetuating. I felt like a Hallmark card when I suggested he deal with his troubles one day at a time. What was this, a meeting of Alcoholics Anonymous?

I said, "Let's talk about something else."

He was silent, still brooding. "You know how all this started, don't you?"

I shook my head.

"With Audrey Vance."

"Audrey?"

"Yeah, I thought you must have figured it out. I was there the day of her arrest. I borrowed Dodie's Cadillac late afternoon to take a little spin and got busted on a DUI. Audrey was brought in about the same time."

"You knew her?"

"Oh, sure. Her and me go way back. I did a couple jobs for her and don't ask what because I'm takin' that to my grave."

"Did you talk to her?"

He shook his head. "I only seen her in passing so I never had a chance. Next day she called in a panic because of what she witnessed that night."

"Which was what?"

"When she came out of the station after her boyfriend posted bail? There sat Cappi in a parked car with Len. She knew who he was because she worked for his brother. Didn't take a rocket scientist to know Cappi was on the police payroll, telling Priddy everything he knew. She knew she was dead meat if he realized she'd seen 'em together. Guess he must have done just that or she'd still be here."

"So who threw her off the bridge?"

"Who do you think?"

"Cappi?"

"Of course. He had to shut her up or she'd have told Dante. Priddy may be corrupt but he wouldn't go that far. Yet. Anyway, subject closed. I shouldn't have let on, but I figured you must be concerned how I'd get caught up with the likes of him."

"I did wonder," I said.

"That asshole Cappi's not going to get away with this. I get my hands on him, he's dead."

"If he's on the run, he might leave the state. You don't even know where he is."

"I can sure as shit find out. I got street connections and I know where he lives. A guy like him can't disappear. He's not smart enough. He couldn't even get a job on his own. He's reduced to working in his brother's warehouse. That's how he gets the lowdown on all the stuff he's passing to the cops."

"Just stay out of it."

"Oh, no. No, no. He's not getting off that easy. I got ways to get even."

"You can't afford to get even. You'll only make things worse."

"You don't know worse. I know worse. I ought to plug him full of holes and let him see how it feels."

"Come on, Pinky. I can understand your wanting revenge, but that'll put you back in prison and then what? Dodie's in trouble. She needs you. It's self-indulgent to brood about striking back when you've got more important issues to worry about. Leave him to the police."

"After I get through, they can have him."

"Forget that and focus on Dodie. I think we should hold good thoughts just in case it helps."

"I am focused on Dodie. That's the point. What he did to her, he pays for. Plain and simple."

I gave up. The more I argued, the more determined he became. No point in fueling his rage by putting up resistance. At 9:00 he agreed to go inside, and it was nearly 11:00 when the surgeon finally appeared. Judging from his ID tag, he was foreign-born with a surname I wouldn't know how to pronounce. I took one look at his face and left the two of them to confer. I wanted to hear what the doctor had to say, but it seemed tacky to listen in. As I watched Pinky's expression change, the news probably wasn't good. As soon as the surgeon departed, Pinky sank into a chair and wept. I sat down beside him and patted his back. I didn't think she'd died, but I was afraid to ask, so I simply murmured and patted and waited him out. The woman at the desk saw what was going on and she appeared with a box of tissues. Pinky grabbed a handful and mopped at his eyes.

"Sorry. Oh man, I'm not long for this world."

"What'd the doctor say?"

"I don't know. He had an accent so thick, I couldn't understand a word. The minute he started talking, it was like I went deaf because I was so afraid he'd have bad news."

"Is she going to be okay?"

"Too early to tell or at least that's what I think he said. He didn't seem all that happy and when he threw in all that medical gobbledygook my ears went out on me. His eyes were so sad, I nearly busted up right then. I think he said he'd know better in the next twelve hours . . . or some amount of time. She's been moved to ICU. I can stay if I want."

Talking seemed to help, and by the time he'd pulled himself together, I felt like I was on the verge of collapse myself. Of course, Pinky opted to spend the night in the waiting room down the hall from ICU. I wanted to stay as well, but he urged me to go home. It didn't take much in the way of persuasion. I told him I'd get in a few hours' sleep and check with him in the morning to see how she was doing. Before I left, I volunteered to go down to the cafeteria and buy a couple of cups of coffee, for which he seemed grateful. I was the only one who seemed to be wandering the halls. I knew the location of the cafeteria from other occasions. The place would be closed, but I remembered a row of vending machines that would be humming with choices. When I reached the corridor, I took out two singles from my wallet and slid the bills into the slot, one by one. I punched the button for coffee, punched a second button to add cream, and picked up some sugar packets from a small cart nearby that stocked napkins and wooden stir sticks. I paid for a second coffee and carried the two Styrofoam cups with me back to the ER.

As I reached the waiting room, I saw a black-and-white pull into one of the parking spaces outside the entrance. An officer got out of the car and came in through the sliding doors, glancing at Pinky in passing. I did an about-face and remained in the hall while the mini-drama played out. I knew how it would go. The cop would ask the desk clerk for the victim's name and next of kin. He'd be directed to Pinky, after which he'd quiz him for however long it took to complete a detailed report about the shooting. I didn't want to participate. I was tired. I felt itchy and out of sorts and too impatient to put up with an interview. I'd be happy to tell the cops what I knew, but not right then. In any event, the officer would leave his business card with Pinky in case he thought of anything he wanted to add. I'd get his name from Pinky and go into the station in the morning. If he was off-duty, someone else would take my statement.

I peered into the waiting room where the two sat in one corner, Pinky slumping forward, talking with his head in his hands, while the officer took notes. I dumped the two cups of coffee in a trash bin and found an exit in another wing. The walk to the parking lot was longer but worth every step. I retrieved my car and drove home through the dark, deserted streets. I turned up the heat in the Mustang until it felt like an incubator and I still couldn't get warm. Once home, I crawled under the covers without bothering to undress.

In the morning, I skipped my run. After I'd showered and dressed and downed my usual bowl of cereal, I pulled out the telephone book and looked for Lorenzo Dante's name. There was no home address given, but I spotted a listing for Dante Enterprises, which was located downtown in the Passages Shopping Plaza. Though it was strictly in the none-of-your-business category, I thought it was time to bring Cappi's brother into the equation. I had no idea what the relationship was between the two, but if Cappi wasn't going to take responsibility for what he'd done, then maybe his brother would step up to the plate. With a police report now on file, the judicial system would grind into gear, eventually pulling Cappi into its maw. His parole officer would file a notice with the parole board, and he'd be picked up and detained until a Morrissey hearing could be held. As the shooter, he'd be entitled to counsel and would be accorded any number of constitutional rights. Meanwhile, Dodie, as victim, had no rights at all. If Cappi's parole was revoked, he'd be sent back to prison while Dodie would be sent into a rehab facility for a long, slow, and painful period of recovery—assuming she survived. Pinky would pay a stiff price either way and that didn't sit right with me.

I drove into the underground parking garage that ran the length of the shopping center. Stores weren't yet open, so all of the parking spaces were available. I chose one at the far end of the lot, close to the elevators. I ran an eye down the wall-mounted directory, which listed the companies with offices on the second and third floors, above the retail establishments. Dante Enterprises occupied the penthouse suite.

I took the elevator up. I don't know what I expected from the digs of a loan shark, but the complex was elegant and beautifully furnished, with pale gray short-cut pile carpeting and interior walls of glass and high-gloss teak. The reception desk was empty, and I waited, not quite sure what to do with myself. I took a seat on a lush gray leather chair and leafed through a magazine with one eye on the elevator. Finally, the doors opened and a tall, balding man wearing glasses emerged and crossed to the inner door, pausing with his hand on the knob. "Is someone helping you?"

I set the magazine aside and stood up. "I'm looking for Lorenzo Dante, the younger one. I understand there are two."

"You have an appointment?"

I shook my head. "I was hoping he could see me. I just took a chance he'd be in."

"He's usually here by now, but I didn't see his car in the garage. Is this something I can help you with?"

"I don't think so. It's a private matter. Do you have any idea what time he'll be in?"

The man checked his watch. "Should be soon. If you take a seat, I can have the receptionist bring you a cup of coffee while you wait."

By then I was feeling anxious, suddenly uncertain what I was doing there and what I hoped to accomplish. I can tattle with the best of them, but I prefer to do so when I know my audience. Here, I had no idea what sort of reception to expect. "You know what? I think I'll run a couple of errands and come back in a bit."

"If you change your mind about the coffee, let the receptionist know," he said. He disappeared into the inner corridor just as the receptionist came out and returned to her desk. I had already moved to the elevator, where I pressed the down button. I was intent on exiting before Dante showed up, so it was only by chance that I glanced back at her as she took her seat. She noticed I was staring at her and she gave me the blank look of someone who hasn't yet registered what's going on.

I said, "Aren't you Abbie Upshaw?"

Still the blank look. "Yes."

"I'm Kinsey Millhone. I met you the other day at lunch. You're Len Priddy's girlfriend."

Her gaze locked on mine, and I could see her formulate the recollection of who I was and where we'd met. It dawned on her that I was a friend of Cheney Phillips's and someone who now knew more about her than I should. I was still putting the pieces together but I'd already gotten the picture. It was *her* house Pinky had broken into when he stole Len's packet of pictures. She'd probably taken the photographs herself, documenting the link between the vice detective and Dante's brother. What I knew without even asking was that she'd been planted in Dante's office to pick up the same sort of inside dope that Cappi was spilling to the cops.

I heard a soft ping. The elevator doors opened and I stepped in. She watched, transfixed, as the doors slid shut. She was pale and her expression had turned from fear to dread.

It was a moment I enjoyed perhaps more than I should have.

# 29

# DANTE

In the rear of the limousine, Dante donned his reading glasses while he studied the spreadsheet Saul had sent to the house by messenger the night before. This was a comprehensive view of his finances, pages he'd shred when he'd absorbed the content. He'd meant to go over the report when it first arrived, but he was distracted by the revelation from Nora's offhand remark at the beach house that day. He wondered if there was any way he could have known she'd been married to Tripp Lanahan, of all people. Dante could count on the fingers of one hand men who'd come to his defense. Tripp had seen value in him, had successfully challenged bank policy for him, an unprecedented gesture of trust and confidence. Tripp had also taken a raft of shit from the bank for approving the loan, but he'd shrugged off the criticism and stuck to his guns. Dante was never sure why he'd done it, but it meant the world to him. In his mind, buying the big old house made him almost respectable, and he'd never missed a payment. In fact, he'd paid it off six years early and now owned it free and clear. Since then he'd worked hard to erase the taint of gangsterdom that dogged his days. It was a reputation he couldn't seem to shake. He was tired of the burden and tired of trying to free himself from the power struggles and the necessity for domination. Until recently when he'd pictured his escape, it was always in the vague and cloudy future. It had helped immensely to know he had a way out, but now that the reality loomed before him, he was reluctant to act. It would make all the difference if Nora agreed to go with him, but what were the chances once she knew the part he'd played in Phillip's death? He was doomed if he stayed and doomed if he left without her. Uncle Alfredo was another loss he wasn't ready to face. Alfredo loved him as his father never had, and even with his life slipping away, he was Dante's anchor. Dante couldn't imagine leaving while the man could still draw breath.

Then there was the end of his relationship with Lola, and that depressed him as much as anything. That morning, when he'd finished showering and getting dressed, he'd come into the bedroom to find her already up and in her travel clothes. She had a suitcase open on the bed and a garment bag hooked over the open closet door, with the inner flap unzipped. She'd already moved a number of dresses, skirts, and suits still on hangers into its interior.

"What's this about?"

"What's it look like? I'm packing my things."

"You don't have to leave so soon."

"Of course I do. The whole world doesn't revolve around you. I have needs and desires of my own."

"Where are you going?"

"Haven't decided yet. I'm having a car take me down to Los Angeles. I'll stay at the Bel-Air until I make up my mind. London for sure and after that, who knows?"

"You need cash?"

"No, Dante. I have a fortune in gold coins stashed under the mattress. I thought you knew."

He smiled in spite of himself. "How much?"

"Fifty grand should do for now."

He took out his money clip and counted off a number of bills that he handed to her. "That's ten. I'll have Lou Elle get the other forty to you at the hotel. After that, she'll set up an account for you."

"Thanks. I'm charging everything to you anyway, but there's always tips and incidentals. You might alert American Express so there's no hassle. I hate when the assholes refuse a card. They're always so smug about it."

"No problem." He sat down on the edge of the bed, which was still unmade. The covers were thrown back and the sheets were warm with her scents: cologne, bath salts, shampoo. He felt a sharp pang of anxiety. What would he do with himself when she was gone? After eight years, he couldn't even picture the empty place she'd leave in his life.

She secured the elastic bands across the hanging clothes to hold them flat and then closed and zipped the inner flap. She added a few items to the big suitcase and closed that as well. "Could you haul that down for me? I don't want to give myself a hernia."

He crossed to the closet door and lifted the garment bag off by its hook. He placed it on the bed and watched while she zipped it up. "This is all you're taking? Doesn't look like much."

"I gotta be prepared to tote everything myself. The bags have wheels, but there's a limit to how many I can manage at one time."

"That's what redcaps and bellboys are for."

"Only when I get where I'm going. In between, I got cabs and airports and who knows what. Better to travel light so I don't end up loaded down like a pack mule," she said. "What about you? I figured you'd be taking off with your new lady love. What's her name?"

"Nora. How'd you find out about her?"

"I know how you operate and I can get information from the same sources."

"She hasn't agreed to go with me and now something else has come up."

"Uh-oh. That doesn't sound good."

"It's not. Two years ago I loaned a kid some money on a gambling debt. He owed a casino in Vegas and he came to me for cash to cover him. We made a deal and shook hands. I ponied up and then he tried to weasel out of paying. He offered me his Porsche in lieu of payment and I told Cappi to take care of it. I meant take a look and see if the car was okay. Cappi tossed him off the parking garage."

"I take it Cappi didn't get caught or he'd still be locked up," she said.

"That's not the problem. Turns out the kid was Nora's only son. I knew her husband years ago, Tripp Lanahan. Guy drops dead of a heart attack at thirty-six. She mentions his name and I put it together in a flash. I thought I'd have a heart attack myself."

Lola sat down beside him. "What are you going to do?"

"What are my choices? I have to tell her."

"No, you don't. Are you nuts? Keep your big mouth shut. Otherwise all you're going to do is fuck it up."

"What if she hears about it from someone else? Then I'm really fucked."

Lola's expression was pained. "Oh, please. You know what this is like? Having an affair and then making a full confession. Leaves the guilty party feeling just fine, thanks. You get it off your chest and your conscience is clear. Meanwhile, you put the whole load of shit on your significant other who hasn't done a thing."

"I want to be honest with her. Do things right."

"Get serious. She's not going to forgive and forget. You tell her and it's over. Is that what you want?"

"I can't live the rest of my life wondering if she's going to find out."

"How's she going to find out? You're taking her out of the country. It's a big world out there. What are the chances of running into someone who—lo and behold—knows what went on? You got what, a handful of people in on the story, all of 'em on your payroll. I wouldn't sweat it if I were you."

He turned and looked at her. "I live with you all these years and this is how you think?"

"It's called common sense. Using the old noggin. Looking before you leap."

"It's a rationalization. Finding a way to save your own skin at someone else's expense."

"It's not costing her anything. How's she going to know?"

And that was the question she left him with, last thing out of her mouth before he helped her carry her bags down to the car and watched her disappear down the drive. End of Lola. Over and done.

Through the tinted windows of the limousine, the quality of the light changed, and he realized Tomasso had slowed at the mouth of the parking garage and was nosing the limo down the incline. Dante returned the report to his briefcase and idly watched the concrete walls slide by, support posts, low ceiling, the exit ramp coming up on his right. Tomasso pulled to the curb near the entrance to Macy's. The backside elevators to the office floors were located to the right, often unnoticed by shoppers as they passed the spot, intent on something else.

Hubert got out on the passenger side and came around to the rear to open the door for him. As Dante emerged from the car, the elevator doors opened and a young woman stepped out. Dante took in the sight of her—jeans, black turtleneck, and a big slouchy shoulder bag—with a curious sense of familiarity. It was unusual to see anyone in the parking garage at so early an hour. Hubert shifted his weight, automatically, blocking her access to his boss. The woman stopped and Dante saw recognition flicker in her eyes as she looked from his big bodyguard to the limousine. Dante couldn't remember ever seeing her, but she seemed to know him.

He was about to move past her when she spoke up. "Could I talk to you?"

"About what?"

Hubert said, "Miss . . ."

"You're Lorenzo Dante. I was just in your office looking for you."

"Who are you?"

Hubert was saying, "Please, Miss. Could you step away from the car . . ." These were standard phrases he'd learned. Anyone hearing him would think he knew English well, but as it turned out, in his job, fluency wasn't required unless it came to guns and hand-to-hand combat, at which he was truly gifted.

"Hubert, would you cool it? I'm having a conversation here."

He said, "Sorry, boss," but kept a watchful eye on the interchange.

"I'm Kinsey Millhone. I'm a friend of Pinky's."

"What's that have to do with me?"

"Last night Pinky and your brother got into a shoot-out and Pinky's wife was hit in the crossfire. She's in bad shape and Pinky's worried sick about her medical bills."

"I'm not seeing the relevance."

"Pinky had a set of photographs to give you, only your brother got there first and destroyed both the prints and the negatives."

"Photographs of what?"

"Cappi and Len Priddy chatting together in a parked car on six different occasions. Your brother sold you out."

Dante stared at her for a moment while he decided what to do and then he said, "Get in."

He stood aside while she slung her shoulder bag into the back of the limousine and slid in after it, shifting both herself and her bag over to the long side seat. When she was settled, he ducked in and took his usual place. To Tomasso, he said, "Take a drive. I'll tell you when it's time to bring us back."

Before Tomasso pulled away, he triggered the mechanism that closed the panel between the front seat and the rear of the car. By then, Hubert was back in the front seat. Dante was intent on the woman sitting to his left. She was somewhere in her thirties, more girl than woman as far as he was concerned. He couldn't decide what to make of her. She was small-boned with a ragged mop of dark hair she must have chopped off herself. Hazel eyes, her nose ever so slightly crooked. He could tell she'd been banged up, but he couldn't imagine why. He said, "How do you know Pinky? You don't look like the lowlife type."

"I'm a private eye. He gave me the first set of key picks I ever owned and I owe him for that. I'm also fond of him, rascal that he is."

"And he hired you to do what?"

"Not him. The man engaged to Audrey Vance."

He was getting it. "You're the one took my money and gave it to the cops. You and her landlady up in San Luis Obispo. That was a bad thing you did."

"Hey, you sent guys to break into my studio. You violated my privacy and that's just as bad."

He couldn't believe she had the nerve to sound indignant when she was the one who'd wronged him. He nearly smiled but thought better of it. "We're talking about a hundred grand you cost me."

She shrugged. "The courier service handed it over to Audrey's landlady. Why am I to blame?"

"Wait a minute. Now I know where I heard your name. I read about you in the paper. You blew the whistle on Audrey."

"What was I supposed to do? I saw her steal underwear and stuff it in her bag."

"You could have looked the other way. Audrey was a peach. She worked for me for years."

"I'm surprised she wasn't better at her job."

"You've also been following a friend of mine and it's upsetting her. Where do you get off pulling shit like that?"

"Oh, right. Helping Hearts, Healing Hands. That's a crock," she said. "You want to talk about Cappi or go on trading recriminations? You ask me, we're even."

"You got a hell of a nerve. Why'd you come to me with bullshit about Pinky? What the fuck do I care? The guy's a punk."

"He needs help. I thought maybe we could work a trade."

"A *trade*?"

"Sure. I'll tell you what I know and you pay his medical bills and living expenses until Dodie's back on her feet."

He stared at her with amazement. "I'm a bad man. Didn't anybody tell you?"

"You don't seem bad to me."

"I'm not someone you come to with a deal," he said. "That's the point."

She looked at him with . . . he wouldn't call it insolence, but maybe cockiness. "Why not?"

"Why *not*? Take a look at the other players in this game. You tell me Cappi's sold me out. You know what kind of guy he is? A claim like that can get you killed."

"Len Priddy's worse."

"Than Cappi? How you figure?"

"Len's a cop, sworn to uphold the law. If he's corrupt, then what happens to the rest of us?"

"Oh, I see. You figure I'm corrupt to begin with so what difference does it make."

"Not at all. I suspect you play straight and you're a man of your word."

"Based on what?"

"Based on the fact that you have power and you've had it for years. You don't need to dick around."

"Nice talk, but it's not going to help. You've got nothing to trade. Cappi's snitching is not exactly late-breaking news. I've been suspicious about him since he got out of Soledad."

"Well, now you know for sure. I saw the photographs."

"Your word against his. You said he destroyed them all, so where's your proof?"

"Doesn't matter. You won't be taking him to court, so the evidence is irrelevant."

"Two corrections. A, you don't know what I'll do with him, and B, you don't have a clue what's relevant. Tell me something I don't know and maybe we'll do business. Believe it or not, I'm fond of Pinky myself."

She held his gaze and he could tell there was something more she wanted to say. She was debating the wisdom of it and for the first time, he was truly interested.

"Come on. Out with it."

"Are you aware Abbie Upshaw is Len Priddy's girlfriend?"

He could feel his focus sharpen. "Says who?"

"I saw them at the Palms a week ago. That's how she was introduced. You can ask her yourself."

"You saw her in my office."

"Of course. I was looking for you when I ran into her."

"And she's in on the deal, whatever it is. With these pictures you're talking about?"

"For starters, I think she took them. Len stashed them at her place. She was out of town last weekend, no doubt humping his bones. Pinky looked for the photographs at Len's and when they didn't turn up, he decided to try her place. He walked away with her home safe and when he drilled it, he hit pay dirt."

"What's his stake in this?"

"Len was using another set of photographs to keep him in line. Those are the ones he was after at the time. The shots of Len and Cappi were a bonus. Dumb luck on his part. He was hoping you'd forgive his two-thousand-dollar debt in exchange for them."

Dante took a moment to assimilate the information. "Fair enough," he said. "You tell Pinky to come see me and I'll take care of him. You have a car?"

"I'm parked in the underground garage."

Dante reached up and pressed a button on the console. "You can take us back now. We'll drop the lady at her car."

. . .

He took the elevator up. When the doors opened, he crossed the reception area and paused at Abbie's desk. Beautiful girl, no doubt about it, with that long dark hair. Sometimes she wore it up, caught in an oversize tortoiseshell clip that looked like a set of spring-loaded teeth. Steady, responsible, a valuable employee. She was watching him carefully, trying to read his mood. Maybe it had occurred to her that he and the private eye might have crossed paths downstairs.

"I have a job for you," he said, his tone matter-of-fact.

"For me?"

Her warm olive complexion had taken on a gray cast, and he knew if he reached out and touched her hand, her fingers would be cold. "I need two first-class seats on a flight from LAX to Manila. I'll need a limousine to take us down to the airport."

Her face went blank as the request sank in. A frown created two parallel creases between her eyes. If she did that often, they'd be permanent.

"Is this a problem?" he asked.

"I was wondering why you chose Manila."

"I like the Philippines, okay?"

She licked her lips as though her mouth had gone dry. "When did you want to leave?"

"Thursday. Make it late so I can get in a full day's work. I'll be at the warehouse first thing. Have a limo pick us up at the house for the trip down to the airport."

"You don't want your driver to take you?"

"He's entitled to three weeks' paid vacation. I'm giving him the time off. Same with my bodyguard."

She hesitated. "Lou Elle usually handles travel."

"And now you do. Think you can manage it?"

"Yes, sir."

He leaned down and pulled over the notepad where she recorded phone calls. He preferred a different system, one with automatic carbons so the top slip could be torn off and left on his desk. He jotted two names and a series of numbers on the lined page and pushed it back to her.

She glanced down. "Mrs. Vogelsang?"

"You have an opinion, you can keep it to yourself."

"Won't I need her birth date and passport number?"

He pointed. "What do you think that is?"

"Oh, sorry. What airline?"

"Surprise me. I want the itinerary in hand by the end of the day. Also, call the police department and ask to speak to Sergeant Detective Priddy. That's *P-R-I-D-D-Y.* Set up a meeting here as soon as possible. Within the hour if he can make it."

He crossed to the door and pushed into the inner corridor without looking back, but he could picture her dismay. What would she do with Len Priddy in the office? Admit she was in bed with a vice cop? Pretend she didn't know the guy?

He stopped in Lou Elle's office and found her tapping on her computer keys, her glasses low on her nose.

"Sorry to interrupt. I've asked Abbie to book some airline tickets. I don't want you to think she's treading on your turf."

"Appreciate the information. Anything else?"

"That's what I like about you. All business."

"That's what you pay me for."

"Who do we know at St. Terry's?"

"Medical records or administration?"

"You tell me. I need everything they got on these two." Again, he jotted information on a scratch pad, tore off the leaf, and passed it to her. He continued writing while Lou Elle read the note he'd given her. "Pierpont? That's a good one."

"I didn't name the guy. His mother did. Set up an account in his name. A hundred grand for starters. We'll see how it goes from there. You make sure he's taken care of regardless."

Her gaze came up to his. "Regardless of what?"

"Life's a crapshoot. You never know what's coming down the pike."

"Is this deductible?"

He smiled. "Good question. Talk to Saul and see if he can make it work," he said. "As long as you're at it, there's something else you need to set up. A little switcheroo." He handed her the second piece of scratch paper.

She glanced at it. "Ooo, for me?"

"I thought you and your hubby could use the time away."

She folded the note in half and slipped it under her desk calendar. "Thanks. Very sporting of you. I'll let Saul know about the rest of it since it's his department."

He said, "Everything is Saul's department."

"Understood."

He spent the rest of the morning taking care of odds and ends. When Abbie buzzed him at noon, he'd almost forgotten what he wanted until she told him Sergeant Priddy was in the lobby. "Give me a few minutes and then bring him in. It won't hurt him to cool his heels."

"Would you like coffee?"

"Why not? Make the guy feel welcome."

He took his finger off the intercom. No reason to chafe about Abbie's deception. People did you in. People turned on you in a heartbeat. Pop always told him it was like that. His advice was to play the hand you're dealt. No point wishing things were different just because the truth cut you as clean as a razor blade.

He got up from his desk and crossed to the wall safe, ran the combination, and opened it. He put his Sig Sauer in the inner pocket of his sport coat. When he sat down again, he buzzed Abbie and told her she could bring Priddy in. A few minutes passed before the two arrived. If he'd had a surveillance camera in the lobby, he might have been entertained by their shenanigans.

She tapped on his door and as she opened it, he reached forward and pressed a button on the answering machine. She and Priddy had apparently decided to play it cool. She kept her expression bland and indifferent, and Len made a point of ignoring her. Dante got up and shook Len's hand, inviting him to take a seat. He'd never liked the guy's looks. Something smarmy going on. His hair was a slick gray, combed back from his face, which was big and square. His skin was crepey, with an unbecoming puffiness along his jaw. He had bags under his eyes and his upper lids sagged until it was a marvel he could see. He couldn't imagine what a gorgeous girl like Abbie was doing with a guy like him. Maybe she needed a sugar daddy and he got off being sexually serviced by someone half his age.

Dante said, "Sergeant Detective Priddy, it's nice to see you again. It's been a while."

"You seem to be holding your own," Len said.

"I was until recently."

"Oh?"

"Yeah, 'Oh.' Let's cut to the chase here. My brother's been seen in conversation with you. I've heard it from more than one source and it doesn't sit well."

Len continued to look at him. Dante could see that he was reluctant to confirm the claim and too smart to deny it. Len said, "I'm not sure this is a conversation we should be having."

"Why not? The place isn't bugged. I have it swept every other day," Dante said, and went on: "I imagine you've come into all manner of information about how I run my business. Not that Cappi's a reliable source."

"I don't think that warrants comment. You know your brother better than I do."

"Here's something he hasn't been told and therefore hasn't had the opportunity to pass along. I'm closing up shop. I've been meaning to get out for years, but it was never the right time."

Len smiled. "You're closing up shop because you're under indictment and you know you're going to jail."

"I wasn't aware we were discussing my motivation," Dante said. "I admit my retirement is self-serving, but keep this in mind: I'm a good businessman. I believe in sound financial practices, the same as a bank. I've also kept the violence to a minimum and what there was of it was Cappi's doing."

"You've never ordered a hit," Len said facetiously.

"No, I have not. Killing makes for bad public relations. Not that Cappi would agree. He can hardly wait to step into my shoes. Once that happens, you got a real problem on your hands."

"I think I can deal with it."

"The deal is the issue we're here to discuss. He might be willing to slip you your share, but he won't be as generous as I've been. You'd be wise to broker an agreement up front and make sure it's on your terms, not his."

"Is that what this meeting's about? Unsolicited advice from a fucking gangster?"

"I don't think of myself as a gangster. The term offends me. I've never been convicted of a crime."

"You will be."

"You're entitled to feel smug because you win either way. I'm out, he's in, it's all the same to you. You think you've got your hands full with me, wait until Cappi's in the driver's seat. He'll turn this town on its ear."

"So why don't you do us all a favor and get rid of him?" Len said.

Dante smiled. "Why don't you? I've got enough problems as it is without adding murder to the list."

"You only have one problem, buddy. We are taking you down."

"Oh, please. How long has this investigation been going on? Two years, three? You're playing patty-cake with the FBI and who else? DEA? ATF? All government grunts, a bunch of jack-offs. I already told you I'm out of here. Cappi's the one you should worry about. Take him out and the business is all yours."

Len got up. "Meeting's over. Good-bye and good luck."

"Think about it. That's all I'm saying. Retire from the PD and live in style for a change. You could do a lot worse."

"I'll take it under advisement," he said. "What's the time frame for this departure of yours?"

"That's no concern of yours. I'm telling you this much because I want to be fair since you've been such a help to me."

Dante left the office early. He was restless, obsessing about Nora, trying to decide what to do. He wanted to tell her what happened to Phillip, but he knew it would be the end of their relationship. On the other hand, what was love about if not honesty and openness? He had Tomasso drop him at the house, where he picked up his car. He drove to the Vogelsangs' in Montebello and swung the Maserati into the courtyard, then parked it next to Nora's Thunderbird. It was Wednesday and he assumed Channing was back in Los Angeles. Dante was heavy-hearted, a phrase he'd never understood before.

He crossed to the front door, aware of how ordinary all of his actions felt. He was playing the part of Lorenzo Dante, not fully inhabiting his body, but removed as though watching from outside himself. She must have heard his car pull in because when he rang the bell, she opened the door. Her face was stone. She held on to the door, forcing him to remain outside.

Someone had spilled the beans. "Who told you?"

"Two FBI agents came to the house in Malibu. I can't believe you didn't tell me yourself. How long were you going to let this go on?"

"I had no idea you were married to Tripp until yesterday at the beach house."

"Yes, you did. I saw it in your face. Why didn't you speak up?"

"I couldn't. When it finally dawned on me, all I could think was I didn't want to lose you. I knew if I owned up, it was over."

Nora said, "You're despicable."

"I didn't mean to deceive you. I came here because I want to be straight with you whatever the cost."

"Well, aren't you the noble one?"

"Nora. God's truth. I never laid a hand on your boy. I'm not excusing myself. He died because of me. I'm responsible, but not through any intention on my part. I made an offhand remark and Cappi took it for something else. He's vicious and he has no impulse control. He's been that way since he was a kid. I should have had him taken out. I couldn't bring myself to do it, but I should have done it anyway. I didn't understand how dangerous he was."

"Yes, you did. You knew perfectly well, but you looked the other way."

"I don't want to argue with you. That's not why I'm here. You're right. Whatever you say, I accept. I should have turned him in two years ago when I found out he threw Phillip off that roof. I thought his being my brother mattered more than justice. I was wrong."

"You could have turned him in yesterday. I might have believed in your sincerity if you'd done that."

"I'll make it right. I'll talk to the DA and tell him everything."

"Who gives a shit what you do now? He's still your brother. I don't see why you should suddenly see your way clear to doing what you should have done long before now."

"Listen to me. Listen. All bets are off. Cappi sold me out to the cops and that's the end of anything I owe him."

"Are you hearing yourself? You're saying if he'd been loyal, you'd have gone on protecting him. So what if he killed a few people, you'd have shielded him as long as there was some benefit to you."

"I carried him because Pop would've died if anything happened to him. I thought if I looked after him, my old man would eventually bring me in out of the cold."

"Oh, you're out in the cold, all right."

"Fine. I'm out. I won't fight you on this. As long as we're putting our cards on the table, there's something else. You do whatever you have to do, but fold this into the equation while you're at it. Phillip was a good kid, but he was off track. He told me he gambled all through college. He bragged he made money at it, but that was bullshit. All poker players say that. It's a distortion . . . filtering out the losses and exaggerating the wins. Did you ever stop and calculate how much you and Channing paid out to cover his debts? You'd be paying to this day because he would never have given it up. He couldn't. That was his fix . . . how he took care of whatever pain and anxiety he felt."

"You don't know what you're talking about."

"Yes, I do. I see guys like him all day long. I lend them money so they can try to bail themselves out of whatever hole they've dug. You and Channing were always going to be picking up after him. He was weak."

"How dare you criticize my son! He was a *child*! Twenty-three years old."

"Nora, he had big problems. He was up and down, immature, grandiose. Which was fine as long as he lived in the bubble he created for himself, but in the real world, he was floundering."

"How do you know he wouldn't have straightened out? He lost any chance he had. He lost his life and for what?"

"Maybe he *would* have straightened up. I don't know that and neither do you. He didn't deserve to die. What happened to him was my fault and I don't deny the part I played. I know you can't forgive me. I'm not asking you to. I just don't want you to pretty up who Phillip was and what he did. I'm sorry he died. I mean that. I know how much he meant to you and I'm sorry."

"Anything else?" she asked, her tone flat.

Dante took a deep breath. "As long as I'm being honest, I might as well give you the rest. I set him up. I meant to teach him a lesson, something Tripp might have done if he'd lived."

"A lesson? What the hell are you talking about?"

"I put a woman at his table, one of my employees. Georgia's a world-class poker player. I knew he'd go down in flames if he came up against her. I wanted him to hit rock bottom so he'd see the error of his ways. He was never going to figure it out if he had people coming to his rescue. That was truly my intent, to put him back on the straight and narrow."

She started to close the door.

He put a hand out, stopping her. "Listen to me. My brother killed your son. Phillip didn't kill himself. His death had nothing to do with you. Blame me, if it helps. You've been through a loss no parent should have to bear and nothing will make up for it. But Phillip's dead either way. At least you know now he didn't die through any will of his own."

"Enough. You've had your say. Now get away from me. I'm tired."

"Hell, Nora. We're all tired."

She closed the door. He stood on her doorstep for one minute more and then he turned and went back to his car.

He thought their conversation was the low point of his day, but there was worse in store. When he reached home, the upstairs rooms were dark. Lights in the kitchen, dining room, and living room were ablaze, but there was nothing cheery waiting for him. Lola was long gone. He left his car in the driveway for Tomasso to put in the garage and entered the house through the front door. He was relieved to see there was no sign of his father. He went into the library and fixed himself a drink. He left the house by way of the back door, greeting Sophie briefly in passing. She gave him a long look, apparently aware that Lola had packed up and departed. While she knew better than to commiserate, she was in the process of preparing all of his favorites: beef Wellington and haricots verts. Chunks of potato were simmering on a low burner and he knew she'd mash them with butter and sour cream. The tureen was set out for the fresh tomato soup she'd made. She'd also made a green salad she'd be dressing just before she served him. This was the only form of mothering he knew—someone cooking his supper, fixing everything he loved. He paid her handsomely, but so be it. Nurturing was nurturing.

Sophie said, "Your uncle's been asking for you. Cara's been in here six times."

"I'm on my way now. I should be back in half an hour or so. Pop on the premises?"

"He took the limo. Tomasso drove. He said he'd swing by Cappi's house and take him out to dinner."

Dante made no comment. What did he care what Pop did with Cappi?

It was still light out, but the day was fading, which made the lights in the guesthouse look cozy. He could smell wood smoke and imagined Cara had laid a fire to warm the old man, who was growing more feeble by the day. When she opened the door for him, she kept her voice low. Over her shoulder, he caught sight of his uncle, whose chair was pulled up as close to the hearth as she could place it.

She was looking at him oddly. "Are you going someplace? Your uncle keeps talking about your leaving. He's been agitated."

"No plans at the moment. Lola's gone. She left for Los Angeles this morning, so he might have caught sight of her going down the drive and thought I was in the car."

"Well, do what you can to calm him. This is as bad as I've seen him."

Dante crossed to the fireplace, where Cara had set out a chair close enough for easy conversation. Alfredo was swaddled in a comforter, his head sunk on his chest. Only the occasional light snore suggested he was still among the living. Dante hated to wake him, so he sat and sipped his drink. Better to wait in companionable silence than to leave and suffer the silence of the main house. He watched the fire and when he next looked at his uncle, the old man's eyes were open, fixed on him with an intensity Dante hadn't seen for many years. Dante said, "How's it going? You still hangin' in there?"

"I had a dream about you going on a journey. You kept looking back, motioning like I was supposed to come with you." He paused to smile. "One of those dreams where I worked hard to catch up, but I couldn't close the distance. Like walking in deep water up to here." He laid a trembling hand on his chest.

"I feel like that sometimes when I'm awake," Dante said. "Meantime, I'm not going anyplace, so you can rest easy on that score."

"Time's getting short and there's something I need to get off my chest."

"You don't have to do this now . . ."

Alfredo shook his head. "Listen to me. This, I know. Shadows are getting longer and I'm cold. My blood pressure's dropping. Cara won't talk about it, but I can feel it in my soul. Those hospice people can tell you to the minute, which is why I didn't want them hovering over me. Cara's better-looking and she's got those big tits."

Dante smiled. "I thought you'd appreciate her attributes."

"What I'm saying, you don't want to know or you'd have figured it out years ago. I don't tell you this to cause you pain, but in order to set you free. You think you're not going anywhere, but time's getting short for you the same as it is for me."

"I'm here now," Dante said.

"Thing about you is you've always broken my heart. You've been burdened by more sorrow than any boy deserves except maybe me so let me say this while I can."

Dante could feel his face grow tense with his effort to hold back tears.

"This is about your mother."

Dante held up a hand. "Let's keep this about us, about our relationship. You're the one I'm going to miss."

"Not like you missed her. You remember the day your father drained the swimming pool?"

"Spite on his part. Even at twelve, I knew that much . . ."

"Because her blood was in the water."

Dante felt his body grow still. The image was as clear in his mind as though he'd been there himself, which he knew he had not. "He killed her?"

"Killing was what he did best. Not like he is now, a wreck of a man. You remember his temper back then. Terrible. Man was a maniac when he was enraged. I don't even remember now what set him off. Nothing she did. It was all in his head. I was there. I tried to intervene, but he was out of control. You kids were asleep. He made me help him bury her and then he disposed of her clothes and everything else she loved. You were her favorite and that's why from that time on he beat you bloody every chance he got. He wanted to crush you to get back at her."

"How'd he do it?"

"He slit her throat."

"Ah, god."

"She never would have left you. You should know that about her. How much she loved you kids and how devoted she was. Over the years, I thought you'd ask. I thought you'd realize it was something he did, that it had nothing to do with her. Now I understand with her gone, all you had to hold on to was him. That's a special hell for a kid. The more you tried to please him, the more you reminded him of what he did."

Dante felt all the cells in his body rearranging themselves, felt memories shift, felt truth ricochet through his soul. He knew. He did know. What else made sense in his life except his mother . . . beautiful, young, and faithful to him after all.

Alfredo said, "I wish I could help, but I can't. I have no counsel. No advice. Take it in and do with it as you will. I couldn't leave you without letting you know. I should have told you years ago, but I'm a coward. Ashamed of myself, but always proud of you. You're a good man and I love you more than I can say. If you'd been my son, this would have all turned out differently. You need to leave the country while you can. I'll be fine. I don't have long anyway and I don't want you hanging around on my account. This is our good-bye. You go. I'll cover your back. I'll be like the guy left in the fort while all the others escape certain death. I'll rest easier knowing you're safe, so you do that for me."

Dante nodded. He reached out and the two men gripped hands tightly as though they might find a way to give immortality to the bond. Dante felt as fierce and as strong and as clean as he'd ever felt in his life. It was Alfredo's parting gift.

# 30

Late Wednesday afternoon, a uniformed officer finally stopped by my office to pick up copies of the report I'd passed along to Cheney Phillips. In point of fact, what I'd given him was my one and only copy—except for the carbon, which I confess I used to run off additional pages after I talked to him. I knew he'd feel better if he thought he'd corralled all the paperwork in my possession, so I handed the officer two more copies and we were all satisfied. The carbon I returned to its hiding place. As soon as the officer left, I put through a call to Cheney, hoping to fill him in on Len's attack, the exchange of gunfire between Cappi and Pinky, and my subsequent conversation with Dante. He didn't pick up the call and I made a note to myself to try again later.

I arrived home from work to find a message from Henry on my answering machine. He'd tried me at the office, but I must have been out the door by then. He said he was on his way to the nursing home to visit Nell. The doctors expected to release her sometime in the coming week. The purpose of his call was to let me know he was flying home the next day. He gave me his flight number and time of arrival—4:05 P.M. He said if I had prior plans and couldn't get to the airport, he'd take a cab and not to worry. He also said he'd treat me to dinner at Emile's-at-the-Beach if I was free. This was cheery news. I knew without even looking my calendar was clear, and I was excited by the prospect of having him home. I popped over to his house to make sure his plants were alive and well. It was also time to clean up the mess Pinky'd left in the hall when he dashed off. The tidying up didn't take long. I dusted, dry-mopped, and vacuumed, and then opened the back door to air out the place.

I made a run to the supermarket and stocked the few items he'd need so he wouldn't have to worry about shopping for groceries right away. The rest of Wednesday went by in a blur. I called the hospital twice for updates on Dodie, who seemed to be holding her own. The reports were superficial and didn't contain much in the way of medical data, but since I wasn't a family member, I couldn't push for more. Pinky was impossible to track down. The floor nurses didn't have the time or the inclination to roust him out of the waiting room and steer him to a phone. If he managed to get home for a shower and a few hours' sleep, the last thing I wanted to do was disturb him.

It wasn't until Thursday morning I had time to make a trip to St. Terry's. I stopped by my office en route, sitting down at my desk just long enough to try Cheney again. In the wake of Len's attack, I was losing my fear of him and anger was taking its place. When Cheney finally picked up, he was short with me. I wouldn't say he was rude, but I knew by his tone he was in no mood to talk. I said I'd catch him later, but the call left me wondering what was going on. I'd no more than returned the handset to the cradle than the phone rang.

I answered, hoping Cheney had repented. Instead, I found Diana Alvarez on the line.

"Hi, Kinsey. This is Diana." She'd adopted the breezy, good-natured tone of a close friend, and I didn't have the energy to remind her she was no such thing. "Has Cheney said anything to you about some big deal coming down?"

"Like what?"

"I'm not sure. I was talking to one of my sources at the PD and got the impression there was something major in the works. I'd love to get the heads-up so I can file a story."

"Can't help you there. He hasn't taken me into his confidence," I said.

"Must be hot stuff, whatever it is. You know how cops are when it's time for fun and games. If you hear anything, would you let me know?"

I said, "Sure." We even exchanged brief pleasantries before she signed off. I sat and stared at the phone while a cartoon question mark formed above my head. Cheney was preoccupied about *something*. No doubt about that. I'd postulated the existence of a task force and an investigation that predated and superseded mine. Were they ready to make a move? If so, how had Diana picked up a hint of it when I was still in the dark?

The drive to St. Terry's was an easy ten minutes. I found parking in the same lot I'd used Tuesday night when Dodie was admitted. I was hoping she'd be out of ICU by now and in a room of her own. At the very least, I hoped to connect with Pinky to see how he was holding up. I looked forward to telling them that Dante'd agreed to cover their bills and living expenses, which I hoped would be a source of relief. I wasn't sure how much fast-talking I'd have to do to convince Pinky the offer was something other than charity. I regarded it as fair payment for services rendered. He'd provided Dante with valuable confirmation of his brother's duplicity, which Dante could deal with in any manner that suited him, the more punitive the better as far as I was concerned.

I stopped in the lobby and asked the volunteer at the desk for Dodie's room number. She checked her roster, which was revised and reprinted daily as patients were admitted, moved, or discharged. She was a woman in her seventies, probably a grandmother and a great-grandmother, though quite the looker for someone her age. She seemed momentarily confused and made a phone call to ICU for Dodie's status, since her name wasn't readily available. When she hung up, she said, "Mrs. Ford passed."

"Passed what?" I said. I thought she was talking about a test. Then my mind skipped to the notion of a blood clot or a kidney stone. This seemed like an odd piece of medical data to be sharing with me. She was clearly uncomfortable at my pressing the point.

"She passed over first thing this morning, but that's as much as I was told."

"Passed over," I repeated. "You mean, she died?"

"I'm terribly sorry."

"She *died*? But that can't be true. How could she do that?"

"I wasn't given an explanation."

"But I called twice yesterday and I was told she was fine. Now you're telling me she *passed*? What kind of word is that anyway, *passed*. Why don't you call a spade a spade?"

The woman's cheeks were suffused with pink, and I noticed that two visitors seated in the lobby had turned to stare at me.

"Would you like to speak to the chaplain?"

"No, I don't want to speak to the chaplain," I snapped. "I want to talk to her husband. Is he here?"

"I don't have information about next of kin. I'd imagine he's meeting with a funeral director about services. Really, I'm so sorry to upset you. If you'll take a seat, I'll have someone bring you a cup of water."

"Oh, for god's sake," I said.

I turned and headed for the door. I didn't doubt her word. I just thought it was ridiculous that Dodie had died when she'd been fine last I checked. Ever quick with the old defense mechanisms, I was using anger as a counterweight to my surprise. I didn't feel sorrow. I didn't know Dodie well enough to experience the loss. Pinky would be devastated, and what sprang to mind was his vow of retaliation if anything happened to her. Now that he was faced with the worst-case scenario, he'd go off on a rampage, and Cappi would be his target.

I drove the four blocks to the duplex. I had no idea the state I'd find him in or what I'd say to him. I parked across the street, noticing that Dodie's gaudy yellow Cadillac was gone. I felt a prick of anxiety, like the tip of a knife touching me between the shoulder blades. I took the porch steps two at a time and knocked on the front door while simultaneously ringing the bell. There was no response, so I did the next best thing, which was to try the knob. The door was unlocked. I opened it and stuck my head in. "Pinky?"

The house had that empty air of lingering food scents and humming appliances. I called his name again, though I was silly to do so when I knew he wasn't on the premises. I moved into the living room. One of the couch cushions had been tossed on the floor and Pinky's gun was gone. I sat down abruptly and put my head in my hands. There was no doubt in my mind he'd gone after Cappi. It was exactly the sort of rash move he'd make. What chance would I have of reaching Cappi before he did? More important, how would I find him? Rapidly, I ran through my options. My first impulse was to dial 9-1-1. And say what? I could describe Dodie's car. I could describe the man driving it, but that was that. I could call Dante and warn him Pinky was on the loose. He was the man most likely to know where his brother was. Maybe he could put out a companywide alert and let him know what was going on. My third option was to warn Cappi myself if I could figure out where he was.

I tried to clear my mind of chatter. I remembered Pinky mentioning something in the course of his morbid ramblings the night Dodie was shot. What had he said? That Cappi couldn't find a job so he'd been reduced to working in his brother's warehouse, which was how he was able to leak Dante's business to the cops. I'd been to a warehouse in Colgate that I surmised was associated with the retail-theft ring. I roused myself and returned to my car.

I merged with traffic on the 101. Time must have skipped six beats, because I couldn't remember traveling on surface streets to reach the access ramp. My impulse was to jam the gas pedal to the floor, which with a Mustang is the equivalent of being shot out of a cannon. However, as I pressed down with my foot, I caught sight of a black-and-white passing on my left. I eased off, marveling at my good luck. Nothing worse than peeling out when you've got a cop car next to yours, equipped with radar. I stuck to the middle lane, so bound by good behavior that I almost missed the appearance of a second black-and-white sailing by on my right. Neither patrol car was traveling at great speed, but the driver closest to me was *intent*. There was something purposeful in his posture, as though he didn't want to be late for festivities I hadn't been told about. A party, parade, some coplike activity requiring him to be punctual.

The two patrol units left the highway at the Fairdale exit, with me bringing up the rear. What was the deal here? When I spotted a third patrol car coming up on my tail, I pulled into the right-hand lane and let them catch up with one another. I reached the intersection, where the red traffic light inspired a stop on my part while the police cars slowed briefly and slid through. By the time I turned right, the three patrol cars seemed to have vanished as suddenly as they had appeared. I continued half a mile until I passed the oversize screen of the now-defunct drive-in theater, popular when I was a kid. I turned right onto the adjacent side road. The orchard of speakers on stands had been removed. I glanced at the empty acres of cracked asphalt and nearly ran off the road. The entire lot was being used as a staging area for patrol cars and unmarked vehicles. Two dozen uniformed officers were milling around, law-enforcement personnel in an assortment of jackets reading FBI, POLICE, and SHERIFF. I was guessing all wore Kevlar vests under their shirts. I jerked my gaze back to the road, but I knew the significance of what I'd seen. Diana had heard something big was going down and this had to be it. No wonder Cheney had been short with me. The only location of significance in the area was the Allied Distributors warehouse. The joint police agencies had to be gearing up for a raid. Whatever intelligence gathering they'd done over the previous months and years had now culminated in an armed response. My heart was thunking and a rush of adrenaline coursed through my frame, making me feel electric. Pinky, the gunslinger, if he managed to catch up with Cappi here, would find himself in the midst of a cadre of officers and FBI agents more hyped up than he was.

A quarter of a mile farther down the road, the warehouse appeared at the end of the cul-de-sac. Crisscrossing lines of railroad tracks ran behind the building. It was possible in times past, goods were moved from the warehouse by train, a miniterminal devoted to the business of commercial transport. Now the tracks were the sole domain of the Amtrak freight and passenger trains that went through town three and four times a day. Abruptly, I put my foot on the brake. To my right, Dodie's yellow Cadillac sat at an angle, wheels off the side of the road and slightly sunk in the grass. Pinky hadn't bothered to park carefully. Then again, he was on his way to shoot a man, so perhaps the finer points of roadside etiquette had escaped him.

The wide metal gates to the warehouse property stood open. The employee parking lot appeared on my right with the warehouse itself on the left. Six tractor-trailers had been backed up to the loading docks and all the rolling metal doors stood open. Five or six guys seemed to be enjoying a smoke while two forklift operators wheeled in and out of the warehouse with loads. At the far end of the building, two white panel trucks sat side by side, back doors open while men shifted boxes from the pallets on a flatbed and into the interiors. I scanned for Cappi but didn't see anyone with his build and body type. I didn't see Pinky either, and I didn't know what to make of it. Dante's employees were caught up in an ordinary day at work, no urgency, no threat, no cause for alarm.

I parked in the employee lot and crossed to the main building. The two-story structure was a quirky blend of the old and the new. Parts of the building were aging brick and frame, with a newer steel addition affixed to the front. The whole of it was probably twenty-five thousand square feet of space. I entered by way of a side door, avoiding the receiving area, which had to be hazardous if you didn't know what you were doing. At the mezzanine level, I could see the business offices. Around the perimeter, catwalks were affixed to the ceiling by a series of cables and steel posts. The offices overlooked the storage blocks that were separated by wide aisles. I spotted zigzagging sets of stairs every hundred feet or so, like fire escapes in a tenement. The place seemed well organized, with a system at work that only the practiced eye could assimilate.

I passed the restrooms, a locker room, and then a lunchroom lined with vending machines. The ten tables I saw were sparsely occupied by a smattering of workers on a coffee break. I crossed the concrete floor and climbed the stairs to the offices, moving as quickly as I could. It's hard to remember what I was thinking at the time. Under the circumstances, I shouldn't have been there at all, but I felt I had to intercept Pinky before all hell broke loose. Judging from the fevered activity I'd seen at the drive-in, a raid was imminent. The strategy had been worked out and the cops were suited up and ready to roll. The goal would be to contain and control the warehouse, subduing its occupants by hitting hard, then moving in rapidly before anyone could escape or destroy the evidence they were after. They'd have arrest and search warrants in hand, and they'd seize files, records, computers, and anything else that would provide details of illegal activities. Who knew how many guys they'd round up in the process?

At the top of the stairs, the offices were enclosed in waist-high wainscoting, with glass panels above. The door was open, and a young girl with a mass of frizzy blond hair sat at her desk. There was a computer in front of her and an old-fashioned typewriter on a rolling table nearby. Unlike Dante's downtown offices, this place was grubby—plain linoleum on the floor, fluorescent lights overhead, battered wooden desks, and cheap rolling chairs. The room was rimmed with file cabinets, and I knew the raiding party would be all over them. She looked up at me. "Can I help you?"

I was caught off guard by the calendar on her desk. It was one of those thick blocks of sheets with the date writ large on each page, which would be torn off and discarded at the end of the day. Even upside down, I could see it was Thursday, May 5, and I could barely suppress a yelp. May 5th is my birthday. That's why Henry had made a point of coming home. That's why he'd offered to take me to dinner. The downside of being single and alone is having a birthday come around and catch you by surprise. I was suddenly thirty-eight years old. Still distracted, I said, "Is Mr. Dante here?"

"In there, but he said no interruptions."

Dante opened the door and stepped out of his private office into the reception area. "I'll take care of this, Bernice," he said to her. He turned a flat look on me. "What can I do for you, Ms. Millhone? You have no business being here. I hope you know that."

He'd seemed friendlier in the limousine, but I needed his help, so I decided to overlook his surly attitude. I put my hand in the crook of his elbow while I steered him out of reception and into his private office. "Pinky's got a gun and he's either here on the premises or not far away. Dodie died this morning and he'll kill Cappi if he catches up with him."

I expected him to react, but he was engaged in a more important task. His wall safe was open, and he was transferring thick packets of cash into a soft-sided suitcase that lay on his desk. He didn't seem to care that Cappi's life was in jeopardy or that Pinky was on the verge of bursting in with a loaded gun. His manner was relaxed; his movements efficient and methodical. He had a job to do and he was doing it with no wasted energy.

"Do you know where Cappi is?" I asked.

"I sent him on an errand to get him out of my hair. Sorry about Pinky's wife. I never met the woman, but I know he was devoted. I suggest you get out before he and Cappi cross paths. Neither one of us has a dog in their fight."

"Can't you put a stop to it?"

"No more than you can."

I stared at him, fascinated by his calm when I was in such a state of panic. I said, "It gets worse. You've got three dozen cops down the road about to descend on this place."

"That's Cappi for you. The guy can't keep his trap shut and this is what comes of it. My best guess, he'll make sure he's rounded up with everyone else so it looks like he's in the same jam. He better hope he succeeds. This isn't a business where a snitch gets away with it. If Pinky doesn't kill him, someone else will."

"What are you doing?" I asked.

"What's it look like?"

As though on cue, I heard shouting down below, and Pinky's voice echoed through the vast warehouse space. "Cappi! This is me, Pinky. I got a debt to settle with you. Show your face, you son of a bitch."

I moved toward the door.

Dante said, "Don't go out there."

I ignored him and left the office. I went out on the landing and looked over the rail. Pinky was drunk and weaving on his feet. He looked like he hadn't slept in days, and when he'd managed it, he'd slept in the same clothes. He held the gun in his right hand, relaxed at his side. If Cappi showed up, he probably didn't want him to spot the weapon until he took aim and fired.

I called down to him. "Hey, Pinky? Up here."

Pinky did a lazy visual search until he spotted me one floor up. "You seen Cappi?"

"What do you want with him?"

"Dodie died. I'm going to kill his ass."

"I heard about her. I can't tell you how sorry I am. If I come down, can we talk?"

"Soon as I shoot him, we can chat all you like."

I could feel the despair surging from my feet all the way up my frame. Pinky had nothing to lose. Violence was about to erupt and I didn't want him to die. How was I going to talk him out of this dumb plan of his? He was beyond listening to reason. Worse, I didn't think I'd be persuasive when he had a gun in his hand and murder on his mind.

Across the concrete apron that jutted out from the loading docks, men had stopped what they were doing. Most seemed poised for action . . . most likely, running away. All waited to see if a deadly confrontation would actually develop. Maybe this was nothing more than big talk from a drunk with a gun, or maybe this would turn into a movie-style showdown with real blood and real death.

Cappi appeared at the side door. He stopped in his tracks, surprised at the tableau of guys standing motionless, eyes turned to the man in the center of the floor who swayed unsteadily. Cappi's gaze traveled to the object of their interest. The minute he realized it was Pinky, he took off at a run. Pinky wheeled. He extended his arm, gun pointed at Cappi as he took the stairs two at a time, using the handrail to propel himself upward. I heard his footsteps on the metal treads, the sound half a beat behind the actual impact. The effect was much like a jet flying overhead, the aircraft itself moving faster than the sound that follows in its wake. In a curious way, it was the perfect distraction for the raid, which was suddenly in progress.

Six black-and-whites pulled in and screeched to a halt. Cops poured into the loading area and fanned out. Several were armed with sledgehammers and two hauled a battering ram. Workers scattered in all directions. The officers with sledgehammers began smashing into the wall near a computer terminal, the pounding magnified in the confinement of the metal structure. One man broke through the outer shell of cinder block, wielding the sledgehammer with a force that made his arms quiver from his elbows to his shoulders.

From my vantage point, it was like watching short clips of film. I saw a man in coveralls scale the fence and disappear into the weedy field next door. Three others banged out the back door and scrambled down into the drainage ditch that some of their pals were already using as an escape route. Officers advanced along the ditch from opposite directions, blocking their escape. Though I couldn't see them from where I stood, I heard guys shouting as they scurried along the railroad tracks. None of the warehouse employees were armed. Why would they carry guns when, for most of them, their jobs were so mundane?

Cappi and Pinky were as oblivious as lovers who had eyes only for each other. Pinky scrambled up the stairs after Cappi, who'd pulled his own gun from the small of his back. Both fired randomly to no particular effect. Bullets pinged off the steel beams that supported the roof and ricocheted into the corrugated metal walls at the rear. I backed up, all too aware how wild and inexpert the shooting match was. This was not a gentlemanly duel at ten paces with pistols raised. This was a two-man war. The window next to me shattered and I dropped to the floor. Dante appeared suddenly behind me and grabbed me under the arms, pulling me up, propelling me toward his inner office.

"Stick with me. I'll get you out of here."

"No! Not until I see Pinky's okay."

"Forget about him. He's a dead man."

In all the shouting it was nearly impossible to separate police orders from the uproar on the loading dock. I pulled away and returned to the front windows so I could see what was going on. Dante disappeared into his office. I stood where I was, sick with fear. Violence scares me silly, but it felt cowardly to run off when Pinky's life was at stake. Below, one of the tractor-trailers growled to life. The driver stomped on the gas pedal. The cab shot forward, careening toward the road where two police cars were parked, blocking the exit. Officers took cover, their guns drawn. The driver refused to give ground and plowed into one of the black-and-whites, which seemed to levitate before coming to rest with a bang. The impact smacked the trucker against the steering wheel and he slumped to one side, blood running down his face. I half expected him to open the door and make a run for it, but he was out cold. By that time, most of the workers had had the good sense to give up the fight. They were herded into the open, where they were ordered to get down on the ground, hands over their heads.

Mesmerized, I scanned the loading platform, where I saw Cheney Phillips. Next to him was Len Priddy with his face upturned. Both ducked out of sight and came up on the far side of a semi, using the cab to shield themselves as they popped up in range of the two shooters. I was certain all the officers had been cautioned about the unwarranted firing of their weapons. Pinky and Cappi, of course, were free of such restraints.

Behind me, Dante's office girl had taken cover under her desk, phone in hand. Her instinct was probably to call the police, but the place was already overrun with officers. Meanwhile, Cappi had circled half the warehouse on the elevated walkway. He ran toward me, approaching from my right. He pushed me aside and headed toward the nearest stairway. He must have thought if he could get down to ground level, he'd be close enough to the side door to get out. He was so focused on reaching safety that he ignored the fact that officers were blocking the exit. Pinky was still to my right and closing the gap between them. Cappi turned and fired twice, and Pinky went down, his right leg going out from under him. He couldn't have been more than fifteen feet away from me. Cappi was out of ammunition, and that changed the dynamic of the game for him. Abruptly, he turned, his face set. Maybe having wounded Pinky, he'd flipped from victim to aggressor. He moved toward me at a measured pace, reloading as he walked. Pinky pulled himself up. I screamed. "Pinky, RUN!"

I meant for him to go back the way he'd come, but he hobbled in my direction, his gaze fixed on mine. This put him directly in Cappi's path. My instinct was to grab him and pull him out of the line of fire. Dante apparently had a similar impulse, but he was focused on me. His face was dark with anger. "I told you to get down!"

I glanced back and realized he was two feet behind me, screaming in my ear. He grabbed me for a second time and dragged me toward his inner office.

"Let go!" I broke his grip, desperate to protect Pinky if there was any way I could. In retrospect, it seems pointless, my thinking to intervene. I have no idea how I could have affected the outcome. Far from helping, I was only putting myself in harm's way. Dante turned me with a quick yank that threw me off balance, saying, "Sorry about this."

I stumbled, and I might have caught myself if I hadn't been so astonished at the sight of his fist coming at my face. There was no way to avoid the impact. The blow caught me dead center and he landed a punch to my nose that dropped me to my knees. I put my arms out, tumbling forward until I supported myself on my hands and knees. My brain clanged around in my skull like the clapper in a bell. I collapsed into a sitting position and put my hands to my face. Blood gushed through my fingers, and at the sight of it I could feel my eyes roll back in my head. I heard one more shot fired, but the sound came from a long distance away, and I knew the shooter wasn't aiming at me. I blacked out briefly and then I was dimly aware of officers swarming up the stairs.

# 31

## DANTE

### May 5, 1988

Dante felt his way down the steep set of stairs built into his office wall. One push had activated the touch latch, and he secured the door behind him before he moved on. During Prohibition, his father built the staircase to cover emergencies. For Pop, an unexpected visit from the cops or an angry competitor was the sort of crisis that required a hasty retreat. Dante had played in the underground passages as a kid, long after Prohibition ended, and he knew how to navigate the maze of small rooms in total darkness. Originally the space housed a number of stills for the manufacture of assorted liquors and spirits that could be stored by the caseload before shipment by rail. The corridor extended for a block and a half, with a number of offshoots created to confuse those unfamiliar with the subterranean network. The hard-packed dirt path gradually climbed upward and daylighted in a culvert that skirted the now-defunct drive-in theater. When Dante exited, he was on the second of two side roads that flanked the theater. The other road ended at the warehouse. Dante was well beyond the chaos, and he imagined the raid was in its mop-up phase. On this side of the drive-in there were five three-story buildings that made up an industrial complex with sufficient traffic to make his sudden appearance seem unremarkable.

Lou Elle was waiting in her car with the engine idling. Dante approached on her right, with the big soft-sided suitcase in hand. He opened the rear door and deposited the suitcase on the backseat, then opened the passenger-side door and got in. Lou Elle shifted from park to drive and pulled onto the road, accelerating slowly to a modest twenty miles per hour. At Holloway, she turned right and drove on for a quarter of a mile. Dante glanced back, but there were no police cars in sight and no indication that an alarm had been sounded in the wake of his escape.

He massaged his right hand where the knuckles were bruised and swollen, though not as painful as they appeared.

Lou Elle glanced over at him. "What happened to you?"

"I busted a lady in the chops. I forgot what it's like punching someone's lights out. Hurts like a son of a bitch."

"You hit a woman?"

"I had to stop her barging into the middle of a shoot-out."

"A shoot-out?"

"Cappi and a guy named Pinky Ford exchanged fire while the raid was going on. Talk about a wild scene. Pinky got clipped, but he'll survive. It's a wonder nobody else was hurt."

"I remember him. He came to the office once. Wasn't he that wiry, bowlegged fellow in a satin shirt?"

"That's him."

"Is Cappi all right?"

"Cappi's dead. A cop took him out with one shot to the head. The timing was close. Cappi was about to blow a hole in Pinky's chest."

"You're okay with that?"

"I'm fine. Don't worry about it. Saved me doing it myself. It'll break

Pop's heart and I'm fine with that too. He's getting what he deserves. You talk to Nora?"

"Well, I called, but she didn't seem receptive. I gave her the information, but she didn't jump all over it."

"You tried, at any rate."

He reached into the inner jacket pocket of his suit coat and took out a bulky envelope with a name and address written on the front. "Couple of weeks, deliver this. Tell her to do what she wants with it. The money's compensation for the punch."

Dante slid the envelope into her handbag on the floor at his feet. Lou Elle turned left onto a short street that led to a small fixed-base operating terminal used by charter companies. He told her to pull up to the entrance to the field and press the call button. When the intercom came to life, she gave the name Dante was using for current travel purposes, and five seconds later the gate slid back, allowing her to pass through. On the tarmac, there was a midsized private jet, a Gulfstream Astra, with a range of twenty-three hundred nautical miles, sufficient to deliver Dante to the second plane he'd be taking that day. There was a third flight as well before he reached his destination. Lou Elle drove within twenty feet of the plane.

Dante retrieved his suitcase from the backseat and walked around to the driver's-side window, which Lou Elle lowered. He leaned in and kissed her lightly. "You're a peach. Thanks for everything."

"Good luck," she said. "You want me to wait until takeoff?"

"I'd prefer to picture you at your desk," he said. "Cops are gonna come down on you like a ton of bricks and I'm sorry about that."

"What can I tell them? I don't know anything."

"You're a good friend."

"It was a pleasure working with you. Safe journey. I hope life is good to you."

"I'll touch base when I change planes. Nothing after that."

"Understood."

Dante proceeded to the aircraft where one of the pilots stood near the retractable stairs. The two shook hands and Dante offered his passport for identification purposes. The pilot glanced at it briefly and then returned it to him. The pilot had been paid well and exhibited no curiosity.

"I was hoping a lady friend would be here. Nora Vogelsang. I put her name on the manifest."

"She hasn't arrived. How long do you want to wait?"

"Give it fifteen minutes. She knows time's at a premium. She doesn't show, she doesn't show. Have we been cleared?"

"We will be shortly. You want me to put that bag in back?"

"I'll keep it with me in the cabin."

The pilot boarded the plane, leaving Dante on the tarmac. Dante looked over at the gate. Lou Elle's car was receding and the gate was sliding shut. There were cars parked outside the fence, but no cars coming in or out of the lot. He'd said his good-byes and regretted he hadn't had the chance to say good-bye to Nora. The way things had turned out, maybe it was just as well. With Cappi dead and Lola gone, Pop would rattle around the house on his own. Alfredo might last another week to ten days and then he'd be gone as well. Dante knew his sisters would come to the old man's aid, but he didn't think any of the four would offer to take him in. Saul Abramson had been instructed to keep up maintenance on the estate for as long as he deemed wise. Dante had given him power of attorney with instructions that if the legal bills got out of hand, he was free to list the house for sale. If it sold, so be it. Pop could go into a nursing home and rot.

Dante checked the terminal with its small waiting room and sliding glass doors. No sign of Nora and no sign of the police, so maybe he was home free. He'd given Abbie enough misinformation to throw the cops off the scent. He knew she'd leak it all to Priddy, who no doubt prided himself on having the inside dope. In the meantime, Dante had told Lou Elle to change the first-class tickets to Manila from Nora's name and his to her own name and her husband's. He'd sport the couple to the trip as a reward for services rendered over the past fifteen years. If the CHP intercepted the limousine on its way to LAX, they'd discover the fish had slipped out of the net.

Dante climbed the steps and boarded the plane, ducking to clear the door as he proceeded to his seat. The interior was cream-colored leather and burled high-gloss cherry with a forward galley and an aft lavatory. He carried a toothbrush in his pocket, but aside from that, all he had was the cash. He chose the second forward-facing club chair on the right. One of the two pilots left the cockpit and made his way through the cabin so he could brief Dante about emergency exits and the drop of oxygen masks if the plane lost altitude. He also told him there was freshly brewed coffee and assorted snacks, along with the catered meals Dante had ordered in advance.

"Questions?"

"I'm good. I've flown privately before."

"Let me know if you need anything. We'll be under way shortly."

Dante picked up one of the newspapers that had been provided. He buckled his seat belt and opened the bottle of water offered in the console. The engines came to life and he could see the two pilots go through their preflight routine. The plane began to taxi down the runway. He could almost feel the familiar sensation of the aircraft lifting and climbing. In moments, he'd be gone. He hadn't expected the sense of loss to be so sharp. He was a patriotic guy. He loved his country. Now that departure was imminent, he couldn't imagine that he'd never again set foot in America. There was no compromising his defection. The number and nature of his crimes made it impossible to remain in the United States with his freedom intact. The plane slowed to a stop.

Ahead, in the cockpit, he saw the pilot unbuckle his seat belt and make a second trip into the cabin. When he reached the door, he swung the handle to the left in preparation for opening it. The door pivoted outward and the retractable stairway settled into place. Dante looked out the window and saw Nora's turquoise Thunderbird speed along the runway. The car came to a stop and the engine shut down.

She got out on the driver's side, pausing to remove a garment bag and an overnight case from the trunk. She was as beautiful as he'd ever seen her, in soft-fitting black sweats that looked comfortable for travel. A young man emerged from the passenger side and came around the front of the car to trade places with her. She tossed him the car keys and headed for the plane. The pilot walked out to meet her so he could carry her bags.

As she boarded, she said, "I left Channing a note, telling him good-bye and god bless. I left instructions for my lawyer, so he can handle the rest of it. I ought to have my head examined."

Dante said, "For that, we've got time."

# 32

## AFTER

### Santa Teresa, California

### May 27, 1988

There's always a story that comes after the end of a story. How could there not be? Life doesn't come in tidy packages, all neatly wrapped up with a pretty bow on top. The raid resulted in seventeen arrests, with criminal charges filed against twelve. To all intents and purposes, the theft ring was shut down and the organization at large suffered crippling effects—at least until they gear up again. If it hadn't been for Len, Pinky Ford would be dead, which Pinky claims he'd have preferred. With Dodie gone, he doesn't feel he has anything to look forward to, but that may change in time. Len was put on administrative leave and then decided to take early retirement before Internal Affairs could conduct a review. With thirty officers and an additional two dozen witnesses on hand, the facts about Cappi's shooting death were never in dispute. After consideration, the district attorney's office decided not to pursue the issue. Publicly, Len was hailed as a hero, which annoyed me no end. I remembered all too well the shooting years before, when he'd been called to an accounting for inadvertently killing a fellow officer during a drug bust gone bad. At the time, he was cleared, but I was never convinced he was without blame. Word on the street had it that the other officer had threatened to report Len for certain questionable transactions that he'd observed in the course of their partnership. In the matter of Cappi's death, the consensus was that Len had done law enforcement a favor, so nobody cared if I begrudged him the praise.

As for Dante, he disappeared while I was still bleeding on his scuffed linoleum floor. After he decked me, I remembered seeing him slip into his office, where he grabbed the suitcase from his desk and moved out of my line of sight. When the FBI agents burst in, I expected him to be escorted out in handcuffs. By then, he was gone. There were numerous explanations for his escape. Some said there was a secret room where he concealed himself until the police wrapped up the raid and departed. Others speculated he'd gone out the window and hung on to the frame while he hauled himself and his suitcase up onto the roof and made his way to the fire escape on the far end of the building. Even when the hidden staircase came to light, the man himself had vanished so completely, he might as well have been B. D. Cooper jumping out of that plane.

Len Priddy, on the other hand, was much in the public eye—smug, self-satisfied, and apparently bulletproof. He was a bad man, but a clever one, and he'd managed to dance out of the reach of the law. With Dante gone and Cappi dead, there were no corroborating witnesses to substantiate Priddy's relationship with the crime family. For those who'd hoped to see him behind bars, disappointment was keen that there was no justice in sight.

Three weeks later I had a visitor. I was sitting at my desk when a woman appeared in the doorway, saying, "Hi, I'm Lou Elle. Are you Kinsey?"

"I am." By then, most of my facial bruises were gone and my nose was only mildly swollen, so I didn't feel I needed to explain my appearance. She probably didn't know the difference since I'd never met her before. I said, "What can I do for you?"

"I work for Lorenzo Dante. Or maybe I should say I *worked* for him, past tense. Mind if I have a seat?"

"Be my guest. I hope you're here to tell me what happened to him."

"Yes and no. He got in touch with me once, but says I won't be hearing from him again. It's probably just as well. The less I know about him the better for both of us. Dante Enterprises is out of business."

"But you came out of it okay?"

"I'm fine. He made sure I wouldn't be caught in the mess. I'm not sure you'll appreciate this, but he had Abbie buy plane tickets for himself and a companion, leaving for Manila on Thursday night. He had me buy a second pair of tickets so when the CHP intercepted the limousine on its way to LAX, they found my husband and me in the backseat instead of him. You should have seen the looks on their faces. Talk about disappointed! They were all set to make the arrest. Instead, they had to wave us on our merry way."

"How did he manage to get away?"

"Sleight of hand. In a year or two, I'll fill you in, but at the moment, all you need to know is he's landed safely and he's set for life."

"I hope so. I only met him once, but I liked him."

"He must have liked you too. Despite the punch in the nose," she added.

"I was never so surprised in my life."

"He felt bad about it. I'm sure he would have apologized in person if he'd had time." She opened her bag and took out a thick envelope and passed it across the desk. "For you."

I picked up the envelope and opened the flap widely enough to catch sight of a fat packet of currency, bound by a rubber band. Topmost was a one-hundred-dollar bill and I was guessing the rest were duplicates.

"That's not a gift," she pointed out. "It's reimbursement for pain and suffering."

"No need," I said. "That's what medical insurance is for."

"It's also payment for a job he wants done if you're agreeable."

"A job?"

"Short-term. Nothing egregious. Let's call it a task."

"And what might that be?"

"Check the envelope again. You missed something."

When I opened the envelope the second time, I found a tape cassette wrapped in plain white paper.

"He thinks that should have an airing."

"What is it?"

"I don't know. He says you'll get the idea. He's trusting you to do anything you like with the information as long as it's made public."

"Have you heard it?"

"Nope, but if I know him, it's worth whatever he's paying you."

At that, she got up and headed for the door.

"What if I decide against doing it?"

"The money's yours anyway."

I said, "Why?"

She smiled. "He says you play straight and he thinks you're a woman of your word."

When I heard the outer door close behind her, I opened the middle drawer of my desk and took out my tape player. I hadn't used it for so long, I had to replace the batteries before I could get it to work. Once I was set, I popped the tape into place and pressed play.

The sound quality was excellent. I heard Dante say,

*"Sergeant Detective Priddy, it's nice to see you again. It's been a while."*

*"You seem to be holding your own."*

*"I was until recently."*

*"Oh?"*

*"Yeah, 'Oh.' Let's cut to the chase here. My brother's been seen in conversation with you. I've heard it from more than one source and it doesn't sit well."*

The conversation took six minutes and ended with Len saying,

*"Is that what this meeting's about? Unsolicited advice from a fucking gangster?"*

*"I don't think of myself as a gangster. The term offends me. I've never been convicted of a crime."*

*"You will be."*

*"You're entitled to feel smug because you win either way. I'm out, he's in, it's all the same to you. You think you've got your hands full with me, wait until Cappi's in the driver's seat. He'll turn this town on its ear."*

*"So why don't you do us all a favor and get rid of him?"*

*"Why don't you? I've got enough problems as it is without adding murder to the list."*

*"You only have one problem, buddy. We are taking you down."*

*"Oh, please. How long has this investigation been going on? Two years, three? You're playing patty-cake with the FBI and who else? DEA? ATF? All government grunts, a bunch of jack-offs. I already told you I'm out of here. Cappi's the one you should worry about. Take him out and the business is all yours."*

*"Meeting's over. Good-bye and good luck."*

*"Think about it. That's all I'm saying. Retire from the PD and live in style for a change. You could do a lot worse."*

*"I'll take it under advisement. What's the time frame for this departure of yours?"*

*"That's no concern of yours. I'm telling you this much because I want to be fair since you've been such a help to me."*

And that's where the tape ended.

I sat and pondered the possibilities, rubbing my nose thoughtfully. Cheney would be ecstatic and so would the district attorney. The problem was I couldn't count on either one to push the revelations to maximum effect. They were more likely to delay exposure of the tape until they were ready to take action. In legal circles, this can take years. There had to be somebody out there who was fearless and aggressive, someone who could manipulate the facts and drive the message home while managing to sidestep the repercussions.

I left my desk, pulled the carpet back, and put the packet of cash in my office safe without counting it. I returned to my swivel chair, lifted the handset, and called Diana Alvarez.

When she picked up, I said, "Hey, Diana. Kinsey Millhone."

There was a momentary pause. She must have been assessing my tone, which I confess was friendlier than it had been in times past. Cautiously, she said, "What can I do for you?"

"It's the other way around. Buy me a decent glass of Chardonnay and I'll do something for you."

Respectfully submitted,
Kinsey Milhone

# ACKNOWLEDGMENTS

The author wishes to acknowledge the invaluable assistance of the following people: Steven Humphrey; Jay and Marsha Glazer; Barbara Toohey; Lieutenant Paul McCaffrey, Santa Barbara Police Department; Sergeant Detective Bill Turner (retired), Santa Barbara County Sheriff's Department; and Chief of Police Deb Linden, San Luis Obispo; Andrew Blankstein, *Los Angeles Times*; Renn Murrell, funeral director, Arch Heady & Son Funeral Directors; Dana Hanson, funeral director, Neptune Society; Kelly Petersen, manager, and Cherry Post, Andi Doyle, and Emily Rosendahl of Wendy Foster; Steve Bass; Tracy Pfautch, former manager, Mall Security, Paseo Nuevo, Santa Barbara; Matt Phar, Santa Barbara Loan and Jewelry; Lisa Holt, Kevin Frantz, and Liz Gastiger.